Fool Me Once

FERN MICHAELS

Fool Me Once

DOUBLEDAY LARGE PRINT HOME LIBRARY EDITION

KENSINGTON BOOKS

KENSINGTON BOOKS are published by

Kensington Publishing Corp.
850 Third Avenue
New York, NY 10022

ISBN-13: 978-0-7394-7269-9

This Large Print Book carries the
Seal of Approval of N.A.V.H.

*I would like to dedicate this book
to my lifelong friend,
Betty Hugill Salyan.*

Prologue

Nineteen hundred sixty-six
Oxford, Mississippi

The three of them walked together, their arms linked, as they left the campus of Ole Miss. Their conversation, as they walked along, dealt with the unbearable humidity that blanketed the town—the whole state, for that matter. Their destination was the Moss Teahouse, run by Hattie and Mattie Moss, two spinsters who, if you believed the rumors, had lived forever and were never going to die because they belonged to the Moss Clan, whatever the hell the Moss Clan was.

The reason the trio was headed for the Moss Teahouse wasn't because they craved the watery, flavorless tea or the wilted cu-

cumber sandwiches that the older ladies of the town devoured, but because none of their classmates frequented the teahouse. Who in her right mind wanted to sit in a dusty, moldy-smelling tearoom, staring out grimy windows behind limp ruffled curtains? The reason they were going to the teahouse was that Allison Matthews had something of the utmost importance to discuss with her two best friends. A secret, actually. No, what she wanted to discuss was more than a secret. It was a devilishly clever idea that would put them all on easy street for the rest of their lives. If, and it was a big if, the three of them had the guts to pull it off.

The conversation drifted to final exams and how prepared each of them was. All were among the top five percent of their class, so there were no worries for any of them. Taking a Saturday off to deal with se-cret, devilish plans didn't pose a problem at all. Their situation was far different from that of fellow students who had partied and cut classes, and now had to cram around the clock just to graduate from Ole Miss by the skin of their teeth and leave town with their heads up.

There was nothing notable about the

trio. They weren't preppie, they certainly weren't pretty, nor were they shapely or fashionable. What they were was bookish-looking. Bookworms. All three wore glasses and no makeup, but, then again, makeup wouldn't have helped Allison's hawkish features or Jill's moon face, which was just as round as the rest of her. Gwen's overbite and full lips would have cried out in protest if makeup had been applied.

The three of them had met in the library and, out of necessity, quickly formed a bond. Four years of college demanded you have someone to pal around with, and they'd had good times, the three of them, even though they all lusted in their hearts to *belong*.

In addition to their superior intelligence, the trio had another thing in common—they loved money. Late at night, when they huddled together, they'd talk about how someday they would all be rich and famous. Then they were going to meet up, go to their college reunion, and make all their hoity-toity classmates sit up and take notice. It was a dream, but one they knew would come to fruition if they worked hard and kept at it. Allison, their spokesperson, always said if you persevered, you would prevail. Allison never said anything unless it was true. Well, hardly ever.

It was a pretty little town, not exactly your typical college town but close, and it was full of monster trees with hanging moss that at times looked eerie yet beautiful at the same time. The shops along the thoroughfare were quaint, with brightly colored striped awnings and multipaned windows that glistened in the brilliant April sunshine.

The trio walked past Mulvaney's drugstore, where the scent of Chantilly powder wafted through the open door. The girls stopped to look at the SALE sign on the front window. Prell shampoo and Colgate toothpaste were listed. Two for the price of one, but the girls weren't interested. They shrugged as they continued down the shady street, past a hardware store so quaint it looked just as it would have fifty years earlier. Daniel Hawthorn sat on an old rocker under the front window, smoking his pipe. Next to him was a barrel of rakes and shovels, and huge bags of grass seed, the first and only clue that the building was indeed a hardware store. Mrs. Hawthorn believed in starched curtains, as did most of the shopkeepers. But curtains in a hardware store? Puh-leeze.

"Well, girls, here we are," Allison said, her voice sounding jittery. She made a pretext of looking inside the tearoom before sitting down on the white-painted bench in front of a bow window adorned with limp checkered curtains. Half-barrels that had been painted white and were full of flowers so colorful they looked like a rainbow in a circle graced each side of the bench. Everyone said Hattie and Mattie Moss had a green thumb and would have been better off operating a flower shop instead of a teahouse. Of course, no one said that to their faces.

Jill Davis wiped at her perspiring face. Her hair was plastered to her forehead. "Are we going to stay out here or go inside, where it might be a tad cooler? I hate this damn humidity. Look at me, I'm drenched," she complained.

Allison got up off the bench, looking up and down the street. Her hand snaked out to the ornate doorknob. A bell tinkled as she walked through, Jill and Gwen following. She stepped to the side to allow the others more standing room and give her eyes time to get used to the dim interior. Her hand went automatically to her glasses to adjust them on her sweaty face. Her friends did the same.

Allison led the way to the back of the tea-room, where a small cluster of empty tables waited. Overhead, paddle fans whirred noisily. Even in the dimness, dust at least half an inch thick coated the blades as they whirled around. Gwen sneezed, not once but three times, as she took her seat at the small, round wrought-iron table. Her eyes started to water behind her thick glasses.

"We should have gone to Dominic's Pizza Parlor. This place is disgusting," Gwen grumbled as she cleaned her glasses with the hem of her skirt.

"Too noisy at Dominic's. Look around—no one is here. It's the middle of the afternoon, and we have the place to ourselves. We don't actually have to drink the tea or eat the sandwiches. We've been coming here for years when we had important things to discuss. It's a tradition," Allison said, her voice sounding defensive.

"Well, let's get to it so we can get out of here. It's just as hot inside as it is outside. I swear, I am going to move to Colorado first chance I get, and I'm never coming back to this place," Jill whined. "Well, I'll come back for a reunion, but that's it."

Hattie, or maybe it was Mattie, clomped her way to their table, a pad of paper and a pencil in her hand. Her ample bosom heaved with the effort of having walked across the room. "Hello, ladies," she chirped. "What can I get for you today?"

"We'll have three ice teas, and some of your famous rice cakes," Allison said.

"No rice cakes today, ladies. We do have some store-bought cookies if your sweet tooth can tolerate them," Hattie or Mattie chirped again.

"Ah, no. Just the ice tea then."

Hattie or Mattie grimaced as she painstakingly wrote down the order before trundling off to the back of the teahouse.

"Okay, why are we here?" Gwen asked as she patted at her perspiring neck with a paper napkin. She yanked at the collar of her yellow blouse, which looked soaking wet.

Allison looked across the table at her two friends. She sucked in her breath, then exhaled it in a loud *swoosh*. She took a second deep breath as she leaned across the table. Her voice dropped to a hoarse whisper. "We're going to rob the bank I work in. I can't do it myself, so that means I need your help, and we split the proceeds three ways. Think of it as three for the money. In this case we're talking about bearer bonds. You in or out?" She flopped back in her chair as her classmates stared at her, their mouths hanging open.

Jill's plump fingers grasped the edge of the table. Her whole body started to shake. "In or out of what?" she gasped.

"With me or against me," Allison said. "Gwen?"

"When you rob a bank, you go to jail. Where did you get an idea like this? I wouldn't do well in jail. I think this state makes women go out in chain gangs. The guards rape women prisoners. I don't think so, Allison. I'm not a brave person. You know me, I'm scared of my own shadow. I won't tell anyone if you want to go ahead and do it. No. My answer is no."

Allison stared at her friends. "What if I told you I've been planning this for a year and can guarantee we'll get away with it. This is not a lark. I'm serious—we can do it. We'll be rich. Not right away, because we'll have to wait till the bonds come due. No one can trace them to us. Bearer bonds, girls. At my bank. I have it all down pat. Come on, for once in our lives let's do something radical. There's not a person within a hundred miles who would ever think we pulled it off. I'm telling you, we can do this and walk away with no one the wiser. You know I'm smart enough to plan this thoroughly."

Jill continued to mop at her perspiring face and neck. Hattie or Mattie set down three glasses of tea whose ice cubes had already melted. Gwen reached for her glass just to have something to do with her hands.

"Tell us the plan," Gwen whispered nervously, after Hattie or Mattie had left.

Allison smiled. "It's so simple, it's downright scary. As you both know, I've worked at the bank part-time since I got here. That's four years of employment. Mr. Augustus depends on me. At Christmastime last year he said he didn't know what he would do without me, said I more or less ran the bank, but that was a joke. He just meant that I know everything there is to know, which is true. You also know that he belongs to that Gentlemen's Club with all those old rich, fuddy-duddy pals he associates with. They are all obscenely rich. Everyone knows that, too.

"So here's the plan. Four times a year, regular as clockwork, someone delivers a package of bearer bonds. The man just drops them off in a brown envelope. It isn't even sealed, just clasped. Then Mr. Augustus divvies them up among the men from the club. One time the package sat on his desk for a whole week. He never even opened it. Do you believe that? I always thought they were doing something . . . something illegal.

"Moving right along here. As you know, Margaret, Corinne, and I are the only employees. My hours are never the same, depending on my classes. Corinne works just three days a week. Only Margaret is full-time. Neither one of them pays attention to anything. They're just tellers, and if the bank is empty, they go in the back and drink sweet tea. If someone comes in to deposit or withdraw, I buzz them. Are you following me here?"

Two heads bobbed up and down.

"Mr. Augustus is going on a trip with the Gentlemen's Club next week. This time they're even taking their wives. The courier is due the day after they leave. Now, this is important. No one touches that envelope but the courier. He personally walks into Mr. Augustus's office and puts it on his desk. He closes the door when he leaves. Usually Margaret signs for the envelope, dates it, and gives me the receipt to file.

"All we have to do is substitute plain white paper for the bonds. I'll do that, wearing gloves of course. One of you will come into the bank and put the bonds in your safe-deposit box. I won't log you in, so there will be no record that you went to the vault. You'll do this when Margaret and Corinne are in the back. You leave. The bonds are safe. We won't move them till after graduation and we're ready to leave town. What do you think so far?"

"Robbing the bank, any bank, is a federal offense," Jill squeaked.

"Why aren't the bonds put in the vault?" Gwen asked.

Allison threw her hands in the air. "I don't know. Mr. Augustus must not think anyone would have the nerve to rob him. Either that, or he's stupid. Like I said, I personally think he and those other men in the Gentlemen's Club are doing something illegal. I haven't quite figured out what, and maybe I never will. It's just the way it is. Look, it's a small, privately owned bank. Mr. Augustus does things his way. This is, after all, Mississippi.

"No fingerprints will be on the envelope other than the courier's. All we have to do is cut up newspapers the same size as typing paper. We'll wear gloves. I'll carry everything in my book bag. I have it covered, girls."

"How are you going to hold up against the FBI, Allison?" Jill whispered.

Allison looked around. The bell over the door had tinkled. Two little old ladies with blue-white hair carrying string shopping bags walked in and settled themselves at a table at the front of the teahouse. A few minutes later, a woman dragging a toddler demanding an ice-cream cone entered.

"Time to go, girls. Don't worry about me. I can hold my own. I've been planning this for a whole year. At the risk of repeating myself, are you in or out?"

Two heads bobbed up and down.

"If we do this, and if we pull it off, does it mean we finally qualify as being the downtown girls who become the 'uptown girls'?" Jill asked.

"It definitely does," Allison said, her eyes sparkling behind her glasses as she counted out change and left a small tip on the table. "Now, let's go get some pizza."

Chapter 1

Five years later
Winchester, Virginia

Sandy-haired Dennis Lowell bounced his way into the small hospital, a huge smile on his face. He was the father of a baby girl. He hadn't seen her yet, but he knew she was going to be the most beautiful baby in the whole world. What, he wondered, had he done to deserve this happiness? His dark brown eyes sparkled at the thought.

Names for his new offspring flitted through his mind. He had been unable to get Allison to settle on one before she gave birth. He rather thought it was because she didn't want to be committed to a girl's name, then deliver a baby boy. Well, she wasn't going to be able to procrastinate much longer. A baby's name was going to go on the birth certificate. He hoped she'd go with Olivia—after his mother. But in the end, it didn't matter what the choice was. He was just grateful that the newborn was healthy and had all her toes and fingers.

Dennis straightened his tie, smoothed back his thinning hair, and took a deep breath as he made his way to the maternity ward. Childishly, he crossed his fingers, hoping that Allison would welcome him with a smile. But he knew in his gut there would be no smile. Possibly, a tirade awaited him. When the call had come into the office, he'd been going over a very muddled tax return with a client. A high-profile, high-paying client. There was no way he could bolt out of the office leaving a client so furious at the Internal Revenue Service. That had been three hours ago. His brand-new daughter was already three hours old, and he hadn't so much as seen her.

No, there would be no smile on Allison's face.

He stood outside the door of his wife's room. He could hear voices inside. He frowned. Was it possible his wife had visitors so soon? Maybe it was a nurse, and they were cooing over the new baby. He brightened a little at the thought.

Dennis knocked softly. At the same time, he pasted a smile on his face and pressed down on the latch of the door handle. He tried for a joke, but it felt sickly even to him when he said, "Ready or not, here comes the new father!"

Dennis took it in all at once; two strange men standing at the foot of the bed, his wife sitting propped up in the bed like a princess and, of course, the nurse, a red-haired, red-faced woman who looked to be flushed with anger. There was no sign of a bassinet or his new daughter. He looked around, instinctively knowing something was wrong. He managed to gasp out one word. "Baby?"

"Dennis, it was nice of you to come. It's been, what, four hours since I had the baby."

Dennis looked at his watch. "Three and a half hours," he managed to croak. The fear he was feeling escalated as he looked at the nurse and her cartful of medical equipment as well as medicines. The men had briefcases. What did that mean? Suddenly he felt light-headed in the small private room they couldn't afford but Allison had insisted on. He wasn't sure, but he thought he recognized one of the men standing by the foot of the bed. He'd seen him at the Rotary Club. A lawyer. What the hell was a lawyer doing in his wife's hospital room? The other one must be a lawyer, too. What the hell were two lawyers doing there? Whatever it was, he knew instinctively it wasn't going to be good for him.

Allison's voice was cool and detached when she made the introductions. "Dennis, this is Jason Carmichael and his partner, Oliver Barrows. They are my attorneys. I'm divorcing you and giving you sole custody of the baby. These two gentlemen will handle all the details. I don't want anything from you. You can keep the house, the cars, and what little we have in the bank. When I'm discharged, I'm walking away from here, and you'll never see me again."

Dennis looked around for a chair. There wasn't one. He struggled with the words he'd just heard. "I don't understand" was the best response he could manage. He felt the red-faced nurse's hand on his arm. It felt warm and comforting, but it did nothing to take away the dizzy feeling. He wondered if he was going to make a fool of himself and pass out.

Allison's voice turned ice cold. "It's simple, really, Dennis. Things haven't been right between us for a long time. The pregnancy never should have happened. You knew I didn't want to have children. So I'm giving you the child I never wanted. I no longer want to be married to you. I can't make it any more simple. Now, if you'll just sign the papers, these gentlemen will handle everything. Grow up, Dennis. This isn't a fairy tale. I don't want to be your princess, and I no longer want to live in a cracker box. With or without you. I do not want to be a mother. I want to be myself and live a life of my own choosing."

Dennis's head was still spinning as he tried to absorb all that he was hearing. He wondered who was paying for these attorneys. What a stupid thought. He looked at the two men, who were eyeballing him. One offered him a pen, and he scrawled his name, as directed, in about ten different places. He heard his wife's sigh of relief. He looked over at the nurse, whose eyes were full of pity. She led him from the room.

In the antiseptic hallway, the nurse took his arm and steered him toward the nursery. She pointed to a small pink bassinet and smiled. "Everything happens for a reason, Mr. Matthews. That's how you have to look at things right now."

Dennis pressed his face against the glass and stared at the tightly wrapped pink bundle. His daughter. Tears rolled down his cheeks. "I'll do my best . . . Olivia."

When the nurse tugged at his arm, he looked up. "You should go home now, Mr. Matthews, and . . . and . . . make some plans. You should be able to take your new daughter home at the end of the week. You need to prepare."

Dennis turned to walk back to his wife's room. He wanted an explanation. The nurse tugged on his arm again. "Your wife left instructions that you weren't to be permitted any other visiting privileges. Just the one. I'm truly sorry, Mr. Matthews."

"Yeah. Yeah, me too."

Dennis left the hospital in a daze. The

nurse was right, he had to make plans. Serious plans.

His shoulders slumped with misery, his eyes wet, Dennis drove home, still trying to make sense of what had just happened to him and his brand-new daughter.

Chapter 2

He was her client.

A superrich paying client.

And, said client was ticked off, big-time.

A murderous glint in her eyes, Olivia Lowell took one step backward, then another. "I refuse to tolerate this type of behavior, Cecil. I will not be intimidated. I was told you were a gentleman. Ha!"

Alice, the West Highland terrier at Olivia's feet, barked shrilly and showed her teeth. "She's a killer, Cecil, so it might behoove you to rethink your actions. Now, what's it going to be? Be aware that I am a woman whose biggest failing in life is my lack of patience."

Cecil eyed the woman standing in front of him, then the yapper at her feet. And he did what any red-blooded Yorkshire terrier would do. He lay down, rolled over, and barked. Happily. Bounding back up on all fours, he raced across the studio, whirled, twirled, and did a hind-leg jig. His one and only trick. Alice ran after him and somehow managed to swat his rear end with one furry paw. They ended up tussling on the studio floor.

"Now look at you, Cecil! The executors of your owner's estate are not going to like this. I need to take your picture, so let's get with it. You're big news, Cecil. You just inherited the Manning fortune. You're going to live a life of luxury. Don't you want to get your due? It isn't every day a fortune lands in a dog's lap. C'mon, let me take your picture. I promise it will be painless," Olivia pleaded.

Cecil hopped onto a stool and did his jig again, to Alice's dismay. Olivia resigned herself to the fact that she wasn't going to get a portrait of the famous dog but would have to go with action shots, which probably wasn't a bad thing at all. She'd tried to explain to the dog's handler, a lawyer named Jeff Bannerman, that Cecil had a mind of his own, but he refused to listen. What Bannerman had said was something to the effect that you're supposed to be the best of the best—now prove it.

Like that was going to happen! If Cecil had been an ordinary dog, maybe. She'd met Cecil two years before, when Lillian Manning had commissioned her to do a sitting portrait of the dog. The picture, while nice, reflected Cecil's more or less placid puppyhood. Now the moneymen responsible for Mrs. Manning's estate wanted a grown-up picture, and they were willing to pay ten thousand dollars for it. After all, it was going to be shown around the world, and it would aid her career, they said.

Olivia reached into her pocket and withdrew a whistle, the kind that emitted a loud, piercing sound that only dogs could hear. She blew it three times and shouted at the top of her lungs, "Cecil, get on that bench and pose! *Now!* Or . . . or you are going back home with that *stiff* who brought you here."

Cecil stopped pawing through the wastebasket, turned to look at the object of his torment, then pranced over to the bench and hopped up. He posed, he preened, he looked haughty, he looked devilish, then he lay down. Alice barked her approval as

Olivia's Nikon clicked and clicked. Then, ham that he was, Cecil stood up on all fours and bowed. He actually bowed. Olivia burst out laughing—until Cecil showed his teeth, which meant the gig was over. He hopped down and chased Alice around the room until the female terrier collapsed. The Yorkie pounced on her and barked shrilly. Alice ignored him. With nothing else to entertain him, Cecil lifted his leg and defiantly peed on the legs of a tripod. Then he walked back to Alice. He lay down and was asleep within seconds.

Olivia smiled as she looked at the two sleeping dogs. She adored Cecil but felt sorry for him. He was now destined to live out his life in a fancy mansion with servants catering to his every whim. The servants wouldn't love him or play with him the way Lillian Manning had. Poor, poor Cecil. Maybe the money people would allow Cecil to have play dates with Alice. How silly was that? How silly was leaving a hundred-and-fifty-million-dollar estate to a dog? Pretty damn silly, in her opinion.

Olivia Lowell, photographer to the canine world, looked at her watch. Lunchtime. Yogurt, a banana, and a cup of coffee, and she'd be ready to photograph a seven-year-old English whippet named Sasha for her owner's Christmas card. Christmas was ten months away, but the owner said she didn't want to have to wait till the last minute.

It was a lucrative living, and Olivia enjoyed every minute of it because she was a devout animal lover.

As Olivia spooned the yogurt into her mouth, she thought about her father. She missed him but understood his desire to retire to the islands and rent out his fishing boat to tourists. He was happier these days than she'd ever seen him. Of course, that might have something to do with his new love, Lea. Maybe she would call him later in the day to ask him how things were going.

Tears pricked Olivia's deep-green eyes when she thought of her father and how he'd raised her on his own. He'd sacrificed so much for her, even giving up his accounting practice and going to night school to learn photography so he could open a studio in their home to be with her during the day. A studio that he himself built on the side of the house, with its own entrance, bath, and minikitchen. The studio even had a plaque beside the door that said LOWELL

AND LOWELL, and underneath their names, the word PHOTOGRAPHY.

Her father had never remarried, despite her urging as she grew older. Not that he didn't, as he called it, "keep company" with various and sundry ladies. Some of those ladies were to Olivia's liking and some weren't, but she kept her own counsel where they were concerned. Until Lea came along five years ago. Lea was the mother she never had. They were friends, good friends. Maybe now that both her father and Lea were in a less stressful atmosphere and retired, they might think about getting married. At least she hoped so, for her father's sake.

Three things happened simultaneously when Olivia tossed her empty yogurt container in the trash. Cecil and Alice raced into the kitchen; Sasha, the English whippet, arrived wearing a huge red and white Santa hat, granny glasses that were tied to her ears, and a Christmas neckerchief; and a distinguished-looking gentleman carrying a briefcase rang her front doorbell.

Olivia strode to the front door. She really needed to make some rules around here. The least Sasha's owner could have done was take the dog to the studio door instead of the kitchen door. Now she had to contend with some door-to-door salesman, the barking, howling dogs, and her own frustrations. Her father would have had the situation under control in a heartbeat. All he ever had to do was look a dog in the eye, wag his finger, and he was rewarded with instant obedience. Her clients walked all over her.

"What?" she snapped irritably. "Whatever you're selling, I'm not interested." She was about to shut the door when the man held up a small white business card. She paused to read it. He was Prentice O'Brien from the law firm of O'Brien, O'Malley and O'Shaughnessy. A nice Irish firm, Olivia surmised. Or else it was some kind of song-and-dance act, and the man standing in front of her was a scam artist.

"What?" she said again, yelling to be heard over the din. "Is someone suing me?" Sasha's body slammed against the locked storm door. Prentice O' Brien stepped back, his face showing apprehension.

"No!" the lawyer bellowed in return. "Can we go somewhere to talk where it's a little more quiet?"

Olivia brushed at her blond curls. "I'm

afraid not," she bellowed back as loudly as the lawyer had. "I'm running late, and, as you can see, I seem to have lost control here. Why don't you call me later, around five."

The lawyer frowned. "Ms. Lowell, this really is important, urgent even. We need to talk."

Olivia turned around when she heard a sound reminiscent of a waterfall. Sasha was peeing on the hall carpet runner. Damn. She noted the look of disgust on the lawyer's face.

"Some other time. *This* situation is *really* urgent. Good-bye, Mr."—she looked down at the card in her hand—"Mr. O'Brien." She shut the door in the man's face and raced to the kitchen for a roll of paper towels.

Thirty minutes later she was still searching for Sasha's glasses and Santa Claus hat. *My father would have this under control, too. Damn.*

At three o'clock Sasha and all her gear were gone. Cecil's handler still hadn't picked him up. Anna Logan, the owner of Logan's Bakery, arrived with a basket of new kittens. She wanted pictures to put up on the bakery bulletin board in the hope that some of her customers would adopt them.

It was ten after five when Anna and the kittens pulled out of Olivia's driveway. Cecil's handler still hadn't arrived to pick him up, which probably meant he'd forgotten about him. Just the way Alice's owners had forgotten to pick her up three years ago. That had been Alice's lucky day. Olivia loved Alice the way mothers love their children.

At five-thirty the doorbell and the phone pealed at the same time. Ignoring the doorbell, Olivia answered the phone while Alice and Cecil raced to the front door and barked. Cecil's handler was on the phone, asking if Olivia could possibly keep Cecil overnight, and he would be picked up in the morning by "someone."

"Well, sure, for fifty dollars an hour, Mr. Bannerman. I don't operate a dog-sitting service. This is a photography studio." She was told the fee would be no problem. After all, Cecil was the richest dog in the United States. She hung up the phone wondering what she was going to prepare for dinner as she made her way to the front door. She opened it. Prentice O'Brien.

"What is it, Mr. O'Brien? It's the end of the

day, I'm tired, and if no one is suing me, I can't imagine what you want to talk to me about. Make it quick."

"Can I at least come in, Ms. Lowell? It's rather cold out here, and it is snowing."

It was *snowing*. How had she missed that? Maybe she'd build a fire later, snuggle with the dogs, and think about Clarence De Witt's marriage proposal. Then again, maybe she wouldn't think about Clarence De Witt's marriage proposal. She didn't want to be Mrs. Clarence De Witt. She didn't want to be Mrs. *Anybody*. She liked her life just the way it was, thank you very much. "All right. This better be good and quick. Come in. Just so you know, Mr. O'Brien, I hate lawyers."

"Until you need us," O'Brien quipped. "Nice house," he said, looking around as Olivia led him to the great room that ran the entire length of the house.

"Thank you. My dad did all the work, even this addition and the entire studio. He can do anything," she said proudly. "This used to just be a two-bedroom ranch house, but Dad added two bathrooms, a third bedroom, and this great room. He remodeled the kitchen, too. He built the playhouse in the back for me when I was little."

"Your father sounds like an extraordinary man, Ms. Lowell."

"Oh, he is. He raised me when my mother died. If she'd lived, I can't imagine her doing a better job. Now, tell me why you're here and what I can do for you."

The attorney removed his overcoat and laid it on the side of the sofa. He looked puzzled. "Did I hear you right just now? Did you say your mother died?"

"Yes, the day I was born. Thirty-four years ago. That's her picture on the mantel. It's the only one we have. Her name was Allison. Why are you here, Mr. O'Brien? Does this visit have something to do with my dad?"

"Not directly."

While O'Brien walked over to the fireplace and studied the picture on the mantel, she eyed the briefcase on the sturdy pine coffee table. It looked old and well used, with scuff marks and gouges in the cowhide. She wondered how many lawsuits it repre-sented. She waited, her gaze taking in the familiar room, while the lawyer, who had re-turned to stand by the coffee table, riffled through his case for whatever it was he was going to show her.

She loved this room, she really did. One wall was her own personal rogue's gallery, as her father called it. Every inch of space on the wall was covered with pictures of her from the day she was born. The massive stone fireplace, with a hearth so wide and deep she could have positioned a sofa on it, took up another wall. Her father had allowed her to carry the irregular fieldstones in from outside, making the building of it a joint effort. In the winter they made roaring fires, popped corn, and toasted marshmallows. They even grilled weenies on sticks on occasion. The green plants and fica trees were her contribution. She trimmed and watered them weekly. All were lush and green, thanks to the three skylights that graced the ceiling.

She'd had sleepovers in this very room when she was young. She wondered where all those old friends were these days.

Olivia was jolted from her thoughts when the lawyer cleared his throat. "What I have here in my hand is the last will and testament of your mother, whom you probably know as Allison Matthews Lowell, although she changed her name to Adrian Ames soon after divorcing your father. I can read it to you, or you can read it yourself."

Olivia threw her hands in the air. "See? See? I knew this was a mistake. You have the wrong person. My mother died when I was born. I guess there's some other Olivia Lowell out there. I'm sorry you wasted your time, Mr. O' Brien."

The attorney cleared his throat again. "I didn't waste my time, Ms. Lowell. I'm sorry to be the one to tell you this, but your mother did not die thirty-four years ago. She died two weeks ago and left her entire estate to you. And whoever that is in the picture on the mantel, it's not Adrian Ames."

Olivia's heart thundered in her chest. She reached out to grasp the arm of the chair she was sitting on, only to see Cecil perched there. She picked him up and brought him close to her chest. She was so light-headed she couldn't think. "No! No! Don't tell me that. My father . . . my father . . . would never . . . he wouldn't lie . . . This must be some kind of cruel joke, and I don't appreciate it. No, you're wrong."

Prentice O'Brien inched the will in its sky-blue cover across the coffee table. It glared up at Olivia like an obscene blue eye. She made no move to reach for it. She struggled with her voice. "I think you should leave now, Mr. O'Brien."

"Ms. Lowell, I'm sorry about this, but my firm represented your mother for many, many years. This is not a mistake. Once you know the story behind all this, I'm sure you'll understand it is not some cruel hoax. I understand your being upset, so I'm going to leave. I suggest you contact your father and talk with him. After you've done that, please feel free to call me."

Olivia watched in a daze as the attorney stood up and put on his overcoat. Faster than a lightning bolt, both dogs chased him to the door. Olivia heard the little pinging sound made by the alarm system when the door opened and closed.

She burst into tears.

If what the attorney said was true, her whole life was a lie. A big, fat lie!

She cried harder. She had a mother. *Had* had a mother. A mother she never knew. A real, live, flesh-and-blood mother like all her friends had, like Sara Kelly's mother. Olivia bolted from the chair and raced to the powder room off the great room. The dogs huddled and whimpered at the strange sounds emanating from behind the closed door.

Ten minutes later Olivia literally crawled out of the powder room on her hands and knees, her face splotchy and red. She crawled across the slick hardwood floors she'd helped her father install. Tongue-and-groove. She'd thought that phrase so funny as a child. Her father had allowed her to hand him the pieces of wood and showed her how to lay them down. She'd been so proud that he allowed her to help. *"It's just you and me, kid,"* he always said after they finished a project. *Just you and me, kid.* Yeah, right. I think you left someone out, Daddy.

It wasn't until she was back in her favorite chair that she saw that the will was still on the coffee table. Well, she certainly wasn't going to touch *that*. No way was she ever going to touch *that*. Absolutely, she was never, ever going to touch *that*.

Alice pawed her mistress's leg for attention. When there was no response, the dog ran to the kitchen for her food bowl, carried it back, and dropped it at Olivia's feet. Cecil barked. Olivia looked at her watch. It was time for Alice's supper. Cecil, too, since she was dog-sitting. She felt a hundred years old when she heaved herself to her feet and made her way to the kitchen.

Olivia reached into the cabinet for the dog food. Her father had allowed her to screw the knobs into the cabinets. *Just you and me, kid*. A duo instead of a trio. She started to cry again, the tears rolling down her cheeks like a waterfall. She sniffed as she scooped out the food into two bowls and watched as both dogs gobbled it down. She let them outside. It was snowing harder. It always snowed in February. Her father was probably basking on the deck of his boat, sharing a glass of wine with Lea at this hour. It was probably warm and balmy, and they were probably both wearing shorts and T-shirts.

She needed to call her father. What should she say? How should she say it? *Just you and me, kid*. Now it was her father and Lea. And, she wasn't a kid anymore.

Nothing was what it seemed. Not even the picture of "her mother" on the mantel.

Alice scratched against the door as Cecil tried to nip her ear. Olivia opened the door, towel-dried the dogs, handed each of them a treat. She should think about her own dinner. She reached for a box of Cheerios and carried it back to the great room. She set the box down and made a fire.

Olivia was a little girl again as she hugged her knees to her chest and watched the flames dance behind the ornate grate. She picked at the dry cereal, sharing it with the two dogs sitting next to her. She had to think, but her brain suddenly wasn't working.

Just you and me, kid.

Liar! Liar!

Both dogs crawled into Olivia's lap and snuggled with her. How warm and comforting they felt. Suddenly, a red-hot streak of rage, hot as the fire she was looking at, ripped through her. What kind of mother would . . . would . . . ignore her daughter for thirty-four years? Who was this woman who had left her entire estate to a daughter she'd ignored all her life?

Well, the only person who could answer those questions, other than possibly the attorney, was her father. And only he could tell her who was in the picture on the mantel.

Olivia got to her feet and rummaged between the sofa cushions for the portable phone. For some reason she always stuck it between the cushion and the arm. Most times the battery was dead, and she had to recharge it or use her cell phone. She took a mighty, deep breath and dialed her father's cell phone. She wasn't surprised when Lea answered, sounding happy and relaxed. Well, why the hell shouldn't she sound happy and relaxed, with her father and all that warm sunshine?

"Lea, it's Ollie," she said, using her father's favorite nickname for her. "Is he there?"

"Honey, you sound . . . funny. Are you all right? Do you have a cold or something? If you do, you need to start taking care of it. I saw on the news that it's very cold and snowing in Winchester."

"Or something," Olivia responded. "Is Dad there?"

"He was until about ten minutes ago. He's down on the pier watching some fisherman haul in a huge marlin. Can I have him return your call, or would you like me to go get him? I don't think he'll be too long. Let's face it, how long can you stare at a dead fish?"

Olivia knew she was supposed to laugh at Lea's little joke. She didn't. She wondered if she would ever laugh again about anything. "No, that's okay. Tell him to call me when he gets in. It's important, Lea."

"Is there anything I can do, honey?"

"No. But thanks for asking." Olivia clicked the OFF button and replaced the phone in its stand instead of letting it slide down between the cushions. She walked back to the fire, carrying an armful of pillows. She was so cold she ached. The dogs curled up next to her, and she fed them the crunchy cereal, one morsel at a time.

Just you and me, kid.

Chapter 3

Three hours later, the dogs sound asleep on the pillows, Olivia's phone finally rang. She looked at it through narrowed green eyes that were little more than slits. The rage she'd felt earlier was still with her. Getting up carefully so as not to wake the sleeping dogs, she barked a greeting into the phone.

"Ollie, Ollie, how are you? I'm sorry I missed your call. Daimon brought in this glorious marlin, and we all had to stand around and watch him gloat. Then we had to go to Finnegan's to make a toast. What's up, honey? Lea said you sounded funny and wasn't sure if you were sick or something was wrong."

There's something wrong all right. "A lawyer came to see me this afternoon."

"Good Lord, don't tell me someone is

suing you! When are people going to understand the camera doesn't lie? They look the
way they look. Call up our attorney, offer to
redo the photos, then touch them up. That
should work. You aren't upset over this, are
you, Ollie? You know it goes with the terri-
tory. It happened so many times to me, I lost
count."

*How cheerful and upbeat his voice
sounds*, Olivia thought, *when my own is so
chilly and hateful. Just you and me, kid.* "It
wasn't about a disgruntled client, Dad. It
was about my *deceased* mother—your *deceased* wife. The woman whose picture is
not on the mantel. It seems she rose from
the dead and died all over again two weeks
ago. Well, *Daaadd*, what do you have to say
about *that?*"

The silence on the other end of the phone
was so total, Olivia had to prompt her father
for a response. "Well?"

"I'll get the first plane out in the morning.
I should be there by midafternoon. This is
not something to discuss over the phone."

"Why the hell not, *Daaadd?*" Olivia
wailed. "How could you? More to the point,
how dare you not tell me? How dare you let
me think that woman in the picture was my

mother? How dare you, Dad?" With shaking hands, Olivia pitched the phone across the room. She watched as the small cover that held the batteries bounced off, and the batteries rolled across the tongue-and-groove floor. She cried harder but made no move to fix the phone. Instead, she went back to the fire and curled up with the dogs, where she cried herself to sleep.

Olivia woke with a stiff neck. She struggled to her feet, all the while massaging her neck. She hoped a hot shower would work out the kink. The dogs raced to the back door, then did a double take when they saw the night's snowfall piled up against the sliding door. Game little rascals that they were, they did their best to plow through snow that was taller than them. They peed quickly and raced back to the house. Olivia handed out treats, made coffee, and trudged off to the shower, where she stood under the pelting spray until the water ran cold. After dressing quickly in a fleece-lined blue sweat suit, heavy socks, and sneakers, she pulled back her hair in a ponytail and tied it with a red ribbon. The last thing she did before leaving the bathroom was to apply some face toner in the hope it would reduce the redness and puffiness around her eyes. Like she really cared how she looked.

What she needed next was coffee. Lots and lots of coffee. As she sipped her second cup, she stared out the kitchen window, knowing that by eight o'clock, all her customers scheduled for the day would call to cancel. Considering her frame of mind, she thought it was a good thing. The only way she would be able to catch up was to work weekends. That wasn't so bad, because she rarely did anything on the weekends except maybe go to dinner or the movies with Clarence.

In order not to dwell on her immediate problem, Olivia tried to shift mental gears and think about her personal life. With the exception of Dee Dee Pepper, all her old friends were married with families. Most of them had moved out of state, and she'd lost touch with them. Christmas was always an eye-opener, when the cards came in with newsletters, new-baby pictures, and family updates. She hated reading the details. Someday she was going to meet a guy who was going to sweep her off her feet. A guy who would like animals and respect what she did for a living. A man with whom she would want to start a family. She shrugged when she realized her biological clock was ticking. "If it's meant to be, it will be," she muttered to herself.

The phone rang in the kitchen. Olivia looked at the clock. Five minutes to eight. It was Cecil's handler, Jeff Bannerman, pleading for her to keep Cecil another day, what with the snow-clogged roads. Olivia agreed, reminding Jeff that her services were fifty dollars an hour. As on the previous day, he readily agreed and said he would bring a check for the full amount when he came to pick up Cecil.

The phone rang three more times, her three morning clients canceling and rescheduling. Outside, the skies were gray, and it looked like more snow. Her father was going to be in for a shock when he stepped off the plane. He was also going to have to take a taxi. There was no way she was going to the airport with road conditions what they were.

Olivia refilled her coffee cup and carried it to the table, positioning it on one of the cheerful place mats she'd made last winter.

She loved this kitchen, with the white cabinets and colorful greenery on the counters. She loved the whole house and was delightedly stunned when her father had deeded it to her when he and Lea went off to the islands. The hanging plants were thick and lush, thanks to a weekly dose of plant food and a good water spritzing every other day. Her collection of saltshakers and pepper grinders graced the tops of the cabinets. Her father had built a special shelf on top of the cabinets when she said she was going to start collecting something. He'd always acquiesced in everything she wanted and got right on it, making it happen. He'd been a wonderful father. Until now. Now she thought of him as a liar. He'd betrayed her in the worst possible way. How could she ever forgive something like this?

Was there a reason for his deception? Surely he had a reason. She wished she knew more about motherhood. All she knew was what she read in magazines and stories and what she'd observed as a child with her friends' mothers. The bottom line in those magazines and stories was about mothers loving their children more than life itself. Why did her mother give her away? Maybe she hadn't wanted to be pregnant. Maybe she hadn't been mother material. Or maybe Olivia had been an ugly baby. Maybe something had been wrong with her when she was born that offended her mother. But then she snorted at such thoughts.

Was she blaming the wrong person? It was possible, she supposed, that her father only did what her mother wanted. Since she didn't know anything about her mother—not even what she'd looked like—she couldn't really say. What she was sure of was that her father loved her with all his heart. She was certain in her own mind that he still loved her and that there had to be reasons why he'd done what he did. And now he was on his way to her to try to make all this right.

Olivia felt like crying, but she bit down on her lower lip. Crying was for wimps. At least that's what her father said. She leaned over and turned the radio on just to have some sound. Music filled the kitchen and lifted her spirits. Since her father was going to be there, maybe she should think about what she was going to make for dinner. She eyed the Crock-Pot sitting on the counter. With her busy schedule, it was a lifesaver. But today, even though she had the time, she didn't feel like cooking. She'd just dump stuff in it from the freezer, and whatever it turned out to be, she and her dad would eat.

It took her all of ten minutes to drop a package of chicken parts into the oversize pot, along with celery, carrots, frozen peas and corn, and a can of chicken broth. At the last minute she opened the cabinet over the stove and sprinkled every spice she had on the rack into the mess. She covered it, adjusted the cook time, then dusted her hands dramatically. Done.

Olivia opened the freezer again, withdrew a Boston cream pie, and set it on the counter to thaw out. Her father loved Boston cream pie. These days, Lea made the pies from scratch.

Just you and me, kid.

Somehow Olivia managed to while away the hours by tidying up the studio, playing with the dogs, checking the Crock-Pot, and washing a load of towels. She looked at the time on her watch at least a hundred times until she heard the pinging sound of the doorbell. With the dogs at her heels, she ran to the foyer, where she skidded to a stop, opened the door, and stared at her father.

He looked wonderful, tanned and fit, wearing heavy winter clothes that looked brand-new. But there was such sadness, such regret and weariness in his eyes that she knew he hadn't slept. She burst into tears. He reached for her, and she fell into his arms. He held her so tightly she wanted to squeal with the pain, but she didn't.

"I have no words to tell you how very sorry I am, Ollie. This was never supposed to happen. *Never!*" he said vehemently. "Let's go into the kitchen and have something hot to drink."

In the kitchen, Olivia reached for a cup and poured coffee for her father. She'd been making pot after pot of coffee since ten o'clock, then throwing each one out because she wanted the coffee to be fresh when her father arrived.

Olivia waited until her father had taken his first sip before she whispered, "Tell me everything."

He did.

"I didn't know what to do, Ollie. I was numb. All I could think of was that you were just a few hours old, and I was the only one who wanted you. I signed everything they put in front of me. I was full of fear and panic. I think the look on your mother's face told me there was no hope that she would change her mind. She had some pretty highfalutin lawyers back then. To this day, I don't know how she paid for them. She said she wanted a divorce, didn't want you, and didn't want anything from me. She also said she was taking back her maiden name. All that was in the . . . the contract I signed. Allison agreed never to interfere in your life. I insisted on that when I finally got my wits about me. She readily agreed. She didn't want either one of us. I know that must hurt you unbearably, Ollie, but I can't change what is. From that day on, I never heard a thing about her. She kept her word.

"I talked to our minister, your grand-mother, anyone who would listen or who I thought could offer advice. They all agreed that telling you your mother had passed away would be best. I tried to be both mother and father to you. I did my best, Ol-lie. It was really rocky in the beginning, but you were too young to remember. I did what I thought was best for both of us."

"You did, Dad. I just wish you had told

me. I'm not faulting you for the care you gave me. I loved our life. I love you. I just think I should have known."

Dennis Lowell ran his fingers through his sun-bleached hair. "I always planned to tell you, but that time never came. And, of course, I had put that picture on the mantel and told you it was your dead mother. I didn't know what would happen if I told you the truth and admitted to the deception.

"You were so happy-go-lucky. I thought you'd become sad, upset . . . maybe even try to search her out or something. That was the selfish part of my thinking. I never, ever thought something like this would happen."

Olivia got up from her chair and started to pace the kitchen. The dogs tracked her until they got dizzy. "But it did happen, Dad. That lawyer wants me to call him back. He left *her* will. I didn't even look at it. I don't want anything from her. Can you take care of it, Dad?"

Dennis stared at his daughter before he got up to lift the lid of the Crock-Pot. "You just threw stuff in here, eh?" Olivia nodded. "I'm afraid, Ollie, it doesn't work like that. I guess your mother wanted to make amends for what she did. She can't hurt you anymore. Just deal with it, then forget about her. I know that sounds easy for me to say, but it's the best thing for you to do. If she left you an insurance policy, donate it to some worthy cause. You're nothing like her, Ollie. You're *my* daughter, and don't you ever forget it. Now, where is that damn will? We might as well get started on this so we can lay it to rest. Do you forgive me, Ollie?"

Did she? Did she have a choice? She forced herself to nod. "It's on the coffee table in the great room." Her heart thumped in her chest as she stared at her father's back. His shoulders were slumped as he made his way into the great room.

Olivia remained at the kitchen table, a table built by her father. She'd helped to sand it. She clasped and unclasped her hands as she tried to come to terms with what her father had just told her. The part that bruised her heart was that her mother had refused even to see her when she had been born. She'd just signed her away, all nice and legal. What kind of woman would do a thing like that?

Time crawled forward as Olivia waited for her father to return to the kitchen. What was taking so long? She started to get angry all over again as she entered the great room. Her father was staring off into space. Fear washed through her as she raced across the room.

"Dad, what's wrong?"

Dennis turned, and for a moment he still didn't seem to be focusing on her. "This is going to be a little more complicated than I originally thought. It seems your . . . Allison changed her name. Does the name Adrian Ames mean anything to you?"

Olivia shook her head.

"How about Adrian's Treasure Box? Does that ring any bells?"

"Oh, yeah. It's some big mail-order catalog. I think I ordered stuff from there a few times. Why, Dad? Why are you asking me these questions?"

Dennis Lowell took a deep breath. "Your . . . Allison is . . . Adrian Ames, owner of that mail-order company. It's a multi-million-dollar business, and she left it all to you."

Olivia's jaw dropped. "What?" she asked in a strangled voice.

Dennis looked down at the will in his hands. "It's all spelled out right here. Much to my surprise, she lived just forty miles from here. At least she had a house here. Seems she has property all over the world. She never remarried. It says right here that when you turned sixteen, she started taking an interest in your life. She hired a private detective to send her monthly reports, and obviously that was done right up until the time of her death. She never did anything about those reports, Ollie. She stuck to our bargain, for whatever that's worth."

Olivia wiped at the tears starting to gather in her eyes. It was starting to snow again, she noticed. "What was she like, Dad? Not that story you made up for me when I was little. The real story."

Dennis leaned back on the sofa and closed his eyes. Both dogs hopped onto his lap. Absentmindedly, he stroked their small heads. "I met Allison during her last year at Ole Miss. She worked part-time in a small bank that was privately owned. One day I bumped into her at a local pizza joint that was off campus. I worked a few doors down from the place and used to go there for lunch. She was with two friends. She dropped her book bag, and I picked it up. They invited me to sit with them, so I did. One thing led to another, and I finally asked her out. At first she said no because she didn't want to get involved with anyone when she would be leaving at the end of the term. I finally wore her down.

"There were no bells or whistles, no wild passion or anything like that. We were just comfortable with one another. That fall we got married and moved here. Allison had a job in Washington, and I worked locally, as you know. Sometimes when I think back I realize perhaps I was too old for her. I was thirty and ready to get married. She was just out of college. And I was her first boyfriend.

"It was a pleasant enough existence for the first few years. Never having been married, I thought it was supposed to be like that. She traveled a lot in her job. That, I didn't like. She'd always come back from those trips with an attitude. Things got worse when Allison got pregnant. She blamed me, said I didn't care about her, I should have done this or that. She wasn't ready for motherhood, that kind of thing. She moved out of the bedroom, and that was pretty much the end of our relationship. I thought all pregnant women acted like that. Then came the day of your birth, and she crippled me. She was so cold, so heartless, so uncaring. I felt like I'd been run over by a train. I probably would have had a nervous breakdown, but I had you to think about.

"I went back to the hospital to try to talk to her several times, but they wouldn't let me in to see her. When I went back the last time, she'd been discharged, and she paid the bill herself. I never saw or heard from her again.

"I was stupid, Ollie. It wasn't till that last time that I realized she'd taken all of her things out of the house. I don't know when or how she did that. It was like she'd never been there, like the whole thing was just a bad dream. That's my story."

Olivia's head bobbed up and down as she tried to come to terms with everything. There was just so much her weary brain could deal with. "Still, Dad, you should have told me at some point."

"To what end, Ollie? I didn't want you to have to deal with her rejection. I did what I thought was best. I'm sorry if you feel I was wrong."

"I can forgive you, Dad. Now, what are we going to do?"

"I guess you and I are going to call Mr.

Prentice O'Brien and see what the next step is. You okay, Ollie?"

Olivia smiled. "Sure, Dad. I'm a big girl now."

Liar, liar, liar.

Chapter 4

It was almost like old times, Olivia thought, as she and her father cleaned up the kitchen. Even though they had a dishwasher, Dennis washed the dishes, and Olivia dried them. It was something physical to do other than sit across from each other in the great room—Olivia with accusing eyes, Dennis's filled with guilt and shame.

Dennis squeezed the yellow sponge until it condensed into a tight little ball in his hand. His voice was low, little short of a whisper. "I can't change anything, Ollie. If you want the truth, if I had to do it all over again, I'd do it the same way.

"Do you know how many sleepless nights I've had over this? Thousands. I don't think I had a good night's sleep until the day of your eighteenth birthday. I always had this fear that Allison would show up and whisk you away. As hard as I tried, I could never convince myself otherwise. Now, to see that Allison took an interest in you when you turned sixteen . . . Well, that more or less confirms that my fears were justified."

Olivia snapped the dish towel against the dishwasher before she straightened it out and hung it up. "C'mon, Dad, lighten up. In time, I'll get over it. It just came out of the blue, and I wasn't expecting it. Never in a million years. You have to let me blame you for a little while till I get it out of my system. Right now I think we need to talk about how I can make this all go away. I don't want anything from her. We have to figure out a way to give it all back. I refuse to accept it."

"It doesn't work that way, Ollie. The will has to go to probate. There are inheritance taxes, all kinds of legal issues that have to be resolved. If Allison was as wealthy as it appears, I'm sure she had a battery of attorneys who have everything in place. Then there's the estate planning . . . just so many things. Tomorrow, I'll go with you to the lawyer's office. In the meantime, we can talk it to death, or we can sit on the couch with the dogs and watch television. I have to warn you, though, I'll probably fall asleep within five minutes."

"Go to bed, Dad. I'm fine. I'm going to go out to the studio and do some paperwork. Don't forget to call Lea. You said you were going to do it before dinner but forgot."

Dennis grinned. "Yes, Moth— Damn, I'm sorry, Ollie."

"It's not a problem, Dad."

"Honey, are you sure you don't mind if I go to bed? I promise to get up early and make us breakfast. Eggs Benedict if you have all the ingredients."

Olivia stood on her tiptoes to kiss her father's cheek. "I have everything."

Dennis hugged her. Tightly, as though he'd never let her go. To Olivia, the hug didn't feel as comforting as past ones had.

With a heavy heart, Olivia scooped both little dogs up in her arms and carried them into the great room. She'd made up that little story about going to the studio so her father would go to bed. Together, she and the dogs settled themselves on the deep, comfortable sofa to watch an inane television show about people on an island eating bugs to survive.

The house was cloaked in silence as

Olivia slumped into the corner of the sofa. Outside, the snow continued to fall. Within minutes, she joined the two dogs in slumber, tears drying on her cheeks.

Dennis Lowell was as good as his word. When Olivia woke, she could smell fresh coffee and other tantalizing aromas coming from the kitchen. The dogs leaped off the sofa to race to the door. Today, though, there was a difference. Dennis had shoveled a path across the patio for the dogs. The new snowfall amounted to little more than a few inches. The sound of work crews and snowplows could be heard as they lumbered down the main and side roads. By midmorning, traffic would be back to normal.

"Good morning, Ollie. How did you sleep?" Dennis asked warily.

"Fairly well, Dad. Listen, are we always going to have this . . . this uneasiness between us?"

Dennis thought about the question for a minute, his brow puckered in concentration. "I think that pretty much depends on you, honey. I can't turn the clock back. What's done is done. I can keep saying I'm sorry from now till the end of time, and it isn't going to mean anything until you are ready to accept the situation and forgive me in your heart of hearts. I would be lying if I said I know what you're feeling. I don't know, but I can imagine. You feel I deprived you of a mother, and I know, Ollie, how special mothers are. Allison just wasn't the kind of person who . . . who would have made a good mother. You'll never know that, though, and you only have my word for it."

Olivia stared at her father. "I know, Dad. I'm not stupid. I was devastated yesterday until you told me your side of things, but now I understand more." Looking at the breakfast her dad had prepared, she said, "Just give me a minute. I want to brush my teeth. Everything looks good, and it smells even better."

"I aim to please," Dennis said lightly.

Olivia was back in the kitchen in five minutes. She sat down and shook out her napkin. Her father had always been big on cloth napkins, the kind that would wrinkle and have to be ironed. Her father had always set a good table. He was also big on manners. She'd learned just about everything she needed to know about life from her father.

She owed everything to her father. Not to the woman who gave birth to her.

"How did you sleep, Dad?"

"Soundly for a few hours. I woke up around three and couldn't get back to sleep. Do you have any clients today?"

"Three unless they cancel. If the roads are clear, I imagine they'll show up. Why?"

Dennis placed a plate in front of Olivia before he carried his own to the table. "I think it might be a good idea to cancel today's schedule so we can go to see Mr. O'Brien and get this over with. I have to leave by the weekend because I have a big paying charter for Monday. I want to see and hear for myself what you're up against. For some reason I don't see this as a simple inheritance. I say this because I know Allison." He corrected himself. "Knew Allison. By the way, when did you get another dog?"

Olivia explained Cecil's story. "He loves Alice. She's going to miss him when he leaves. I think he's going to be one unhappy little dog. I wish I could keep him. He's a real cutie and has a mind of his own. And he's smart."

"Why don't you offer to keep him? I don't see his handler minding too much. Just don't ask for money. He might be willing to give up the responsibility. Not the money, though. On the other hand, you might have to go through the lawyers who represented Cecil's owner. Do you want me to kidnap him?" he joked.

Olivia's head snapped up. "I know you're joking, but don't kid yourself, I already thought about it. I have to call Jeff today. He's Cecil's handler. I don't know if he lives in Mrs. Manning's house or if he just carts the dog to the vet and groomer. I'm not sure what he does. He didn't balk at paying me fifty bucks an hour to dog-sit Cecil. I'm not going to take the money. I just said that to him to make him aware of his responsibility. It didn't faze him in the least. Cecil is going to die of loneliness when he has to go back."

"I can take him and Alice with me when I leave on the weekend. I'm up for a little dognapping. It's your call, Ollie."

Olivia's eyes almost bugged out of her head when she realized her father was serious. "Dad, Cecil is the richest dog in America. He's news. They'd probably call in the FBI."

"How about this? We get another dog

that looks just like him and pass the new dog off as Cecil. I take both dogs with me, and no one will be the wiser. When we get back from the lawyer's office, we can check the Yorkie Rescue, the pound, and all the pet shops. I bet it would work. The best part is you'll be giving a rescue dog a good home, and Cecil won't care one little bit. Then when the smoke clears, you can come to the islands and pick them up. Alice knows Lea, so she won't be homesick. Cecil, I'm thinking, will adapt as long as he's with Alice. Lea loves animals."

"And if we get caught?"

"Then we deal with it at that time. Why don't you call the handler now and see what he says about your offering to keep Cecil for a few more days."

Olivia looked down at the two dogs sleeping at her feet. They were curled up side by side. She rose from the chair. "I can't believe I'm willing to do this. Damn, I can't believe I'm even *thinking* about doing it."

"We make a good team, Ollie. You know what I always say, it's just you and me, kid."

Yeah, Dad, that's what you always said.

Olivia looked up at the small calendar

taped to the wall above the kitchen phone. She ran her finger down the long column of numbers she'd penciled in on the side. She punched out Jeff's number and waited. When he answered, he sounded like he'd been running, or else he was just one of those people who was always harried. "This is Olivia Lowell, Jeff. I was wondering if you would mind if I kept Cecil for another day or so. I'd like to get some action shots of him out in the snow. You know, showing him at play with my dog. People love to see dogs playing. Cecil is such an interesting dog, and he's so very rich. People want to know he isn't being treated . . . you know . . . differently. By the way, I was just jerking your chain when I said I was going to charge you fifty bucks an hour. What do you say, Jeff?"

"I think that would be okay. So when do you want me to pick him up? I hate to say this, but that dog is controlling my life."

"He just needs a playmate. Why don't you get him a companion? I bet those trustees would applaud you for being so conscientious."

"Do you think so? A companion, huh?"

"I could get you one, if you think it will be

okay. I know someone who has Yorkies," Olivia lied through her teeth.

Suddenly, old Jeff wasn't sounding so harried. He was sounding relieved and happy. "I'll call you back later this afternoon. I'm sure it will be all right, but I do have to run it by the trustees. So what you're saying is, I should pick him and his companion up on Monday."

Olivia sighed and held up her thumb for her father's inspection. "Yes, that's what I'm saying. It will free you up for the week-end, and I don't really mind watching the little guy."

"Okay, Olivia, I'll be there sometime Monday afternoon."

Olivia burst out laughing when she hung up the phone. "Hey, Cecil, you are no longer rich and famous." Cecil opened one eye, then closed it.

"I'll call the airlines and make arrange-ments for the dogs. Do you have carriers?"

A huge smile stretched across Olivia's face. "Dad, I have everything but the re-placement dogs." Sobering, she added, "I sure hope we don't get caught. This is seri-ous stuff."

"I think it's worth the risk, don't you?

Some people don't realize dogs have feelings. They suffer separation anxiety. They miss the people who care for them when they're taken away. Their personalities change. Cecil already went through one trauma when Mrs. Manning died. He's attached himself to Alice and you. What do you think would happen if he had to go back to that lonely house without Alice? Is it worth the risk? Ask yourself if Mrs. Manning would approve."

"The end justifies the means, huh? You know what, Dad? She would approve. She loved that little dog. As long as he's happy, warm, and well fed, I don't think she'd have a problem with what we plan to do."

"Good. Then it's a go. I'll clean up here, Ollie. Go take your shower."

As Olivia stood under the steaming spray she wondered what was happening to her. One day she was the heiress of a criminal and the next day she was a criminal herself—almost. She wondered what it would be like in jail. The eggs Benedict in her stomach started to protest at the thought. *Just think about the good life you're going to give Cecil and the two new dogs. Assum-*

ing you can find two new dogs, she cautioned herself.

Not wanting to dwell on criminal activities, Olivia hopped out of the shower. She dressed quickly, applied makeup, and blow-dried her hair. She didn't, as she put it, "dude up" for Mr. O'Brien. She was wearing camel-colored wool slacks, rubber-soled boots, and a cherry-red sweater. Her unruly hair was gathered into a loose bun and fixed in place by tortoiseshell combs.

Dennis Lowell was brewing a fresh pot of coffee when Olivia walked into the kitchen. He was dressed in the winter clothes he'd left behind before leaving for the islands with Lea. He looked distinguished, and he also smelled good. Olivia said so. Her father smiled, but Olivia noticed the smile didn't reach his eyes. He looked worried.

"I'm going to call my clients and cancel," Olivia told him. "I can be ready to leave anytime you're ready. I'm sure the roads are clear by now. Do you think I should call Mr. O'Brien, or should we just show up?"

"I think we should just show up. Go ahead and make your calls. I'll take the dogs outside for a little while. Give a shout when you're ready to leave."

* * *

The law firm of O'Brien, O'Malley and O'Shaughnessy was a small one. But what it lacked in size it more than made up for in elegance. Even the address was an elegant one, on P Street in Georgetown, home to senators, congressmen, and diplomats. The sidewalk had been cleaned professionally, and little pebbles of salt could be seen between the cracks. Aged oak trees, bare now, lined the street on both sides. At first glance the building could have been a private residence. The polished brass plaque, though, was a giveaway as to what the three-story edifice housed.

Like most structures in Georgetown, it was narrow, with a small patch in the back that served as a lawn, and neighboring buildings so close that the inhabitants could have leaned out their windows and touched each other.

A desirable, high-end parcel of real estate.

A buzzer emitted a fuzzy sound as Dennis pushed open the door. Olivia gasped. Everything seemed to be green. Green marble walls, green marble floor so shiny she could see her reflection. A half-moon desk of polished mahogany had a top made from the same green marble. It was as glossy and shiny as the floor under her feet. The only things on the desk were a phone console, a computer, and a huge basket of fresh yellow tulips. *Fresh tulips in February*, Olivia mused. She stayed where she was as her father walked toward the receptionist and said, "I'm Dennis Lowell, and this is my daughter, Olivia. We're here to see Mr. O'Brien."

The receptionist resembled a polished, lacquered mannequin dressed in designer wear. Olivia wondered if she wore a wig. No one's hair was that perfect except maybe Ted Koppel's, and everyone knew he wore a rug. Olivia continued to stare at the receptionist as her father carried on a conversation with her. False eyelashes long and curly enough to balance a pencil. Makeup so perfect it looked like it would crack if she smiled. Olivia felt dowdy next to her.

"It seems we're supposed to have an appointment," Dennis told Olivia after walking back to where she stood waiting. "That young lady said this establishment is not a storefront, walk-in legal office."

"Oh," was all Olivia could think of to say.

"Would you like to leave, honey? He can make the trip to Winchester to see you."

The mannequin held up a hand with blood-red, inch-long nails. "Mr. O'Brien will see you in five minutes. Please, take a seat."

Five minutes stretched to ten minutes, then fifteen. When the hands on the clock registered twenty minutes, Olivia got up in a huff and marched to the door, her father behind her.

Dennis was unlocking the car door when a mousy young woman with thick glasses ran up to them. She was breathless and full of apologies as she pleaded with them to follow her back to the office. Dennis shrugged in acquiescence. "I hate lawyers," Olivia hissed as they followed the young woman back to the law offices.

"Me too, honey. Me too."

Prentice O'Brien's offices were just as elegant as the lobby. The deep, comfortable client chairs were rich Corinthian leather; the desk, mahogany. The sofa was covered in a nubby wheat-colored material that blended perfectly with the ankle-deep carpeting and ceiling-to-floor draperies. There was even a real fireplace with a real wood fire. The file cabinets were custom-made and built into the rich paneling. An entertainment center and portable bar graced a far wall. The lawyer's desk was cluttered, and the man sitting behind it was in his shirtsleeves. He got up and walked around the desk to greet them. He introduced himself, then motioned for them to be seated.

Dennis and Olivia waited for him to speak. He spoke slowly, almost irritably. "If I had known you were coming in this early, I would have carved out a period of time. I'm sorry I had to keep you waiting. We're going to have to zip through this because I have another appointment in a few minutes."

Olivia was on her feet in an instant. "You didn't have an appointment with me yesterday. You just showed up. If it's all right for you to do that, why isn't it all right for us to do the same thing? Time is money, is that it? Well, I'll tell you what, Mr. O'Brien, when you can carve out some time for me, give me a call. If I can fit you into *my* busy schedule, perhaps we can resolve this. I'm not into billable hours like you are. Personally, Mr. O'Brien, I don't care if I ever see you again. I want nothing to do with Adrian

Ames's will. Come on, Dad, we're outta here."

When the attorney realized they were indeed leaving, he said, "Ms. Lowell, Mr. Lowell, please." Father and daughter ignored him and kept walking.

"At least take this with you," the lawyer said, scrambling across the wide expanse of office space with a letter in his hand. He held it out. "Your mother wrote this letter to you, and she instructed me to hand it to you personally." Olivia made a very unladylike sound and gesture as she continued out of the office. She literally ran through the elegant lobby toward the front door. She didn't see her father reach for the letter and tuck it into his pocket.

The seventy-six-mile ride back to Winchester was made in silence.

Chapter 5

The dogs barked a joyous greeting when Olivia and Dennis returned to the house a little past noon. Olivia made a production of hanging up her coat and dropping to her knees to play with the two happy dogs. She watched her father out of the corner of her eye to see if he would take anything out of his pocket. He did. She started to tremble with nervousness when she saw him fold a white envelope and stick it in his back pocket.

Let him deal with whatever was in the envelope. She wanted no part of it.

Dennis smacked his hands together. "What shall we do now, Ollie? Do you need any help in the studio, or should we start calling around to see what we can come up with in regard to Cecil? Maybe we should make some coffee first to get the chill out of our bones. I swear, being in the islands has thinned my blood. I can't tolerate this cold. I think my tan faded overnight, too."

Olivia forced a laugh she didn't feel. She was surprised at how normal her voice sounded when she said, "Let's do the coffee first. You can use the phone in the kitchen, and I can use my cell phone. And, yes, I'd like your opinion on the photographs I've chosen for this year's canine calendar. I had the idea to do a special section between June and July. A group shot, a collage of some of the action shots I took of all twelve dogs. You know me, I think each one is perfect. I need an independent eye to keep me on track. I'm thinking of it as a kind of bonus for the calendar lover."

She realized she was babbling. "I'll make the coffee," she repeated, heading for the kitchen. "You can turn the heat up in the studio if you don't mind. I'm thinking of getting a space heater for out there. What do you think, Dad?" *Damn, I'm still babbling.*

"Sure, honey, whatever you want. Are we ever going to talk about what's in my pocket?"

The response to her father's question blasted from her mouth like a bullet. "No!"

Dennis shrugged as he moved toward the studio. "Maybe the ducts need cleaning in the studio. Let me take a look at them before you invest in a space heater. Those things are dangerous. Don't forget all the chemicals you store out there for the darkroom."

Olivia spooned coffee into the paper filter. "It was just a thought, Dad. If you want to check the ducts, be my guest."

While she waited for the coffee to drip into the pot, Olivia pulled out her address book and dialed Alice's vet. Within minutes she had the names and phone numbers for the Yorkie Rescue and two Yorkshire breeders in the immediate area. Twenty minutes later she ran out to the studio to tell her father she had two hot leads for Cecil's replacement. "Do you want to go, or should I? It seems this particular rescue is operated by three women and one man. They keep and care for the dogs at their own homes. I wrote everything down."

Dennis was on a ladder peering into one of the ducts. "I don't think this duct has been cleaned since I installed it. Must be a hundred years old," he quipped. "I think you should go. You know more about dogs than I do. I'll hold the fort."

Both dogs sat on their haunches, watching Olivia with bright eyes as she bundled up yet again. The moment they saw her reach for her purse, they scampered to the studio, where they would probably pester Dennis for attention. Purses and jangling keys meant they were being left behind.

Outside, the sun was shining, casting a silvery hue on the piled-up snow. The roads, Olivia noticed, were still wet, and slick with patches of ice that hadn't melted. She drove carefully up and down the streets, her homemade map on the seat next to her.

She'd never been a serendipity kind of person. If anything, she was one of those people who had to make a chart, then think about it for days, weigh everything, then nine times out of ten squash whatever the idea was she had in the beginning in favor of something that was tried-and-true. She even did it with Clarence. One of these days she had to decide what she was going to do about Clarence. It was so hard to feign interest in his IRS audits. If he had told her once, he had told her a thousand times how good he felt exercising his authority over people. The truth was, she had her own fear that he'd audit her for her entire life, as well as her father and all of their friends, if she broke off their mundane relationship. Alice didn't like Clarence. Smart dog.

Olivia slowed the car as she approached the intersection that would take her to Anita Wellesley's sprawling ranch home, where she was caring for eleven Yorkshire terriers and two poodle-Yorkie mixes.

The moment Olivia parked in the driveway she could hear the clamor indoors. She smiled. Dogs always knew when someone was coming. They would consider her an intruder. She was surprised to find a ramp going up to the front door. Maybe Anita Wellesley was handicapped. She rang the bell. The door was opened by a plump, pleasant-looking woman wearing a red smock over faded jeans and an infectious smile.

"I'm Olivia. I called you a little while ago."

"Yes, yes, come in. This is my mother, Anna Pellecone," she said, motioning to a woman sitting in a wheelchair and holding three adorable little dogs. "She helps me with the dogs. My husband does, too, but he works during the day. Come, I'll show you the others. I warn you, it's going to be hard to pick one."

Olivia oohed and aahed as she watched the herd of little dogs behind the gate that separated the great room from the rest of the house. She saw plenty of toys, dog beds, rawhide chews, and water bowls. She climbed over the gate and waited to see which dogs would seek her out. They all did.

"I'll leave you for now. Take all the time you need. I'm going to fix my mother some lunch. Can I make you a sandwich? Perhaps offer you a cup of tea?"

"No thank you. I'm fine. If you don't mind me asking, exactly how does your mother help you if she's confined to a wheelchair?"

Anita laughed, a pleasant musical sound. "She has nothing to do all day but read, watch TV, and love the dogs, and not necessarily in that order. All the dogs love her because they know instinctively that she genuinely loves them. My mother is a jewel."

Olivia heard the whir of the electric wheelchair and turned. "Is my daughter singing my praises again?" Anna Pellecone laughed.

Tears pricked at Olivia's eyelids when she saw Anita bend over to kiss her mother's cheek.

"This lady," Anita said proudly, "is the reason you are seeing all these dogs in my house. She simply cannot stand to see an animal not being loved. She was that way with us kids growing up. She was the mother of the entire neighborhood. Our house was where all the kids came when there was a problem. Mom would soothe them, feed them, and love them. It's what motherhood is all about, you know."

No, she didn't know what motherhood was all about, but she wasn't going to say anything.

An hour later, Olivia made her choice. The Yorkie named Loopy, according to his collar, looked so much like Cecil he could have been his brother, and his color as well as his markings were identical. For Loopy's playmate she chose a female Yorkie-Poo named Bea.

It was another hour before Olivia completed the paperwork, signing her name in a dozen different places. She was reminded that Loopy had been neutered and Bea had been spayed, and both dogs had received all their shots. Anita and her mother told Olivia what the dogs' likes and dislikes were. Olivia cuddled them to her and at the last minute before leaving walked over to the wheelchair so that Mrs. Pellecone could give the animals one last hug.

"You be good little dogs for Ms. Olivia, you hear?" said the older lady. The dogs barked happily. Anna reached for Olivia's hand and gave it a hard squeeze.

So that's what it feels like to have a mother touch you, Olivia thought. Impulsively, she leaned over and kissed the woman's dry, powdered cheek. She smelled wonderful, like fresh flowers on a warm spring day. Something caught in Olivia's throat when she tried to smile. She had to get out of there. *Immediately!*

"Remember, now—call if there are any problems. We're here to help."

"I will," Olivia gulped as she practically ran to the car.

On the drive back to the house, with the dogs cuddled in her lap, Olivia thought about motherhood and mothers in general. Obviously, she had missed a great deal by not having a mother. She knew in her gut, though—and there were her father's words to back it up—that Allison Matthews, Adrian Ames, or whoever, was no Mrs. Pellecone.

As Olivia swerved into the driveway, she saw her father and the two dogs waiting for her. All of them crowded around the car as she climbed out with the two new guests. Alice and Cecil sniffed, stared, barked—then barked some more. Inside, they raced around chasing each other, snapping and snarling. Finally, Olivia blew her whistle and was rewarded with instant silence. "Okay, here's the drill, so listen up. . . ."

Dennis laughed until his sides hurt. "This is just an observation on my part, honey, but I don't think you're going to be able to give those dogs to Jeff. Now, would you like ham and turkey or turkey and ham on your sandwich? I just made fresh coffee. Your ducts are clean, and your studio is toasty warm. Don't thank me"—he twinkled—"that's what fathers are for."

Olivia sat down at the kitchen table. That's when she saw the white envelope. If she closed her eyes, she wouldn't have to look at it. "I met the rescue lady's mother, Dad. She was in a wheelchair. She had the sweetest disposition, and she smelled so nice. It . . . it was easy to see how much she and her daughter loved each other. They both love the dogs, too."

Dennis turned toward her, his face sad. "And your point is . . ."

"Didn't your wife show any . . . you know . . . loving qualities? How can you be so sure she wouldn't have made a good mother? Maybe in time—"

"Stop right there, Ollie. Allison never wanted children. We didn't love each other the way most couples do. I'm not even sure we liked each other, which doesn't say much or explain why we got married. I always thought she considered me a safety net, and I'm not sure why that was. Just a feeling. She didn't want to see you when you were born. She didn't want you, period. Based on that, no, I don't think she would have made a good mother. Allison did love herself. She thought she was smarter than everyone else. She graduated summa cum laude. Her main goal was to be rich and famous. She constantly reminded me of that when we were married. She said she couldn't depend on me to make her rich, so she would have to do it herself. Now, why don't you read the damn letter and get it over with. Maybe all the answers to your questions are right there."

"I'm sorry, Dad, I didn't mean to upset you."

"Well, you did. You are. We can't change anything. I say, read the letter, make decisions, and move on. Refusing to acknowledge things isn't going to help. Deal with it, Ollie," Dennis said, slapping the plate down in front of her. "I'm going to take the dogs out back. Do what you want." Dennis stuck his head back in the door for one last parting shot. "And make a damn decision where that guy Clarence is concerned. For once in your life, stop waffling and take the bull by the horns. I know that's a cliché, but you damn well know what I mean."

Shit. Now my father is angry with me. The last time he used that tone of voice with me I was twelve years old.

Olivia bit into the ham-and-turkey sandwich. It tasted dry. She lifted off the top slice of bread. Her father had forgotten the lettuce and mayo. He must really be upset with her. Dutifully, she ate the sandwich anyway and washed it down with coffee. All the while her gaze stayed on the white envelope.

Clarence.

Cecil.

Adrian Ames.

She was getting a headache.

Olivia picked up the letter by the corner, as if touching it would somehow contaminate her. She walked through the house till she came to a small room that at one time had been a guest room and was now her in-home office. She had a desk, a computer, two colorful, small canvas chairs, a fax machine, and a state-of-the-art color copier. The first thing she did was drop the envelope on the desk. Then she settled herself in her ergonomic chair, turned on the computer, and headed for the Net. She typed in the name Adrian's Treasures, figuring there was a Web site. She remembered ordering from the catalog before but had never been to the Web site. It was impressive, definitely a high-end one. She reared back in her chair when the screen in front of her flashed her mother's picture. It was a close-up, airbrushed, to be sure. Olivia leaned closer to see if she could see any resemblance to herself. She couldn't. The woman didn't look anything like her or the woman in the picture she'd removed from the mantel.

Thank God she took after her father. Adrian Ames didn't look the least bit like a mother—not even coming close to looking like Mrs. Pellecone. Adrian Ames was hard-looking, with bleached hair and too much makeup. She had small eyes and thin lips and a real honker for a nose. Not any kind of pretty.

Olivia scanned the categories on the side of the screen. She checked them all. Her mother's history, presented in an interview format, was a short summary of how she had gotten started in the business and the trials and tribulations of a woman trying to make it in a very tough market. She catered to housewives. Women who had to watch their pennies. She herself, she declared, liked fine things and had found a way to sell cheap imitations the housewife could afford. No, she wasn't a housewife, but she understood the mind-set of a woman both raising children on a limited budget and wanting fine things. On holidays, the interviewer said, Ms. Ames offered free shipping.

How had it all started? Baby bracelets. Those little beads new babies were given at birth to identify them. "I took it one step further by making the beads colorful and sizing them accordingly, with a tough, resilient elastic," Ames said. "A money-back guarantee was offered. One has to stand behind one's products. The bracelets led to other articles until I had enough for a full-featured catalog. I bet my shirt and gambled. It worked."

The article went on to ask if she'd ever married. Ms. Ames said she was married to her business. Did she regret not having children, a family? She said her customers were her family, and one couldn't miss something one never had.

And the rest was history.

There was a little more to the article. The long hours, doing things herself. Her confidence. Her philanthropy. Her collection of cars, her many houses. Her incredible wealth. How her employees adored her. The lavish Christmas presents she bestowed on her faithful staff. She had no immediate family.

"What a crock." Olivia clicked on a button to bring up pictures of the home of Adrian Ames, a.k.a. Allison Matthews Lowell. She whistled approvingly. "Way to go, Mommie Dearest," she mumbled as she scanned the lavish estate and its designer rooms. Obviously mail-order was the way to go.

Olivia clicked on the BACK button and proceeded to print out the articles and pictures for her father's benefit. Certainly not hers. After he looked at them, she'd toss them into the fireplace.

Olivia reached for the envelope. It felt heavy. Great. It was probably Adrian Ames's life story—a missive. She opened it. No, not a missive. A missive was many pages. There were only three sheets of paper, lined paper ripped from a legal pad. The writing was large, taking up two lines for each sentence. She was surprised to see a tissue-wrapped square among the three pages. She opened it carefully and was stunned to see her baby bracelet. It said, BABY MATTHEWS. Olivia tossed it onto her desk before she leaned back in her chair and propped her feet up on the desk. She looked down at the letter. It was dated ten months earlier. It was written in April, Olivia's favorite month of the whole year.

> *Dear Olivia,*
>   *I can only imagine how shocked you must be at this intrusion into your*

life. By now I am also certain that your father has explained things to you. I know he never would have divulged our secret to you, but things changed in my life, and I regret that I am the one breaking our pact.

Six weeks ago I received some bad news in regard to my health and knew after the initial shock that I had to put my house in order. There's no need to bore you with the details.

I know you've had a good, wonderful life. I know this because your father is a kind, caring man. He couldn't wait for you to be born. He talked endlessly of the things he was going to do with his son or daughter. I know he named you after his mother. It's a beautiful name. I didn't become involved in your life until you turned sixteen, at which time I hired a private investigator who sent me weekly reports. I'm very proud of you, not that that means anything.

I'm leaving everything I have to you. Not because I feel guilty but because it is the right thing to do. It's that simple. I wish I could say I feel something maternal, but I don't. I never have.

Now, I want you to do something for me. Because it is the right thing to do. It doesn't affect your inheritance in any way. I would take care of these matters myself, but unfortunately, time doesn't permit it.

Before I met your father, the spring of my last year at Ole Miss, I worked in a small, privately owned bank. I worked there for four years. I liked being around money even then. I robbed the bank with the help of my two best friends, Jill Davis and Gwen Nolan. We didn't go up to the teller and demand money or anything like that. We just helped ourselves to a package of bearer bonds. We held on to them for five years. That's how long I was married to your father.

Jill, Gwen, and I met up two weeks after I walked out of the hospital after giving birth to you and divided up the bonds. That's how I started my mail-order business. We agreed not to keep in touch, though we did take each other's phone numbers and ad-

dresses in case of emergency. We eventually lost track of one another, although Gwen once asked for a loan. I want you to find them, and I want you to return the money to the bank anonymously. When you take possession of my house, go to the safe in my bedroom, and you'll find what little information I've been able to gather in regard to Jill and Gwen. The combination to the safe is under the blotter on my desk.

If for some reason Jill and Gwen balk about paying the money back, I want you to be stern with them. It was wrong what we did. It has haunted me all these years. I'm sure it's haunted Jill and Gwen, too. Paying the money back is the best way for them to deal with the guilt. If they don't cooperate with you, repay all the money from my account. I would like you to do one last thing for me even though I have no right to ask. Buy your father the boat of his desires. Anonymously, of course. I owe him that much, and he deserves so much more. Have a good life, Olivia.

All best wishes,
Adrian Ames (Allison Matthews)

Olivia bolted off the chair, the letter clutched in her hands. "Daaaaaddddd!" she screamed at the top of her lungs. "Daaaaddd!"

Chapter 6

Dennis Matthews shrugged out of his down jacket and ran to his white-faced daughter, who was shaking from head to toe. The jittery dogs at his feet danced and pranced as they tried to make sense out of the high-pitched babble around them. "What? For God's sake, what happened, Ollie?"

"Read this! Just read this!" Olivia shrieked. "Your wife is a thief!" She corrected herself. "Was a thief. Her friends are thieves! She robbed a damn bank! She wants me to . . . she wants me to . . . Read the letter, Dad!"

Dennis reached for the yellow sheets of paper in his daughter's hands. He had to pry her fingers loose. "Ease up, Ollie. Ease up." Olivia relaxed her hold on the letter and handed it over. She started to pace as her father read the letter. "Well?" she shouted. "Say something, Dad."

Dennis sat down at the kitchen table. "I don't know what to say, Ollie. I never had a clue. Not one. For some reason, though, it doesn't surprise me. Allison was never afraid to take risks. What does surprise me is that she convinced Jill and Gwen to go along with her. Obviously, that little caper was something she couldn't pull off on her own. Don't look at me like that, Ollie. Don't blame me for this."

Olivia ran her fingers through her hair. The color was coming back into her face. "I'm not blaming you, Dad. She wants me to . . . The nerve, the gall of the woman! She said she had no maternal feelings. She made these arrangements because . . . because it was the right thing to do. Damn her to hell! I'm not doing it! No one can make me do this. Almost forty years later she wants me to return the money, anonymously. She's still not willing to take responsibility for what she did. Explain that to me, Dad."

"I can't, honey. No one can make you do anything you don't want to do. The letter was sealed. That has to mean the lawyer doesn't know what's in it. I seriously doubt

Allison, I mean Adrian Ames, would have confided in her attorney even though the communication would have been privileged. Don't even think about buying me a boat anonymously."

Olivia continued her frantic pacing to the annoyance of the four scampering dogs as they circled and whined at her feet. "We need to make some coffee, and we need to put *something* in it." She ran water until it cascaded over the pot and down to the floor. The dogs lapped it up. Then she spilled coffee grounds all over the counter. Her father reached for the paper towels to clean it up. "How much brandy do we need to dull our senses to make this all go away, Dad?"

"It's not going to go away, Ollie. You have to deal with it. Like it or not, she was your mother. I hate to say this but . . . a person's last wishes should . . . *be honored*."

Hands on her slim hips, eyes dark with rage, Olivia glared at her father. "Okay, you do it! You were the one who was stupid enough to marry her! Oh, God, Dad, I'm sorry. I didn't mean that. Well, I did sort of mean it. How in the hell did she get away with robbing a bank? Think, Dad."

The phone took that moment to ring, saving Dennis from a reply. He turned around to pick it up and growled a greeting. "Lea!" Dennis listened, a frown building on his face. "Let me talk to Ollie, and I'll call you back. Oh, yes, it's cold here. There's a good bit of snow on the ground. It might snow again before the day is out. Give me an hour or so, and I'll call you back."

"Is something wrong?" Olivia asked after her dad hung up the phone.

"Not really. My fishing party is arriving early. They want to add a couple of extra days to their itinerary. If I want the charter, I'll have to leave tonight. Otherwise, I'll have Lea turn it over to Daimon."

Olivia felt her eyes well up. "It's okay, Dad. Since I'm not going to do anything, it won't make any difference if you're here or not. Go on back to Lea and your charter, and don't worry about me. I'll just . . . you know, roll with it."

Dennis looked like he was torn as he gazed at his daughter. "Are you sure, honey?"

No, she wasn't sure, but she sensed her father wanted to get as far away as he could from the memories of his ex-wife. "I'm sure," she fibbed.

"Well, all right. But if you change your mind, call Lea, and she can get me on the ship-to-shore. I can always come back if you need me." His demeanor made it clear he hoped that wouldn't be necessary. "Do you mind if I use the office?"

Olivia poured two cups of coffee. It looked blacker than coal. Dennis looked at it and grimaced. "I'd say this is strong enough to grow hair on my chest." Olivia managed a sickly smile in response.

"I printed out some things from *your wife's* Web site. I left them on my desk. You might want to take a look before I burn them."

Olivia glared at the ugly-looking coffee in her cup. She couldn't drink it. She tossed it and made a fresh pot. While she waited for the water to drip down, she squatted on the floor with the dogs. They ran to her to be cuddled. At that precise moment, as she stared at Loopy and Cecil, she panicked. Where was Loopy's collar? Which one was Cecil? She couldn't tell. She tried calling them by name, but they both responded. Markings? They were the same. Teeth? She pried open their respective mouths. Teeth were teeth. Her heart started to thunder in her chest. "Alice, which one is Cecil?" Olivia asked in a jittery voice. Alice looked up at her, then at the two Yorkies in her arms. She barked playfully. Panic-stricken, Olivia up-ended both dogs. Two pink bellies. Boys, obviously. Both neutered. "Do I need this? No, I do not need this. Absolutely I do not need this," she mumbled as she continued to search for a difference in markings on the dogs. She drew a blank.

"What's wrong, honey?" Dennis asked as he set his cup on the counter. It was still full of the horrible-looking coffee.

"Loopy's collar is gone. One of the other dogs must have loosened it. Now I can't tell them apart, Dad. Can you?"

Dennis squatted next to his daughter. He eyed both Yorkies. He did everything Olivia had done, with exactly the same results. He finally threw his hands in the air. "I don't know, Ollie. I can't tell. Which ones am I tak-ing with me?"

"None, Dad. I can't do that. I have to give Cecil back. I'm going to try to talk to Jeff, or maybe the trustees. I don't know, maybe we can work something out."

"So now you have four dogs!"

Olivia managed a rueful laugh. "Looks that way. I . . . I suddenly have no desire to break the law. So, did you manage to change your flight?"

"Yep, leaves at eight this evening. I'll take a cab. I don't like leaving you like this, Ollie. But the charter is important to me—it will take care of the lean months. I hate reducing it to dollars and cents, yet I really don't have much of a choice. Ah, fresh coffee. I'll have a cup after I pack. I called a cab. It'll be here in an hour. With all the security at Reagan National, I have to be there extra early. Are you sure you don't want me to take the dogs?"

"I'm sure. I must have had a brain freeze even to suggest it. That would put me in the same category as your ex-wife if I went through with it." She looked up at her father from her position on the floor. He was somewhere else. Probably planning his charter. She'd never felt more alone in her life. A second later she was on her feet and handing out dog chews. The dogs accepted them and trotted into the great room, where they lay down by the fire and chewed contentedly.

With nothing else to do, Olivia made her way to the studio, where she reached for her appointment book. "I must be crazy," she muttered over and over to herself as she called to cancel a month's worth of appointments. She made the last call just as her father called her from the kitchen.

Dennis poured coffee for them both. "Now, let's talk seriously, Ollie. I can only imagine how you feel. I see the bitterness and sense of betrayal in your eyes. You have to leave that behind you—otherwise, it will fester like a bad sore. I want you to do whatever feels right to you, but be sure that whatever that turns out to be, you can live with it. When you hit a rough patch, you have to slow down and think it through. Whether you know it or not, you're a very strong, capable person. You *can* deal with all this. You really can, Ollie. Plot out a course of action and go on from there. Do it the same way you plan a photo shoot. Set it up. You're the one in control, and don't ever forget it." Then he started to laugh and couldn't stop. "The first thing you have to do before you do anything else is figure out which dog is Cecil."

Olivia groaned, but she, too, started to

laugh. "Hey, I hear a horn. I guess your taxi is here." She ran to the window. "Yep, it's here. He's gonna love you—a trip to Reagan. Big fare, big tip."

Dennis zipped up his jacket, then hugged his daughter. "I love you, Ollie, and I'm sorry you have to go through this. Call me if you need me. If you want someone to come and stay with you, I'm sure Lea wouldn't mind." He squeezed her so hard she squealed for mercy. The horn blew again.

And then he was gone, and Olivia was alone.

Again.

So much for good intentions, Olivia thought as she tossed the pictures from Adrian Ames's Web site onto the coffee table. The letter followed, the one she knew by heart. She'd planned on burning the lot, but somehow she couldn't bring herself to drop the pages into the fire. She wondered why that was. There should be somebody she could ask, but there wasn't. Her father would say the letter was the only thing she had of her mother's, which was pretty damn sad if you considered that she was thirty-four years old. No, no, that was wrong. She had the bracelet. In the blink of an eye she ran down the hall to the desk where she'd thrown it. She reached for it and clutched it in her hand. Now she had two things. A letter and a bracelet. But the bracelet was *hers*. Some kindly, smiling nurse had probably put it on her wrist within minutes of being born. Such tiny beads. Today they put little plastic strips that passed for bracelets on babies. Today they put them on the baby's ankle instead of the wrist. She'd read that in some dentist's office.

Olivia frowned. Didn't her father tell her that Allison had never seen her, refused to see her after she'd given birth? Of course he'd said that. *So how did she get my baby bracelet? And why did she keep it all these years?* Her father had never shown it to her. He was sentimental and would have kept it if he'd had it. He'd kept her first baby booties and her pink blanket. Why wouldn't he have kept the baby bracelet? She made a mental note to ask him the next time she spoke to him.

Everything came back to one thing, the letter. Since she knew it by heart, Olivia folded it up and shoved it into the drawer of the coffee table. The pictures of the estate were shuffled into a neat pile, and she placed them on top of a stack of books. She dropped the baby bracelet into a crystal candy dish that had held Cisco candies until her father had eaten them all.

Feeling churlish and out of sorts, she decided she shouldn't be sitting there alone at eleven o'clock at night with only four dogs for company. But then her mood lightened when she looked at the contented dogs. A smile crept across her face—until she remembered her problem. Fortunately, she had kept Jeff's phone number. So what if it was eleven o'clock on a Friday night? She punched in the numbers. His voice wasn't harried when he offered up a greeting. It was sleepy and lazy-sounding. She heard a giggle in the background. A female giggle.

"Well, hi there, Jeff. This is Olivia Lowell. I'd like to talk to you about Cecil."

"Now? You want to talk about Cecil now? It's after eleven o'clock."

Olivia heard a voice chirp, "Who's Cecil?"

"Well, yes, Jeff. Eleven is just a number. Tomorrow is Saturday. I'd like it if you'd come out here now, please."

"Wait just a damn minute, Olivia. It's almost midnight, it's cold as hell outside, and you want me to get into an ice-cold car and drive seventy-six miles out to your house?"

"Uh-huh."

"Why? Oh, God, is something wrong with Cecil? Tell me there's nothing wrong with Cecil. Olivia, please tell me nothing's wrong with Cecil."

The voice in the background chirped again, "Who's Cecil?"

"It took you long enough to ask about the dog, Jeff. He's fine. I guess you have other priorities. Yeah. I want you to crawl out of your nice, warm bed—that's where you are, right?—and get into your nice, cold BMW and drive seventy-six miles to my house. Now. You coming or not?"

The voice chirped in the background once again. "Jeffie, baby, this is the last time I'm going to ask you who Cecil is."

Olivia looked at the pinging phone in her hand. Then she laughed. The dogs woke, and she let them out. Jeff was right, it was frigid outside. She could see icicles hanging from the roof. They glistened like diamonds in the light from the patio. She shivered. The dogs trotted back indoors. She still couldn't tell who was who. She handed out treats and returned to the sofa, but not before she replenished the fire that was starting to subside. The shower of sparks racing up the chimney reminded her of fireworks on the Fourth of July. Her father had always bought her one box of sparklers, then took her and Dee Dee Pepper to see a display in town. She'd loved it, thinking it was somehow magical. She'd had such a wonderful childhood. So many special memories to cherish.

Now they were tainted.

A lone tear escaped her eye, followed by another, until she was crying openly. The dogs, tired out from their busy day, slept through her torment, and she finally joined them, dozing until the doorbell pealed. Then all hell broke loose as the startled dogs woke and raced to the front door. Olivia rubbed her eyes and opened the door. "It's about time," she snapped. *It must have been hard to leave that chirping, whiny voice,* she thought uncharitably.

For some reason, she was surprised to see how tall Jeff Bannerman was. The only time she'd met him was when he'd come to the studio door, bent down, and let Cecil out of his carry crate, leaving immediately thereafter. Talking to him on the phone hadn't quite prepared her for his tall, rumpled good looks. Right then he looked pissed to the teeth. Olivia stood aside to let him enter the foyer. She continued to observe him. Nice tight jeans, scuffed Nikes, Ralph Lauren jacket, baseball cap on backward. A hunk.

"You look different. I guess it was your suit that first day."

"I'm a lawyer. Lawyers wear suits. I'm on my own time right now. I'd like to get back to my own time, so tell me what the problem is and I'll get out of your hair."

"Come in where it's warm," Olivia said, leading the way to the great room. The dogs leaped and tried to chew at Jeff's leg as he scrambled to follow Olivia. *Pissed to the teeth* was probably an understatement.

"Do you want a beer, a cup of coffee, maybe some wine?" Olivia asked. Her hands were twitching so badly that she shoved them into the pockets of her sweatpants.

"No thank you. Just please tell me what the problem is so I can go back home. I have company, not that you care."

"Oh you mean, chirp, chirp, chirp, and

this is the last time I'm going to ask you who Cecil is?" Olivia imitated the woman's voice in an obnoxious falsetto.

Jeff Bannerman clenched his jaw. His face turned pink. *Men blush. How interesting,* Olivia thought. "I thought you just had one dog," he blurted.

"I do. Did. I went to get a playmate for Cecil and ended up getting another one for . . . for other reasons. Now I can't tell them apart. Can you?"

"Me? I'm no dog expert. Look, the president of our law firm, one of the trustees of Lillian Manning's estate, *appointed* me to care for Cecil because Lillian Manning requested me specifically. I'm the one who drew up her will. I did not volunteer. With a rather nice stipend, I might add. All I had to do was bring him here for his photograph and take care of him until Mrs. Manning's estate was settled. I agreed. However, the dog has ruined my apartment. He chewed everything in sight, he poops anywhere he feels like it, and he hates my guts. He's a fussy eater, too. He doesn't like dog food. He wants a meal. A meal! I have to bring takeout home for him. The dog eats better than I do. Did I mention, the dog hates my

guts? That's the sum total of my involvement with that little terror. Oh, yeah, one
other thing—he's screwing up my social life.
What in the damn hell do you mean, you
can't tell them apart?" Dark brown eyes that
matched his unruly hair sparked dangerously with the question.

Olivia twirled a hank of hair over her ear
with her index finger. "I can see why Cecil
would hate you. You have to love a dog. The
dog needs to know you love him. You need
to care for him, walk him, feed him at regular times, and—of course—you have to play
with him. That's another way of saying I
don't give two hoots about your social life.
You have a responsibility to the richest dog
in the United States, maybe the world, and
you're getting it on with some bird who
chirps in the background. Let's get real
here. We, and I stress the *we,* have a problem. Why isn't this dog living in his owner's
mansion the way it says in the newspapers?
Those very same newspapers said Cecil
was being catered to twenty-four/seven and
was living like a king. Ha! You all lied. I
wouldn't trust a hamster with you, Jeff Bannerman."

The baseball cap had been turned

around. He fiddled with it. And he looked uneasy. Nervous and jittery. "Well . . . they're . . . repainting or something. They let Mrs. Manning's rather large staff go, and they're going to get a person to live there with Cecil. I'm just—"

"An appointee. In other words, you lied, and the trustees lied to the public. I'm going to report you to the newspapers. I've been taking care of this dog. You were only too willing to let me do it for you. Chirp, chirp, chirp. Mrs. Manning must be spinning in her grave. I bet you could lose your law license or whatever it is lawyers have. I hate lawyers. You're scum of the earth. My father hates them, too. Now, let's get back to the problem at hand. Pick up Cecil."

"Which one is he?" Jeff said, bending over to peer at the two dogs that looked alike.

Olivia looked helplessly at the young lawyer. "You tell me. You can take them both. Cecil needs a playmate. I was going to give you Bea, but I've become attached to her. That means you have to take Loopy."

Bannerman continued to twirl the baseball cap in his hands. "Yeah, well, I may have spoken too soon. My boss vetoed the idea. I was going to call you tomorrow to tell you. And, on top of that, the condo association doesn't allow dogs. I more or less sneaked Cecil in, but he blew it when he started to bark. He did it on purpose because he hates me. I did mention that, didn't I? I was hoping I could make arrangements with you to take care of him. He seems to love you and the other dogs. No one would have to know," he pleaded.

Olivia's heart soared. She might get to keep Cecil after all. "You're trying to bribe me! For shame!" she said dramatically. "Then, of course, you would pretend you still have him and obviously keep that generous stipend. You lawyers are all alike."

"Yes. No. I would continue, but I wouldn't spend it. If it's in Cecil's best interests, why not?"

"See? See? That's why I hate lawyers. You twist everything around till you can make it work for you. In this case, me taking care of Cecil. Covering your ass so you can make Brownie points with your boss. No dice, Counselor."

The lawyer shifted from one foot to the other. "Let me put this another way, Ms. Lowell. I know nothing about dogs. I'm not even sure I like dogs. I work sixty, sometimes seventy hours a week. That's what new lawyers do. I have to go home at lunchtime and take him out. I don't get home till late. It's no life for a dog. You've got the perfect setup here. Never lose sight of the fact that I was *assigned* this gig. Cecil is happy. Isn't he?" Bannerman asked anxiously.

Olivia could feel hot tears start to prick her eyelids. "Of course he's happy," she said in a choked voice. "That's why I hate it that you have to take him. My dog Alice loves him. Bea and Loopy love him. They all bonded instantly."

The man standing in front of her sat down. "Look, under other circumstances, I think I could be a real animal lover. I just don't have the time right now. Help me out here, Ms. Lowell."

Olivia then made the mistake of sitting down, her gaze going to the pile of printed pages on the coffee table. She turned, her eyes full of unshed tears. "Say it, damn you. Just have the guts to say you don't want the dog, you're rejecting him because . . . because you have things to do and places to go, and a dog doesn't fit into

your schedule—after you agreed, for a generous stipend, to care for him. You know
what? That's what my mother did. Now take
your dog, and get the hell out of my house.
Now, damn you!"

Bannerman reared back, then jerked forward. "*Whoa.* Whoa. Whoa. Okay, okay.
Which one?"

Deep, gut-wrenching sobs ripped from
Olivia's throat. It was all the little herd of
dogs needed. They attacked in full force,
clawing, snapping, biting, and sniping until
Bannerman shouted at the top of his lungs.
"Enough! Sit! That means you, too, Olivia!"

Olivia, her vision blurred by tears, picked
up the crystal candy dish that held her baby
bracelet and heaved it at the lawyer before
she turned around and marched out of the
room. "Take your dog and go!"

The four dogs defied him to get up.
Bannerman knew he wasn't going anywhere. He sighed, removed his jacket, and
stretched out on the sofa, but not before he
picked up the crystal candy dish, which
miraculously had not broken, and the baby
bracelet. He clutched it in his hand. He slept
that way, his fist curled into a tight ball un-

der the pillow. He'd think about all this in the morning.

He really would.

The last thing he saw was four pairs of eyes watching his every move as he drifted into sleep.

Chapter 7

Olivia woke and knew instantly that it was still dark outside. She rolled over so she could see the digital clock on her nightstand—5:30. Where were the dogs? Alice and Cecil liked to sleep on the bed. Maybe it was too cold in the bedroom. She swung her legs over the side of the bed and headed for the bathroom and her robe. Then she remembered what had happened before she had fallen into a tearful sleep. She raced down the hall, skidding to a stop when she saw Jeff Bannerman sitting up on the couch.

"Well, good morning, Ms. Lowell," he snarled. "I really have to go to the bathroom, so I'd appreciate it if you'd call off these hounds and point me in the right direction."

Hounds. She didn't like the sound of that. "I thought I told you to leave last night. I'm not doing you any favors, Jeff Bannerman."

"What? You're just going to let me sit here until I—? Well, lady, it's your couch!"

Olivia's eyes widened at the implication. "Come on, guys, let's go into the kitchen. Ohhh," she trilled to the dogs as she looked out the window, "it's snowing again. I just love snow." While the water dripped in the coffeemaker, she slapped bacon into a fry pan and cracked eggs into a bowl. Normally, Olivia didn't eat more than a bagel or muffin for breakfast, but on weekends she made it a point to have either scrambled eggs or pancakes. When she was growing up, her father had served skimpy breakfasts during the school week but always managed a super, colossal breakfast on weekends, and she continued the tradition. Weekend mornings were a special time to eat slowly while reading the newspapers.

As she turned the bacon, Olivia pondered her day. If it continued snowing, and it looked like it might, maybe she'd stay in, make some chicken soup and even a cake. She did have a sweet tooth. Maybe she'd use her father's secret recipe—triple chocolate mousse cake. The one he'd entered into her eighth-grade bake-off for parents. He'd come in seventh out of eighty-eight entries. When they called his name for honorable mention, they called him Denise instead of Dennis. Her father had laughed, and she'd cried. The only father in the bakeoff.

The dogs barked to be let in. She obliged, then dried them all off with a towel from the dryer. She looked up to see Jeff watching her. She wished she knew what he was thinking. "Why are you doing that?" His voice sounded curious.

"So they don't get sick. Dogs get sick just like humans. It's wet and cold out there. Dogs like to be warm. Watch this bacon, and don't let it burn while I replenish the fire. They like to lie by the fire and chew on their treats."

"Oh."

Olivia wondered if Bannerman was this articulate in the courtroom. She built up the fire, handed out dog chews, and returned to the kitchen, surprised to find the table set.

"Let me cook," he said. "I know how. My mother made all of us boys learn early. She taught us to do our own laundry and how to clean house. I have five brothers."

Well, that was certainly more than she needed to know. Olivia just looked at him as he rummaged for a clean fry pan, greased it, then dropped the whisked eggs into it.

"They all live in Pennsylvania. On a farm. In a town called Ebensburg. They raise corn and alfalfa."

That was *definitely* more than she needed to know.

"Two of my brothers are dentists. They have a partnership. One brother is a thoracic surgeon, Jack is an architect, and Kirk farms with Dad. I'm the only lawyer. Think about it," he babbled. "I get a lifetime of free dental care. I have the best teeth in the family. No cavities, no veneers, no bridges. And I still have my wisdom teeth, but they have to come out. Jack is drawing up plans for a house for me. It's going to be a work of art. I just have to come up with the money to build it. If I ever need a thoracic surgeon, I just have to call my brother. I get corn on the cob and other vegetables free all summer long."

"And I need to know this . . . why? I don't remember inviting you for breakfast."

Jeff whirled around. He was still wearing the baseball cap. He shrugged. "You seem to have an unfavorable opinion of me, like the dog. I'm really a nice guy. You can even ask my mother." At the murderous look in his host's eyes, Jeff cut off whatever else he was going to say. He scrambled the eggs and pressed the plunger on the toaster at the same time. "I invited myself. I'm starved. I can pay you for it if money is the issue."

Olivia waved her hands in frustration. She felt like crying and wasn't sure why. She looked down at the plate he put in front of her. The bacon was just right, extra crispy, not a speck of grease anywhere. The eggs were fluffy and golden. The toast expertly buttered, not too much, just right. "Thank you," she said grudgingly.

"My pleasure. I'm sorry if I said something . . . Obviously, I hit a tender spot somewhere along the way. Does it have anything to do with this?" he said, withdrawing the baby bracelet from his pocket. "When you pitched that bowl at me last night, it fell out. I picked it up." He slid the little bracelet across the table. Olivia made no move to pick it up but couldn't take her eyes off it.

Olivia licked her lips. She nodded. "It has everything to do with my . . . attitude. I guess I should apologize. I said 'guess,' and that doesn't mean I'm going to do it. Shouldn't you be leaving? Don't you have company waiting for you at home?"

Jeff blushed again. The sight pleased Olivia. "I don't think so," he hedged. "You pretty much took care of that." He grinned. In spite of herself, Olivia laughed.

"So, you take dog pictures!"

"Yep."

"Nice in-home business. That overhead can kill you, though. How long have you been doing this?"

He sounded like he really wanted to know. "Forever. I took over from my dad when he retired. He lives in the islands and takes charters on his fishing boat. I do calendars, too. A dog a month, that kind of thing. All breeds. I'm working on next year's right now. I'd like to put Cecil on it, but I'll need permission. In case your next question is 'which one is which,' I still don't know."

Jeff groaned. "I don't do dishes," he said, to avoid discussing the dogs. "I use those shiny plastic things you just toss in the trash. Listen, if you want to talk about . . .

whatever it is that's bothering you, I'm a good listener. If you pay me a dollar, we can log it under attorney-client privilege. I was just going to hang out today and write a brief."

She didn't mean to speak the words, but they tumbled out of her mouth anyway. "I was going to make chicken soup and maybe bake a cake. My dad always did that on bad-weather days."

Jeff's eyebrows shot upward. He removed his baseball cap, suddenly aware that he was still wearing it. He shoved it in his back pocket. Olivia noticed how the cap had mashed down his unruly curly hair. "My mother does the same thing. If it isn't chicken soup and cake, it's stew and a pie. We had a lot of bad weather back in Pennsylvania growing up, so we did eat hearty in the winter."

Again, words she didn't mean to utter tumbled from her mouth. "What's your mother like?"

Jeff leaned back in his chair. He didn't know how he knew, but he knew nonetheless that he was treading on troubled ground. "I wrote an essay on her once for school when I was little. I got an A. Mom framed it. She hung it up in her bedroom. I think my dad was a little miffed. She has a wonderful smile. I kind of look like her, or so my dad says. She's the one with the curly hair. All us boys have curly hair. My dad's hair is poker straight. She wears glasses, and her hair is gray now. She says she's a little heavier than she'd like to be. She's active in church stuff, 4-H and the like. She enters all the cooking contests when they have the county fair. She wins, too. She helps Dad and can drive the tractor. Sometimes she mows the lawn. She never went to college, never had a job outside the house. Six boys were enough to handle. On Thanksgiving we always had to have two turkeys. When we'd get brave enough to take a girl home for the first time, we always knew right away if Mom liked her or not. If she was polite and formal, that meant a no-go. If she was herself, that meant the girl was okay. None of us ever pushed our luck in that department.

"When we'd get sick, she'd sit by our beds and read to us, play checkers, stuff like that. She made more noise at our graduation than the whole stadium combined.

You can't be embarrassed when it's your mother."

Tears flooded Olivia's eyes.

Jeff ran his fingers through his hair, then rubbed at the stubble on his cheeks and chin. "What did I say? Talk to me. I'm a lawyer, I'm trained to deal with problems. If there are taboos, tell me."

Olivia blinked away her tears. She got up and carried her plate to the dishwasher. With her back to him, she said, "I never had a mother. The day I was born, she told my father she didn't want me and that she wanted a divorce. My dad told me she'd died. Then a few days ago a *lawyer* showed up at my door and said my mother had just died a few weeks ago and left me her fortune."

Jeff was suddenly at a loss for words. When he finally found his tongue, he said, "Well, that damn well sucks."

Olivia busied herself unplugging the toaster, wiping it off, and sliding it back under the counter. She tied a twist-tie on the package of bread and put it, along with the bacon and eggs, back into the refrigerator. "Yeah. It does. I called my dad, and he flew up. He left last night before you came. He said he was sorry."

Jeff struggled for words. The only thing he could come up with was, "You didn't pay me a dollar." Olivia reached into the cookie jar and withdrew a dollar bill. She handed it to him. Jeff shoved it into his pocket. "We are now lawyer and client."

"I hate lawyers," Olivia said.

"Yeah, yeah, everyone hates lawyers until they need one. Is there more? There is—I can tell. You might as well spit it out right now."

Olivia's eyes narrowed suspiciously as she stared out the kitchen window at the falling snow. "How do you know there's more?"

"My fine legal intuition, which is honed to a sharp point. Nah, it just stands to reason there's more."

Olivia poured more coffee into her cup. Jeff held his out for a refill. She obliged before sitting down. "My mother changed her name from Allison Matthews to Adrian Ames. Does that ring a bell with you?"

Jeff looked perplexed. "No. Should it?"

"She is Adrian Ames of Adrian's Treasures. It's a huge mail-order house. Wait here a minute." Olivia ran into the great room and returned with her printouts and the letter. She had no idea why she was suddenly confiding in a total stranger. No idea at all.

Minutes later Jeff said, "Wow! What are you going to do?"

"Nothing. I don't know. One minute I think I should do what she asked because 'it's the right thing to do.' Then the next minute I say, screw it, she did it, I'm not making it right for her. What would you do?"

Jeff's eyes almost bugged out of his head at the question. "I don't know, Olivia. I guess it would depend on how much hate I was carrying around. You look to me like you're carrying a bushelful."

"I had such a nice life before I was bombarded with all of this. I had wonderful memories. I had this fantasy that my mother gave up her life so I could live. In my mind she was a martyr. Her picture—well, not really her picture—was on the mantel. My whole damn life was a lie. If that wasn't bad enough, then I find out not only was my mother alive all those years when I hungered for a mother, but that she was a thief. I hate feeling like this. I don't know if I can . . . I just want it all to go away, but, like my dad said, that isn't going to happen. I have to deal with it.

"In addition, I have to deal with you and the dogs. Before I do anything else, I have to square that away. So let's get to it. What are we going to do in regard to Cecil?"

"I do my best thinking in the shower. Do you mind if I take one in your bathroom? By any chance, do you have a razor?"

"Everything you need is in the downstairs bathroom in the linen closet. I'm going to take my own shower. I sure hope you come up with something."

"Yeah, me too. . . . *Who am I kidding*?" Jeff mumbled to himself as he made his way to the bathroom.

Olivia was the first to return to the kitchen. She'd dressed quickly, in jeans and a bright yellow long-sleeved shirt. While she waited for her houseguest, she got out her soup pot and a frozen chicken from the freezer. She worked like a robot as she added frozen stock and water to the huge pot. She pared vegetables and proceeded to chop with a vengeance. Everything was simmering nicely when Jeff entered the kitchen, the four dogs at his heels.

"Smells good."

"It gets better as it cooks. I love the smell. One of my friends used to say our house always smelled like celery and parsley. I think it was a compliment."

"Our house always smelled like apples and cinnamon. Mom did a lot of baking. It was nice to smell when we came in from school. It still smells like that."

Olivia looked out the window. "Let the dogs out, okay? While you're out there, you could sweep off the patio before the snow piles up again. You need to earn that dollar I paid you."

Jeff looked at his hostess. *Really* looked at her and was stunned. *She's beautiful,* he thought. And she smelled so good! *She smells like soap and water, green grass and flowers.* He thought then about the woman he'd been with the night before. She'd smelled like nothing he'd ever smelled before. A hair-spray smell, a makeup smell, a perfume smell, and a deodorant smell. For a split second he couldn't remember her name. Then it came to him. Melanie. Melanie something. A paralegal from his law firm. They'd gone out for a drink at the end of the day with a few coworkers and somehow ended up at his place, which hadn't been his intention at all. Everyone at the office said Melanie was a manipulator. They were right. He'd never been a one-night-stand kind of guy. Hell, he wasn't much of anything in the romance department. He was married to his job. It worked that way when you put in sixty to seventy hours a week. Any leftover time was spent sleeping and eating. Just another way of saying he was a dud, romantically speaking.

"They aren't going to attack me, are they?" He wondered why his voice sounded so strange. It looked to him like Olivia was wondering the same thing. He marched to the door and opened it. The dogs barreled through, barking and squabbling, almost knocking him over. Olivia tittered behind her hand.

The phone rang. Probably her dad calling to see what was going on. She almost said, "Hi, Dad," but changed her mind and simply said, "Hello."

"It's Clarence, Olivia. How are you this snowy morning?"

Olivia winced. "Fine, Clarence. How

about you?" *Please, please, don't regale me with details of your latest tax cheat.*

"Fine. I'm fine. I was wondering if we could get together this evening. I could pick up some Chinese or maybe some Italian. What do you say?"

Olivia crossed her fingers and fibbed. "Gee, Clarence, my dad is in town. I have to spend time with him. Can we make it some night next week? I'll cook." As an added incentive, she continued, "I'll even make you a pie." She had to get off the phone before Jeff came back into the house.

Clarence laughed heartily. Olivia shuddered at the sound. "Well, I can't turn that down." *Didn't think so,* Olivia said to herself. *Cheapskate.*

"Okay, it's a date. I'll call you on Monday to set up a time. I have some great stories to tell you. You aren't going to believe some of it."

"Oh, I'm sure. Okay, Clarence, call me Monday." *I need to get Caller ID.* Olivia made a mental note to call the phone company first thing Monday morning, then uttered her good-bye and hung up the phone. It wasn't that she didn't like Clarence. As a friend, he was okay. But he was incredibly boring, and, as a suitor, which was what Clarence wanted to be, he was sadly lacking. She saw him from time to time because she didn't want to hurt his feelings. She really had to break it off with him. Maybe she could do that gently over the pumpkin pie she would bake him next week. She shivered at the thought of an IRS audit if Clarence didn't take rejection well.

As Olivia gulped her coffee, her gaze fell on the tall man wielding the broom on the patio. The dogs were trying to catch the broom and the snow at the same time. She could hear the lawyer laughing through the closed door. He looked like he was having fun. For some reason she felt buoyed at the sight and sound of him.

The moment Jeff opened the door, the dogs bounded through and headed for the laundry room. Jeff followed, reached for a towel, and dried them off the way he'd seen Olivia do it. He looked up and grinned. Olivia felt her heart start to melt. Then it hardened immediately when she thought about the chirpy voice she'd heard the night before.

"Did I earn that dollar? Where are the treats? I have these," he added, scrutinizing the Milk-Bones Olivia handed him. "That's how we can tell. Cecil won't eat these. He wants those bacon strips." Olivia laughed as all four dogs gobbled the treats.

"Guess that shoots down your theory. Come on, sit down. We have to figure out what we're going to do about Cecil."

Jeff felt his heart start to flip-flop in his chest. "Look, if I go to my boss and complain, he's just going to give Cecil to someone else to take care of. That's the unknown. Everyone is in the same position I'm in. Too many hours at work, not enough hours in the day. Most apartments don't allow dogs. It's best, I'm thinking, if we keep this between us, with Cecil's best interest being our main goal. It's obvious he's happy here. He likes the other dogs. Since we don't know which one is which, here's what I think. If you agree to dog-sit him, the stipend is yours. I know you said you don't care about that, but fair is fair. It's the best situation for Cecil, considering the circumstances. I'll try to make it out here a couple of times a week plus weekends to do my share. In return, I'll help you with your . . . your situation. If you want me to. If you want to drive to your . . . to the house you inherited tomorrow, I'll go with you. I need to see the information she said is in her wall safe in regard to the robbery. What do you think?"

What did she think? It sounded like a win-win situation. Still, she didn't want to appear too eager. It was best for Cecil. She couldn't argue with that. She wondered if they would be breaking any laws but was afraid to ask. It would be nice to have some company, some legal company, when she traveled the forty or so miles to the nearby estate Adrian Ames had left her.

Olivia brought her gaze up to meet Jeff's. He had incredible brown eyes. Soft and caring. "Okay. But you have to do your share. I don't want any money. I would like . . . it very much if you would agree to go to that house. If the snow lets up, that is."

Jeff's sigh of relief was so loud, Olivia sighed in response. Little did she know her own sigh was equally loud. Jeff stretched out his hand. Olivia grasped it. He had a handshake just like her dad's.

Maybe this was a good thing after all.

Time would tell.

Chapter 8

"I guess I should be leaving," Jeff said as he eyed the falling snow through the window.

Olivia found herself grimacing. She'd be alone if he left, the balance of the day looming ahead of her. Still, she felt awkward asking him to stay. She wished she was a more forceful kind of person. Her one big flaw, her father always said, was trying to please everyone and never putting herself first. Her snappy comeback to that comment had been, "You taught me to always think of others first instead of myself." To which he replied, "I was trying to instill . . ." whatever it was he was trying to instill in her.

"Be careful on the roads. I don't think there will be any real accumulation. It's more or less just snow flurries now. If it freezes, it might become a problem." How dull-witted that sounded.

Jeff bunched the wilted-looking baseball cap into a ball, straightened it out, and bunched it up again before putting it back on his head. "I need a change of clothes, and I want to get a head start on that brief I have to write. I'll gather up all of Cecil's gear and bring it with me when I come back. What time do you want me to come tomorrow? And, are we in total agreement that I am not taking Cecil with me?"

Olivia took a deep breath and inhaled the fragrance of the simmering soup. "An early start would be good if you can make it out here. Since the weather is iffy, we should plan for contingencies." Damn, that sounded like something coming out of a schoolteacher's mouth. "Maybe if you bring Cecil's gear, he'll dig in, and we'll be able to tell which one is which. If you feel like making the trip back out here this evening, I'll wait dinner for you. The soup isn't finished—otherwise I'd give you some to take with you."

"You know what, Olivia, I'll give that some thought. Should I call you if I plan on coming back tonight? You're right about the iffy weather, too. I'll pay attention to the weather reports and get back to you." Suddenly he yelled, "Hey, Cecil, I'm leaving now."

Four dogs came on the run and skidded to a stop. They eyed him with suspicion. When he dropped to his knees to coax them toward him, all four scampered off. Olivia shrugged.

"Told you that dog hates my guts," Jeff mumbled as he pulled on his jacket.

Olivia felt sorry for him. "He doesn't hate you. He misses Mrs. Manning. She used to carry him around like a baby. She'd play with him for hours. That was all he knew. Then, suddenly, she's gone, and there you are. You know squat about dogs, and he knows it. He did all those destructive things to get your attention, but you were too busy. I told you, dogs have feelings. Think about that on the ride home."

Jeff nodded. And then he didn't know why he said what he did, but he said, "What are you going to do when I leave?"

Olivia laughed. "Shovel my driveway. Not really shovel, I have a snowblower. I might make a cake. Then I'm going to go on the Net to see if I can find Jill and Gwen."

"Sounds like you're going to be busy. Okay, I'll see you when I see you. Bye."

Olivia stared at the solid mahogany door after it closed. He was nice. She liked him. He could make her laugh, something Clarence couldn't do. She shrugged as she headed to her office instead of the kitchen. The cake could wait. So could the driveway.

Olivia looked at the time on the computer when she logged on—10:30.

It said 2:30 when Alice started to paw at her leg. Olivia rubbed at her eyes and stretched her neck and arms. She'd been at it for four hours. She got up, let the dogs out, checked the soup, then got out everything she would need to bake the cake. It was still snowing lightly, but there was no real accumulation.

Her thoughts raced as she worked steadily. She'd found forty people with the name Jillian Davis and twenty-seven with the name Gwendolyn Nolan. She was unable to tell if any of the women had attended Ole Miss. She'd e-mailed the Alumni Association of the university to see if she could get any information about the two women. If she'd had Adrian Ames's social security number, she would have been able to log on to the site, but she'd been blocked. Maybe on Monday, after she explored the contents of Adrian Ames's safe, she could call the association and get more details. Unless, of course, Jill and Gwen had cut all ties to Ole Miss.

The bank where Allison had worked was still where it had been almost forty years ago and was currently run by the grandson of the man Allison had worked for during her student years at the university. On Monday Olivia planned to take a trip to the library and go through old newspapers to see how the bank had handled the robbery. How had those three women gotten away with robbing a bank? They must have had nerves of steel. Just the thought of the guts it would take to rob a bank blew Olivia's mind.

She turned off the mixer, scraped the batter into a cake pan, and slid the pan into the oven. After cleaning up her mess, she called her father, having fogotten that he was probably out with his charter. She'd hoped he would call when he got home, but he hadn't. *Out of sight, out of mind.* The thought saddened her. She felt even sadder when the answering machine spoke to her.

She hung up, not bothering to leave a message. She felt so desperate to talk to someone she was tempted to call Clarence just to hear a human voice other than her own. That particular thought lasted all of two seconds before she put on her jacket and headed for the garage and the snowblower.

Olivia was back in the house in thirty-eight minutes, just as the buzzer announced that the cake was done. She put it on a wire rack to cool and turned on the television to see what was going on in the world. Nothing was happening that could be characterized as a crisis, so she headed back to her little office and the computer and worked till it was time to feed the dogs, at six o'clock.

Had Jill Davis and Gwen Nolan dropped off the face of the earth? Had they changed their names? Were they in hiding? Olivia was convinced that Allison had gone into hiding after the robbery. Why else would she have divorced her husband, abandoned her child, and changed her name?

Fear, that's why.

Olivia set down the dogs' bowls and called her father again. *Surely, he'll answer by now,* she thought as she looked at the clock. As before, she got the answering machine. She called his cell phone. He picked up on the second ring. *He must be at the dock*. The noise in the background was deafening, the raucous laughter of men having a good time. She shouted to be heard over the din. "Dad, it's Olivia."

"Is something wrong, honey?"

"I want to know about Gwen and Jill," she bellowed. When there was no response, she repeated herself. Was it her imagination, or did his voice hold a trace of annoyance when he answered?

"Ollie, that was forty years ago. They were girls. I hardly knew them. I'm sure you're going to find everything you need to know when you speak with the lawyer or go to the house."

Olivia felt like a chastised child. Her shoulders slumped. "Okay, Dad, I guess I called you at a bad time. Sorry," she mumbled. The next thing she knew, the connection was broken. Angry with herself, she hung up the phone and let the dogs back in. They raced through the house, barking and growling at one another.

Now what am I supposed to do? Feel sorry for myself? Maybe what was *really* bothering her was the fact that Jeff Bannerman hadn't called her. It didn't look as if he was going to make the trip back to Winchester. With that in mind, she started to pick the meat off the chicken and drop it back into the pot. Water was boiling for noodles. Chicken soup required noodles.

It was seven fifty-five when she set the table for herself. She was ravenous. She was ladling the rich-looking broth into her bowl when her doorbell rang, causing the dogs to go wild. She ran after them, hoping against hope that it was Jeff and not one of her neighbors. Her smile was of the megawatt variety when she saw the lawyer standing in the doorway with a huge box in his hands. "You're just in time," she said happily. He smiled, and her heart turned over.

"I'm starved!" He grinned as he dumped Cecil's gear out onto the floor. The dogs looked at it, sniffed it, then both males lifted their respective legs and marked it before walking away.

"Oh well!" Olivia laughed.

"Yeah, oh well!"

It was bitter cold when Jeff steered his BMW up the long, winding road that led to

Adrian Ames's estate. Tall, fragrant blue spruces lined both sides of the driveway. "It's like being in a forest," Olivia said as she stretched her neck, trying to see everything.

"Are there people living here?" Jeff asked.

"I don't have a clue. No one has cleared the driveway, so off the top of my head I'd have to say no."

Jeff slowed the car. "Our first obstacle," he said, pointing to an electronic gate. The little hut at the side of the road was empty, the door locked. "I don't suppose you have the code, do you?" Olivia shook her head. Jeff lowered the car window and proceeded to punch numbers to no avail. "I guess we have to climb over and hoof it the rest of the way unless you want to call the lawyer and ask him for the combination."

"Today is Sunday, Jeff. I don't know where he lives. I think we can scale the fence. And then, like you said, we walk the rest of the way."

Jeff got out of the car, waited for Olivia to get out, and locked it. He cupped his hands together for Olivia to boost her up to a bar that would allow her to climb even farther, then scale the top and drop to the ground. With a thump, she landed in an ungraceful heap in the deep snow. A second later, Jeff landed right next to her but stayed on his feet. He reached out to help her to hers. Together, they continued up the driveway.

"Wow, this is gorgeous! Just how rich was your mother?"

"She's not my mother. Well, she did give birth to me, but she's not what I would call a mother. I would appreciate it if you don't refer to Adrian Ames as my mother. I guess she was pretty rich. Bear in mind how she got rich."

Jeff stopped in his tracks. "Point taken. Sorry. Do you know if she lived here alone? My mother would positively drool at the idea of having all this room. Look at that house! I bet it has at least twenty rooms. Maybe ten bathrooms, and probably six or seven fireplaces. Want to bet?"

Olivia shivered and snapped, "No." Looking around, she said, "I wonder if there's an alarm system. Maybe this was a foolish mistake. I don't have a key to get in. I can't imagine the woman leaving a key outside after she went to the trouble to install all this fencing."

"Well, you own the place, so you can break a window."

They heard the noise before they saw the monster dog barreling straight for them. Both Jeff and Olivia froze in their tracks, their jaws dropping when the huge dog ground to a halt and showed his massive teeth.

"Down, Brutus. Hold!" barked a voice from the side of the house.

Neither Olivia nor Jeff moved a muscle until a grizzled old man carrying a shotgun came into view. "We don't hold with trespassers around here, folks. You best be turning around and leaving the same way you got here."

The dog held his stance, his teeth as white as the snow at their feet. Deep, guttural growls could be heard coming from his mouth.

Jeff found his voice first. "I'm Jeff Bannerman. I'm a lawyer. This is Olivia Lowell, Adrian Ames's daughter. She inherited this property. We have a right to be here. We climbed the fence because we couldn't figure out how to work the gates."

"Power's off on the gates. I'll need to see some identification." The shotgun didn't move an inch.

Jeff reached into the back pocket of his

jeans and withdrew his wallet. Olivia took hers out of her shoulder bag and handed it over. The old man studied both driver's licenses carefully. He handed them back. "What is it you want?"

"To go into the house. And any information you care to give us," Olivia said. "I never knew Adrian Ames. She abandoned me the day I was born and divorced my father at the same time."

"I know about you. She talked to me about you. There's no heat on in the house. I'll take care of that and make you both some hot chocolate. You look frozen."

"I'd appreciate that," Olivia said. "What about the dog?"

"Brutus listens real good. He won't hurt you as long as you don't do anything you ain't supposed to be doing."

"Are you the only one working here?" Jeff asked.

The shotgun lowered as the man moved away. "Name's Cyrus Somers. It's just me now. I have a job here for another year, then I'm pensioned off. All the others left after the funeral. Furniture is covered up, utilities are still on. There was no need to keep anyone on, the lawyers said. Miz Ames left generous bequests to all her loyal employees. I'm the oldest, and I been with her from the day she moved in here twenty-five years ago."

They arrived at the back door. A key ring jangled in the old man's hands. He fiddled with it until he found the right key and fit it into the lock. The door squeaked open.

Olivia thought it was colder inside the house than it was outdoors. The man moved to a small hallway off the kitchen to turn up the thermostat. Brutus stood by the door, his ears flat against his head, his long tail tucked between his legs. "Be warm in a few minutes," the old man growled.

They stood around like three boxers warily eyeing each other, hoping to spot a weakness. "I'm not happy having you here without a lawyer present. I suppose you're who you say you are, but I think I need more information before I let you touch things."

"Why don't you call Ms. Ames's attorney if that will make you feel better? I can let you use my cell phone if the phones here in the house aren't connected. Or, if you want to go somewhere else, you can leave your dog to guard us," Jeff said, pulling out a small cell phone from his pocket and offering it to the caretaker.

Cyrus waved away the use of the phone. He looked at the dog, and said, "Hold, Brutus." He left by the back door and returned thirty minutes later, a box of tea bags in hand. *He must have changed his mind about the hot chocolate*, Olivia surmised.

Olivia thought the old man looked like he was sucking on a lemon when he growled, "Mr. O'Brien said you can do whatever you want. He said it's your house now. I'll be leaving you alone. When you're ready to leave, press triple X, and the gate will open." He dropped the box of Lipton tea bags on the counter. The dog followed him out of the house.

"Jolly fellow, isn't he?" Jeff said. "I wonder if he had shells in that shotgun?"

Olivia whirled around to be sure the dog was gone. "Who needs shotgun shells with Brutus?" she quipped. "Ah, it is getting warm in here. Tea?" she said playfully as she pointed to the box of tea bags.

"I'll pass. Let's get to it. Where do you want to go first?"

Olivia looked around at the ugly, cold, stainless-steel kitchen. "Upstairs, or wherever she slept, so we can open the safe. I hope the rest of the house doesn't look like this institution-style kitchen."

"My mother wouldn't like this kitchen. There aren't any plants or homemade rugs on the floor. No color. No curtains. No cookie jar. No, Mom wouldn't like this kitchen at all," Jeff said.

"My dad wouldn't like it, either," Olivia said.

"Well, let's go."

Jeff flicked light switches on as he led the way through rooms with furniture shrouded in white sheets. White sheets also hung over the heavy draperies, blocking all light from outside. Some kind of heavy brown paper secured at the edges with blue painter's tape covered all the floors. It felt like there was thick carpeting underneath the heavy brown paper.

The staircase, when they found it, was of beautiful mahogany and curved. The same brown paper they'd walked on covered the steps. They crunched and crackled their way up to the second floor.

"This reminds me of one of those spook houses my dad used to take me to on Halloween when I was a kid," Olivia said, looking around.

Jeff flicked on light switches at the top of the steps. A hallway that appeared to run the length of the house, as well as the doors to many alcoves, sprang to light. More furniture, more brown paper, more sheets.

They opened doors. Olivia counted seven bedrooms by the time they reached the last room at the end of the hall. It wasn't just a bedroom. It was a suite of rooms—what looked like a bedroom, a sitting room, a dressing room, an oversize bath with its own dressing room, and a huge linen closet. A tiny room off the sitting room held a computer, a fax, and a telephone console. Everything was covered in clear plastic. *The sheets must have run out,* Olivia thought.

She stood still as a statue in the middle of the suite. So this was where the woman who had given birth to her slept. Then nervousness suddenly overwhelmed her. "The combination to the safe is under the blotter on the desk. The safe is behind one of these pictures. She must have liked seascapes. Angry-looking seascapes." She began to pull at the corners of the pictures so she could see behind them. Finally the right one was located in the sitting room. Jeff removed it and leaned it against the wall.

"Turn it to the right for three turns to sixty-seven, then to the left for two turns to forty-four, and then right again for three turns to fifty-one, and then one turn to the left to three, then back to fifty-one right, and it should open."

Olivia turned the handle of the safe. She was surprised when it actually opened. This was no dream. If it had been a dream, she would have awoken before she could open the safe. "There's lots of stuff in here. There's even some money. It says five thousand dollars on the envelope. I guess it's emergency money."

"Bring everything over here. The light on the desk is the brightest," Jeff said.

Olivia dumped the contents of the safe on the desk, shed her heavy jacket, and threw it on top of Jeff's jacket on the plastic-wrapped bed. "You go through a pile, and I'll go through a pile. I'm not interested in her investments or her bank accounts. I want anything that pertains to the bank robbery and anything you find about Jill and Gwen."

Jeff sifted through a pile of packets. "Then this is probably what you're looking for. Looks like a diary. Why is it you women like to write down your lives in a diary? The stuff you put in them comes back to haunt you at some point. I've seen too many of them in my end of the business."

"In this case, that little book just might explain everything. We'll take it with us. Keep digging. Anything on Jill and Gwen? Wait a minute. Didn't I see a file cabinet when we came in here? Maybe they're in a file folder. If Adrian was sick for a year or so, maybe she worked out of this suite of rooms. It stands to reason she would have wanted everything close to her. I'll check while you keep going through this stuff."

When she finally located the filing cabinet, Olivia sucked in her breath in anticipation. She felt like a pricked balloon when she closed the drawer. "There's nothing in the file cabinet except stuff that pertains to her business," she called out.

"Here's a packet of pictures. Someone wrote on the back. It says Gwen, Jill, and Allison."

Olivia dropped to her knees at the side of the desk. She stared at the pictures, trying to find the answers she was seeking. Her final conclusion was, "They look like three bookworms, with those dark-rimmed glasses. I wonder if my dad took this picture. Dad said the three young women didn't have any other friends." While she continued to riffle through another packet of pictures, Jeff let out a whoop.

"This is why you couldn't find Jill. This is a wedding invitation. She married someone named Gill Laramie. Allison, as she still was called then, never returned the RSVP, so that must mean she didn't attend the wedding. Here's another one. Gwen married someone named Ted Pascal. Uh oh, what have we here? Another invitation. Gwen got married again, to William John Hendrix. With these names you should be able to find them now. Unless they married again and didn't send invitations."

"Look what I found!" Olivia cried out. "This is a copy of a bank card. The kind you have to fill out when you rent a safe-deposit box. The signatures are Jill Davis and Gwen Nolan. And miracle of miracles, here are their social security numbers. We hit the mother lode with this. For sure we'll be able to find them now. But why would Adrian Ames have a copy of this bank card? It looks like the original to me." She threw it into her purse along with the three wedding invitations and the diary.

Thirty minutes later they'd gone through everything from the safe with the exception of one thick manila envelope. Jeff undid the clasp and picked away at the red sealing wax. He pulled out the thick wad of papers and whistled. "These are photocopies of bearer bonds. Each one is for ten-thousand face value with another ten thousand in coupons. The stack must be an inch and a half thick."

Olivia could only gape at what Jeff was holding in his hands.

Chapter 9

Jeff fanned out the stack of papers in his hands. His expression rivaled Olivia's. "This," he said, "is downright scary. I've been thinking about all of this since you told me about it, and I have to admit I thought your . . . Ms. Matthews . . . was making all this up out of some kind of belated guilt. Hell, I don't know exactly what I thought, but seeing this . . . this . . . puts it all right up there front and center. Three college girls, and I don't care how smart they are . . . were . . . pulling off a successful bank heist is pretty awesome. And," he said, slapping at his forehead, "they obviously never got caught."

"How . . . how much is there?" Olivia gasped.

Jeff walked over to the bed and sat down.

The plastic gave off a soft *swooshing* sound as he struggled not to slide off the bed. He thumbed through the papers he was holding. "An easy half million dollars. . . . Forty years ago this same batch of bonds would have been worth three, maybe four times that much in sixties dollars." He did a double take as he stared at one of the bonds, then checked another. "Wow, I didn't notice this before. Someone, probably Allison, since she seems to have been the brains of the outfit, wrote all three names on the bonds at the bottom. See? They all have a number. I tend to think she did that to have proof of the other two's involvement in case they got caught. Equal share, equal blame. No one could lie or weasel out. And," Jeff said, holding up his hand for Olivia's attention, "this was also all the proof she would need to get the other two to pony up their share of the money to return to the bank when she decided to do that."

Olivia reached for the stack of photocopies. She jammed them back into the yellow envelope any which way, as fast as possible, as though handling them would somehow taint her. The round glob of red sealing wax glared up at her like an evil eye.

The envelope went into her canvas purse. "I need to think about this . . . Why? Why couldn't she take care of this herself? This is a punishment, Jeff. She did the crime, not me. I don't want to hear that she was sick, either, and didn't know what she was doing. She had forty years to make restitution, but did she do it? No, she did not. Neither did the other two. This is not going to be an easy thing to lay to rest."

Jeff handed Olivia her jacket before shrugging into his own. "Olivia, you can walk away from this if you want. You don't have to do anything. It's not part of the woman's will. The letter she left you is a private matter. She didn't demand you do it, she made a request. Close your eyes and walk away if that's what will sit well with you. Then you can spend the rest of your life pretending this never happened." He winked at her and said, "It goes without saying you'll probably never have a decent night's sleep again, either."

Olivia's eyes were full of fire when she marched over to the desk to gather up the contents of the safe. Shoving everything back inside, she closed the door and spun the dial. Jeff rehung the picture over the safe.

The canvas bag, considerably heavier, went over her shoulder. "I'm outta here. I hope I don't have to come back. Do you think we should turn the heat down or what?"

"We could do that," Jeff said agreeably. "I'm sure Cyrus will check the house and lock up after we leave. That's what caretakers do. He should leave the heat on at least a little so the pipes don't freeze."

Outside in the brisk, cold air, Olivia trudged through the snow to the gate, looking around for some sign of Brutus or the old man, but there was none. Relieved when Jeff opened the car door for her, she hopped in and buckled up. Her teeth chattered with the cold until the heat from the car kicked in.

Neither of them spoke on the forty-mile trip back to Winchester.

Jeff slowed the BMW for the turnoff to Winchester. "How about I treat you to lunch, Olivia, before I head back to the city? It's Sunday—maybe we should do brunch."

Olivia shook her head to clear away her

thoughts. "I'd like that, Jeff. Not too much open on Sunday, though. How do you feel about Chinese?"

Jeff threw his head back and laughed. Olivia loved the hearty sound. Clarence's laugh was more like a titter.

"Are you kidding! Chinese is a lawyer's staple. I'm up for it."

"I think we should stop by the house to let the dogs out first. Damn, it looks like snow again, doesn't it?"

Jeff craned his neck to look upward. Steel gray clouds scudded across the sky. "Yep. The wind is starting to whip up, too. With that in mind, I'm going to head back to the city after lunch. We can make up a schedule over lunch for when you want me to come out here to do my share with Cecil. You're going to have to cut me some slack and be flexible. I *will* do my share, though, and that's a promise. If you don't mind, there will be some nights when I'll have to sleep here. Can you handle that?"

"Okay," Olivia said agreeably.

Jeff steered his car into the driveway and parked behind Olivia's Bronco. They heard the dogs barking as they walked across the snowy lawn to the front door. "Guess they missed us. You more than me," Jeff said.

"You have to win a dog's trust, Jeff. That's another way of saying you have a lot of sucking up to do where Cecil is concerned."

Thirty minutes later, Olivia and Jeff were seated in a black-lacquered booth in the China Jade Restaurant. Hard noodles and sweet-and-sour sauce along with a hot mustard sauce were placed in front of them. They dipped and dug in, asked for a refill, and sipped a lot of green tea.

"Let's talk about anything but business and the dogs, okay?" Jeff said.

"Sure. What would you like to talk about?"

"You," Jeff said succinctly.

"There's not much to tell. I grew up here, with my dad raising me. I went to college— University of Virginia. I majored in childhood education, but after two years of teaching, sad to say, I couldn't take it any longer. It wasn't the kids—I loved them. It was the administration. So Dad took me on, and we became Lowell and Lowell Photography. I love it. I specialize in animal photography, and I've done a few baby calendars. Dad did people. I make a very good living, and I'm my own boss."

"Are you seeing anyone?"

Are you seeing anyone? Her heart fluttered. She chomped down on a hard noodle to cover her sudden nervousness. "You mean romantically?" Jeff's head bobbed up and down. "No. How about you?"

"No. No time. I'm a male pariah when it comes to women. I make a date and end up canceling because of time pressures. Women seem to want a commitment after a few dates. I'm in no position to make one at this point in time. If you're wondering about . . . that night you called me, Melanie is just a colleague. Nothing went on with us." Jeff blushed then. "The truth is, I fell asleep on the couch. Melanie was dozing off, too. She's a colleague. On the aggressive side. Not my type. I'm babbling, huh?"

Olivia laughed. "I think you've established that you're not involved with anyone." Suddenly she felt wonderful. So wonderful, she smiled from ear to ear. "Do you like working in D.C.?"

"It's as good a place as any. Cost of living is high. It's a good firm. I have the same dream most lawyers have of hanging out my own shingle someday."

"What's stopping you?"

"Money. I need to build up my bank account. To do that you need clients. Someday I want to practice family law. My brothers offered to back me, but if I'm going to do it, I'm going to do it on my own, just the way they did."

Their food was brought just then by a tiny woman with eyes as dark as her hair. She smiled as she ladled out their food onto their plates. They ate with gusto, sampling each other's food and laughing over absolutely nothing. They finished a second pot of tea and sat back to wait for the bill and the fortune cookies.

Olivia cracked open her cookie, read her fortune, and smiled. "Mine says, 'Good fortune awaits you.'"

"You gotta believe a fortune cookie." Jeff grinned. He broke open his cookie and laughed uproariously. "Mine says 'You are popular with people and animals.' Oh, if it were only true." He slipped bills from his wallet and placed them on the plate. Then he helped Olivia with her coat. Somehow or other Olivia's hand touched his, and she felt a jolt of electricity. She saw Jeff's eyes widen, his face pinking up.

The ride back to the house on Eagle Drive was tense. Neither spoke until Jeff pulled into Olivia's driveway. All Olivia wanted was to escape into the house so she could think about what she was feeling. Jeff looked like he couldn't wait to leave.

"I'll call you," Jeff said, as she slipped out of the BMW.

"Okay." Olivia ran to the door, opened it, and raced inside. The dogs barked and jumped all over her as she dropped to her knees to pet and talk to them. They allowed themselves to be gathered close and suffered through her smothering hugs. She stayed with them until she felt herself calming down.

Jeff Bannerman was no Clarence De Witt. Not by a long shot.

It was almost three o'clock when Olivia carried the items she'd taken from Adrian Ames's house to her office. She dropped them on her desk and turned on her computer. The diary glared up at her, but she ignored it. Before she allowed herself to read it, she wanted to search for Allison

Matthews's two friends. She did her best to clear her mind and started a search.

By six o'clock she was ready to tear her hair out. Jillian Davis Laramie had married two years after Allison, then divorced Gill Laramie seven years later. She'd given birth to one daughter, named Mary Louise. That had to mean Mary Louise was about the same age as Olivia. Jill moved around a lot. She'd lived in Sladen, Mississippi, then moved to Birmingham, Alabama, and stayed there for several years before moving back to Sladen temporarily. Natchez, Mississippi, was her next home for a few years until she moved to Salt Lake City, Utah. The trail ended there.

Olivia started a new search for a telephone number or e-mail address. In both instances she drew a blank. She realized then she didn't have the capabilities to do a more extensive search. Her shoulders slumped.

There had to be a way to find Jill Laramie. Maybe she was in hiding. Maybe, like Adrian Ames, she had changed her name. There was no point wasting time trying to find Gill Laramie or the daughter, Mary Louise, without having their social security numbers.

Contacting the Alumni Association at Ole Miss, even with Jill's social security number, was an exercise in futility. Jill had a password, which meant Olivia couldn't log on to her info without it. Obviously, Jill had an e-mail address. The Department of Motor Vehicles showed that the last known address on Jill Laramie's driver's license was a Utah one. The license had not been renewed.

Olivia called a halt to her search and headed for the kitchen to feed the dogs. She let them in and out, then heated up some of the soup from the day before. She was back on the computer by seven-thirty and worked till ten, with no better results. Not only was she discouraged, she was disgusted. She knew in her gut she wasn't going to be able to find Gwen Nolan, either. She needed to switch gears, but she didn't know how.

Clarence!

Clarence worked for the IRS. Everyone had to file a tax return. Everyone. Jill and Gwen would be no exception.

Olivia didn't stop to think about what she was doing, she just did it. She called Clarence and asked him point-blank if he could get her the addresses for the two women. "Don't ask me why, Clarence. It's a personal family matter. I'll never divulge where I got the addresses. I have to find these two women. It's very, very important. I tried to find them on my own, but I can't. You're my last hope. I will be eternally grateful, Clarence. I'll bake you a chocolate cake every day if that will convince you." She listened to his excuses, his questions, and answered them as best as she could without really telling him why she needed the information. In the end, Clarence said no.

"Fine, Clarence. I thought you were a friend. Obviously, I was wrong. It would take you ten minutes. Ten minutes. I just want an address. It's important to me. Good-bye, Clarence."

Shit!

Olivia headed for the shower. While she danced under the hot spray, her mind whirled and twirled. Now that she was back to square one, her only other option was to engage the services of a private detective to locate Jill and Gwen. That's what she would do first thing in the morning.

When she woke in the morning, she was surprised that she had slept through the night. A deep, dreamless sleep. After juice, coffee, and toast, she headed back to her office and her computer. It was time to do some research in regard to private detectives.

Only a few minutes later, she turned her swivel chair around, reached for the phone, and dialed the number for "The Private Detective Agency." No originality in that name! The Web site promised a full staff of professionals and guaranteed results or there would be no charge. Along with the latest high-tech equipment for surveillance, dedicated staff members, and reasonable rates, the firm also guaranteed privacy and confidentiality. Daily or weekly reports were offered, depending on the client's wishes. TPDA had offices all over the area, five in all.

After Olivia introduced herself, she was stunned to discover she was talking to the owner, Miki Kenyan, herself. She quickly stated her business while the detective took notes.

"Thanks, sweetie. That should do it. I'll get back to you tomorrow or maybe later this evening. Now, I'll need your credit card number. One last thing, do you prefer e-mail or phone contact?" Olivia said either was fine and rattled off her credit card number and expiration date.

The detective signed off by saying, "I'll be in touch, sweetie. Sit tight. TPDA guarantees results."

Olivia dusted her hands. Done.

Now she turned her attention to some housekeeping chores—washing and changing sheets and towels, cleaning the bathroom and building a fire in the great room, running the vacuum. Next she made herself lunch, then played with the dogs for a while before heading to the office. Before she sat down, she raced back to the kitchen to take out a frozen meat loaf and set it on the counter to thaw partially. Her dinner taken care of, she returned to the office and turned on the computer. Then she turned it off. She didn't want to work on the computer; she wanted to start reading Adrian Ames's diary.

With a shiver of apprehension, she picked up the leather-bound burgundy diary and flipped through the pages, noting there were more blank pages than pages with writing on them. She licked her dry lips as she settled down to read Adrian Ames's small, cramped writing.

The book was old, the pages yellowed.

The leather felt dry and was cracked in places. It was, after all, forty years old. She read the first entry.

> *Jill and Gwen agreed. They were not exactly eager, but when I explained the entire scenario, all the pros and cons, they finally agreed, knowing we would get rich. Jill held out the longest, but she's as greedy as the next one. I wasn't surprised that she agreed. They trust me. I guess they finally realized I'm the smartest of us all. We spent hours telling each other what we would do with our money. It was hard to make them understand that if we succeed, we won't be able to spend the money for five years. They didn't like that one bit, but I finally convinced them we have to wait.*

Olivia read the entry several times. Allison Matthews, as she had been then, hadn't used the word *robbery* or *bank* once. Not spending money for five years could mean a number of things. So what if she said she was the smartest of the three? Maybe she was. So what if she convinced them to go along with her plan? The entry didn't say what the plan was. Waiting five years to spend money could be as simple as waiting for money to gather interest. Spending hours talking about spending the money could be considered girl talk. The fact that there was no date on the entry could mean it was written at any time, not necessarily prior to the bank robbery.

Olivia turned the page to read the second entry.

We did it. Jill and Gwen were magnificent. There wasn't a tremor in either one of them. I was so calm I thought I was going to doze off. I think I missed my calling. I bet I could do this for a living. The three of us are going to celebrate tonight. I am going to tell Dennis I can't see him tonight. This is our night. We three deserve the celebration. Now all we have to do is work on phase two and wait for five years. We made a pact to never discuss this matter until the five years pass.

So they "did it," and the girls didn't so much as twitch. "Did it" could mean a thousand different things. Allison had nerves of steel. They were going to celebrate, and she was blowing off a date with Olivia's father. Nothing incriminating here. Not talking about something for five years could refer to a secret other than a bank robbery.

Olivia walked to the kitchen and turned on the oven. When the oven buzzer pinged to announce the temperature, she prepared the meat loaf and slid it in. Then she carried a can of soda pop back to the office.

The third entry was interesting. Short but interesting.

I'm getting married tomorrow. I asked myself why, and the only response I can come up with is, why not? I don't love Dennis. He's incredibly boring. Nice but boring. He has a good job, and we're going to move to Winchester, Virginia, and live there. All around, it will be easier. A name change could prove to be beneficial. I hope. I told the girls. They were surprised. They were even more surprised when I told them the first thing I was going to do when the five years are up is divorce Dennis. They laughed. That annoyed me. I didn't like the look I saw in Jill's eyes. Gwen asked me how I could marry someone I didn't love. I told her it was easy. She asked me about the sex part. I didn't answer her.

"You were one ugly person, Allison Matthews," Olivia snarled, tossing the diary across the room. The dry pages parted from the leather binding and scattered all over the floor. With no dates, how was she going to put them back in order? "Who cares," she snarled again as she gathered them up in a bunch.

Olivia read other entries, all boring, about Allison's job, Dennis's late hours, keeping house, and grocery shopping. Then she read the entry concerning her. Her tongue was dry. She swigged from the soda can, the soda dribbling down her chin.

I damn well can't believe it. I'm pregnant. I've done everything I could think of that might possibly help me to abort. Nothing works. I told Dennis. What else could I do? The stupid clod was overjoyed. I called Jill and Gwen. Both of them laughed as they offered up aborting remedies. I tried them, but they didn't work either. I'm doomed to have this kid. Jill told me I should take a tumble down a staircase. I told her we don't have a staircase. She laughed like a hyena. I don't want this kid. I made Dennis move out of the bedroom. I will never have sex again. He can have the kid. I certainly don't want it.

Olivia placed the loose pages on the desk. She reached for a tissue. She was an *it*. Allison Matthews Lowell thought of her as an *it*.

"Damn you! Damn you!" Olivia said, breaking into sobs. "Damn you to hell!"

Chapter 10

Olivia woke with a start, all four dogs on the bed nudging her to get up. She rolled over and groaned. She didn't want to get up. She wanted to stay under the warm covers and forget about all the bad dreams she'd had, one after the other, during the long night. As she swung her legs over the side of the bed, her head started to pound. *Damn, now I have a headache.*

Tying the belt to her robe, she shuffled through the house to the sliding glass doors to let the dogs out. There was a light dusting of snow on the patio. Such a long time till spring and warm breezes! The temperature gauge said it was thirty-seven degrees outside. It felt colder. Before she made coffee, she turned the thermostat to eighty.

It. She was an it. Olivia started to grind

her teeth in anger. If Adrian Ames had been standing in front of her at that moment, she'd have punched her silly. Where was it written that a person had to love her mother? Nowhere, that's where. The title of "mother" came biologically, but love for a mother had to be earned.

The last cheerful plop of the water dripping into the pot alerted Olivia that the coffee was done. She poured a cup, swallowed some Tylenol, and sat down just as the phone rang. Her voice turned surly when she recognized Clarence's voice. Before he could say anything more than hello, Olivia said, "Look, Clarence, I'm sorry I called you and asked you to find those addresses for me. It was wrong. I wouldn't want some agent giving out information on me. Let's just forget it. I had a temporary lapse of good judgment."

Olivia listened as Clarence prattled on about everything and nothing. He didn't even accept her apology. "I'm heading out of town for a full-blown audit. A big one, Ollie. I might even get a big promotion on this one. I'm just calling to tell you I won't be able to make dinner this week."

"Fine. I have to go now, Clarence. Say

hello to everyone at the IRS for me." Before he could comment, she hung up the phone. It rang almost immediately. Thinking it was Clarence calling her back, she let it ring four times before she picked it up. It was the detective agency.

Olivia looked at the clock, surprised to see that it was only a quarter after nine. The detective was on the ball. They made small talk until Miki Kenyan got to the point. "Okay, I just sent you an e-mail and a fax. We found Jillian Davis Laramie in Wood-bridge, New Jersey. We're still working on Gwendolyn Nolan with all the many different names. I expect to have something for you later today."

"You actually found one of them! Do you have any details?"

"The report is sketchy. It's all in the e-mail. If you want us to do a more thorough background check, it will cost. Read the report, and get back to me. If you take the Metroliner from Washington, D.C., you can be in New Jersey in three and a half hours. It's a forty-minute flight to Newark. I'll get back to you later today."

Olivia leaned back in her chair. Her headache was just a dull throb. She hoped

with a shower it would disappear completely. A fresh cup of coffee in hand, she
made her way to the office, the dogs following. She took a moment to watch them.
How happy the little pack was. They all got
along, played and tussled and even looked
out for one another. She still had no clue
which Yorkie was Cecil.

When she clicked on her e-mail, there it
was, TPDAgency@earth link.net. She read
all eight lines:

Jillian Marie Davis Laramie
99 High Street
Woodbridge, New Jersey
Time of residence: 19 years
Phone number is unlisted and
there is no e-mail address.
Subject has no driver's license on
record in maiden name or
married name.

Eight lines.

Olivia blinked. She'd hoped for more. But,
she'd hired the agency to find Jill, and that's
what they'd done. No telephone or e-mail
address meant a face-to-face meeting was
called for. Well, she could do that. She

could leave in the morning and come back the same day. Her father's buddy down the street would come in and let the dogs out. Alice liked Tom Hutchins, a retired mailman, because he always carried treats in his pocket when he stopped by. If Alice liked him, so would the others.

Woodbridge, New Jersey. A long way from Ole Miss for Allison Matthews's friend.

Olivia swiveled her chair around so she could watch the dogs growling over a pull toy. Her gaze settled on the diary. She needed to continue to read it. She had to finish it before she went to New Jersey, but first she needed to take a shower and get dressed for the day.

An hour later, dressed in jeans, a shell-pink sweater, and ankle-high boots, Olivia made her way to the kitchen, where she scarfed down a toasted bagel and a container of yogurt. She definitely needed nourishment before tackling the leather-bound diary with Adrian Ames's secrets.

It.

The phone on the desk pealed to life. Olivia looked at it long and hard. A client? Jeff? She yanked at the receiver and brought it to her ear. She heard her father's cheerful voice. The headache that had almost been gone started to pound behind her eyes. "What's up, Ollie?" It was the way he started all his phone calls.

"Stuff," was always her response.

"Details, please."

"Well, I went with Jeff Bannerman, Cecil's handler, to your wife's estate. We almost got mauled by a vicious dog. There's a caretaker there. We opened the safe, and there was a diary, photocopies of the bearer bonds the trio stole, and a few other things. We took the pictures, the photocopies, and the diary. I read some of it last night. She referred to me as an *it*. Did you know that, Dad?"

"Yes. It was a long time ago, Ollie." How defensive her father sounded!

"I hired a private detective to locate Jill and Gwen when my own search didn't pan out. The detective called a little while ago and said they found Jill in New Jersey. So far no luck on Gwen."

"I assume you're going to talk to her." It sounded like a statement, but it was really a question.

"How did she get my baby bracelet, Dad?

I thought you said she didn't want to see me. Me, the *it*."

"I don't know, Ollie. Maybe the nurse gave it to her. All I know is when I picked you up, you weren't wearing it. I asked. The nurse just looked befuddled. I even panicked, wondering if I was taking the right baby home. But then I realized I had the right baby because you were the only girl baby in the nursery. The other four were boys."

"How's your charter going?"

"Fine. They're booking again in September. I have to run, Ollie. They're waiting for me to shove off. They want and expect their money's worth. I love you, kid, and don't you ever forget it."

This was where she was supposed to say, "I love you, too, Dad," but she didn't. Instead she broke the connection. She picked up the diary and started to read.

The most meaningful entry other than the hit-and-miss one-liners dealt with the distribution of the loot.

We met at the Holiday Inn. I carried everything in a big satchel. Before I left to meet with them, I divided the stuff into three equal parts. It was supposed to be a high moment but somehow it was flat. We just looked at each other. Jill was so interested in my divorce she almost seemed oblivious to what we were doing. I've never seen her so hateful. She actually made me nervous because she acted like she wanted to kill me. Gwen was so high she couldn't talk straight. She just babbled. I cautioned them about how and when to turn things over. I suspect they didn't hear a word I said. Jill said she was seeing a man. Gwen said the same thing. Jill said some things about her husband. Neither of the men they talked about impressed me. Jill has gained weight. She looked pregnant to me. Gwen is fat. I think both of them worry a lot.

We agreed not to call or write. It's better this way even though we did exchange addresses and phone numbers. Both of them were upset that I changed my name. Legally, of course. They acted like I was trying to put something over on them. I'm not.

I just want to be done with them like I was done with Dennis and the baby.

We didn't hug or anything stupid like that. We each went our separate ways. No one ate the pastries or drank the coffee I paid for. They're such losers. I don't know why I ever bothered with them. Fifty years from now they'll still be like they are today. Stupid. I'm so glad to be rid of them.

The entries afterward were sporadic, dealing with adapting to her name change, her move away from the Winchester area, which she said was a good thing. Her first sale, her excitement.

The years fast-forwarded with nothing even remotely interesting. There was a brief mention early on about Gwen's wedding announcements. A terse one-liner summed that all up.

Fools, both of them.

Olivia flipped through the pages. She sat up straighter in her chair when she saw a paragraph that referred to her.

I hired a private detective today. I put him on a retainer and he guaranteed me quarterly reports on Dennis's daughter. Even after all these years I still can't think of her as my daughter. She's sixteen today. It's strange how I always remember the girl's birthday. It was such an ugly day for me. I guess that's why I remember it. So why did I get a private detective to find out about her? Curiosity, nothing more.

Olivia winced. *The girl* sounded a tad better than *it. Dammit, I will not cry.* She jumped up and ran to the kitchen. She eyed the coffeepot but decided she had enough caffeine in her to take her through the day and opted instead for a can of apple juice. Her mouth felt like cotton, her eyes dryer than sand. She struggled with herself to take deep, calming breaths. Finally quieting down, she told herself that she needed to finish reading the diary so she could move on.

The next entry that had any meaning to her was one written after her college graduation.

It's hard to believe twenty-two years have gone by. That stupid detective can't understand why I don't want pictures of the girl. I'm paying him for reports, not pictures. I think he's ripping me off, too. The girl sounds as boring as Jill and Gwen. She never does anything exciting. She doesn't date, she isn't involved in anything. Do I really want to see pictures of her with her father hugging and kissing? No, I do not. A teacher for God's sake. It figures. Good old boring Dennis must have put that idea in her head.

Olivia cringed into herself. "You bitch!" she yelled, seething with anger.

Flipping the pages, she saw bank account summaries, brokerage accounts, then this entry:

I love seeing all these zeroes. In my wildest dreams I never thought I would be a millionaire a hundred times over. Gwen wrote and asked me for a loan. I just sat in stupefied amazement reading that letter. A loan. I ripped the letter into shreds. I knew she was stupid.

Gwen asked for a loan. That had to mean she went through her share of the money. How weird was that? Olivia couldn't help but wonder how Jill had done with her share.

More meaningless entries, most of them dealing with foreign imports, new products— and then the ultimate betrayal. A longtime loyal member of Allison's staff had been caught with his fingers in the till:

I'll ruin him. If it takes my last cent I will see that man suffer. You can't trust anyone these days. I was so generous to him and his family, and this is how he repays me. He's going to regret the day he ever came to work for Adrian's Treasures.

"Well, hot damn. Serves you right, you sanctimonious bitch. And I bet you didn't call the cops, either. You handled it yourself. It figures—no cops for you, Adrian Ames, you thief," Olivia muttered.

More blank pages.

Olivia clenched her teeth when she read the next entry.

> *Calendars for God's sake! Dogs! Those filthy, smelly little creatures that lift their legs on everything they come in contact with. I can't believe this. It's Dennis all over again. Calendars! I'm embarrassed for her, and I don't even know her.*

Olivia bit down on her lip. To the best of her knowledge, she'd never been an embarrassment to anyone. *Way to go, Adrian. You bitch!*

No more entries for years. Then the big one. Olivia's eyes widened.

> *That stupid doctor said I'm dying. I should know if I'm dying or not. I feel fine. I'm going to another doctor.*

Another entry.

> *It's been confirmed. Three out of three have agreed I'm dying. I can't believe this. Well, I'm going to fight. Attitude is everything. One of those*

crappy doctors actually had the nerve to tell me to put my house in order. He wasn't smart enough to tell me how to do that. That's a man for you. I'm not going to write in this stupid journal anymore. I'll take care of matters myself. Life is for the living, and I'm still living.

Olivia gathered up the loose pages and fit them snugly between the covers of the diary. She wrapped two rubber bands around the little book, then sealed it in an envelope and shoved it as far back as it would go in the bottom drawer of the desk.

Her eyes burning, Olivia walked out of the office and into the bathroom, where she washed her hands under hot water. She scrubbed her fingers and the backs of her hands with a nailbrush. Now her hands were burning as well. She staggered toward the kitchen, looked around in a daze. *Why did I come in here?* She made coffee, more to have something to do than anything else.

The dogs circled Olivia's feet. She tried to smile at them. All they wanted was to be loved, fed, and kept warm. "Okay, we have a lot of meat loaf left from last night. I'll warm it up for you." The little dogs gobbled it down. Alice burped. Olivia burst out laughing.

Outside, the day was gray and dismal. More snow was probably coming.

Don't think about that miserable diary or the miserable person who wrote it. Make plans to go to New Jersey. Call Mr. Hutchins. Call the airlines and a rental car service.

She did all of the above. She managed to get a 7:00 A.M. flight to Newark the following morning with a return flight at 7:00 P.M. Avis guaranteed a Ford Taurus for twenty-four hours. Mr. Hutchins promised to dog-sit and agreed to stay at the house until her return. He would arrive at five o'clock in the morning. The only thing left to do was to go back on the computer to MapQuest and print out directions to Jill Laramie's house.

I'm doing this because . . . because . . . I don't know why.

Somehow or other, she managed to while away the rest of the day by going grocery shopping, dropping off and picking up her dry cleaning, and stopping at the pet store for some new dog toys with squeakers inside and some rawhide chews. At the last minute she picked up a fifty-pound bag of kibble she knew the dogs weren't going to eat. But she bought it anyway.

On the way home, she stopped at Violino's Italian Restaurant to buy her dinner, including a side order of garlic bread. Her last stop was the liquor store, where she bought a bottle of plum brandy for Mr. Hutchins and some beer for Jeff, in case he stopped by in the next few days.

Olivia was putting the last of her groceries away when Jeff called. He sounded tired. She offered him a brief rundown on Adrian Ames's diary and her plans to go to New Jersey the following day. "I'll be home around nine tomorrow evening if you want to come out."

"Okay, I'll bring dinner. Be careful, Olivia. When it comes to money, people change. If they feel threatened by you, anything can happen. Just be alert and careful."

"Okay, *Daaad*," Olivia drawled.

"I think I missed you today, Olivia."

Olivia's hand went to her heart. She felt suddenly flustered. "You did?" What a brilliant comeback that was!

"Yes. I'm sitting here working on this confounded brief. I've written the same thing four times, and it still doesn't make sense. And last night I dreamed about that dog Brutus chasing me around the Tidal Basin, and Cecil was chasing him. Would you like to go out to dinner Wednesday night? I'll make plans to stay over. How's Cecil?"

"Are you asking me for a date, Jeff?" God, what should she wear? She'd have to get something new. She couldn't remember the last time she'd had a *real* date. Some guy named Brad who was the track coach at the local high school. It hadn't worked out because she wasn't interested in feeding his jock ego. Clarence simply didn't count. "Cecil's fine. So is Loopy. Whichever one is fine."

"Are you sure? Does he miss me?"

Olivia rolled her eyes. "Yes, I'm sure, and, no, he does not miss you. At least I don't think so. It's hard to tell. He's acting normal. By that I mean all the dogs are acting normal. Maybe he does miss you a little."

"I bet!" the voice on the other end of the phone groused. "I gotta go, Olivia. I'll see you Wednesday. No, I said I'd come out tomorrow. Okay, both nights. Howzat?"

Olivia found herself giggling. "Sounds

good to me. I think I might have missed *you*. A little. See ya!"

Olivia ran to her room and yanked open the door to her closet. The contents looked pitiful. Truly pitiful. Her fingers were feverish as she moved hangers, peering behind them as though some wonderful designer outfit would suddenly appear. Truly, truly pitiful. There wasn't one single thing that could qualify as a date outfit.

Olivia's shoulders slumped. Then she brightened almost immediately. Wednesday morning, bright and early, she could go to the mall and pick up something. Maybe she'd get her hair done and even get a facial. The thought excited her. Then again, maybe what she was excited about was the date and not the wardrobe. Yes, the date. She almost squealed with excitement.

Giddy with what she was feeling, Olivia headed for her office and her computer. Her fist shot in the air when she saw an e-mail from the detective agency.

Like its predecessor, this e-mail, concerning Gwen Nolan, was short. A note at the bottom said *Report to follow within 36 hours*.

Gwendolyn Rose Nolan Pascal
Hendrix
246 Indian Drive
Summerville, South Carolina
Subject has lived at this address
four years.
Phone number is unlisted and
there is no e-mail address.
Driver's license is in name of
Gwendolyn Rose Hendrix. It is
current.

Okay, ladies, get set, because I'm coming to see you!

Chapter 11

At eleven o'clock Olivia knew she was lost, even with the MapQuest diagram in her lap. Somewhere she'd taken a wrong turn as she'd tried to keep up with the speeding traffic on Route 1. She hated the eighteen-wheelers that whizzed by her. She made a left-hand turn on Amboy Avenue, wherever that was, just to get off the busy highway, and decided to stop at a gas station and ask for directions. She also needed to use the restroom and get something to drink.

The best-laid plans of mice and men, she thought, and snorted.

Ten minutes later, Olivia paid for her Diet Coke and asked for directions, pleased to hear that she was less than three miles from her destination. The clerk made her a crude map.

Back in the car, she drove slowly on Route 35 until she came to High Street and made a right-hand turn. This was it—Jillian Laramie's street. She rode up and down until she was comfortable with the neighborhood. It was neat and tidy, a lot like Eagle Drive, where she lived. At this time of year there was snow on the ground, but she could tell it would be pretty in the spring and summer, when the trees were in full dress and the flowers and shrubs bloomed.

Ninety-nine High Street was a two-story house with a big screened-in porch. She could see a side door to her left. Six steps led to the screened-in porch. There was a garage, but the door was closed. Then she remembered that Jillian Davis Laramie had let her driver's license expire. How did she get around?

Going over in her mind what she was going to say to Allison Matthews's friend, Olivia continued to stare at the house. All the shades and draperies were closed. What did that mean? Maybe Jill no longer lived there. Well, there was only one way to find out. She got out of the car and marched determinedly up the walkway and the six steps. At the top she was thwarted. The door leading onto the screened porch was locked. There was a bell, however, and she rang it. The draperies on either side of the main door didn't move. She rang the bell again as she tried peering through the foggy Plexiglas of the storm door. There was no response. She rang the bell a third, then a fourth time.

Finally she turned around and walked down the steps and around to the left and the side door, where she banged on the glass in the door since there was no bell or door knocker. The upper portion of the door was a six-paned window with a venetian blind that was closed. Obviously, Jill liked privacy. Olivia knocked again, with no result. Then she pressed her ear to the door, listening for any sound inside such as a radio or television. Silence.

Frustrated, she walked back to the front of the house and out to the sidewalk. Maybe one of the neighbors could tell her if Jill was away, if perhaps she was the type to head south for the winter to get away from the snow and cold. Olivia made her way to the house on the left, walked up the steps, and rang the bell. An elderly man with a shock of white hair and matching beard opened the door and smiled. "What can I do for you, little lady?"

"I'm looking for Mrs. Laramie. She doesn't answer the door. Do you happen to know if she's away?"

The old man cackled with laughter as he hitched up his suspenders. "Come in, come in. It's cold out there." Olivia obliged. "Can I offer you some tea or coffee? I just made a pot for myself. Can't drink coffee first thing in the morning, but by noon my stomach can handle it. Just follow me, and we can talk."

Olivia trailed behind the man through the stiflingly hot house. She smelled licorice and Ben-Gay. The house was neat and tidy, the furniture old but comfortable-looking. The kitchen was warm and full of bright sunshine from the bay window. A small television sat on the counter, tuned to a twenty-four-hour news station. The old man turned the volume down. He held out his hand. "Paul Hemmings."

"I'm Olivia Lowell. I live in Winchester, Virginia. What can you tell me about Mrs. Laramie?" Olivia said, getting right to the point.

The old man raised a bushy white eyebrow at her question as he poured coffee into a pretty flowered cup. A company cup, Olivia suspected.

"Can't tell you a thing. She moved in here about twenty years ago. Saw her go into the house and haven't seen her since. She didn't acknowledge my wife's death or even send a card. 'Course, that was eight years ago, and she didn't really know us, so I might have expected too much. In the beginning the neighbors talked some. Most of it made up, I'm sure. People do that when they don't have the real story, whatever the real story is. Deliveries are made to the side door. The neighborhood used to fret about her, not knowing if she was alive or dead in that house. After a while we stopped fretting and just ignored the whole thing. There's a daughter who lives in Avenel. Someone said she works for the *News Tribune.* Someone else said her name was Mary Louise, but I don't know if that's true or not. Would you like some cookies? They're store-bought, but they're okay."

"No thanks, Mr. Hemmings. The coffee is fine. Does the daughter come to visit?"

"Not that I know of. I've never seen her. Some of the neighbors thought they, mother and daughter, might be estranged, but I don't know that for a fact. Are you wanting to see her about something important?"

"Yes, Mr. Hemmings, it's important. Do you think I could trouble you for a piece of paper and some tape? I'll put a note on her door, then go see if I can find the daughter. Can you give me directions to the newspaper?"

Paul Hemmings ripped out a sheet of paper from a spiral notebook, found a pen and an envelope, and handed them over. "I'll do better than that—I'll draw you a map." Olivia watched as he found a stub of a pencil, spit on the end of it, and proceeded to draw a detailed map that would lead her to the local newspaper.

Olivia scribbled a note identifying herself.

It's imperative that I speak with you at Allison Matthews's request as soon as possible. I am her daughter.

She wrote down her cell phone number and sealed the envelope.

"You come back anytime, little lady. I like the company. Winters are bad for us old folk. Summertime, we can sit on our porches and chew the fat. Now it's just television—though it isn't so bad now that my son bought me a computer. I play poker all day long with my buddies. Still, it isn't the same thing as talking to people."

Olivia shook hands with the old man, thanked him for the coffee, and left the house. She taped the envelope securely on the side door of Jill Laramie's house and knocked as loudly as she could to alert the person inside that she was back. Then she left.

Thirty minutes later she was at the *News Tribune* asking for anyone named Mary Louise. She was told they only had one such person, Mary Louise Rafferty, and she was in Classifieds. The receptionist pressed a number, spoke quietly, and a few minutes later a pleasant freckle-faced young woman bounded into the lobby. She was dressed warmly in wool slacks and a sky-blue sweater. She smiled a greeting. "Can I help you?"

Olivia held out her hand. "Olivia Lowell. I live in Winchester, Virginia. Is there some-place we can go where we can talk in private?"

Green eyes appraised Olivia. Newshound

instincts. "About what?" the young woman asked carefully.

There was a wholesomeness, an air of honesty about Mary Louise. Olivia liked her instantly. "Your mother. I went to her house, but she didn't answer the door. I spoke to her neighbor, Paul Hemmings. He told me to come here. I really need to talk to you. Your mother and my mother were friends a long time ago. Allison Matthews was her name. She died a few weeks ago. She wanted me to find her two old friends."

Frowning, Mary Louise Rafferty led Olivia across the lobby to an ornate bench under a bushy fica tree and a pond of sorts, with trickling water. Both women sat down. Mary Louise clasped her hands together. Olivia noticed the wedding ring and commented on it. Mary Louise smiled weakly and said, "I have seven-year-old twins. I only work the hours they're in school. Now, tell me how I can help you."

"Tell me how I can get in touch with your mother. Does she have a phone number you can give me or an e-mail address? If the number is unlisted, perhaps you could call her and pave the way for me. This really is important. Perhaps *important* isn't the right word. *Crucial* might be more like it."

Mary Louise looked torn. Then, "I can call her for you, but I doubt it will do any good. My mother is . . . Well, she's different. She's reclusive. She never goes outside the house. Never. She won't let anyone in because she's afraid of germs. Very phobic. She's never seen my children in person. I send pictures. I know how weird and strange this is going to sound, but I haven't seen my mother since she moved to High Street, and that's almost twenty years now. Needless to say, we are not close, but she is my mother. I tried for years but . . . I finally gave up. I'm closer to my father. He's a wonderful grandfather to my kids, too. Unfortunately, he lives in Arizona, but I can give you his phone number and e-mail address. My mother has e-mail, and that's how she does her banking and ordering. Deliveries are just left at the door. I guess this sounds pretty bizarre to you."

Olivia made a sound that was supposed to be laughter. "You want to hear about bizarre, try this one for weird and bizarre. My mother gave birth to me, then told my father she didn't want *it*. I was the *it*. That same day she said she wanted a divorce. My father never saw her again. He raised me, told me she was dead. Then a few days ago a lawyer came to the house to tell me my mother had died a few weeks ago. Now, that's weird."

"Damn. You're right, that is weird. I never knew anything about my mother's friends. Maybe there was something in the water in Mississippi back then." Mary Louise gave a rueful laugh.

"There's another friend," said Olivia, "named Gwen. She lives in South Carolina. I'm going there in a few days to talk with her. Do you know anything about her?"

Mary Louise grimaced. "No. I never heard the name. I wonder if she's as weird as your mother and mine. I just bet she is," she said, answering her own question. "My father has a saying, birds of a feather flock together."

Olivia laughed. "My father says the same thing. I agree with you—I bet she's just as strange. I left a note on your mother's door. Do you think she'll read it?"

The young woman shrugged. "I don't know. I used to worry about her, but I got over that real quick when she didn't even want to see my kids. My husband gets very upset if I even mention her name. Wait here, Olivia, I'll go back to the office and give her a call, and I'll write down my e-mail address for you."

Olivia walked around the spacious, drafty lobby, looking at framed headline pictures that graced the walls. She whirled around when she heard her name being called.

Mary Louise shook her head to indicate her mother wouldn't agree to talk to Olivia. She handed over a piece of paper. "I put my home phone number on here and the number here at the paper if you want to call me. I know my dad will talk to you. My mother said to tell you the past is past, and she doesn't care one way or the other that your mother died. I'm sorry. My mother is very blunt."

Olivia's shoulders slumped. "Will you at least give me her e-mail address? I'll never say where I got it. I promise." Mary Louise looked torn again, but then she nodded and added the address to the bottom of the slip of paper. Olivia thanked her profusely and promised to stay in touch.

Leaving, Olivia suddenly thought of something and whirled around. "Mary Louise, do you have a cybercafé around here any-where?"

"Sure. There's one in Woodbridge Mall, and another one on Main Street, in town."

"How do I get there?" Mary Louise reached for the paper and scribbled directions to both cafés. They said good-bye again.

Olivia headed out toward Route 1 and followed the directions Mary Louise had given her. Studying the map, she realized the mall was less than a mile from where Jill Laramie lived.

It took her a good thirty minutes to find the cyberstore after she parked her car in the humongous parking lot. She signed on for computer use, paid the fee, and sat down to write e-mails to both Gill Laramie, Jill's ex-husband, and Jill herself. Ever mindful of the time, she figured she could wait at least two hours for a return of the e-mail, assuming either Jill or her ex was logged on. After that, she would have to immediately head for the airport if she wanted to avoid rush-hour traffic on the turnpike, return her rental car, and check in. She had no desire to spend the night in New Jersey. She wanted to see Jeff.

First she wrote to Gill Laramie and gave him her home e-mail address. Assuming he was logged on, he could respond to her there at the cybercafé. She offered a brief rundown of what she wanted but avoided any mention of the bank robbery.

Olivia anguished over the e-mail to Jill. If Jill was as weird as Mary Louise said she was, there was every possibility she would simply delete the e-mail and not even read it unless Olivia came up with a shocker of an opening line. She also needed a real grabber for the subject line. She finally settled for two words on the subject line. She typed both words in bold, oversize letters. **BANK ROBBERY**. Her message was short and to the point.

Think Federal Bureau of Investigation. Think back forty years. I came to your house to talk to you. My mother, Adrian Ames, who you knew as Allison Matthews, died a few weeks ago. She wants me to return her share of the money to the bank in Mississippi. She said she wants you and Gwen

to return your shares. Bank robbery is a federal offense, as you know. I need to speak with you. And, you need to think of me as the eight-hundred-pound gorilla where this matter is concerned. I'm enclosing my home phone number and my e-mail address. I will be going to see Gwen this week. You can't hide from this, Mrs. Laramie. If you decide to run or hide, the FBI will find you. I found you. If you decide to run again, I will find you.

Olivia signed her name and added her phone number and e-mail address before she logged off and walked out to the mall. At best she had two hours. She shopped, but her mind was someplace else. She walked out of the St. John store five hundred dollars poorer with a delicious cranberry-colored dress that hugged her body as if it was made for her. In Lord & Taylor she found the perfect shoes and bag. Usually on the frugal side, Olivia realized she'd just spent her entire clothing allowance for the year for a date with Jeff Bannerman.

She told herself everything was classic and would last for years and years and she'd get tired of the things before they wore out.

Olivia made her way back to the cyber-store, paid for computer time, logged on, and was not surprised to find no messages. She logged off, gathered her shopping bags, and headed for her car. It was time to go home, back to Winchester and her dogs. Back to the house to wait for Jeff.

Olivia grinned from ear to ear when she pulled into her driveway and saw Jeff's car. She reached for her bags and ran to the house. She was still smiling when she opened the door to see Jeff and the dogs waiting for her. Home sweet home.

It was a wonderful evening, what was left of it. Jeff had dinner on the table—takeout, but that was okay. It was the company, Olivia thought, that made the meal. They talked about everything and nothing as though they were old and dear friends. They had a beer while they watched David Letterman, laughing and poking each other at some of the silly jokes. It was one-thirty when Olivia showed him to one of her guest rooms. It had been decorated by her father for a male guest, with deep hunter greens, rich browns, and lush burgundy. A man's room. Even the towels in the bathroom matched the decor in the bedroom. Another one of her father's favorite things to do—decorating.

They said good night in the hallway. Just good night, all smiles and shuffling of the feet by both parties until Jeff reached for her and kissed her until her teeth rattled. When they broke apart they eyed one another with stunned surprise. Olivia backed up, and so did Jeff. A moment later he was in his room with the door closed. Olivia found her feet, ordered them to move, and raced to her own room. She was panting when she closed and locked her door. A moment later, she unlocked it. All four dogs were on the bed sitting up on their haunches, looking at her expectantly. Maybe this was a new game.

She was a sixteen-year-old again as she leaped on the bed. She giggled and laughed as she played with the dogs. Finally, exhausted, she undressed and brushed her teeth before crawling between the covers. She was drifting off to sleep when she realized she hadn't checked her e-mail. "Who cares," she muttered sleepily. The dogs moved, circled, scratched, then finally settled down, the two females on Olivia's right, the two males on her left, their little heads pointed outward. Guarding their mistress.

At five-thirty in the morning, Olivia and Jeff eyed each other warily until Olivia burst out laughing. Jeff joined in, his face pink.

"Do you want some breakfast?" Olivia asked.

"Can't, Olivia. I have to make an appearance in court today on a probate issue. I want to be there early, and it's snowing out right now. I'll see you this evening. We're still on, right?"

"I'm looking forward to it, Jeff. If things change, call me."

Jeff wrote down his e-mail address at the law firm on a scrap of paper, grabbed his coat, and ran toward the door. He turned back and kissed her on the cheek. "E-mail me if you get a response to your e-mails yesterday."

"Okay." Two kisses. One real, one hit-and-run. *I'll take it.* Olivia felt like singing.

Olivia ran with the dogs to the sliding

door. The quartet yipped and yapped as they tried to catch the swirling snowflakes falling down faster than Olivia liked. She stood in the open doorway, watching the dogs scampering about, her thoughts a million miles away. The moment the dogs raced inside, she dried them off and made coffee even though she itched to get to the computer.

It was almost light outside when Olivia entered the great room to build a fire. Outside, the wind howled as snow swirled against the windowpanes. Maybe another storm front coming through. Another inside day. She thought about her father, pictured him basking in island breezes under a golden sun. She shrugged off the image as the fire blazed upward. Satisfied that the dogs would be warm enough, she headed back to the kitchen, poured coffee, grabbed a strawberry-filled Pop-Tart, and headed to the computer. Childishly, she crossed her fingers, hoping there would be e-mails. There were, about seventy, at least sixty-five of which were pure spam. She deleted them, then clicked on one from Gill Laramie. There was no e-mail from Jill Laramie. Maybe she hadn't read Olivia's e-mail yet.

But she should have gotten the note taped to the door.

Gill Laramie's e-mail was a one-liner and simply said to call him at a certain phone number.

Olivia gulped down the coffee in her cup before she dialed the Arizona number. The answering voice was deep and pleasant-sounding. "Gill Laramie here."

Olivia sucked in her breath. "Mr. Laramie, this is Olivia Lowell, Adrian Ames's aka Allison Matthews's daughter. I e-mailed you yesterday from New Jersey. Your daughter, Mary Louise, said you lived in Arizona and gave me your e-mail address."

"Yes. My daughter called me last night. She explained the situation to me. Now, how can I help you?"

"I'm not sure, Mr. Laramie. Do you have any idea why your ex-wife is so reclusive, why she won't talk to people? I spoke to one of her neighbors, a Paul Hemmings, and he said she never leaves the house, never even goes outside. Then your daughter confirmed that. . . . I really need to speak with your ex-wife. It's important."

"Jill isn't exactly on my speed dial, Ms. Lowell. I haven't spoken to my ex-wife since we divorced. She was a strange one, that's for sure. I always thought she was trying to imitate Allison Matthews. I never met the woman. I did meet Gwen, however. Jill was always paranoid. I could never understand it. Mary Louise . . . It was hard on her, growing up. One day Jill was what passed for normal for her, which was strange even back then, then the next day she refused to leave the house, wouldn't talk to anyone. She virtually lived in one room. When it got to the point where I couldn't take it anymore, I filed for divorce and took Mary Louise with me. Jill didn't care."

Olivia digested the information. "Did something happen? Some sort of crisis?"

"Everything was a crisis with Jill. She was upset when Allison didn't respond to the wedding invitation. Gwen gave us a silver tea service, but Allison didn't send a present. Jill was livid. Then she seemed to get over it. A couple of years later, when she became pregnant with Mary Louise, she started acting strange again. I thought it was her pregnancy. But it got progressively worse after she gave birth. To this day, I don't know how I put up with it all. When it finally started to affect Mary Louise, I made the decision to leave. At first Jill panicked. She didn't want to be alone. She promised to see a therapist, but was afraid to leave the house. The therapist came to the house for a while, but then that stopped. It was incredibly expensive, but Jill has a trust fund. When I left, she gave me fifty thousand dollars for Mary Louise. Has any of this helped you?"

"I'm not sure, Mr. Laramie. Did Jill stay in touch with Allison and Gwen?"

"For a little while. But that stopped shortly before Mary Louise was born. She said they turned on her. Whatever that meant. Gwen didn't bother her as much as Allison did. She used to mumble and mutter about Allison, saying awful things like, she'd get even, she'd fix her, stuff like that. One time she called her a selfish bitch, saying she'd ruined her life. I didn't waste time trying to figure out what it was all about. I simply chalked it up to female stuff."

"Well, I appreciate your talking to me, Mr. Laramie. If I need to call you back, will that be okay?"

"Anytime."

Trust fund, my ass, Olivia thought.

The rest of the day and evening passed in

a blur. There was still no response from Jill Laramie. When Jeff arrived around eight, they batted around what she had learned from Gill Laramie before playing with the dogs, then retiring for the evening.

Chapter 12

Olivia woke with a start on Wednesday morning. It was already 9:20. She bolted from the bed, pulled on her robe, and raced down the hall to wake Jeff, thinking they had both overslept. The dogs whined and growled as they circled her feet. The guest room door was open and the bed neatly made. Thinking Jeff was in the kitchen, she hurried through the family room, shivering, her teeth chattering. The dogs barked louder. She quickly let them out and returned to the kitchen. The red light glowed on the coffee machine. The coffee itself looked black as pitch. She poured it down the drain as she looked this way and that, hoping to see a note. Then she saw it, taped to the microwave. Her sigh of relief was so intense she felt light-headed. She held the note as she walked back to the sliding door to let the dogs inside. That's when she noticed the snow. Lots of snow. A mountain of snow. Her spirits plummeted, but they perked up again when she read the note.

> *Good morning, Olivia,*
> *I couldn't sleep last night so I thought it might be a good idea to get on the road. I'm leaving now, it's four o'clock, and it's snowing heavily. I'll call you at some point and do my best to keep our date. I don't know why I couldn't sleep. No, that's a lie, I do know why.*

A big capital J was the signature.

Olivia smiled. She kept smiling as she dried off the dogs, then made a fire in the great room that she hoped would last the morning. The dogs claimed their space near the fire and lay down, each content with his or her chewy.

Olivia read the note six more times. He couldn't sleep. She, on the other hand, had slept like a baby. Had even overslept.

It was still snowing. Another gray-white day. Damn. Later, she'd turn on the weather to see what the forecast was. It was just her luck. A new dress, new everything, depleted bank account, and now this. Still, the road crews might have the roads cleared by this afternoon, especially the major highways in and out of the District.

"Guess I won't be going into town for a haircut and facial," Olivia muttered as she carried her coffee back to her office. She could hardly wait to see if there was a message from Jill Laramie. She sipped at her coffee and clicked the mouse at the same time. She saw the floating envelope on her screen informing her she had an incoming e-mail. She clicked the mouse and blinked. The subject line read *Re: BANK ROBBERY*. Jill Laramie had returned her e-mail.

"Guess that finally got your attention, huh, Mrs. Laramie?" She clicked on the e-mail and it popped up on the screen. Olivia had to read it twice before she could comprehend what she was reading.

Ms. Lowell,
    How dare you send me such a message! How dare you come poking around my home to invade

my privacy! How dare you! I don't know what you're talking about. Your mother's death has nothing to do with me. For the record, I hated her guts. Yes, I knew your mother when we were in college, but that ended upon graduation when we each went our separate way. Your threats of an FBI investigation mean nothing to me. How dare you threaten me! Stay out of my life and look into your mother's life, not mine. She was a hateful, conscienceless woman. I suspect you take after her to be doing such things.

It was signed Jill Davis Laramie.

Olivia rummaged on her desk until she found the slip of paper with Jeff's e-mail address at his law firm. She forwarded the message, sat back, and waited for a response. The response from Jeff appeared almost immediately.

Sorry I cut and ran, Olivia, but when I saw all that snow I figured

I better get on the road. I thought about you the whole time I was slipping and sliding on the highway. I'm going to do my best to make it out there this afternoon. If there is any way I can get out of here early, I will. I've got my portable radio here in the drawer tuned to the weather station.

As for Jill. It sounds to me like she's getting ready to take it on the lam. That's lawyer-speak for her doing a disappearing act. She's in some serious denial. Perhaps you should e-mail her back and tell her about the proof Allison left in her safe. Gotta run. Jeff

Olivia printed out the e-mail so she could read it again and again. She then pulled up Jill's e-mail to type a response.

Dear Jill,

Thank you for taking the time to answer my e-mail. I will take your comments one by one and address them. How dare I say and do the things I did? How dare you rob a bank? How dare you deny it? I have the proof. Allison Matthews photocopied all those bearer bonds. Your share is clearly marked, as is Gwen's. Denial on your part is no longer an option. You don't have a trust fund; you lied to your husband Gill and your daughter. You gave Gill fifty thousand dollars for Mary Louise's care when you divorced. I understand your feelings for Adrian Ames. She wasn't a nice person. I also understand the idea to steal the bonds was Allison Matthews's. But you and Gwen were willing participants. I have the bank card where both you and Gwen signed for the safe-deposit box. That card has your social security number on it and Gwen's as well. That's where you three stashed the bonds until things blew over. In addition, Adrian Ames left a diary. I have all these things in my possession. I also have your wedding invitation and two from Gwen. For some reason,

Adrian Ames saved them. I want to
talk to you so we can resolve this
with the least amount of trouble.
You and Gwen, should this go public, could spend time in a federal
slammer. Bank robberies are always
on the books. I gave you my phone
number but here it is again.

Olivia read and reread her message before she added her phone number and then
typed in her name. She wondered if what
she'd just typed was true. Somehow or
other she thought bank robberies had
statutes of limitations. She pressed SEND,
and the e-mail was gone.

After showering, she dressed warmly in a
fleece-lined sweat suit, knowing she was
going to snowblow the driveway and patio.
But not yet—it was still snowing. It looked
to her like there was at least five inches of
new snow on the ground. In the kitchen, she
made herself scrambled eggs, bacon, and
toast, which she shared with the dogs. Her
eyes on the falling snow, she opened the
freezer and debated taking something out
for dinner since she didn't know if Jeff
would make it. She opted for a pot roast.

She hadn't made one of those in ages. Carrots, string beans, potato pancakes. Hmmmm. She tidied up the kitchen, knowing she was stalling. Finally, she couldn't stand it any longer and ran to the computer.

There were no personal messages, but there were nine spams. She deleted them. She must be really stupid to have thought Jill Laramie was sitting there waiting for an e-mail from her. The lady didn't scare easily. For some reason that surprised her. Well, she could wait. She had all the time in the world.

With nothing else to occupy her time, Olivia went to MapQuest and requested directions to Gwen's home. She printed out the response. A trip to South Carolina might require an overnight stay. Then again, maybe not, if she could catch an early-morning flight. She called the airline and made a reservation for Saturday morning at 6:05, with a change in Charlotte, arriving in Charleston a little before ten. A half hour to pick up a car rental and get on the road, and she should be able to make Summerville no later than noon, possibly earlier. She scheduled her return flight from Charleston at 8:20 P.M. If all went well, she would be home and in her own bed by 2:30 A.M.

If Jill knew where Gwen was, there was every possibility Jill gave her the heads-up and the trip would be fruitless. Still, she had to try.

Back in the kitchen, waiting for the coffee to warm up, Olivia wrestled with her conscience. Why was she doing this? Why did she even care? *I don't owe those women a thing.* She had said she wanted no part of this, yet here she was threatening Jill Laramie. She'd probably threaten Gwen, too. Adrian Ames said if they didn't cooperate, she was to repay the whole amount out of her own funds. Maybe Adrian's estate did deserve to repay the whole amount of money, since the idea to rob the bank was Allison's. As her father always used to say, right is might.

Olivia argued with herself. *Just look at you, Olivia Lowell. You were so willing to steal a dog and lie about it. What makes you any different from those three women? On top of that, you imposed on your friendship with Clarence to ask him to do something illegal for you.*

Olivia hung her head in shame. Yes, she'd

wanted to do those things, but—she lifted her head—in the end she hadn't done either of those things. She still had Cecil, but with Jeff's okay. As soon as they resolved that issue, Cecil would be taken care of. Those women—her mother and Jill and Gwen—were greedy and selfish. They robbed a bank for their own personal gain. *All I wanted was to make a little dog happy. And I'm doing the best I know how in regard to my mother's last wishes. Why, I don't know. Yes, I do know. Dad raised me always to do the right thing. And the right thing to do here is to return the bank's money—and to honor Adrian Ames's last wishes, because at the end the woman who was my mother cared about those other women's lives and the guilt she was sure they bore. So it isn't apples and oranges, but it's damn close.*

Olivia spent the next few hours washing the dogs' beds, then snowblowing the driveway and patio, knowing full well she'd have to do it again in a few hours, and running back and forth to the computer to see if there was a message from Jill Laramie. There wasn't. There were no messages from Jeff, either.

At three o'clock, after a second bout with

the snowblower, Olivia eyed the thawing meat on the counter, glad that she'd taken it out of the freezer. Even if Jeff did make it over to her house, they wouldn't be going out to dinner in this weather. She worked steadily in the kitchen for the next half hour, braising the meat, paring vegetables, and baking a coconut custard pie. Midway into her dinner preparations Jeff called her. She literally danced around the kitchen while she talked to him. Later, she couldn't remember what they said. All she heard was that the office was closing, and he was leaving in five minutes.

"Expect me when you see me. I don't know how long it will take, but I'd like a big cup of hot chocolate with some brandy in it, a roaring fire, and some warm clothes on my arrival," he announced, laughter ringing in his voice.

"Yes sir. Drive carefully."

"You bet. See ya."

A grin stretching from ear to ear, Olivia walked over to the sliding doors to stare out at the snow. She crossed her fingers that it would continue. Being snowbound with someone like Jeff . . . well, what could be better?

*   *   *

At seven o'clock, dinner was ready. All she had to do was fry the potato pancakes. The table was set with her best dishes and silver. She'd even added a pair of sweet-scented vanilla candles to the table. A date was a date. So what if she was wearing a sweat suit.

It was also still snowing.

Olivia wearily donned her parka and headed for the garage and the snowblower to clear the driveway for the third time. She was just finishing when a pair of headlights approached. Jeff! She backed up, pulling the blower with her. She ran back down the driveway just as Jeff climbed out of his snow-covered car. He looked so good she wanted to hug him. She would have if his leather-soled shoes hadn't slipped on the packed snow the blower couldn't move. He reached out, and they both went down.

Both their arms and feet moved as they tried to get traction. Olivia was close enough to smell his aftershave and minty breath. Snow continued to fall as they ended up rolling down to the end of the driveway. He kissed her because her face was mashed against his. Olivia heard him groan. The kiss was every bit as wonderful as the one the night before last, with a slight difference. This kiss held the promise of things to come.

Olivia rolled away and struggled to her feet. She held out her hand to Jeff. He grasped it, and together they walked into the garage.

"Olivia . . . is something happening here? All I did was think about you today."

Olivia licked the snowflakes off her lips. "I think so," was the best she could manage in response. Arm in arm, they walked into the kitchen.

Jeff looked around, sniffed, observed the table, all the while trying to pet each one of the dogs. "This is nice. This is really nice. Did you do this just for me?"

"Sort of, kind of. Yeah, yeah, I did. Hey, a date's a date. I'm keeping up my end. You made it here. It's a date. I put some warm clothes out on the bed in your room—I mean the guest room. Take a hot shower so you don't catch cold. I'll have dinner on the table by the time you're finished. It's going to snow *all* night," she added happily.

"*All* night?" Jeff called over his shoulder.

Olivia, her back to him, didn't see his clenched fist shoot in the air.

Curled up on the comfortable sofa, both Olivia and Jeff were dozing, the dogs curled alongside them. The phone rang sharply in Olivia's ear, startling her. She grappled behind her for the portable, clicked it on, and muttered a sleepy greeting.

"This is Paul Hemmings. Is this Olivia Lowell?"

Olivia jerked upright. "Yes, Mr. Hemmings, this is Olivia. Is something wrong?"

"I don't rightly know, little miss. I was standing on my front porch waiting for the boy to finish shoveling my walkway so I could pay him when I saw a car pull up to Mrs. Laramie's house. We're having a bit of a snowstorm here in Woodbridge. Saw on the TV that you're having the same storm, little miss. It was one of those fancy town cars from Arrow Service. He tootled his horn and out comes Mrs. Laramie, carrying her purse and a shoulder bag. Neither one looked heavy to me. I thought you might want to know. I never would have known she was gone if I hadn't been standing on the porch. Me and all the neighbors would go on thinking she was still in there. I talked to a few of the neighbors on the phone, and they agreed I should call you. Now, mind you, we don't want to know her business, but it certainly is strange for that woman to leave after twenty-some years right after you come here looking for her. Mighty peculiar."

"Thank you for calling me, Mr. Hemmings. You did the right thing. I appreciate it. Have a good night, Mr. Hemmings."

After she hung up the words tumbled out of Olivia's mouth so fast, Jeff had to tell her to slow down. "What do you make of it, Jeff?"

Jeff's chest puffed out. "Didn't I tell you she sounded in her e-mail like she was going to split, take it on the lam? If she hired a car service, that means she's either taking the Metroliner or heading for the airport. Man, is that lady going to be shocked at the outside world if she hasn't left the house in twenty years. It's amazing how fear can goose a person. What are you going to do, Olivia?"

All romantic thoughts vanished from Olivia's mind as she started to pace the great-room floor. She stopped her frantic pacing to toss two oak logs on the fire. "I don't know. Does this mean I write her off and concentrate on Gwen? Or do I go back to the detective and have them try to track her? Jill must still have the money. Living like a hermit for twenty years probably means she didn't spend much other than that fifty grand she gave to her ex-husband for her daughter's care. The daughter said her mother did her banking online, so that has to mean she has investments. She might have a sizable portfolio if she's invested wisely. Remember those high interest rates in the eighties? I wonder if the daughter knows. Do you think I should call her, Jeff?"

"Olivia, I don't have a dog in this race. The daughter will certainly ask you questions. Are you going to want to answer them? Estranged or not, the woman is her mother."

Olivia paced, wringing her hands. "I know, I know. I guess I really spooked her. That has to mean Jill isn't giving up her share. Assuming she still has it. She shouldn't get away with it, Jeff. Neither should Gwen."

"Your mother got religion late, when she

learned she was dying. Even though the statute of limitations for the robbery expired decades ago, going public could seriously embarrass the two living participants. And that's not what Adrian Ames wanted. She wanted them to agree to return the money to help them *overcome their guilt*, not to see them held up to public ridicule."

Olivia stopped her frantic pacing, her eyes wide. "That was just a threat. I'm not turning them in. I just want them to pay it back. Unless . . . unless . . . Would the fact that I know about this make me guilty of obstruction of justice? I don't know anything about the law. Well, would it?"

Jeff threw his hands in the air. "Think, Olivia. If they cannot be prosecuted for robbing the bank because it was so long ago, you cannot be prosecuted for obstruction of justice for doing nothing about it now. As far as the law is concerned, there *is* nothing to do about it. So you're in the clear."

Olivia started to pace again. "This can't be happening to me. How could that woman do this to me? Even if the law isn't concerned, now I'm part of her ugly past. I'm going to see Mr. O'Brien as soon as I can to find out when Allison Matthews's money will be available. The big question is, how will I get all that money in cash to pay it back? Someone is sure to notice that kind of withdrawal and start asking questions. I'm thinking it was a hell of a lot easier to steal it than it will be to return it. Oh, God, I have such a headache."

Headache. The magic word that alerted Jeff that he might as well go to bed. Tongue in cheek, he said, "You just keep right on pacing, and I'll let the dogs out."

Olivia nodded.

Why was this bothering her? Why?

"I hate you, Adrian Ames. You had no right to ask me to do this. I don't owe you a damn thing. Not love, much less respect. You were too gutless to return the money yourself, so you brought me into it to do your dirty work. Damn you! Oh, damn you!"

Olivia heard the sliding door shut, heard the snick of the lock, heard the dogs racing to the laundry room for Jeff to dry them off. She heard the parade walking down the hall to the guest room. Then she heard Jeff call out, "Good night!"

"Night," she mumbled.

Some date this turned out to be.

Shoulders slumping, Olivia walked back

to the office. Like she could sleep. Maybe she'd never sleep again and would eventually wither and die.

Turning on her computer and opening her e-mail, she wasn't really expecting any incoming mail, but there were three, one from Gill Laramie, one from his daughter Mary Louise, and one from Paul Hemmings.

Olivia clicked on the mail from Gill Laramie first.

Dear Ms. Lowell,

My ex-wife e-mailed me today. She berated me for talking to you. Whatever you stirred up is not sitting well with Jill. She said she was leaving the area because she doesn't wish to be harassed. She said she was going to file a complaint against you. I thought I should warn you. I don't know why. Something tells me there is more to your visit to her than a simple deathbed wish of your mother to communicate with her. Having said that, I don't want to know anything about it. Mary

Louise is terribly upset. She thinks she was wrong to give you her mother's e-mail address. She has always hoped Jill would come around where the twins are concerned. Now, that's not going to happen. Please, I respectfully ask that you stay out of our lives. Whatever my ex-wife was involved in, or is still involved in, Mary Louise, her family, and I do not wish to be involved. Jill belongs to our miserable past, not our glowing future.

Olivia blinked back tears as she opened the e-mail from Mary Louise Rafferty. There was nothing on the subject line, nor was there a greeting. Just a short message.

I don't know what your game is, Ms. Lowell, but I want you to know my mother left town. I worry about her out in the world since she's been such a recluse all these years. I don't know if she can cope. And, you dashed all hopes of her ever coming around where my little family is concerned. I'm sorry I gave you the e-mail address. Please don't call or write to me ever again.

Olivia reached for a tissue to wipe her drippy nose. "Yeah, well, I just wonder what you'd think if you knew what I know. I was trying to spare you and be discreet," she mumbled as she opened Paul Hemmings's e-mail.

Little lady, this is Paul Hemmings. It's late, and I didn't want to call and wake you. I'm one of those night owls. An hour or so after Mrs. Laramie left, a young woman went to the house and carried out four large cartons. I don't know if that's important to you or not, but I thought I should tell you. I was taking my trash out because I don't like leaving it in the house overnight when I saw her. I waved, she looked at me, but she didn't wave or say anything. It was

**real nice talking to you, little miss.
You perked up my day. If I hear or
see anything else, I'll let you know
by e-mail.**

Olivia sat in her swivel chair and cried into
the wad of tissues.

Chapter 13

It was still dark outside when Olivia felt a gentle nudge to her shoulder. She mumbled something under her breath and tried to roll over. Soft, cushiony material pressed against her face. Her eyes snapped open. She was on the couch, and Jeff was standing over her. The dogs were whining and snarling to go outside.

"Olivia, wake up. You need to see the snow outside. What do you want me to do with the dogs? They're not going to be able to maneuver, the snow's too deep. Do you want me to get the snowblower out and do the driveway first so they can do what they have to do?"

Olivia struggled to get her wits about her. "What . . . what time is it?"

Jeff looked down at the oversize watch

on his wrist. "Almost five. It stopped snowing a little while ago."

Olivia swung her legs over the side of the couch. "A little while ago? Didn't you sleep?"

"Not much. I did doze off from time to time. The dogs slept with me. Do you believe that?"

Olivia stood up. No, she didn't believe that. *Little traitors*, she thought uncharitably. "What was the question again? Never mind, I remember. That sounds like a good idea. Let me get my jacket and boots and help you."

"No, no, I can do it. I'm just going to clear a spot for the dogs. You can make breakfast if you don't mind. When it gets light out, I'll finish up the job. I heard snowplows earlier, so that means the end of your driveway is socked in, which also means I have to shovel. It's okay, I need the exercise."

Olivia watched as Jeff pulled on his outer gear, the dogs dancing impatiently at his feet. "I'm sorry about last night. I really am. This . . . this mess is starting to consume me, take over my life, and I don't like it one little bit."

Jeff nodded understandingly. "See you in a while."

Olivia went to the kitchen to make coffee before she headed back to her bathroom, where she took a quick shower and dressed for warmth. She was wearing a new lavender sweat suit her father had given her for Christmas, heavy wool socks, and slippers. When it was time to go outside she'd switch to rubber-soled boots.

She quickly thawed frozen pancake batter, fried up some frozen link sausages, and warmed some syrup, which also came in a frozen packet. She absolutely refused to read the list of ingredients on the package labels.

The day moved forward until all practical matters were taken care of. It was late afternoon when the couple stood face to face by the kitchen sink, and Jeff said, "Why do I feel like we're some old married couple without all the marital perks?" He grinned mischieviously.

Olivia linked her arm with his and smiled as she led him over to one of the kitchen chairs. She popped open a soft drink and split it two ways. "I need your help, Jeff. I don't know what to do. My father is no help.

Like you said, you don't have a dog in this race, so you should be able to be objective—give me some insight here."

Jeff crumpled and uncrumpled a wad of paper napkins. "I can't tell you what to do, Olivia. Once you read the letter from Adrian Ames, you became a part of her past life. No one knows what's in that letter but you. Me too, of course, but I'm your lawyer, so I cannot divulge anything. Client confidentiality. Nothing on this earth, no agency, can force me to divulge a thing. You can drop everything, pretend you don't know anything, walk away from it. I suspect you aren't that kind of person, though. If you *were* that kind of person, you wouldn't have gone to New Jersey. You wouldn't be planning on going to South Carolina on Saturday. I did e-mail my friend Sean, and posed a hypothetical to him about your problem. He's a criminal lawyer and in the middle of a trial. He'll have the straight skinny on the legal aspects. Like I said, I'm a probate lawyer and rusty on anything in that vein. The information I gave you yesterday is straight out of Criminal Law 101, and needs to be verified by someone in the field.

"Olivia, just because you're angry with the circumstances, you can't go around threatening people to get what you want. In this case, you don't even know what you want. The can of worms is open. You can't stuff them back in. Legally you have no obligation to go to the authorities and tell them everything you know. If you decide to do so anyway, then tell them you are prepared to pay the entire amount of money back from the estate, plus whatever fines or penalties are involved, although I doubt that even that's required. I do not think there is anything the authorities can do to Jill and Gwen.

"If and when you decide to go to the authorities, you can say that it took some time before you decided what to do about the information in the letter Adrian Ames left you and what you found out from the items in her safe. Just because you read it right after Mr. O'Brien gave it to you does not mean you had to bring the information you acquired to anyone's attention immediately. I don't see them, whoever 'them' turns out to be, going to your father. His life with Allison ended the day you were born. The bank robbery occurred before they were married. As I've already told you, I'm pretty sure any statute of limitations has run out, which means no one can be prosecuted after forty years."

"Could I really be that lucky? You'd think that if Adrian Ames was as smart as she thought she was, she would have known she was safe as far as the time element goes. It's a lot to think about, isn't it?"

"You could be right. Obviously, when she found out she was dying, it became a moral issue, not just a legal one. Maybe Jill knows that, too, and that's why she could snub you like she did. Maybe Jill has some mental problems. I just don't know, Olivia," Jeff said with a groan.

Olivia got up and watered the plants sitting on the counter. "I'm tired of thinking. I never asked for this. I don't want Adrian Ames's fancy house, her money, or any legacy. I don't want anything from her. Damn, it was forty years ago." She moved over to the kitchen window to stare out at the blinding white snow.

Olivia felt his presence, felt his warm breath on the back of her neck. Her heart started to pound inside her chest as her feet took root on the floor. She felt herself being turned around, then he was kissing her, and she was kissing him back.

A long time later she couldn't remember walking down the hall to her bedroom. Maybe Jeff carried her. But for the rest of her life she would remember what happened when they arrived at their mutual destination, physically as well as emotionally.

Jeff Bannerman was her destiny. She was almost sure of it.

Olivia closed her eyes the moment she buckled up. Her mind seemed to race as fast as the plane she was sitting in. She'd made the decision to wait until she talked to Gwen Hendrix before she made any concrete decisions in regard to Adrian Ames's request. She had, however, called the detective agency to start an additional investigation into Jill's whereabouts. She was promised a report within thirty-six hours, which would make the report due sometime on Sunday. Or, if private detectives didn't work Sundays, she would have to wait till Monday. That was okay, too.

Sooner than she expected, the flight attendant tapped Olivia on the shoulder to indicate she should bring her seat back to the upright position. The descent was short and smooth. When she deplaned she had to run to the gate to make her connection since her flight was thirty minutes late. After racing down the gangway, she barely made it. Buckled up, she closed her eyes again, and this time she thought about Jeff Bannerman and all her new feelings. She could hardly wait to get back to Winchester. She wondered how he was making out with the dogs and all the snow. Her lips still felt hot and bruised from the lip lock he'd planted on her before she left the house. She smiled to herself. Her destiny. She hoped Jeff felt the same way.

The fifty-minute flight was made with no turbulence. The landing—which she always dreaded—was smooth. She loved this small airport, the kind it was impossible to get lost in. Stopping long enough to buy herself a cold drink, she headed for Avis and her rental car and was on the road in less than ten minutes. A right turn on Dorchester Road took her to Old Trolley Road, where she made another right—and a mental note to stop for pizza at a shop called Pies On Pizza on the way back. She continued until she came to a five-street intersection, where she turned right on 17A. The car grew stuffy, and she rolled down her window, amazed that it was so warm here in South Carolina. And green in February. It looked like winter had forgotten about South Carolina. She thought about the frigid temperatures she'd left back in Virginia just hours ago.

As she whizzed down 17A, or Main Street, Olivia admired the pretty little town of Summerville. It reminded her of home—in springtime. Thoughts of home brought thoughts of Jeff front and center. She pushed the thoughts out of the way. She had to think about Gwen Hendrix and what she was going to say to her.

Fifteen minutes later she made a left-hand turn onto a rutted road that led to a run-down trailer park. Straggly shrubs, rusty bikes, and cars littered the roadway. Skinny dogs and stray cats abounded. She wasn't sure, but she thought she saw two chickens trying to outrun a bushy-tailed cat. The noise of a motorcycle revving up sounded close, then another, and finally a third and fourth. A motorcycle gang. Her stomach churned at the thought. All at once four motorcycles roared past her. She had to pull onto something that passed for a road shoulder, half scrub weeds and a dangerous-looking ditch.

The address for Gwendolyn Hendrix was 246 Indian Drive. Olivia looked for some sign of oleanders, but there weren't any. She finally found Oleander Drive and turned to avoid a deep rut that would have ruined the underbelly of the rental for sure. Stopping the car, she looked across the road at a grimy, dilapidated trailer. Three wooden steps led to the door. The middle step was missing entirely. A sickly looking Christmas wreath still hung on the filthy front door. A broken screen hung from one of the front windows. The mesh part of the screen was hanging in tattered strips, its metal border rusted through in places.

Olivia sucked in her breath and walked over to the trailer, then hopped up to the top step, careful not to slip through the opening where the second step should have been.

She heard a game show going on inside. The television seemed extra loud. Maybe Gwen had a hearing problem. She rapped sharply to be heard over the noise inside. When there was no response, she shouted Gwen's name. The sudden silence was startling. Then the door opened. The tall woman standing in front of her didn't have any of the features Olivia recalled from the photographs Adrian Ames had left behind. "Mrs. Hendrix?"

"Who wants to know?" The voice was hoarse and sounded cracked—what her father would call a whiskey-cigarette voice.

Olivia found it hard not to stare. Who was this slovenly looking creature? There wasn't one thing about the woman's features that resembled the photograph in her purse. Not one little thing. She said, "I'm Olivia Lowell. Allison Matthews gave birth to me. Dennis Lowell is my father. I'm sure you remember him from your college days. Allison . . . passed away a few weeks ago. Do you think I could come inside so we can talk?"

The woman fiddled with the buttons on her blouse, a threadbare white blouse that was on its last legs. "Depends on what you want to talk about. Why would Allison send you here?" So this *was* Gwen!

"Maybe because the three of you robbed a bank in Mississippi," Olivia said bluntly. "Now, can I come in or not?"

The big woman moved aside, allowing Olivia to step through the opening. She was surprised to see that the rooms, while shabby, were clean, neat, and tidy. Gwen motioned her to an old corduroy Barca-lounger, the best-looking chair in the room. A small herd of cats materialized from somewhere and settled fearfully near their mistress.

"Talk," Gwen said succinctly.

Olivia cleared her throat. "Adrian Ames, the woman you knew as Allison Matthews, asked me to try to get in touch with you and Jill. It seems she had an attack of con-science before she died and wants to repay the bank-robbery money. She was . . . she was meticulous about her record keeping. There was a copy of the bank card you and Jill signed, with your social security num-bers on it. That's pretty much how I was able to find you. That's where you . . . where you stashed the bonds until graduation, when Allison said it was okay to move them.

Obviously, she was the one who held on to them until the division of the spoils, since she had copies made of all the bonds. She also made a separate list of the bond numbers and which ones you got and which ones Jill got. She asked that the return be made discreetly."

The woman sitting on a spindly stool across from Olivia laughed, a raucous, phlegmy sound. "You're a little late, sweet cheeks. That money is long gone. Do you think I'd be living in this dump if I had money? I made some bad decisions. What that means to you is I married a bum the first time, and he spent half of it. You'd have thought I learned my lesson but, oh, no, I turned around and married an even bigger bum, who cleaned me out completely. I tried to borrow money from Adrian Ames, but she didn't even respond when I wrote her. I just could never get back on my feet. I'm lucky I have enough money to buy cat food for my kitties. I tend bar three nights a week. Doesn't pay much. I baby-sit once in a while. So, what does this mean? You're going to turn me in and collect a reward? What?"

Olivia ignored the question and asked

one of her own. "What about Jill? Wouldn't she help you?"

Gwen laughed again, the same deep raucous laugh. "I lost touch with her early on. She was a piece of work, that one. Even when we were at Ole Miss she was decidedly odd. After we graduated, she began worrying about germs and getting contaminated. If it was possible to live in a bubble, she would have. She told me how she used to wash her money with soap and water. Tell me that isn't weird, or a sign of something. I have no idea where she is. So, does that mean I swing in the wind for that little caper?"

Olivia answered truthfully. "I don't know."

"You know, kid, your mother was strange. I don't think she had a conscience. All she was interested in was money and more money. She would have sold her soul to the devil for money. I think she did. Sell her soul, I mean. I don't know if she was smart or just downright conniving. She planned the whole thing, and we pulled it off. Hell, I'll never deny it. If you plan on turning me in, you better find Jill and turn her in, too. Wouldn't you know, Allison, I mean Adrian, beat the system by dying! I know that must sound cruel to you but, tough noogies. And, she ended up on top, name change and all. I read somewhere that she was worth tens of millions of dollars. Is that true?" Gwen asked bitterly.

"It could be. The lawyers never gave me an accounting."

"If she was that rich, let her estate pay back the money. I don't feel like I owe her anything. If they want to put me in jail, let them. It's time someone took care of me. Sweet cheeks, why do you call her Adrian Ames or Allison Matthews? You never once referred to her as your mother. Are you sure she was your mother? You don't look a thing like her. Of course, that's probably a good thing. Allison was no raving beauty. None of us were. Today young people would call the three of us nerdy. I guess we were back then."

"You know the reason as well as I do. As she told you the day you split the bonds, she gave me up to my father as soon as she gave birth to me. She told him that same day that she wanted a divorce. My father never saw her again. He told me she was dead. I didn't know I had a mother all these years until her lawyer showed up at my door to tell me she died."

"Yeah, I knew that. Tough break, kid. Listen, you wouldn't have liked her. Trust me on that. Everything back then was about Allison. What she wanted, when she wanted it. She made sure she got it, too. She told us to jump, and we asked how high. The only thing I feel bad about is that my son is going to find out about this. I did my best to try and save a little for him, but that last weasel, Hendrix, conned me out of it. My son lives in Columbia. He's a cop. Do you believe that? He has three little boys. He works two jobs, and his wife works so they can save for college. Oh, well, guess this was all meant to be, otherwise it wouldn't be happening. What do you want me to do?"

A good question. The woman sounded like a runaway train. Olivia looked up at all the religious pictures hanging on the wall. Gwen noticed her gazing at the pictures. "I got religion late in life. That's why I'm ready to take my punishment, whatever it is."

"Well . . . I'll get back to you, okay? Do you have a phone number?"

"No. I live a bare-bones existence. I use the phone at the convenience store down at the corner. I call my son every other Sunday. Other than that, I don't need a phone. If you want to get in touch with me, you can call the store, and they'll come and get me. I can call you back, but it will have to be collect."

"It's okay to call me collect." Olivia watched as Gwen tore a corner off a brown paper grocery bag and wrote down the number of the convenience store. She pocketed the piece of paper.

Before she left the trailer, Olivia reached in her purse and handed Gwen fifty dollars. "For cat food," she said.

The woman reached out to hug Olivia. She smelled of cats and cigarettes. "You aren't going to believe this, Olivia, but I'm actually relieved to have talked about all this. It's been like a festering sore inside me all these years. I wish we had never done it, but wishing won't do a thing for you. But like I said, whatever the punishment is, I'll take my share. You have a safe trip home, young lady."

Olivia stood poised on the top rickety step, knowing she was going to have to jump to the bottom. She turned around. "Gwen, was there even one good thing, one decent thing that you liked about Allison Matthews? Surely she had one redeeming quality."

Gwen straightened her shoulders. "I would be lying if I said there was. You're nothing like her, if that's your next question. She was evil, that one."

Olivia carried that statement with her when she left. It was still with her when she stopped for pizza. She ordered three slices with the works—pepperoni, green peppers, garlic, and onions—and a Sprite. She devoured it all, then ordered a second Sprite to take with her.

One good thing was she didn't have to rush. She wasn't heading into any kind of rush-hour traffic, since it was Saturday. Olivia drove in a leisurely manner to the airport, her thoughts whirling and twirling.

After she returned the car rental, she walked into the airport and browsed the shops. She ended up buying Jeff a cap that said STINGRAYS on the bill, and a few rubber toys that could have been baby bath toys or dog toys—they'd serve as the latter. She also bought a bag of salted pecans for herself. Having checked in for her flight, she headed to the bar area, settled herself into a corner, ordered a beer, and called . . . her destiny. That's how she now thought of Jeff. A smile as wide as the whole outdoors stretched across her face when her destiny said "Hello."

Chapter 14

It was one o'clock on Sunday afternoon, the weekend almost over, when Jeff suggested they go outside to play in the snow and pretend they were kids again. "My last clear memory of doing that was with my brothers when I was thirteen years old. My brothers, of course, were older, but they humored me. I think they knew somehow that it was my last go-round as a kid. We really got into the whole thing hot and heavy. Mom and Dad came out and joined in. It's one of my most favorite memories.

"We were out there in waist-high snow for three or four hours. Frozen stiff, soaking wet, but no one wanted it to end. Finally Mom put her foot down, and we all trooped inside. She made us take showers, put on warm clothes, then she made hot cocoa with tons of those little marshmallows and toast with lots of butter and her own home-made strawberry jam. If I close my eyes I can still picture it all and even taste the jam."

"That's a really nice memory. I have some like that with my dad. Unfortunately, I never had any siblings. It was just him and me. He always used to say, 'It's just you and me, kid.' He was always up for everything, no matter what it was. He didn't want me to feel cheated in any way. I needed him, and he needed me. We were a good team," Olivia said, her eyes particularly bright.

Seeing Jeff's attentive expression, she continued with her own reminiscing. "I have this one really fond memory of going sled riding in Handley Park with my friends. I think I was sixteen, and I had this enormous crush on a guy named Danny Salyan. He was four years older, a college boy, and he was there with his friends. Even though they were older, we were all the same age that day. I almost fainted when he invited us all back to his mom's house. She was such a sweet lady. She made us hot chocolate and gave us big, thick slices of cake. Her name was Betty Lou and she looked just the way a mom is supposed to look. His dad was named Bill, and he was just as nice as my own dad. Betty Lou was all cozy and warm, and she smelled so good. She sews. Today you would probably call her an expert seamstress. She even hugged me when we left. I often wondered if she knew what a crush I had on her son. He joined the navy and is married now and lives in Florida. He has a new son, named Connor William. I saw the announcement in the *Winchester Star* a week or so ago."

His voice soft, Jeff said, "And now?"

Olivia smiled, but it was more of a grimace. "Now it's Dad and Lea. He doesn't need me anymore. That's the way it should be. He deserves his own happiness. I have the dogs. If you mean Danny, I got over my crush that spring." Her voice was so flat she had a hard time believing it was her own.

Jeff's eyes were diamond bright, almost as bright as Olivia's. "You have me now. You know that, don't you?" he said gently.

She'd hoped to hear something like that but hadn't been sure she would. What she was feeling right then was nothing like the schoolgirl crush she'd had on Danny Salyan years ago. Was Jeff making a commitment to her? It sure sounded like it. She felt light-headed at the thought. She didn't trust herself to speak, so she nodded.

Jeff's eyes twinkled. "You know what else, Olivia? If you marry me, you will be married to Cecil's handler. That would certainly solve our problems where he's concerned."

Married. "Whoa. Whoa. Slow down. You hardly know me. I hardly know you. You can't just jump into marriage. That's what my parents did, and look at the outcome."

"My parents only knew each other for two weeks. Look at *their* outcome. Six handsome, strapping big boys. It's one for one. I'm not like your father, and you aren't like your . . . like Adrian Ames, or Allison Matthews. My parents will love you. I know that. I'm positive you will like them, too, and my brothers. My mother's biggest disappointment in life was that she didn't have any daughters. Did I ever tell you she made us wear aprons when we cleaned up the kitchen? She did, and we didn't argue, either."

Aprons. Maybe it had some kind of secret meaning. Her head bobbed up and down as she tried to figure out what boys wearing aprons meant. She didn't even own an apron. Neither had her father. When either one of them needed an apron they tied a dish towel around their waist. "Okay, let's go out in the snow. I gotta warn you, Jeff, I have a powerful pitch. The sun is out, so the snow should be wet, perfect for snowballs. My throwing arm was better than my dad's. Did you ever build a snow fort?" How high and shrill her voice sounded. *Why is that?* she wondered.

"Yeah, when I was little. Wanna do it? We can build one big enough for us and the four dogs."

"Let's do it!" Olivia chortled as she grabbed her parka and raced for the sliding door. The dogs barreled out right behind her, Jeff bringing up the rear. Olivia scooped a handful of snow on the run, whirled, and let it fly. She was rewarded with the sound of a loud *ooof* as Jeff doubled over.

The fight was on, and they pummeled each other for a solid half hour. It was clear when Jeff threw up his hands that Olivia was the winner. Their arms around each other, they squared off an area of the yard for the fort, then rolled snow into huge, round balls. Two hours later, exhausted, they had a two-room fort, one room for the dogs and one for themselves.

They crunched themselves in half as they struggled to fit into the room they'd carved out. "Seems to me we had more room when we were kids," Jeff groused. "Where's the fun sitting here scrunched up like a Gumby?"

Olivia laughed. "We were half our present size back then, and it was the thing to do when it snowed. We must be old, because I would rather go inside and watch a movie on TV."

"Yeah, me too," Jeff said, grinning. "Guess you can only be a kid once in your lifetime. I wish I had known that back then. I would have had more fun. Come on, I'll help you up." He reached for Olivia's hand.

Olivia dug her heels into the snow, bracing herself to be pulled to her feet. Her left foot skidded, and she toppled backward, the fort collapsing around her. With the mountain of snow covering her, she could barely hear Jeff's frantic voice shouting, "I'll get you out. Stay calm, I'll dig you out. Stay calm, Olivia!"

When she was free of the snow, Olivia's eyes were wild. "Now I know what it feels like to be buried alive. Snow is heavy!" she gasped.

"Are you okay? Say you're okay. Swear to me you're okay," Jeff said, his voice rising in panic. The dogs reacted immediately, snapping and snarling as they tried to bite Jeff's ankles and rip his boots to shreds. They only calmed down when he scooped Olivia into his arms to carry her back to the house. The dogs looked at one another as they tried to figure out if this was a new game that didn't include them.

Her heartbeat back to normal, Olivia helped dry off the dogs, wrapping them in lemon-yellow towels before settling them by the fire. She crooked her finger at Jeff as she wiggled her eyebrows.

Jeff was no fool; he followed her to the shower.

It was just turning light out Monday morning when Olivia, her arms crossed over her chest to ward off the frigid cold, waved good-bye to Jeff from the open doorway. She waited until she could no longer see the red taillights of his car before closing the door.

It seemed exceptionally quiet with Jeff

gone. Why was that? He certainly wasn't a noisy person. Maybe *quiet* wasn't the right word. *Empty* seemed to fit the situation a little better. Olivia looked around. The dogs were nowhere to be seen. She went in search of them. When she found all four of them curled up in the covers on the bed Jeff slept in, she clamped her hand over her mouth so she wouldn't laugh out loud and wake them.

The day stretched ahead of her. She needed to give some thought to her business and get back on track. She argued with herself about getting back to work on her photography business versus settling Adrian Ames's business. What she *really* wanted to do was just sit and daydream about Jeff and their weekend. She knew she couldn't do that, and she couldn't go back to her little business, either—not with Adrian Ames on her mind.

She hoped that Jeff was right about the statute of limitations, which meant they would all be home free legally. It certainly made sense that forty years afterward would be too late to prosecute for bank robbery if priests couldn't be prosecuted for child molestation after five or seven years. Morally was something else.

As she walked back to her office, Olivia realized that somewhere in the past few days she'd made the decision to return the money Allison Matthews had stolen from the bank. No matter what. She also knew she would have to do it anonymously as well as discreetly. Any other way would hurt too many innocent people—Mary Louise Rafferty and her little family, Gwen's son and his family. And last but not least, herself. She knew she was tough enough mentally to handle the fallout, but was Jeff? If he really was her destiny, how would it look to the world if he married a thief's daughter? It certainly wouldn't help his career. His employment might well be terminated, raising another problem—Cecil.

The full amount of money had to be returned with or without Jill Laramie's share, but she wasn't going to give up on convincing Allison's old partner in crime to cooperate unless there was no alternative. Allowing Jill to find some sort of peace was one of the reasons for this project. Since Gwen had found religion and was prepared to take her punishment if necessary, Olivia assumed that there was nothing left to do on that front, except maybe see if she could do something to help Gwen financially.

Olivia turned on her e-mail and let out a subdued whoop of pleasure when she spotted an e-mail from The Private Detective Agency admidst all the spam. She let out another whoop when she read the message. Jill Laramie had returned to the scene of the crime, Oxford, Mississippi. An address followed with the words, *This is a three-bedroom, three-bath rental condominium. Subject signed a year's lease.*

The phone was in Olivia's hand in a second. She made an airline reservation for the following morning. She would be able to check out the family bank the three women had robbed. How cool was that? Damn cool, she decided.

After e-mailing Jeff about her intentions, she called her neighbor to see if he would stay with the dogs. He agreed.

She looked down at her watch. It wasn't nine o'clock yet. Promptly at nine she would call Prentice O'Brien to ask him to set up a special bank account with two million dollars in it. She hoped it would be enough to repay the bank. Somehow she had to figure out what the bearer bonds would be worth forty years later. Never a whiz at math, she realized she would have to find a good accountant to figure it out for her. At least she had time to do it all properly and not go off half-assed in all directions, one of her father's favorite expressions.

Olivia spent the rest of the day reading and rereading Adrian Ames's will and poring over the copies of the bearer bonds. This time she paid attention to Allison's assets. She whistled at the extensive list. She hadn't known there was that much money in the world. From mail-order, no less. She groaned out loud when she turned the pages to read the intricacies of the mail-order business. Was she expected to take over the reins of the company? Like hell. She wondered if any of Adrian Ames's competitors would be interested in buying her out.

She leaned back in her chair and closed her eyes so she could think about all the problems facing her. Instead, she drifted into a deep sleep.

It was late afternoon when Olivia woke with a deep ache in her neck and shoulder.

She worked at massaging the tender spots until the pain lessened. Stretching her neck, she reached for the phone to call a local accountant she'd gone to school with. She rattled off what she referred to as a hypothetical problem, promised to pay for his time, and waited for his response. He in turn rattled off every CPA's February mantra— that this was the height of tax season, and he'd get back to her as soon as possible. Olivia shrugged, knowing she should be grateful for small favors.

She returned to the computer to send an e-mail to her father and Lea, telling them what she had done thus far about Adrian Ames's instructions to her. Her father hated the computer, so it would be Lea who would respond. If she responded. She then went to MapQuest to search out Oxford, Mississippi. Once more she lost track of time until she noticed it was almost dark outside. She turned on the lights, checked her e-mail again, but there were no waiting messages. It was time to let the dogs out. Then she fed them and fixed a sandwich and some soup for herself. The evening news told her nothing new was going on in the world. Disgruntled, she took a shower, washed her hair, and was in bed by eight o'clock. She set the alarm for 4:00 A.M. and was asleep within seconds.

Olivia slept through three calls, one from her accounting friend, one from Jeff, and one from her father. In the morning she was in such a rush she didn't bother to check her messages. She was out the door the moment the dog-sitter arrived. Zipping down the interstate on clear roads, she made it to Reagan National in time to buy herself a cup of coffee before boarding her flight.

With no seat companion, Olivia was able to spread out the photocopies from her bulging carry-on bag. She read, reread, then committed to memory those points she needed to remember.

By the time she arrived in Mississippi, she felt a scorching anger ripping through her. This wasn't her fight, yet here she was. She hated what she was feeling, hated what she was doing. She wanted her old nice, placid life back. She shrugged out of her denim jacket before she climbed behind the wheel of her rental car. After spending several minutes acclimating herself to the workings of the four-by-four, she slipped it into gear and headed away from the airport.

At Wendy's she bought a salad and a soft drink before she got back on the road. *I wonder what this area was like forty years ago,* she mused, *when Allison Matthews and her friends were here.* She shrugged away the thoughts. Thinking about the three women would cause her to become more involved than she already was. She wished the whole thing had been as simple as three wild and crazy college girls pulling a heist on the spur of the moment. But, no, this was planned, premeditated, and carried out with incredible precision. And they'd gotten away with it. Surely they would have gotten caught if it had been a wild, crazy, spur-of-the-moment thing.

Olivia clenched her teeth, so angry at her circumstances that she missed a turnoff that would have taken her to Jill Laramie's leased condo. It took her forty-five minutes to backtrack, which only made her angrier. By the time she parked her car in the area reserved for visitors she knew she was in the right frame of mind to take on Jill Laramie and whatever excuse she might come up with. She was also prepared to bang on the woman's door until Jill either called the police or went deaf from the noise. But at this moment, Olivia hated herself almost as much as she hated Jill Laramie.

She walked up four steps to a small, covered entryway, pressed her finger on the doorbell, and held it there. She knew an eye was staring at her from the peephole in the middle of the door. She pressed harder on the bell. If necessary, she would lean against it and ring it till it wore out. She was stunned when the door opened wide to reveal an attractive woman staring at her. Olivia found herself blinking at Jill Laramie, who looked nothing like her college photos.

"You don't look like an eight-hundred-pound gorilla," Jill Laramie observed.

"You don't look like a bank robber," Olivia shot back.

"*Touché*. Come in. I didn't think you'd find me so quick."

"Yeah, well, let's just say I'm motivated, okay?"

Jill Laramie was tall and angular. Thin but not skinny. She wore designer clothes and sported a fashionable haircut. So much for being a recluse. Her manicure was professionally done. Olivia would just bet she had a pedicure, too. There wasn't the faintest hint of the old, moon-faced Jill Laramie in the pictures Adrian Ames had saved. A face-lift for sure. A definite nose job. She was probably nipped and tucked all over the place. The thought irritated Olivia for some reason.

Jill motioned Olivia to follow her into a living room that looked like it had been decorated by a professional in white wicker, golden yellows, and lime greens. There was nothing personal lying around, not even a book or magazine. There was, however, an ashtray and a package of cigarettes on the glass-topped table. A stopover place.

"Would you like coffee? I just made some."

Olivia grimaced. "What, so you can doctor it up and skip out again? I don't think so."

The woman laughed. It was an unpleasant sound. "That's something Allison would have said. I guess the apple doesn't fall far from the tree. What do you want?" she asked coldly.

"Your share of the money, so it can be returned to the bank, where it belongs."

Jill laughed again, this time with amusement. "My dear," she drawled, "what planet have you been living on? The statute of limitations has run out on that little caper. I'm in the clear. That means no prosecution, and I can keep the money. Allison knew that, but she never chose to tell either Gwen or me about it. I did some research. Gwen, on the other hand . . . What can I say."

The woman's words rocked Olivia. She hoped her expression didn't betray what she was thinking and feeling. She grappled for something to say. Leaning back in the lemon yellow chair she was sitting on, she pulled words out of the air. "Well," she drawled in return, "there is the moral aspect of the whole thing. And the civil suit you could be facing by the grandson of the man who now owns the bank. Everyone knows, even an idiot, that insurance companies *never* give up. They're going to want *their* money back. A trio of women pulling off a heist like you three did is great human interest. The press will have a field day with it. Remember that civil suit against O.J. Simpson? The press fed on that for over a year. You need to think about that, Ms. Bank Robber." Olivia wondered if anything she said was true. It looked to her as if Jill was wondering the same thing.

"Guess I'll just have to deal with it," Jill said coolly.

"I wouldn't get my passport ready just yet if I were you. I'm prepared to watch you twenty-four/seven. All I have to do is make one phone call, and this place will be under surveillance night and day. You will be forced to become a real recluse. Not that pretend deal you had going on back in New Jersey."

Jill leaned forward and reached for a cigarette. She blew a stream of smoke in Olivia's direction. "Why are you doing this? What will it take to make you go away?"

Olivia wished she'd accepted the offer of coffee. Holding a cup would be something to do with her hands. "Nothing."

The woman's eyes narrowed. She blew another stream of smoke in Olivia's direction. Olivia waved it away. "Come on, money makes the world go round. How much?" she demanded. "Oh, I get it, you inherited Adrian's estate. You have no need of money. Are you some kind of do-gooder, or is this some kind of vendetta against your mother? She did give you up the day you were born."

"Yes, she did. But then you did the same thing to Mary Louise, just a little later, didn't you? You're just like Allison. Gwen was different. I met her, you know. She's really down on her luck. She hardly has enough money to feed her cats. Guess what? She's contented with her life. Did I say she lives in a trailer?"

"Is that supposed to mean something to me?" Jill snapped. Olivia shrugged.

"Just out of curiosity, Jill, did you give up your daughter because that's what Allison did? Did you divorce Gill because Allison divorced Dennis, my father? You envied her, didn't you? You wanted to be just like her. That's what she thought. She left a diary. She thought you and Gwen were stupid. She didn't even like you."

Jill's nipped and tucked face tightened as her eyes sparked with anger. "My reasons for my actions are none of your business. I never liked your mother. Actually, I hated her guts. To me she was evil personified. I didn't much care for Gwen, either, but she was way better than your mother. A girl needs friends at college. I'm going to call your bluff, Ms. Lowell. Do what you want. That whole scene was a lifetime ago. No one will be interested at this point in time."

"Oh, that's where you're wrong. The media will be very interested in how Allison Matthews started up that mail-order business. Think trickle-down. You can't run fast enough to outrun an insurance investigator. They're like dogs with bones, and they probably get a percentage of whatever they recover. Remember, I told you Allison left a diary. It's all in there."

Olivia didn't think it was possible for the woman's features to turn even tighter and colder, but they did. "Do you really expect me to believe you'd turn your own mother in?"

"You better believe it, Jill. This is my pound of flesh. You see, my father told me my mother died giving birth to me. Then one day a week or so ago, a lawyer showed up at the door and told me about Allison Matthews. And then I read her diary. She thought of me as an *it*. Yet she left her entire estate to me. Out of guilt, I suppose. She also left a letter for me asking me to return her share of the money to the bank. She asked me to locate you and Gwen and to get you to return your share of the money, too. She seemed to think you two would be carrying a load of guilt, and she wanted to get you to return the money so that you could assuage your consciences.

"Since Gwen doesn't have two cents to her name, and, incidentally, has found religion and is prepared to take whatever punishment comes her way if I go to the authorities, I'll return her share out of Adrian's money. You, on the other hand, seem to have no conscience at all, so you're going to swing in the wind for your share. The civil suit might even ask for punitive damages. You could be wiped out. The first things they'll ask for are all your bank and brokerage statements."

Jill reached for another cigarette. Olivia was pleased to see that the woman's hand trembled when she fumbled with the lighter. Olivia waited . . . for what, she didn't know.

"The whole thing was Allison's idea. Gwen and I didn't want to do it. Back then Gwen didn't have enough sense to come in out of the rain. I wasn't much better. Allison never let us forget how smart she was. She set it all up, but it was Gwen and I who actually picked the package off her desk and put it in the safe-deposit box. All she did was substitute plain paper for the bonds in the package on Mr. Augustus's desk and put the bonds in the package we stashed. She was smart enough to parlay that into the fortune you inherited. When we met the last time to divide up the bonds she said we should go our way, she would go hers, and we should never get in touch with each other again. I thought she was scared, that maybe she knew something we didn't know, so we did what she said. Gwen and I stayed in touch for a short while. I saw what she was all about rather quickly, so I cut her loose the way Allison had cut us both loose."

Olivia frowned. It all sounded so rehearsed, so clever. She didn't believe any of it for a minute. "It doesn't matter. You're all equally guilty," Olivia said.

"How much is the payback?" Jill asked suddenly.

Chapter 15

Olivia was momentarily stunned at Jill's question. Somewhere during the past thirty minutes she'd obviously managed to hit a nerve. She wondered if the spur had been her mention of a civil suit or perhaps the words "insurance fraud." She rummaged in her bag for the paper where she'd done her calculations. She pretended to study it as her mind went in all directions.

"Well?" Jill asked irritably, her eyes narrowed, her jaw tight and grim.

Once again, Olivia plucked words out of the air. "If we settle up now for the face value, and that includes the twice yearly attached coupons, I'm out of your life. This," she said, extending the sheet of paper that had Jill's name sprawled across the top, "is your share." Jill winced as she read the number. She didn't say a word. Instead, she got up and walked out of the room. When she returned she had a check in her hands drawn on a New York Goldman Sachs brokerage account.

"I'd like it if you'd leave now," Jill said coldly. "Don't come back, either. I never want to see your face again."

"Why?" Olivia asked suspiciously. "Are you planning on leaving?"

"No, I'm not leaving. I just never want to see you again. You remind me too much of your mother. This is finished. Get out of my life." Jill walked to the door, opened it, and tapped her foot impatiently as she waited for Olivia to shove all her papers back into her bag.

Jill watched Olivia cross the pavement to the parking area and get into her car. She moved then, faster than lightning, to the laptop sitting on a small desk in her bedroom. She clicked and clicked until a summary of her brokerage account appeared on the screen. She clicked furiously until the screen showed nothing but zeros. The window that appeared said, *Funds successfully transferred*. She then tapped out a message to her broker telling him to cancel check number 5694. She smirked with satisfaction. Now all she had to do was wait until it got dark so she could leave again. The girl was smart, but not as smart as her mother was. Allison would never have fallen for such a blatant about-face on Jill's part.

There was no doubt in Jill's mind that whoever had tracked her to this place, probably some private detective who'd spoken to the old busybody that lived next door to her in Woodbridge, hadn't investigated beyond the end of his or her nose. Everything these days was done by computer. Little did they know, whoever they were, that she held temporary leases on the two condos on each side of the one she was sitting in right then, but only on paper. All she had to do was go out the back door, into one or the other of those condos, after dark—disguised, of course—and leave.

And everyone thought Allison was the smart one. Jill grudgingly admitted she had learned one thing from Allison Matthews. It wasn't enough to have Plans A and B. You also needed Plan C. She was operating on Plan C.

She poured herself a glass of wine and settled down to watch an afternoon filled with stupid soap operas. She got up several times during the course of the afternoon to look out the window. There was no sign of Olivia's car. Jill was smart enough to know that didn't mean anything. The girl could be lurking anywhere.

At five o'clock, after turning on all the lights in the condo, she called for a pizza to be delivered. All part of Plan C. Her food arrived at 6:20. She paid for it and carried it inside and dumped it down the trash chute. Trotting into the bedroom, she changed out of her designer clothes. Fifteen minutes later, she looked like a sloppy male teenager with a backpack. Faux dreadlocks hung to her neck. On top of the faux hair she plopped a grungy baseball cap that was even grubbier than her jeans and jacket. Now she looked like half the college students at Ole Miss.

It was 6:50 when she entered the condo on the left by way of the back door. She turned on the light in the kitchen, then the bathroom light, and waited exactly seven minutes before she turned on a lamp in the living room. For the benefit of anyone who might be watching outside, she ran back and forth turning on other lights, then turning them off. Finally, at 7:35 she slipped on the backpack, which contained her laptop and little else, and prepared to leave the condo, making a point of jingling a ring of keys and locking the door. Shoulders slumped, she slouched down the four steps and proceeded to shuffle away from the condo. She was just another lazy-looking, sloppy college kid. No one gave her a second glance.

Jill Laramie smiled to herself in the darkness. So she had just lost fifteen thousand dollars with the three minimum down payments and security deposits on the condos. She could live with that. Plan C. "Thanks, Allison," she chortled.

Olivia drove up to the small bank where Allison Matthews had worked during her college years. It didn't look much different from the picture in Adrian's safe. It had a new red tin roof, and the paint on the white columns looked fresh. She remembered how those same columns had gleamed in the sunshine earlier. Surely the furnishings inside had been replaced at some point during the last forty years. But there were no additions since Allison had worked at the bank except for a drive-through window and a polished brass drawer outside for night deposits. There were still only two tellers and one man, probably the grandson, sitting in a room that was all windows. The desk in the lobby looked as though some-one sat and worked there. Although it was empty, a yellow sweater draped on the back of the chair confirmed that particular thought.

Olivia brazenly walked into the bank and asked the teller to change a hundred-dollar bill. She stared at the teller, wishing she could ask her how long she'd worked at the bank. The teller smiled and asked if she was a visitor. Olivia nodded. "My sister goes to Ole Miss. I just popped down to see her. It's her first year, and she still gets homesick."

The teller adjusted her glasses and smiled. "I see a lot of the students who go to Ole Miss. Quite a few of them bank their allowances here. We hire some of them in the summer."

It was the opening Olivia had hoped for. "A friend of my sister's mother used to work here when she went to Ole Miss. Maybe you knew her. Allison Matthews." Olivia made her voice as cheerful-sounding as she could. "Of course that was forty years ago."

"Well, that was before my time. We're just a small bank. You're probably talking about Margaret's era. She had my position before she retired and I took over."

"I hope she's enjoining her retirement."

The teller's voice matched Olivia's for cheerfulness. "Not really. She's dead."

"Oh dear, I'm sorry to hear that. Have a nice day," Olivia said, stuffing the bills into her pocket.

And that had been the end of that.

Olivia spent the remainder of the afternoon wandering around the Ole Miss campus, wondering if the places she was walking to and looking at were some of the same places Allison and her friends had traveled. Not that it was important in the scheme of things. She then whiled away another ninety minutes ordering a late lunch before she made the decision to head back to the airport.

Even though it was close to midnight when Olivia made the seventy-six-mile drive to Winchester, she felt elated. She'd actually gotten a check from Jill Laramie that she would deposit first thing in the morning. She was so proud of that little fact, she gave herself a mental pat on the back. Now all she had to do was figure out a way to return the money to the bank anonymously. Once she accomplished that, she could get back to running her business and spend some serious time with Jeff. She would sit out the probate period of Allison Matthews's will and deal with the fallout later on.

Olivia sighed with satisfaction. Tonight she was going to sleep like a baby.

Once again, she didn't check her voice mail but tumbled into bed the moment she finished brushing her teeth. As her eyes started to close, she took a second to wonder where her destiny was and what he was doing.

Jeff Bannerman shuffled the papers piled high on his desk. He looked around at the yellow plant standing in the corner. His mother would pitch a fit if she saw the way he'd neglected it. Who had the time to water plants? He reached for a manila folder and opened it. He really didn't want to write a brief. He didn't even want to be here in this cluttered office. He wanted to be in

Winchester with Olivia and the dogs. Where the hell was she? She should have called him by now to report on her trip to Oxford. He reared back suddenly as a thought hit him. What right did he have to expect Olivia to report to him or call him the moment she had news. He was only part of her life because of Cecil. No, no, that wasn't true. It was more than Cecil. They'd eaten together, played in the snow together, slept together. That definitely had to count. He didn't sleep around, and he knew Olivia didn't, either. They'd crossed the line in the sand that would lead them down a road to marriage. At least he thought it would lead to marriage. The big question was, did Olivia think the way he did? Maybe he should call her. He shook his head. He'd already left three voice mails and sent three e-mails with no response. In all his life he'd never chased after a girl or a young woman. They'd flocked to him for some reason, and not because he'd encouraged any of them.

Olivia was different. So different, he wanted to take her home to meet his parents and brothers. But she wasn't answering his phone calls or his e-mails. It was obvious he needed some expert advice.

Who better to give him advice than his mother. Without stopping to think, he dialed the number and waited. He'd know his mother's voice anywhere in the world—it was all warm, cozy, and welcoming. "Hi, Mom, it's Jeff." Like she didn't know his voice, too.

"Jeff, what's wrong? Are you all right? You aren't sick, are you? Tell me you didn't have a car accident with all that bad weather we're seeing on television. You never call during the day. Oh, God, Jeff, you didn't lose that little dog, did you? Jeff, I'd really like it if you would say something."

"Mom, I'm fine. I didn't want to interrupt you, and no, I did not lose Cecil. Really, everything is fine. How are you and Dad? What are you guys doing?"

"Your dad is reading the paper, yesterday's paper. He's reading it all over again because we didn't get one today. I'm making vegetable soup. You know how your dad likes vegetable soup. I swear that man could eat soup every day. What's wrong, Jeff?"

"Mom, I need some advice."

"Well, I need a break from all this vegetable chopping. Go ahead, tell me your problem."

The words tumbled out of Jeff's mouth in a rush. He ended with "and the dog hates me. Well, maybe hate is too strong a word. He, whichever one he is, slept with me. He might be coming around. So, should I call or e-mail her again or wait it out? I don't want to be pushy. She's not like that, Mom."

"Do you really like this girl, Jeff?"

"Mom, I wouldn't be calling you if I didn't like her more than a lot. I think she likes me, too. Is she in love with me? I don't know, Mom. The question is, should I call her again or send her an e-mail? Do you think I should wait? I should just wait it out, right? Thanks, Mom. I knew you'd steer me straight. Tell Dad I said hello. I'll call over the weekend. Enjoy the soup."

Jeff went back to the brief that was staring up at him. Olivia would call or e-mail him when she was ready. He was sure of it. Still, it wouldn't hurt to send an e-mail to inquire about Cecil's well-being. He fired off a one-liner inquiring about Cecil, signed his name, and went back to his brief, but his heart wasn't in what he was doing. He knew he was falling in love with Olivia Lowell, and it was scaring the pants off him.

Olivia woke, stretching luxuriously. She'd slept like the proverbial log. How warm and cozy it was under the covers with the dogs snoozing alongside her. She turned to look at the clock—3:30. *In the afternoon*. It had to be afternoon since it was light outside. She'd slept more than twelve hours. Damn, now she'd never sleep tonight.

Suddenly the dogs were all over her, so she played with them until they yelped to go out. She got out of bed, walking with her eyes downcast for little puddles or surprises. She was relieved that there was nothing to clean up. How good they were. Twelve hours was a long time for a dog to hold it. She must be doing something right with their training.

While she made coffee and toast, she ran through a mental list of things she'd planned to do that day. She realized it was too late now to make it to the bank to deposit Jill's check. Tomorrow would have to do. Alice had a vet appointment to get her teeth cleaned that morning. Well, she'd blown that and would have to reschedule.

She couldn't remember all the other things that were on her schedule, so obviously they weren't important. She should call Jeff, though, and report yesterday's activities. She just knew he was going to be as shocked as she was that Jill had paid up.

Olivia fixed coffee and buttered toast with the phone clamped between her ear and neck as she listened to her voice mail messages. She smiled at Jeff's four messages, grimaced at the one from Lea, and frowned at the one from the accountant she'd called. She saved the four messages from prospective clients before she called Jeff at the office.

"Bannerman," he barked into the phone.

"Lowell here," Olivia barked in return.

Olivia heard his sigh on the phone. She smiled. "I've been calling you, Olivia. I was worried about you going to Oxford. How's Cecil?"

He was worried about me. How sweet. Endearing, actually. "Cecil's fine. You aren't going to believe what happened. Jill paid up. I came home with a check. I can't tell you how shocked I was. She paid up, Jeff! I was so tired, I went straight to bed and just got up a few minutes ago. I wanted to take the check to the bank, but now I'll have to wait till tomorrow. Pretty cool, huh?"

Olivia's heart started to flutter in her chest when she heard Jeff ask, "Did you get a certified check?"

"No, should I have? She just wrote me out a check from her brokerage account. Oh, God, do you think it will bounce? That was really stupid of me, wasn't it? What was I thinking? I got a little cocky and started to spin this tale about a civil suit and insurance fraud. She looked scared and finally asked me how much she owed. First, though, she tried to bribe me. Damn, I can't believe I was so stupid. Now I'm going to worry until tomorrow morning."

"I'm a lawyer—it's natural for me to be suspicious. As a layperson, I can understand you being happy with a check and not thinking twice about it. But, yeah, I think you should be worried about that check, considering the circumstances. Hell, I wouldn't be the least bit surprised to hear that she split again. If she did, the trail's cold by now. You don't have a Paul Hemmings to alert you to her comings and goings this time around. Listen, we can talk this through later. If it's okay with you, I'll come out after work. Are you sure Cecil is okay?"

"He's doing a lot better than I am right now. Okay, I'll see you later."

The dogs greeted Jeff as though he were their long-lost owner showing up to save their furry little bodies. Olivia grinned at the greeting when Jeff dropped to his haunches, then rolled all the way across the foyer into the family room, the dogs nipping at his ears and lathering his faces with wet kisses. "Does that answer your question, Mr. Bannerman?" she teased.

"It'll do," Jeff gasped, as all four dogs settled themselves on his chest. "Did you miss me half as much?" he finally managed to gurgle.

"A whole lot more! Did you have anything to eat?" Now that sounded romantic.

"I ate a whole pizza on my way out here. I'm wearing half of it, can't you tell? I could use a beer if you have one," Jeff said, pointing to the white T-shirt he had on under his down jacket. "At least I didn't get it on my jacket. My car seats are wearing it, too."

When Olivia returned with two beers and an afghan Lea had made for her, Jeff was sitting by the fire with the dogs on his lap. Either Cecil or Loopy was sitting on his shoulder, and Jeff seemed to be loving every minute of it. *But he looks so tired*, Olivia thought. Her heart swelled with what she was feeling.

They sat huddled together for a long time, holding hands and just looking at each other until Olivia wiggled free of their tight cocoon, threw three logs on the fire, and brought over cushions from the sofa before snuggling against him. An instant later Jeff's eyes closed, and he was sound asleep. One by one, the dogs crawled and maneuvered their way closer to the fire. Even though she'd slept the better part of the day, Olivia closed her own eyes and joined Jeff, sleeping to the beat of his heart.

It was 9:20 when Olivia walked into the National City Bank with Jill's check in her hand. Instead of going to a teller, she went to one of the bank officers and asked him to call Goldman Sachs to see if the check in her hand would clear. The young officer looked her over, although he tried not to be obvious about it. The amount on the check didn't seem to faze him one way or the other. Bankers saw huge sums of money every day. He did, however, excuse himself, preferring to make the phone call out of her sight and hearing.

Olivia settled back in a comfortable chair that hundreds of other people had sat on and let her gaze swivel around the bank's lobby as she compared it to the bank she'd visited in Oxford the day before yesterday. It seemed like it was weeks ago.

National City Bank was a big bank, recently merged for the third time. It had been refurbished in the summer after the latest merger. Everything was now royal blue—drapes, carpeting, and the tile in front of the tellers' counters. Unlike the small bank in Mississippi, this bank had six busy tellers shuffling money. The tellers never made eye contact with the customers. The customers were just numbers. Watercolors hung on every available wall. Pictures of Winchester's Apple Blossom Festival's queens going back forty years. She wondered if any of the bank customers ever really looked at the pictures.

Since the latest merger the bank had screwed up her business account three different times, forcing her to sit for hours behind the glass walls until the matter was straightened out. It also seemed as if their computers went down at least once a day. Big-time banking. She made an ugly sound in her throat just as the bank officer returned to his desk. His nameplate said he was Anthony Bortellie. He looked unhappy. Olivia felt her stomach muscles tighten. She knew what he was going to say before he said it.

"I'm sorry to tell you this, Ms. Lowell, but this particular account at Goldman Sachs was closed the day before yesterday, at one-thirty, to be precise. I'm sorry."

Olivia blinked, feeling incredibly stupid. "Are you saying Mrs. Laramie stopped payment on this check, or are you saying she . . . ?"

"Mrs. Laramie transferred the money out of the account day before yesterday at one-thirty, then closed the account. Is there anything else I can do for you today?" He spoke as though he were a teacher explaining a math problem to a dim-witted pupil.

Olivia reached for the check and replaced it in her purse. Another piece of worthless paper. "No, there's nothing else. Thank you for your help."

Olivia called herself every name in the

book as she made her way back to her car. She knew in her gut that Jeff was right and Jill Laramie was long gone from the temporary condo in Oxford. How stupid could one person be? Pretty damn stupid when it came to her.

Shit!

"I'll get you, you witch!" Olivia snarled as she put the car in gear and backed out of her parking space. "You aren't going to get away with this." She seethed over her stupidity all the way home. She would have to fall back and regroup.

The first thing she did when she returned home was call the detective agency and initiate another search. She was so grouchy, her voice so angry-sounding, the dogs ran and hid.

Her second call was to return Lea's phone call. She knew right away that something was wrong. She groaned inwardly at the sound of Lea's voice, which was so totally foreign she felt herself shivering.

"I'll get right to the heart of the matter, Olivia. Dennis told me that his ex-wife asked you to buy him a top-of-the-line boat anonymously and that he declined the offer. Well, I want you to do it. The engine on his boat went out, and it's going to cost a fortune to fix. A fortune we don't have. These are his golden years, and he should be able to enjoy them. And it would be nice if you'd open an account for him with some of those millions your mother left you. Dennis deserves something for all those years that he spent raising you on his own." The woman's voice was so flat and businesslike she could have been discussing the price of beef.

Olivia didn't know what she'd been expecting, but this certainly wasn't it. She didn't know how to respond. What she said was, "Does Dad know you're calling me?"

"No, and I don't want you to tell him, Olivia, because he'll just say no. I can control the money and make things easier for him. He doesn't have to know until the time is right. Gradually, in time, he'll come to accept the money and not think twice about where it all came from. It would make our lives so much easier, Olivia."

"I'll . . . I'll work on it, Lea. I have to go now. Someone's at the door."

"If someone's at the door, then why aren't the dogs barking?" Lea asked, suspicion ringing in her voice. "You just want to get me off the phone, don't you?"

"I have to go, Lea. Bye."

Olivia fought the tears that were starting to burn her eyes.

Just you and me, kid.

Hot tears rolled down Olivia's cheeks. Then she sobbed. The dogs came on the run to circle her feet. She slid off the chair she was sitting on to gather them close. They loved her unconditionally. They didn't care about money.

"I knew in my heart something like this was going to happen," she sobbed to the dogs. "I knew it!"

Chapter 16

Jill Laramie ducked into the restroom of the first gas station she came to on her walk into Oxford. She ditched the clothes and the dreadlocks in the filthy trash can before dressing in clean jeans, sweat shirt, and denim jacket. A dark blue wool hat covered her fashionable hairdo. The backpack containing her laptop secure, she ventured out of the restroom and started walking again.

As she ambled along the road into town, her mind raced. She'd looked forward to her return here to Ole Miss. She'd loved her college life, loved everything about the area.

Maybe, if she was lucky, she really would be able to come back again at some point in time to attend the yearly William Faulkner conference. She loved Faulkner and Eudora Welty. Ole Miss now owned Faulkner's

Rowan Oak, his old home. She wanted to see it, to ramble through the rooms, to get a feel for where he created his masterpieces. Allison always made fun of her when she caught her with one of his books. Gwen just shrugged off her passion for the two authors.

In just a few months Ole Miss would host the Jazz Reunion. The Reunion was on her list of things to do, too. *Had* been on her list of things to do. Her dream, if she could ever get up the nerve, was somehow to wrangle her way to a volunteer position teaching for the Center for the Study of Southern Culture. She longed to teach and research all aspects of Southern culture. That particular dream was one she'd never shared with either Allison or Gwen.

She belonged here. She'd known it the first day she'd set foot on the campus. Ole Miss, a mecca for writers, Mississippi blues musicians, and artists, and she wanted to be a part of it again. She'd been away too long. If that miserable daughter of Allison's hadn't shown up when she did, Jill would be working right now to make her dream come true. Instead she had to run again. How like Allison to reach out from the grave to torment her even now, to prove once again that she was the great master brain. If Allison said jump, the only response she would tolerate was, how high?

Jill adjusted her dark glasses before she stepped into a coffee shop filled with bookish-looking students. From there she could call a taxi to take her to a boardinghouse she knew of from her college days. No point in even attempting a stay at a motel or hotel. It was getting late, and she was hungry. She thought about the pizza she'd dropped down the trash chute. Her mouth started to water when she took her place at the counter and ordered a hamburger, french fries, a glass of chocolate milk, and a cup of coffee. She looked around, saw that all the tables were full of chattering students. She removed her sunglasses and rubbed at her eyes. Wearing sunglasses was stupid. She wasn't thinking clearly, that was for sure.

A young man with a mess of red pimples dotting his face slid her food down the counter. She ate it quickly and debated ordering another burger but didn't. Having paid her check, she headed for the wall phone near the restroom. She hated the smell of Pine-Sol or whatever disinfectant the establishment used in the bathrooms. She knew there would be a card on the bulletin board for a taxi service, and she was right. She called. A taxi would pick her up in ten minutes. She elected to wait outside—it wasn't that cold.

In another month the two-thousand-acre campus at Ole Miss would come alive with magnificent magnolias, delicate dogwoods, brilliant azaleas, and hundreds of ancient oaks that dripped Spanish moss. She wondered if the twenty-two thousand students would view springtime with the joy she had. At present, though, she shivered in the chill night air as she waited for her taxi.

Her life at Ole Miss hadn't been so wonderful until she met Allison Matthews. It was Gwen, her best friend, who'd introduced her to Allison. She remembered how flattered she'd been when the brainy young woman offered friendship even though they had very little in common. She, along with Gwen, had been interested in the arts; Allison's only interests were finance and money. Once she'd said she worshiped money. That was the reason she worked part-time at a bank—just to be near money. Jill, on the other hand, like Gwen, knew she would never be rich and would have to work for her money. They both tried to ignore their friend's passion for riches.

During the last year of their studies at Ole Miss, things started to change. Allison started to talk about what great lives they could all have, talking about how Jill and Gwen could be patrons of the arts, attend all those wonderful cultural events Ole Miss sponsored. She'd been relentless, pounding away about how they could live the lives of true academics. All they needed was money. Lots and lots of money. It was only natural that Jill would eventually huddle with Gwen and talk about it in hushed voices. To say Jill and Gwen were like lambs going to the slaughter was to put it mildly. The two of them had been like ripe apples just waiting to be picked when Allison unveiled her plan for the riches that would make all their dreams come true. All they had to do was do what she said.

Even now, to this very day, Jill still didn't know the intricate details of how the owner of the bank got the bearer bonds and why he'd been so sloppy as to leave them on his desk. And why he'd never reported the theft, preferring to have a detective agency from Memphis, Tennessee, conduct the investigation. She and Gwen had whispered, stewed, and fretted over that. Was old man Augustus involved in something illegal? Obviously Allison thought so, they whispered, which just made it a plus for the heist.

Jill could see the headlights of what looked like her taxi. She hitched her backpack tighter against her chest. Crumpled bills to pay the fare were in her hand.

She had never thought about insurance fraud until Olivia Lowell showed up. If you did something illegal, how could you insure the fruits of that illegal action against detection? The girl had to be lying, trying to scare her. But because Jill wasn't sure, she had no choice but to run again. The big question now was, where should she go?

The cab pulled to the curb, and Jill climbed into the backseat. "I'd like to go to Mandal's Boardinghouse, please. I don't know the address."

The driver was a young college kid probably working his way through Ole Miss and working the night shift. He nodded and pulled away from the curb.

Fifty minutes later Jill was ensconced in a sparsely furnished but clean room with a shared bath. No television or radio. She climbed into bed wearing her clothes. As soon as the stores opened on the Square, she'd buy some clothes and a piece of luggage and anything she could pick up that would help disguise her person until she could make a plan.

She leaned back into her nest of pillows. Maybe it was time to think about heading out of the country. Then again, maybe she should follow one of Allison's old rules, which was when you're trying to hide something, hide it front and center because no one ever, according to Allison, looked at the obvious. That old adage probably applied to a person hiding out, too. She could dye her hair, restyle it, get a pair of clear glasses, wear baggy clothes, carry around an armload of books. She'd look like half the women in Oxford. An academic.

If she wanted to, she could relocate to Holly Springs, which was just forty or so miles from Oxford, or she could head for Beldon. If she felt the need to go farther afield, she could go to Memphis, Tennessee, which was less than fifty miles away.

In the morning, she'd use her laptop to

see what she could find out about insurance fraud and how worried she should be. Just then she was too tired to think clearly. She finally fell asleep, a troubled sleep invaded by people from her past. In one dream she was smothering Gwen with a blanket the two of them were hiding under. That dream faded to one where she was digging up Adrian Ames's grave, looking for a list of instructions. That dream took an even more bizarre turn when she saw herself walking arm in arm with Dennis Lowell, who was pushing a baby stroller with his free hand. He was spitting mad about something, but she couldn't figure out what he was saying. She tried, but she felt like she was wearing earplugs.

Jill woke, her forehead beaded with perspiration. It was still dark outside, not quite morning yet. She must be really stressed out to be having nightmares like she'd just had. Dennis Lowell. Why would she be dreaming about Dennis? Adrian and Gwen she could understand, but Dennis?

While Jill Laramie was trying to come to terms with her dreams about Dennis Lowell, Dennis was sitting on his boat, the *Olivia*

Lea, waiting for the sun to come up. He was sitting in a canvas slingback chair, smoking his pipe, a new habit he'd picked up with the move to the islands.

God, how he loved it here. Life in the islands, his reward for working hard his whole life, raising his daughter with no help from anyone. He'd been a model citizen, a good neighbor, a good Christian. And now this.

He couldn't give this up, he couldn't go back to Winchester a failure. He'd used every cent he could scrape together to get this boat. With Lea's pension and his modest social security, the two of them had been living an idyllic life that was virtually stress-free. They'd made wonderful friends. Their charter fees covered that little extra for a dinner out, a new dress for Lea, a new shirt for him. Maybe steak more often. They had agreed that all charter money would be divided two ways. Half to spend and half to save. But the second half was almost gone. The *Olivia Lea* needed a whole new hydraulic system. He'd lost two charters to Daimon, who'd accepted them regretfully. All the other boat owners, friends now, had offered manual help, but hydraulics were beyond their capabilities. Most of them, like him, were retirees trying to fulfill their dreams on a small fixed income.

As if that wasn't bad enough, Lea was acting peculiar. She was short-tempered, angry most of the time, and not socializing. Just yesterday she called the place they lived in a dump. When they signed the lease, she'd said she loved it and could fix it up on a shoestring. And she had.

Money. It always came down to money. In this case, the lack of money. He still hadn't told her the bank turned him down yesterday when he went to apply for a short-term loan. With no collateral other than his inoperable boat and no guarantee of future charters, the bank felt it couldn't commit to a loan. Short of considering a loan shark, his options were zip. He couldn't even sell the boat with the hydraulics shot.

Dennis was never one to spend his life wishing and hoping. He worked at making things happen, but just short of seventy years old, he knew this was beyond his capabilities. Even if he'd had any friends with money, he wouldn't have wanted to hit them up for a loan.

Damn, it couldn't end like this. It just couldn't.

Dennis got up and went down to the galley to make coffee. His mind raced as the water dripped. God, what would he do if they couldn't make the rent? He could live on the boat, but Lea couldn't. She liked to take long, scented baths. The skimpy shower on the boat would drive her insane in two days' time.

The coffee sloshing over the side of his cup, Dennis sat back down in his canvas chair. It was almost light out, his favorite time of the day. He loved watching the sun come up, seeing the boats all lined up in the marina. The gentle rocking of the boat sometimes lulled him back to sleep until the sights and sounds of the marina came to life. In one good sniff, some mornings, provided the wind was right, he could smell a blend of coffee, frying bacon, and the pungent odors of the brackish water and seaweed. Once in a while he'd get a whiff of someone's aftershave, or sometimes it was perfume. The breeze was warm and gentle, the skyline a beautiful shade of lavender. So peaceful, so beautiful, so wonderful.

Overhead a flock of seagulls swooped down for an early breakfast. He always left half a loaf of bread on the dock when he left for the night, just for the gulls. They'd come to expect it and most days, weather permitting, they joined him to start the day.

Dennis felt like crying. How was he going to give up this peaceful existence? How?

He was on his second cup of coffee when he looked down the dock to see Lea approaching. His shoulders tightened instinctively. She looked angry. Her walk was angry-looking. She wasn't carrying anything, so that meant no breakfast. In the early days after their arrival, she'd always walk to the donut shop and bring back either fresh donuts or bagels. Of course, those were the nights early on when they both spent the night on the boat relishing their newfound paradise.

Lea waved listlessly as she hopped onto the boat. She didn't sit down in the matching canvas chair but elected to stand with her back against the rail. "Why didn't you come home last night, Dennis?"

Dennis didn't choose his words the way he had in the past. "I didn't want to get into another row with you. It's obvious you aren't happy. Well, guess what, I'm not real happy right now, either. Just so you know, the bank turned me down yesterday. I simply wasn't ready to talk about it with you or anyone else. I needed to wallow in my own misery. Before you can ask, I'm going to go to some of the bigger owners and ask them if they can take on an extra hand. It would help if you'd get a job, Lea. We can save every penny, and in a year or so maybe we can start some repairs. Or I can try to sell the *Olivia Lea,* and we go back home. I'm doing the best I can."

She was a pretty woman for her age, with short blond hair, bright blue eyes, and a body she took care of, but right then, Dennis thought she looked like a shrew who was getting ready to spit and snarl.

"I'm not going out to work, Dennis, so get that idea right out of your head. I retired, the way you retired. I agreed to all this because you made it sound so wonderful. You don't know enough about boats, because if you did, you wouldn't have bought this lemon. They saw you coming. You spent all our money, and now we're broke with no means to get any more. Unless—"

"Don't go there, Lea. The answer is no. I said I'd get a job. You're half of this team, too, you know. It wouldn't hurt you to get a job to help out."

Lea's lips set in a grim line. Her blue eyes sparked dangerously. "Dennis, Olivia said *she* wanted to buy you a top-of-the-line boat. Why won't you accept the offer? You're being incredibly stupid. If you'd use the brain you were born with, you'd realize you could pay *her estate* back with all the extra charters you'd get with a new boat. Think of it as a loan and forget where it came from. We're talking about our very survival here, Dennis. I hate it when you act like this."

"I don't much care for the way you're acting, either. What's happened to you?"

"What's happened to me?" Lea screeched as loud as the gulls were screeching. "We're broke! We might not have a roof over our heads! We only have a few hundred dollars in our bank account, and our pensions won't do more than feed us. Do you even know how much you owe for all the gas you charged for this boat? Thousands, that's how much. They're dunning us, Dennis. Everyone is dunning us. I can't take it."

Dennis bit down on his lower lip so he wouldn't cry. "Say it, Lea. Just say it."

Lea leaned forward, her shoulders

hunched over, her face a mask of hate. "All right, I will, Dennis. You promised me so many things. I believed you. I put all my money into that boat of yours, and now it's all gone. Ask your daughter for the money. She's sitting on hundreds of millions of dollars. That's what you told me. What can she possibly do with all that money? You certainly, of all people, have a right to share in it. You raised that bitch's daughter. Now collect on that. Get over that imagined shame you're feeling. Give me the life you promised. I'm going home. I expect an answer from you by this afternoon, Dennis." She tossed him the cell phone. Dennis caught it in his lap.

This time when his eyes filled with tears, Dennis didn't blink them away. He was oblivious to the screeching gulls and the sights and sounds that made up the marina. He just sat there and cried.

Chapter 17

Olivia was staring out the kitchen window when the phone rang. Maybe she should just let it ring, she thought, her shoulders sagging. Nothing was going right. Whoever was on the other end of the line was probably someone with more depressing news. Still, she wouldn't know that for sure unless she answered the phone. It was also possible it could be Jeff, and she did want to talk to him. She picked up the portable phone on the seventh ring.

"Ollie! It's Dad. How are you, honey?"

Olivia cleared her throat. Her thoughts ricocheted backward to her conversation with Lea. Was her father calling for the same reason? Suddenly, Olivia felt sick to her stomach. "Hello, Dad. I'm fine. How are you?" Her voice came out flat and cool.

"Ollie, I'm having a bit of a problem here. The hydraulics on the boat went out. I need to ask you something. Can you take out an equity loan or a second mortgage on the house? I'll make the payments. I've got some outstanding bills that are past due, and the creditors are dunning me. I've lost quite a few charters. Can you see your way clear to helping me out here, honey?"

Olivia felt so light-headed with the question she had to reach out to grab hold of the back of one of the kitchen chairs. *He doesn't want Adrian Ames's money. Thank you, God. Oh, yes, thank you, God.* It took her several seconds before she could get her tongue and lips to work. "Okay, Dad. I'll go online and see what I can do. You can do all this stuff online these days. How much should I borrow?"

"As much as you can. I hoped it wouldn't come to this, but when you buy a second-hand boat you buy someone else's problems. Guess that's why the guy wanted to get rid of it. Thanks, honey. You're saving my retirement life. I want you to know that."

Just you and me, kid. "Glad to help out, Dad." This was where she would ordinarily ask about Lea. Instead, she clamped her lips shut and waited for her father's next comment.

"How is everything, Ollie? Are you getting more snow? How are the dogs?"

Olivia stared out the kitchen window again. It was another gray day, and the weatherman had promised light snow by evening but with no real accumulation. She said so. "The dogs are fine. Jeff has been coming out to help. He's really nice, Dad, and I like him a lot."

"That's nice, Ollie. When do you think you can go online?"

Olivia winced. "When we hang up, Dad. I'll send you an e-mail, is that okay?"

The silence on the other end of the phone was unnerving. "Well, honey, I'm thinking it might be better if you call me on my cell phone. I'm staying on the boat for a little while. I would hate for any vandalism to occur with it being disabled. I can't expect the other boat owners, nice as they are, to spend all their free time watching my boat. We've had a few incidents with some unsavory characters during the past few weeks."

Olivia didn't believe him for a minute. She ground her teeth together so she wouldn't blurt out what she was thinking. It didn't

work. The words slipped out: "Is this something Lea isn't supposed to know about,
Dad?"

Another unnerving silence. "For now,
Ollie."

Olivia knew her father. He wasn't going to
say any more. They said their good-byes.
Olivia stood staring out the window for a
long time after she broke the connection.
She thought she saw snowflakes starting to
fall. Would this winter ever end? She could
feel tears filling her eyes as she made her
way down the hall to her little office.

An hour later, Olivia stared at the screen
in front of her. The bank would give her
$165,000 on a second mortgage, thanks to
her excellent credit and timely mortgage
payments. All she had to do was go to the
bank in the morning, sign the papers, and a
check would be issued in her name. She
crossed her fingers the way she had when
she was a child, hoping her father would be
able to make the payments every month. If
he couldn't, her less than robust savings account would fade away very quickly.

Olivia knew her father was sitting on his
boat waiting for her return call. *Just you and
me, kid.* She eyed the phone on her small

desk but didn't pick it up. Instead, she whistled for the dogs. "Suppertime!" she called out in a choked voice. The dogs, as one, flew down the hall to the kitchen.

Their supper over, Olivia opened the sliding door. While the dogs played outside in the snow, Olivia paced, clenching and unclenching her fists. She alternated between anger, sadness, and frustration. Life had been so wonderful before Prentice O'Brien showed up on her doorstep to tell her she'd inherited Allison Matthews's estate. Now everything was so cockeyed she was no longer sure about anything. Even her own feelings.

Olivia chewed on her thumbnail as her thoughts ran wild. The Private Detective Agency should have called her. Jeff should have called. Right now she'd accept a phone call from anyone not involved in this mess, even Clarence. Well, maybe not Clarence. She opened the door for the dogs to come back in. They lined up like a mini-parade to await their dog treats, then scurried off to devour them as Olivia walked back to the office to call her father.

She wasn't the least bit surprised when her father answered the phone on the first ring. He also took the initiative. "I hope you have good news, Ollie."

"I guess I do, Dad. How much do you need?"

"As much as you can get me. Did you have a problem?"

Olivia's mind raced. She could tap into the money in the account Prentice O'Brien had set up. She hated the desperate sound in her father's voice. "The bank said they could give me two hundred thousand," she fibbed. "Is that enough, Dad?"

Another unnerving silence. "If it was just the hydraulics, it would work, but Lea wants me to sell the boat and give her back what she invested. By the time I pay all our out-standing bills, I'm going to be down for the count. Do you think you could borrow on the business, Ollie?"

Olivia's heart fluttered. *Just you and me, kid.* "I can try, Dad, but it won't be that much. You know that. Do you want me to wire the money into your account? If you do, you have to give me the account num-ber."

"No, no. I want you to send me a certified check and send it by overnight mail. Send it to the marina. I can pick it up there."

"Dad, what's going on? I've never heard you like this. Are you and Lea having problems?"

The sensor lights outside flickered to life. Olivia could see swirling snowflakes in the yellow dimness. She waited for her father's response.

"You could say we've hit a rough patch. She gave me an ultimatum this morning. I don't do well with ultimatums. That's why I'm staying on the boat. Look, Ollie, this isn't your problem. I'll work it out somehow."

"How, Dad? How much money did Lea put into the boat?"

"Lea put in eighty-six thousand. She put in another twenty thousand on the cottage we bought, so it's a total of a hundred and six thousand."

"Look, Dad, I know you won't accept money from Adrian Ames's estate, but that doesn't have to mean Lea can't accept it. I can send you a check for the hundred and six thousand on top of the two hundred thousand from the home equity loan, and you can pay her back. She doesn't have to know where it came from. Just say we took out a second mortgage. What you do after that is entirely up to you. Did you make a mistake, Dad?"

"Let's just say there's no fool like an old fool. I'm so sorry, Ollie. Okay, send two checks. Make them both out to me. I'll deposit them and write her out a check for her investment. You're saving my life, kiddo. You know that, don't you?"

"It's not *my* money, Dad. I don't want you to sell the boat. I know how much you love it. It's your dream. Are you going to live on the boat or what?"

"I think so. Most of the old codgers like me without a spouse live on theirs. We're all good friends. It will work for me, and there won't be any overhead. With no overhead, I can get a leg up. Of course, it might take a while to sell the little house, and mortgage payments still have to be made. I'll try to rent it out until it can be sold. It will be dicey, but I think I can make it work for me."

"Okay, Dad, I'll take care of everything. What are you going to do now?"

"Ollie, I'm going to sit here on this old, ratty canvas chair and wait for the stars to come out. I'm going to see if I can find the Ollie Lowell star and stare at it until I fall asleep. I haven't been sleeping, kiddo—I've been too worried. I think I'll sleep really good tonight. Thanks for helping your old dad."

"Okay, Dad. Stay in touch."

Olivia tapped her fingers on her desk. It always came down to money. Life was getting more complicated by the second.

Olivia looked at the clock on the mantel. It was almost midnight, and she still hadn't heard from Jeff or the detective agency. She'd never felt more alone in her life. She'd spent the entire evening thinking about her father and his problem. She knew he was devastated with what was going on in his life. What would Lea do? Would she hang around because of Adrian Ames's money, hoping Dennis would agree to accept what she would consider to be his share of his ex-wife's estate? If that was her thinking, she didn't know Dennis Lowell very well. She wondered if her father had told Lea where Adrian Ames's money had come from. Probably not. Her father didn't like to think or talk about his ex-wife. She also wondered what Lea would do with that information if she did know. Would she consider blackmail as a possibility?

Damn, no one was who she seemed to be.

She should go to bed and try to sleep. Like that was going to happen with everything swirling around in her brain! A glass of wine, a big glass, might be the answer. Or maybe a whole container of ice cream. A fried bologna sandwich might do it, too. Ice cream, a bologna sandwich, and a glass of wine. For sure she'd have nightmares all night long.

In the end, Olivia did nothing but add some extra logs to the fire before she curled up with the dogs on a mound of pillows. She eyed the all-cotton afghan Lea had made for her. In a fit of anger, she tossed it into the fire. Then she stomped her way back to her bedroom for a quilt. She gathered the dogs close. Within seconds she was asleep, the heat from the fire drying the tears on her cheeks.

Olivia woke grimly determined to make the day count for something in her quest to get her life back on track. As she prepared her breakfast she reviewed the past weeks. There was nothing more she could do for her father. She'd found Gwen, and now

Gwen was more or less out of the equation. Jill was in the hands of the detective agency, and until they came up with something, Jill too, was on the sidelines. Jeff was busy with his own career. Until he made a move in her direction, he was also on the sidelines. Cecil was safe for the moment and being well taken care of. That just left Olivia herself and Adrian Ames.

She crunched down on a crisp slice of bacon, surprised at how hungry she was. She literally wolfed down three scrambled eggs and two slices of toast, sharing the last slice of bacon with the dogs before tidying up the kitchen and turning on the dishwasher.

She knew what she was going to do next. The minute she took care of her father's banking needs, she was going to climb into her car and drive to Adrian Ames's estate. It was time to see exactly who Adrian Ames really had been in life. The sooner she came to terms with the woman who gave birth to her, the sooner she could put all this behind her.

Olivia was out of the house and on her way to the bank in an hour's time. She waved to the dog-sitter. Her banking business took all of twenty-two minutes. Her hand shook slightly, later in the car, when she wrote out the checks to her father, and her sigh of relief when she sealed the FedEx envelope in the car was so loud it startled her. She drove to a drop box to deposit the envelope.

Done.

Move on to Adrian Ames, she told herself.

The caretaker and Brutus were waiting on the other side of the gate when Olivia pressed in the code. She'd called ahead to have the heat turned on in the house. Driving slowly, she talked to Cyrus Somers through her car window as he accompanied her up the driveway.

"Made a pot of coffee for you, miss. You said you wanted to talk to me. I talk better with coffee. You here to stay?"

"No, I'm not here to stay. I need . . . I want . . ."

"To know the woman who left you all this," he said, waving his arms about.

"Yes. I would appreciate it if you can tell me everything you know about her. You worked for her for a long time, so you must have formed opinions. Did she share her life with you? Her secrets? By the way, where is she buried?"

The old man tugged at the earflaps on the fur-lined cap he was wearing. He looked to Olivia like he was trying to figure out what to tell her and what not to tell her. "I was wondering when you were going to ask me that. Most daughters would have asked that right off."

"I'm not your regulation daughter, as I'm sure you know very well. I was told she died thirty-four years ago. In my mind, she was buried somewhere in Mississippi. I don't know why I thought that. It probably had something to do with her going to Ole Miss. As I got older, I never asked. What would have been the point?"

"She's buried in the back under an oak tree. She used to sit out there sometimes in the summer and read. Brutus would sit with her. Sometimes she'd read aloud to him. The dog liked her. She didn't want a tombstone. She thought gravestones were macabre. I carved a small cross at the base of the tree. Moss grows there now. Brutus won't even go near the tree. He will stand on the periphery and stare. He does that a lot in the winter. I don't know why. She had a hard time trying to decide if she should be cremated or buried. She finally decided on burial. She knew no one from the outside world would be coming to . . . visit or pay their respects. Brutus and I stop by every day."

Well, she'd asked the question. It didn't mean she had to like the answer.

Olivia was relieved when they reached the cleared parking area by the garage. As she got out of the car, the cold biting at her cheeks made her anxious to get indoors.

"She was afraid, you know. There at the end. The whole year, really."

Olivia snorted, an ugly sound. "Don't try to con me, Mr. Somers. The woman didn't have a bone of fear in her body. Trust me when I tell you she wasn't who you thought she was. She wasn't really Adrian Ames, either, but then I suspect you already know that."

"You're wrong, miss. She was scared out of her wits. I saw her cry when she thought no one was watching. I took care of her."

"Well, Mr. Somers, you have your opinion of her, and I have my opinion. I'm sure we're never going to see eye to eye on Adrian Ames."

"God forgives all his children. If He can do it, why can't you?" the old man growled. "Do you want to go through the rest of your life feeling bitterness and hatred? It's such a wasted emotion."

Olivia shed her coat and walked over to the coffeepot. She reached for two cups and proceeded to pour. Brutus dropped to his haunches and stretched out by one of the heating vents. She sat down across the table from Cyrus Somers. "Tell me about Adrian Ames. Don't gild the lily, either. All I want is the truth as you know it."

Cyrus cupped his hands around the mug of coffee in his hands. "At first I didn't like her. Not even a little bit. She was what my generation would call hoity-toity. None of the staff liked her, either. She was very demanding. There in the beginning I was taking the help back to town and bringing someone new on almost a daily basis. One woman, a cook who came highly recommended, really told her off when Miz Ames fired her. The cook got the others heated up, and they quit, too. My ears burned with the name-calling. For almost a year we had no help. I was doing everything. Your mother didn't know how to deal with people. She thought if she paid them well, she could treat them like dirt. I had to explain that to her by threatening to quit myself. Finally, she managed to get some domestic help from Jamaica. They were here till the end. She was very generous in her bequests to all of them. All four of them cried when I buried her."

Olivia stared at the old man over the rim of her coffee cup.

Cyrus drained his own cup and said, "She came to depend on me, and we formed a friendship. She allowed me to speak my mind on just about anything. Once she was comfortable with that trust, she started to ask my opinions about her business, what products to buy at various trade shows. She used to test dog products on Brutus. If he took to it, she'd order it. If not, she scratched it, whatever it was.

"One time, years and years ago, she casually mentioned that she had a daughter. She said she'd never seen you. At that time I didn't ask any questions. Later, the year you turned sixteen, she started showing me reports some detective agency sent her on you and your father. She asked me what I thought of your pictures. I told her I thought you were a pretty young lady. She agreed, and said she was glad you didn't look like her. That's when she told me she gave you up to your father because he would give you a good life. She said she wasn't mother material. She looked me right in the eye, and said, 'Cyrus, I'm not a nice, loving person. Dennis is a nice, loving person, and a child needs a nice, loving person to raise her. It was probably the best thing I ever did in my life, but Olivia will never view it that way. I'm sure Dennis hates me. But, Cyrus, look, just look at the superb job he's done with Olivia. I know Dennis must be proud of her. I sent money and gifts over the years, through my lawyer, but Dennis always sent them back. I could never understand that. He wouldn't accept a dime. For some reason, that pleased me,' she said. 'That's when I knew I did the right thing for all of us.'"

Olivia shrugged, not liking what she was hearing. Her features showed her disgust.

"She always sent the money and gifts twice a year, your birthday and Christmas. She attended your high school graduation and your college graduation. I know this for a fact because I was with her. She stayed out of the way. She just wanted to see you. When you walked across the stage to accept your diploma, she squeezed my hand so hard, I thought she broke my fingers."

Olivia hated hearing such nice things about Adrian Ames. She wanted to hear mean, ugly things, so her hatred would be justified.

Cyrus got up to replenish their coffee cups. "I only ever heard your mother laugh aloud once in all the years I knew her. I don't think she ever smiled, either. But she did laugh once when I fetched her your first calendar, the one with the dogs. She never hung the calendar but kept it in her desk. I saw her looking at it many times. She said you had a good eye."

Olivia licked her dry lips. "Did Adrian ever tell you where she got the money to start up her mail-order business?"

Cyrus leaned across the table. "She told me she robbed a bank. At first I thought she was joking. She told me shortly after she got her final medical diagnosis. I can't tell you how relieved she looked after she told me. She knew she could trust me."

Olivia was stunned at the old man's reply.

"Did she tell you about her cohorts in crime? Jill and Gwen?"

"She told me everything. She also said she was making provisions in her will for the money to be paid back to the bank. She said she had lost touch with both women. She said that was probably a good thing. The bank robbery and her two friends weren't important to your mother during the last year of her life. She concentrated on getting through the days, one at a time. She did say that if she had one wish, that wish would have been to talk to you at least once."

"Thirty-four years too late," Olivia snapped.

"During the last six months, I paid the household bills for your mother, and that included the phone bill. There were numerous calls to your home phone number in Winchester, Virginia. I suspect, but I never asked outright, that she did call and that when she heard your voice, she hung up. If you think back, I'm sure you'll recall a series of wrong numbers or hangups."

Olivia fiddled with the handle of the cup clutched in her hands. She did remember a series of calls with someone listening but not speaking on the other end of the line. "Guilt does strange things to people. I'd appreciate if you'd stop referring to Adrian Ames as my mother. She was not a mother in any way. A person has to earn that title. Giving birth simply doesn't cut it."

"You have to let your bitterness go. She tried to make things right in the end. That has to count for something. Did your father ever tell you anything about your . . . about Miz Ames' past?"

"No. He said she died. Period. There was nothing to talk about. I don't think he knew about her past. When he visited me a week ago, we talked, and he didn't say anything."

"She didn't have a good life. Shiftless parents, father was a drinker, mother was. . . a . . . a lady of the evening. They lived in a trailer with no heat in the winter. She had to scrounge for food. She told me one of the neighbors, a kindly old lady, always gave her a bath on Saturday night. Her clothes came from the Salvation Army. She left the trailer when she was fourteen and made her own way by working as a waitress. She had . . . she had several benefactors along the way, and I don't think I have to spell out to you what that meant. With all that going on in her life, she somehow kept up with her studies. Her dream was to go to college and make something of herself. She had a good work ethic during those years. She told me she graduated summa cum laude."

"And the bank robbery was her reward for studying hard during those four years," Olivia snarled.

"Something like that. She did say the owner of the bank was involved in some sort of shenanigans with a few of his banking friends. She was worried about the insurance company, though, during the early years because Mr. Augustus and his friends had insured those bonds. That's one of the reasons she changed her name and turned reclusive. That's all I can tell you, unless you have any questions."

Did she have questions? "Did she ever say anything specific about my father?"

"Only that he was a good person. She never said a bad word about him. He was beyond excited about your birth. He wanted a lot of children, she said. She did tell me she married your father to get out of the area, away from the bank and the insurance company. A new name, that kind of thing. Then she changed her name again when she divorced your father. She professed amazement that the three of them got away with it so cleanly. Yet she was always looking over her shoulder, waiting for someone to tap her on the back and cart her off to jail. Miz Ames wasn't a happy person. This is just my opinion, but I don't think she knew how to be happy. All that money, all that success, all her possessions didn't help in that department one bit."

Olivia had heard enough. "I'm going to go through the house, Mr. Somers. I'm going to remove all the dust covers. I don't know why, but I want to get a feel for the house she lived in. I'm not sure yet, but I might spend the night."

"Do you want me to stay and help you?"

"No, Mr. Somers, this is something I need to do myself."

"Well, if you need me, just call me on my cell phone. I'll keep it on."

"Do you by any chance know the name of the insurance company that insured the bonds?"

"Great Rock of Mississippi."

"Thanks."

Chapter 18

There was a frenzy to Olivia's movements as she raced through Adrian Ames's house, ripping at the sheets covering the windows and furniture. She tossed them onto a pile in the middle of the floor. She was breathless by the time she unveiled the entire downstairs. She lowered her head to take deep, gulping breaths as she looked around at the chaos she'd created.

Did Adrian decorate this house, or did some professional designer do it? Everything looked costly, elegant. Olivia was reminded of a movie set, where everything was positioned perfectly, and everything shouted dollar amounts. Silk, satin, brocade, gilt. She assumed the area carpets were Persian.

Looking around for something personal,

she found nothing—no photographs, no mementos of travel to a place one wanted to remember. She walked over to the fireplace. It looked like it had been scrubbed clean with a brush. No cozy fires had been laid there. She tested a sofa. It was so firm, so stiff, she knew no one had ever sat on its gold brocade.

Olivia stood, hands on hips, looking around, hoping she would gain some kind of insight into what she was seeing. The best she could come up with was that this was about as far as you could come from living in a rusty trailer with no heat and less than caring parents.

Her feet lagging, Olivia retraced her steps to the kitchen and the room-sized pantry she'd seen earlier. She knew before she checked the pantry that she would find a virtual grocery store. Wall-to-wall, floor-to-ceiling shelves were packed with canned goods and boxed products. The freezer was filled to capacity. She'd bet her life it held a side of beef, packaged and labeled. She was proved right when she opened the lid. Adrian Ames had no intention of starving. Someone who'd had to scrounge for food in her teenage years would make sure that never happened again.

Olivia made a mental note to have Cyrus check the expiration dates on the packages. If they hadn't expired, she would have him take them to a local food kitchen to feed the homeless. She closed the door on the way out. She didn't want to look at this room. She didn't want to stand in it, either.

In the middle of the kitchen, she stopped in her tracks to pull out her cell phone. She called Cyrus's cell. "I have another question, Mr. Somers. When Ms. Ames's lawyer turned over a letter she had written to me, my baby bracelet was in the envelope. Do you happen to know where she got it? It was my understanding she never wanted to see me when I was born. If that's true, where did she get the bracelet?"

The old man's voice sounded even more gruff on the phone. "She told me she asked the nurse to get it for her the day you were to be taken home. What she said was she wanted a memento of the horrible experience of giving birth. She told me she had no desire to see you. Does that answer your question, miss?"

"Yes, it does, Mr. Somers. Thank you."

Eyes dry, jaw tight, Olivia made her way through the house to the beautiful carved, circular staircase. She hated walking on the taped-down brown paper. The sounds her shoes made were just as bad as fingernails scratching a blackboard.

Olivia stomped her way down the hall, ripping at the cotton and plastic sheets covering the hallway furniture. She backtracked to the end of the hall to tackle the guest rooms. She assumed they were guest rooms, since Adrian Ames had lived alone. Where did the Jamaican servants live? She whipped out her cell phone a second time and asked Cyrus Somers.

The voice that sounded like it was mixed with gravel and molasses said, "Miz Ames converted the original garage to make it into a four-bedroom carriage house. The building has a kitchen, two full baths, a large living room with a big-screen TV. The four women were cousins and wanted to be together. You can see the building from Miz Ames's sitting-room window. It's just beyond my cottage. Is there anything else, miss?"

"No. Thank you."

Olivia shrugged as she yanked at the sheets and plastic covering the furniture, paintings, and drapes in the four guest bedrooms. All four rooms were bright and cheerful, with vibrant colors. Feminine and frilly. Beautifully decorated. The color scheme of each guest room was carried out in the adjoining bathrooms. There were no hanging towels, but there were thick, thirsty towels that matched the bedcoverings in the linen closets. Olivia shrugged again. It was all for show. She couldn't grasp the point of it all.

She was in her mother's suite of rooms. The painter's plastic she and Jeff had removed on their first visit was still lying in crumpled heaps on the floor. She removed the rest of it and looked around.

These rooms were lived in. Adrian Ames's lair. The furniture in the sitting room was neutral in tone, deep and comfortable. The wheat-colored draperies were thick and lined and went all the way to the floor. An ottoman sat at the foot of an oversize chair. Adrian must have liked to put her feet up when she watched television. Olivia looked around for a stereo system but didn't see one. Maybe Adrian didn't like music.

The moment Olivia settled herself behind Adrian's desk, her cell phone chirped to life. She broke into a smile when she heard Jeff's voice. She thought his voice sounded shy but warm. She hoped her own voice matched his in warmth. "How are you?" she asked.

"Tired. I really wanted to get out to Winchester last night but couldn't make it. When I got back to the office I was dead on my feet. I meant to call when I got home, but I sat down, closed my eyes, and didn't wake up till this morning. What's going on? Anything new?"

Olivia brought him up to date. "I'm sitting here in her office. I'm going to copy her files onto a CD-ROM and take them home with me. I was prepared to spend the night, but that idea is waning. I think I just might take the whole computer with me and do it all at home." Her voice turned shy when she said, "I'd rather spend the night with you. If you're serious about coming out to the house, pick up dinner. I'll pack up everything from here and head on home. How's the weather?"

"It's raining now, but it's melting a lot of that ugly black ice. Okay, I'll see you this evening. Is Cecil okay?"

"Cecil is fine. I'll see you this evening."

The cell phone still in her hand, Olivia called Cyrus Somers one more time. "I'm going to be taking some things with me. Can you find me some boxes so I can pack up what I want to take?"

An hour later, the cargo hold of Olivia's Bronco was full of cartons as well as Adrian's computer. She'd cleaned everything out of the safe and the desk drawers. What she'd hoped to find was a mystery to her.

Olivia shook hands with the caretaker and scratched Brutus behind the ears as she prepared to climb into the Bronco. "Mr. Somers, you don't have to retire or leave here if you don't want to. I'd like you to stay on if you're up to it. The estate will continue to pay your salary. You don't have to give me your answer right now. Think about it and get back to me when you can. You have my home phone number." Olivia wasn't sure, but she thought she saw relief in the old man's eyes. He nodded as she slipped the Bronco into gear and drove away.

It was four o'clock when Olivia realized she was starved. She cruised into the parking lot behind Kosco's, parked the Bronco in front of the Sleep Inn, and headed for the Daily Grind Coffee Shop, where she ordered a large coffee and a sandwich. She could have eaten more, but Jeff would be bringing dinner so there was no point in stuffing herself now. She liked eating with Jeff and talking about everything and nothing.

Olivia was home forty minutes later. She debated carrying in the boxes, but it was raining. Maybe Jeff could do it later. He needed to earn that dollar she'd paid him. She grinned at the idea. She really liked the guy. No, no, that was wrong—she was falling in love with Jeff Bannerman.

Inside the house, she paid the dog-sitter and played with the dogs for a while. They refused to go outside in the rain, so she put down pee pads by the door.

Olivia popped open a soft drink to carry into the great room, where she searched for the portable phone that was, as usual, between the cushions on the cocoa-colored sofa. She called her father, her foot tapping on the floor as she waited for him to click on his cell phone. The moment she heard his voice, she laced into him, her voice angry. "Why didn't you ever tell me your ex-wife, the woman who gave birth to me, sent presents to me? Why did you send them back? How did you even know they were from *her?* Dammit, Dad, why did you lie to me?"

He didn't hedge. He didn't try to wiggle out of the question. "What would have been the point, Ollie? You thought your mother was dead. They were sent from a law firm. Who else could they have been from?"

Olivia's foot was tapping so furiously, the dogs stopped what they were doing to watch this strange behavior. "Why didn't you tell me when this all came to light? Why did you continue to keep me in the dark? I had a right to know, Dad. I don't know if I can forgive you for that."

"Ollie . . . I know you want me to say I'm sorry, but I can't do that, even for you, Ollie. Look at what you're going through right now. This is what I never wanted to happen. As cruel as it is, she didn't want you, Ollie. She said so, to me, to the nurses, to the lawyers she had there waiting for me, hours after you were born. For God's sake, the woman robbed a damn bank to get what she wanted. Those gifts she sent were guilt gifts. She knew where you and I lived, otherwise how could she have had her lawyers send those gifts? If she wanted to see you, she could have stopped by at any time. If she had done that, Ollie, I wouldn't have turned her away. It was her choice." After a pause, he added, "When are you going to be done with this mess?" Frost dripped from his voice.

"I don't know," Olivia snapped.

"I don't much care for your attitude, young lady. If you have more to say, say it now. I have no desire to go through this every few days. I can't change the past. In fact, even if I could, I wouldn't. I gave you a good life, Ollie, a damn good life, and you know it."

"Well, guess what, Dad, I don't much care for the way you lied to me all these years. I think I have a good reason to have a bad attitude, as you call it. I think we should hang up now before one of us says something we'll regret." Olivia knew her father was angry when the connection was ended without a good-bye. She burst into tears.

Pacing around the great room, stopping only to wipe at her drippy eyes and nose, she thought, *It isn't fair. I didn't ask for this.* And there was no way she could make it all go away. She raised her eyes to the ceiling. "I want my life back! I want to stew and worry about my calendars. I want to budget my money and know when I can or cannot buy something. I want to live here with my dogs, my work, and, most of all, I want to have a relationship with Jeff. Can You hear me?" When there was no response from the ceiling, Olivia threw herself on the sofa and bawled her eyes out, all the while telling herself she was going to have red, puffy eyes when Jeff arrived.

Later, when Jeff got there, he took one look at the miserable woman standing in front of him and took her in his arms. He crooned words of sympathy as the dogs crowded around his legs.

"You're a lawyer, Jeff. I paid you a retainer. Tell me what to do. Tell me how to handle this. That . . . that woman has, in death, done more damage than she did in life. My dad is angry with me. In a way, I don't blame him. He thinks he's right. Then, there's *her,* reaching beyond the grave to turn what we had to ruins. Am I wrong to feel like this? It's never going to be the same again, is it? Maybe that's what I can't accept," Olivia said, sobbing.

"We'll talk later," Jeff said soothingly. "By the fire, with a nice glass of wine. Right now, though, I'm really hungry. I brought Italian. Spaghetti and meatballs in a garlic lemon sauce from Mama and Papa's. The best Italian restaurant in the District of Columbia. Wait a minute! I did bring it—where is it?" he said, looking around.

"Did you set it down?" Olivia asked.

"Yes. Oh no!" Together, they raced into the great room. Four defiant furry little faces gazed up at Olivia and Jeff as much as to say, "It was past supper time, what did you expect?" Then they started to lick each other's whiskers. Plastic containers littered the great room. "Guess they don't like spaghetti. They just ate the meatballs." In spite of himself, Jeff was laughing. Olivia joined in the laughter as she helped Jeff clean up the mess the dogs had created.

The dogs raced off to hide under the bed when Olivia started to wag her finger in front of them.

"Shame on all of you."

"I like scrambled eggs." Jeff guffawed. "Do dogs do stuff like this a lot?"

"Yeah. They're like little kids. Did you see how defiant and guilty they looked?" Both of them burst out laughing again. Suddenly, Olivia felt a hundred percent better.

The following morning, as Olivia was struggling to hook up Adrian Ames's computer, Dennis Lowell was waiting in the marina office for his FedEx delivery. He alternated between pacing and talking to a wizened old man with skin baked to a rich mahogany color. It also looked dryer than shoe leather. He had no idea what the old man was talking about, and he responded with absentminded grunts. He sighed with relief when he saw the red, white, and blue FedEx truck drive into the parking lot. He had to fight with himself not to run out to the truck.

Dennis knew he looked a total mess, his eyes red-rimmed with lack of sleep. He knew in that moment, if Allison Matthews, or Adrian Ames, or whatever she called herself, had still been alive, he would have searched her out and killed her himself. If there had been a way to blame the hydraulics problem with his boat on her, he would have.

Dennis signed for his envelope and walked back to his boat. He needed to get a deposit ticket before heading to the bank. Most important, he wanted to sit in his canvas chair and look at the checks that were literally saving his retirement years. Ollie hadn't failed him. *It's just you and me, kid,* he thought. Why did he ever think it wouldn't be any different with three people in the mix?

As Dennis stared down at the checks in his hands, he was seeing the numbers, but his thoughts were back in Winchester with his daughter. She was upset with him. Well, he was upset with her, too. She was waffling where Adrian Ames was concerned because she couldn't bear to accept the truth. If she had to make him out to be the bad guy, that would have to be okay as long as she could come to some kind of peaceful resolution where her mother was concerned.

There was a spring in Dennis's step when he hopped off his boat and started down the dock to his car, a battered, secondhand, open-air Jeep with a stick shift. He'd chosen the stick shift because Lea didn't know how to drive a stick. She had her Honda. Until two days ago, he hadn't realized how divided their relationship was. This was his, that was hers. Sometimes he was really dense, and things didn't register until it was too late. At least that's what Ollie used to tell him. Certainly that had been the case with his first wife!

Forty minutes later, Dennis walked out of the bank feeling like a new person. He then did two things from his Jeep. He called the hydraulics firm and set a date for the work to begin. Next, he made his way to the local newspaper, where he renewed the ads he ran in hopes of getting more charters.

On his way home, he pulled to the curb and bought a hot dog with chili, sauerkraut, onions, and relish, along with a soft drink. He gobbled the hot dog down, finished off the soda, and kicked the Jeep into gear. The check for Lea felt hot in his pocket.

Lea was sitting on the steps, a paperback novel in one hand, a glass of ice tea in the other. The Jeep's wheels squirted gravel as he pulled to a stop. He climbed out. They eyed each other warily. Lea didn't look angry, just resigned. He felt something tug at his heart, and he straightened his shoulders to get rid of the feeling. Lea moved to the side so he could sit down next to her. He waited to see what she would say, if anything.

"This isn't working, is it, Dennis?"

"I don't think so, Lea. It sounded wonderful when we were planning this way back when. We didn't allow for things like the hydraulics. I guess that was my fault. I'm sorry about that, Lea. I really am. I know you're not happy here. I'm sorry about that, too. I overheard your phone conversation with Olivia. I walked home and came in the backdoor. I heard you ask for the money from Adrian's estate. How could you do that, Lea, knowing how I feel about it? How, Lea?"

All the fight seemed to have left Lea. Her voice was wan when she said, "It would have made our lives so much easier, Dennis. I can honestly say I wanted it more for you than for myself. These are our golden years. What they've turned out to be are tarnished brass." Lea moved on the step, her voice now brisk and cool. "What do you suggest we do, Dennis?"

Dennis reached into his pocket and

brought out the check he'd had the bank make out to Lea. "I called Ollie yesterday and asked her to take out a second mortgage on the house. Here's all the money you put into the boat and the house. There's a little left from the loan to pay off the boat's gas bill and the house bills. I can get some of the minor stuff done on the boat and hire out to Hemmings or some of the other guys. I'll sell the house and live on the boat. It will cut down on overhead."

"You're assuming I'm leaving, is that it?"

"We're too old to play games, Lea. Of course you're leaving. This life isn't for you, we both know that. I'm really sorry it didn't work out. I don't think I could ever come to terms with what you did. Just so you know, Lea, Ollie didn't tell me about your phone call."

Lea nodded sadly. "I'm sorry, too, Dennis. This is all happening so . . . so quick. Are you sure you're going to be all right? Or . . ."

Dennis's eyes narrowed in the bright sunlight. "Or what?"

"Are you getting rid of me so you don't have to share Allison's money with me?"

Dennis stood up and looked down at the little woman sitting on the step. He noticed that the ice cubes in her tea had melted. The tea looked like pale colored water. All he did was shake his head from side to side before he walked over to the Jeep. "Good-bye, Lea."

Chapter 19

"You look cute in the morning," Olivia teased. "Look! The dogs think so, too." She burst out laughing when all four dogs hopped on the bed. Cecil or Loopy nibbled on Jeff's ear while Alice tugged at his arm to get him to move. Bea, ever flirtatious, sat on Jeff's chest, making funny, adoring sounds as she licked the stubble on his chin.

Olivia leaned up on one elbow, drinking in the sight before her. It would be like this every morning if she married Jeff Bannerman. Assuming, of course, that Jeff asked for her hand in marriage. If that did happen, who would take care of the dogs during their honeymoon? Where would they go on a honeymoon? Maybe they would have to take the dogs. Four dogs on a honeymoon should be interesting. She felt laughter bubbling in her throat at the thought.

"What's so funny?" Jeff grumbled good-naturedly as Bea suddenly made a flying leap to land half on the pillow, half on Jeff's head. Alice growled, then swatted the suddenly rambunctious Bea. Jeff made a mighty leap and was off the bed. Thinking the game was ongoing, the dogs followed him to the bathroom. When the door closed, as one, they howled their disapproval.

Olivia reached for her robe. She led the parade to the door to let the dogs out. A quick glance at the kitchen clock told her Jeff had time for toast and coffee. She made both. She was spreading butter and jam on the toast when Jeff entered the kitchen. She almost swooned. He was wearing what she would call a power suit of charcoal gray with a pristine white shirt and red-striped tie. His dark, unruly hair was slicked back and he smelled . . . heavenly. She said so.

"You think so, huh? Do I smell good enough to marry?"

Olivia whirled away from the toaster. "Is . . . is that a proposal?"

"Well, yeah. I guess it wasn't very romantic, huh? Did I do it wrong? You know, I never proposed to anyone before. I could get down on one knee. Should I call your father to ask for your hand? What? Help me out here."

He was so agitated, his face so pink, Olivia took pity on him. She handed him a slice of toast with shaking hands.

"Ah . . . I didn't even brush my teeth yet," she blurted. "You don't have to ask my dad for my hand, and you don't have to get down on one knee, either. I . . . no one has ever proposed to me, so I guess we're starting out even. I accept. I do. I mean, I will marry you. When?"

Jeff's eyes bugged out of his head. "When? Well . . . when do you want to *do it?*"

"We should probably think about a date when we have more time. You have to leave now or you'll be late." God, how brilliant was that?

Jeff looked at the clock. He grimaced as he headed for the door. "I'll leave early and bring some champagne. I'll try to make it more romantic. All I do is think about you, Olivia. I can't concentrate. Is it okay if I call my parents today to tell them?"

Telling his parents would make it official. Olivia nodded, her smile stretching from ear to ear.

"Good! Call your dad, too. Talk me up real good—you know, tell him I don't have any cavities, I'm a hard worker, I'll take care of you. Tell him we'll have beautiful children, and don't forget to tell him I love dogs. Really love dogs! Bye. Oh—I love you!"

Olivia stood in the middle of the kitchen, a blank look on her face. Children. He'd said children. That *really* made it official. He wanted her to call her father. He was going to call his parents. Tonight they were going to celebrate. All he did was think of her. "Wooeee!" she shouted to the dogs. And on top of that, he'd said he loved her. What better way to start the day?

It must be a new game, the little herd decided. They swooped down on her when Olivia crouched down. Soon they were all rolling across the floor with Olivia screaming out her happiness. Yesterday she'd been in a terrible funk—today she felt like she was on top of the world. "Call your dad," Jeff had said. She would. After all, he would be *giving her away.*

Olivia rolled away from the dogs. She

could feel the color draining out of her face. It was just an expression. All fathers gave their daughters away at a wedding. It was normal, it was expected, it was the way of things. Unless you got married in Las Vegas.

Olivia raced down the hall to her bedroom, where she showered, then dressed in jeans and a bright yellow sweatshirt. Her feet had wings when she ran to her office to call her father. The moment she heard his voice, she started to babble. When she finally wound down and there was no comment from Dennis, she prodded him.

"I'm happy for you, Ollie. If it's what you want, then it's what I want. I guess you know it won't be *'just you and me, kid'* anymore."

Olivia's euphoric mood changed with her father's words. Her voice turned cool and flat. "In case you didn't notice, it hasn't been that way for a long time. Since Lea, actually. By the way, how is Lea?"

The silence on the other end of the phone boomed in Olivia's ear. This time she refused to prod her father.

"Ollie, I overheard Lea the day she called

you asking for money. I walked home that day because it was so beautiful out. I went into the house by the back door. I had no idea she felt the way she did. It never, ever, occurred to me that she would do what she did. To make a long story short, I gave her the check, and she's leaving. I plan to sell the house and live on the boat. I just wanted you to know that. I'm happy for you, Ollie. Right now my head is in a hundred different places, so if I'm not coming across the way you'd like, that's the reason."

"It's okay, Dad. I'm really sorry about Lea, but maybe it's for the best? Look, I have to go. Like you, I have a hundred different things on my mind. Stay in touch, okay?" Olivia had to stab at the OFF button three times before she finally broke the connection.

Don't think about this, Olivia. Shelve it— put it out of your mind. Don't even think about crying.

Olivia sat down at the computer, turned it on, and waited to boot up her e-mail. The only e-mail of any importance was the message from Miki Kenyan of The Private Detective Agency. It was short but meaningful.

> **My investigator is on the case
> and has three promising leads.
> Person resembling subject seen at
> Memphis, TN, airport. It's not
> easy getting a passenger manifest.
> We guarantee results, as I've told
> you. Your next report will be sent
> in twenty-four hours.**

The message was signed with the initials MK.

Olivia ignored the rest of the e-mails, going to the Net, where she typed in *Great Rock Insurance Company of Mississippi.* Her printer whirred as she printed out everything that popped on her screen. She searched out the 800 telephone numbers and made a note of them. Maybe, if she was lucky, she could find the insurance investigator who authorized the payoff on the bearer bonds forty years ago.

Olivia left the computer once, around noontime, to let the dogs out and fix herself a sandwich. While she was chewing her ham and cheese, Jeff called to tell her he loved her and was serious about his proposal and couldn't wait for evening. Before he hung up, he asked about Cecil. Olivia laughed all the way back to her office.

Perusing the papers from the printer, she saw that Great Rock was a very large insurance company these days. Forty years ago Mississippi Rock, as it was known then, was a rinky-dink company with five office employees, two agents, and an office in Oxford. Today the home office was in Biloxi and had over four hundred employees, as well as eighteen full-time insurance investigators and four investigators on a part-time basis. A payout like the one they'd made to the bank forty years ago would have hurt the small company big-time. How had they managed to stay in business by paying out close to a million dollars when they insured small life insurance policies and some homeowner policies? Damn, maybe it was all a scam, and the insurance company was in bed with the man who owned the bank? Olivia was smart enough to realize she'd probably never be able to find out the truth.

She leaned back in her chair, propped her feet on her desktop, and tried to think. How hard could it be to track down two insurance agents? If the agents had been in their twenties, or even their thirties, they would be in their sixties or seventies now. There was a good chance that they were dead. She needed names. Without names there was no way she could do a search.

Jeff had said he vaguely recalled seeing something about an insurance company among Adrian's papers. Maybe Adrian had the agent's name. She was certain there was nothing in the diary she'd read in regard to Great Rock.

Olivia looked at her watch. There was no point now in trying to read Adrian's computer files. Tomorrow would be soon enough. She wanted to take a scented bubble bath, get dressed up, and be ready for Jeff's formal proposal. The thought left her giddy and light-headed. What to wear?

A little before three o'clock, Jeff raced home to his apartment, where he quickly showered and shaved, splashing on a woodsy-scented aftershave his brother said would drive women wild. He wondered what a *wild* Olivia would be like as he changed to a fresh suit and clean shirt. He knotted the same power tie at his neck and nearly flew out of the apartment. His first stop was Goldman's Jewelry, where he stewed and fretted over the wide selection of engagement rings, called his mother twice, then chose a two-carat diamond engagement ring that seriously depleted his bank account. It winked and sparkled against the black velvet cloth the jeweler had placed it on. Jeff closed his eyes, trying to picture it on Olivia's hand.

Suddenly Jeff was having trouble with his breathing. Was he going to pass out right there in the jewelry store? He forced himself to take deep, steady breaths. He'd done it! He'd picked out an engagement ring! He'd asked Olivia to marry him. God Almighty!

The red, velvet-lined box felt scorching hot in his hand. He shoved it into his pocket. He started to sweat profusely when he slid into the driver's seat of his car. This was serious business. He'd just committed himself to a woman. A woman he'd known less than two weeks. Did time count when you were in love? He'd always known that someday he'd find someone he wanted to spend his life with. For some reason he thought it would be a long courtship with fights, breakups, then kissing each other and professing undying love. None of that was happening.

Jeff's foot started to shake on the gas pedal. He was getting dizzy again. He needed to keep his wits about him or he was going to go off the road. Think about Cecil. If it wasn't for Cecil, he never would have found Olivia. Good old Cecil. "God, I love that dog," he mumbled. Maybe he should stop and buy Cecil and the other dogs a hamburger at Burger King in thanks. Yeah, yeah, he'd do that. Some french fries, too. Maybe even some chicken nuggets to round out the meal. Yeah, yeah, Cecil loved chicken almost as much as he loved burgers. Lillian Manning always cooked for Cecil—chicken livers, filet mignon, lamb chops.

Jeff fumbled on the seat for his cell phone. He called information for the number of the Colonial Flower Shop on Valley Avenue. He punched out the number, spoke to someone named Mary, and ordered two dozen yellow roses. "Put a big bow on the box, and put lots of that green stuff in them. I'll pick it up in twenty minutes." Before he hung up, he rattled off his credit card number. Candy? Should he order candy, too? Nah. Champagne! With no idea where a liquor store was, Jeff redialed the Colonial

Flower Shop and asked Mary where he could purchase a bottle. A minute later he had the phone number. A man named Peter promised to have a bottle of his best champagne ready when he stopped by before closing. He rattled off his credit card number for the second time.

Jeff wondered if he was losing his mind as he screeched into a Burger King and ordered the little dogs their burger and chicken nuggets. The moment the young boy held out the bag, he snatched it and peeled out of the drive-through.

Damn! Jeff slapped at his forehead. Was he supposed to bring dinner? For the life of him, he couldn't remember. He was nuts, he was sure of it, when he swerved into the lot of a Chinese restaurant called Pagoda. He was so rattled he just said, "Give me some of everything!"

The food smells in the car were so strong, he rolled down the window as he headed for Loudoun Street—the florist's and the liquor store. He was so jittery, he made two wrong turns and had to backtrack before he finally turned onto Eagle Drive. The moment he stopped the car he heard the dogs barking.

Jeff stood still, rain pelting him and his

new suit. He could cut and run if he wanted to. He jammed his hand into his pocket to check the little box. It still felt hot. The dogs were barking louder. The front light came on. He reached into the car for the flowers and the champagne. He tucked both under one arm. The Chinese shopping bag with one of everything and the Burger King bag were in his other hand. He kicked the car door shut with his foot before he ran to the front door.

He felt loved and wanted when the dogs circled his feet, trying to snatch the Burger King bag. He sighed with happiness when Olivia's lips locked on his.

What could be better?

Nothing, he answered himself.

They were both breathless when the kiss ended, both their eyes full of wonderment. Hand in hand, they walked into the great room, suddenly shy. Jeff took charge, feeding the dogs while Olivia ooohed and aaahed over the yellow roses. She put them in two vases, fluffing out the greenery. "They're gorgeous!" she said, awe ringing in her voice. "Champagne! Oh, I have some beautiful glasses to drink this out of. I love drinking out of fragile glasses, don't you?"

Jeff wanted to say a paper cup would do it for him, but he knew it was a girl thing, so he said, "Me too."

They looked at each other.

"Should we get officially engaged before or after we eat? I brought Chinese, and it will get cold if we wait."

"Then let's eat! You're spoiling those dogs, you know that, don't you? I set the table in anticipation of you bringing dinner even though I couldn't remember if you were to bring it or not. If not, it was going to be peanut butter and jelly. There's something about peanut butter and jelly with candlelight."

"I love peanut butter and jelly with or without candlelight. Need any help?"

"Not really. Since they packed everything so nicely, let's just spoon it out onto plates, unless you want to wash a bunch of bowls. Let's put the flowers on the table. They're so pretty, Jeff. Thank you. Yellow is my favorite color."

Jeff's face was full of amazement. "It's my mother's favorite color, too." A girl just like Mom. Olivia smiled at him as she filled his plate.

Jeff slipped out of his jacket and hung it

over the back of his chair as he unbuttoned the top button on his shirt and loosened his tie. Just to be sure the red, velvet-lined box was still in his pocket, he stuck his hand in his pocket to feel it. For some reason, it still felt hot to the touch.

The dogs raced into the kitchen the moment they smelled the food. They circled the table but didn't beg. Sooner or later, they would get *something.* At least that's the way it usually worked.

Jeff, his eyes on the woman across from him, paid no attention to the dogs. Cecil or Loopy started to sniff his shoes, working his way around to the back of the chair where Jeff's coat was hanging. One little paw swatted at the bulge in the jacket pocket. Alice, seeing the Yorkie dancing around on his hind legs, meandered over to see what was going on. She, too, swatted at the bulge in the pocket. When nothing fell to the floor, she stuck her snoot into the pocket and brought out the small red box. All the dogs circled around the prize that Alice dropped to the floor. Food? Treats? Bea wiggled her rear end closer, sniffed the box, pushed it around a little to see if it bit back. When it didn't, she picked it up and trotted out of the dining room, down the hall to Olivia's bedroom, where she once more dropped the box. The other dogs crowded closer, sniffing and pawing at this sudden new treasure. A toy, a new ball that didn't bounce.

The dogs took turns rolling the little red box all over the floor. Cecil snatched it up, biting down hard so as not to lose it, which caused the lid to pop open. He dropped the box and backed away, as did the other dogs. When the four of them realized the box wasn't going to do anything, they moved closer to eye the sparkling gem winking at them in the overhead light.

Alice, queen of 509 Eagle Drive and top dog, stepped forward and picked up the box, ring and all. She headed back down the hall to her basket of toys in Olivia's office. This was her treasure and would go in her basket. Cecil or Loopy, not liking the arrangement, waited until Alice buried it under a fluffy stuffed bird before he snatched it and ran down the hall to where *his* basket of toys rested. He rooted around till he found a spot and dropped it in. Bea barked, as did Loopy or Cecil. Cecil or Loopy growled. Alice swatted him so hard he stopped growling just long enough to give Bea time to snatch the box, the ring almost out of its snug position. Halfway down the hall, the ring fell out of the box, and Loopy or Cecil snatched it up and ran to the bathroom, where he hid behind the toilet. The others growled at him, but he ignored them, enjoying being the center of attention. He did his best to dig into the shaggy carpet to bury his treasure before he pranced out to race down the hall again. Bea dropped the red box, Alice picked it up, and the game was on again as she looked for a better hiding place.

In the dining room, Jeff's heart kicked up a beat when Olivia cleared away the dishes. Dessert was a fortune cookie and the ring. His mouth was suddenly dry, and he poured more champagne into his flute. He eyed the woman bustling about. She looked as pretty as his mother, maybe prettier. Her blond hair curled around her face in little wisps. He'd never really seen her dressed up before. She was what his brothers, all five of them, would call a knockout. She wore a simple lavender dress with long sleeves. In her ears and around her throat were pearls. His mother always wore pearls. She'd gotten dressed up for him just the way he'd gotten dressed up for her. He was still waiting to see if his aftershave would drive her wild. Her perfume was driving him nuts. He felt like a caveman. He hoped she'd catch up soon. He poured more champagne into her glass the moment she sat down.

This was the moment. *The moment!* First, though, they had to open their fortune cookies. He handed Olivia hers. He laughed nervously when she read her fortune.

"Mine says the gods of fortune will smile upon me." Olivia giggled. "What does yours say?"

Jeff broke open his cookie and read his fortune. "Mine says, 'You will eventually find that which you seek.' What do you suppose that means?"

Olivia smiled. She loved fortune cookies. "Did you lose something lately?"

Jeff loved fortune cookies, too. And wouldn't admit it to anyone, but he always read his horoscope in the daily paper. "No, not that I know of." He got up, walked over to Olivia's chair, and dropped to one knee. "I want to do this right. My mom said my dad proposed to her on his knee. So, here I am." He reached for Olivia's hand. "Will you marry me, Olivia? I promise always to take care of you. I promise to love you forever and ever. I'll do everything in my power never to disappoint you. Please say yes so I can get off my knees."

Olivia gurgled with laughter. "Yes, yes, a thousand times yes. You can get up now." She stood up and kissed him, a long lingering, sweet kiss that spoke of wonderful things yet to come.

"Oh my gosh, the ring! I bought you an engagement ring today. If you don't like it, we can exchange it. I picked it out myself. I thought it would . . . Oh, God, where is it?" he said, rummaging in his jacket pocket, then his pants pocket. "It must have fallen out. It was in my pocket when we sat down. I felt it when I took off my jacket. Do you see it anywhere, Olivia? It's a little red box."

An engagement ring. Lordy, Lordy, this was it, what most women waited for from the time they were toddlers. An engagement ring. "Wait a minute, Jeff. Calm down. Are you sure it was in your pocket when you took off your jacket and hung it over the back of the chair?"

"I'm sure, Olivia. I was nervous about giving it to you, hoping you would like it. I touched it. It was there." His voice was so desperate-sounding, Olivia thought he was going to cry.

"I didn't take it, Jeff. Now, think, who does that leave?" Olivia reached behind her to open one of the drawers under the counter. She pulled out a whistle and blew three sharp blasts. The dogs came on the run. "I would almost bet the rent these guys are the culprits! Okay, here's where you have to show them you're the boss. Point to your pocket, show them the jacket. Then tell them to fetch it. Maybe they will, and maybe they won't. I'm betting they hid it."

"They hid it?" Jeff said in a choked voice. "Are you saying we might not find it?"

Olivia shrugged. "There are a hundred places in this house to hide things. They all have a basket of toys, but that's way too obvious. Go on, show them who's boss!"

Jeff felt like a fool when he stood up, his jacket in his hands. "Listen up, you guys. You took something out of my pocket, and I want it back. Right now! Fetch it!"

Alice looked up at him and barked. Bea lay down and closed her eyes. Cecil and Loopy growled, not liking his tone. Then they started to yap. Bea and Alice joined in the barking before they all turned tail and ran out of the room.

"They aren't going to fetch it, are they. They were toying with me, right?" Jeff said miserably.

"Nope. And yep. Told you, dogs are smart. When they get tired of guarding it, they might bring it out. Then again, they might not. I'll take this end of the house, you take the back end."

"This isn't how I wanted us to spend the evening, Olivia. I wanted it to be just a romantic evening."

"Oh, Jeff, it's all right. For sure neither one of us is ever going to forget this night. Let's view it as a treasure hunt. It's going to be a wonderful memory for us in years to come."

Jeff laughed. "Okay. You're a good sport, Olivia. I'm glad you aren't upset."

"Pretending I have a ring on my finger is almost as good as having one. Come on, let's start the search."

Chapter 20

The fire was almost out when the grubby young couple sat down next to each other, glasses of wine in hand. Jeff tossed two oak logs on the fire. A shower of sparks shot upward. "I am so sorry, Olivia. We've crawled over every inch of this house, and we still can't find the ring. What if we never find it?"

Olivia placed a finger on Jeff's lips. "Shhh, don't think like that. We'll find it. We have to figure out a way to trick those four little rascals. Alice doesn't have it, that's a given. She'd give it up in a heartbeat. I haven't had Loopy and Bea long enough to know what all their little quirks are. When it comes to Cecil, I really only know what you and Lillian Manning told me about him. It's one of those three, I'm sure of it. Now, understand this—Yorkshire terriers are incredibly smart. Sometimes they can outthink you. That's what Lillian said. Which means we have to use trickery. Oooh, that fire feels so good."

The dogs cuddled in both their laps. Olivia made a production of taking off a birthstone ring her father had given her on her tenth birthday. She winked at Jeff as she showed it off. Instead of putting it back on her finger, she placed it on the hearth. "Let's see which one of them snatches it up. It's a good chance one or the other of them will take it to their lair and, voilà, hopefully, we'll find the other one. We also have to pretend we aren't watching them."

"Sneaky little rascals, aren't they?" Jeff grinned as Bea wiggled off his lap. The others followed suit. Jeff pretended to lean toward the fire while Olivia slipped off her shoes. Loopy or Cecil snatched up the ring and ran out of the family room and down the hall, the other three dogs right behind him.

Jeff looked at Olivia, his face full of awe.

"We have to be as sneaky as they are. Don't make a sound," she said, and she began running softly down the hall. "Aha!" she called out to Jeff. "The bathroom! Quick!

Quick! Shut the door! Where could they possibly hide it in here?"

Caught in the act, the four dogs lay down. Cecil or Loopy dropped the ring on the tile floor. Olivia swooned when she heard the plinking sound of a ring hitting the tile. "Quick, put it on my finger. I'll never take it off. Never!"

Later, when she was drifting into sleep, Olivia thought of it as a magical moment, one she would carry with her forever.

Her destiny was lying right beside her. It all felt so right.

The following morning after Jeff left for work, Olivia walked back to her studio to begin preparations to resume her work schedule. She spent an hour calling her clients and scheduling appointments. She was going to need the money to buy her wedding dress.

Within an hour, when she was satisfied that she had a full schedule mapped out, she tidied up and walked back to her office. She had a few days left till Monday to work on Adrian Ames's business affairs. After Monday, that business would have to take a backseat to her own work.

Olivia shifted and collated the papers she'd printed out on the Great Rock Insurance Company. Before she hired Miki Kenyan again, she wanted to take a stab at finding the insurance agent herself. Subterfuge was what she needed. Her mind raced, and then she picked up the phone and dialed the 800 number at Great Rock's home office in Biloxi. When the operator came on she asked for Human Resources.

The voice on the other end of the phone was young, warm, and cheerful-sounding. Olivia did her best to match it. She identified herself as Helen Noonan, researching her family tree. "This is my problem, Ms. Berensen, I've managed to track everyone but one uncle. His name was Leroy Sullivan. A cousin seems to recall him working for your company when he was young and your offices were in Oxford, which was some forty years ago. We can't seem to find any information on him. Is there any way you can help me?"

"I'm afraid that was way before my time, Ms. Noonan. I wouldn't even know where to look. I know there is no one here by that name now. Was he an agent?"

Of course there was no one there by that

name—she'd made it up. "Yes, the cousin believes he was an agent. Do you have any employees from that time period, maybe someone I could talk to? It's possible they might remember."

"Let me check, Ms. Noonan. Do you mind holding on for a few minutes?"

"Not at all. I appreciate your help."

While she waited, Olivia stared out the window. She groaned when she saw snow flurries swirling. She let her thoughts drift to Jeff. As soon as the weather got nice she was going to take him on a picnic. She loved picnics.

Olivia was jolted from her thoughts when Ms. Berensen's voice came over the wire again. "I don't know how much help this will be, but you might try Hudson Buckley. I can't give you his phone number, but I can call him and ask him if it's all right to give it to you. He lives here in Biloxi. The company had a retirement dinner for him last year. He's about seventy-five years old. If you don't mind holding on again, I can call him to see if it's all right to give out his number. If he has an e-mail address, do you want that, too?"

"Yes, that would be a big help."

Olivia turned her thoughts to Jeff again as she was put on hold. Would his family like her? Would she like them? What were the brothers like? How would she fit in with that huge family? Would they go to Jeff's family for holidays?

Olivia jerked upright when the voice came back on the line. "Ms. Noonan, Mr. Buckley said it was okay to give you his phone number and his e-mail address. Do you have a pen handy?" Olivia said she did and copied down the information. She thanked the woman again before she broke the connection.

Her eyes on the weather outside, Olivia debated whether she should use the e-mail address or the phone number. Her alias of Helen Noonan wouldn't jibe with her e-mail address, so she opted for the phone. She dialed the number and waited.

The voice was brisk, professional-sounding. "Hudson Buckley."

"Mr. Buckley, this is Helen Noonan. Great Rock gave me your number. I hope I'm not calling you at an inconvenient time."

"Not at all. How can I help you?"

Olivia ran through her family-tree spiel

again. She waited for the retired agent's comments.

"I don't recall a Leroy Sullivan working for Great Rock. I wasn't an agent back then. I started out as a janitor and worked my way up. If I recall correctly, there were two male agents. It was a small company."

"Did you know either of the two agents?" Olivia asked.

The man on the other end of the line chuckled. "As much as a janitor can be friendly with two 'suits.' I do remember their names, though. Nate Clancy and Darryl Spencer. Both of them left about a year after I started working for the company. I saw them last year at a concert at Ole Miss. I go every year. I almost didn't recognize them, but they recognized me. Our wives talked for a while. They're retired, too, but they still live in the area. That's about all I can tell you."

"I appreciate it, Mr. Buckley. I guess I have to continue looking for my uncle in another area or industry. Thank you again."

Olivia got up to stretch her legs. While she was up she made her bed and took a load of clothes to the laundry room. At least she now had two names and a location. If she was lucky, the Information operator might be able to give her their phone numbers. Would they talk to her on the phone? How much should she divulge? Which retired agent had been assigned to the robbery?

Olivia made fresh coffee, and while it was dripping into the pot she stared out the window. It seemed like it was snowing harder. She shivered a little even though she was wearing a toasty-warm dusty rose sweat suit. The phone rang just as she reached into the cabinet for a cup. She snatched at it, wondering who was calling her.

"Jeff!"

"I just called to tell you I love you. I don't think I say that often enough. I do."

Olivia smiled as she cradled the phone against her ear. She hugged her arms against her chest. "I love you, too. I miss you. I spend a lot of time staring at this ring. I just love it, Jeff. You made a wonderful choice. It's snowing again," she said, changing the subject.

"Doesn't matter. I'll be there tonight even if I have to come on snowshoes. I miss you, too, Olivia. I really should go, I have a ton of work on my desk. I just wanted to hear your voice. I'll see you tonight. Love you."

Olivia smiled at the declaration. "I love you, too." When she broke the connection, she looked around, amazed that nothing had changed. The earth wasn't shaking, the sky was intact, the house hadn't blown up. Something should have happened. Then she grinned. She was glad there was no one around to see her just then. She couldn't help but wonder if all first-time loves were like hers.

Coffee cup in hand, Olivia literally skipped her way back to her office, not caring if the coffee sloshed out of the cup, knowing the dogs would lick it right up. She was in love and loved and had the ring to prove it. When you were in love, there were no rules. When she finally settled herself in her ergonomic chair she was shocked to see she'd lost half of the coffee in her cup. She laughed, a sound of pure joy. She looked around, expecting the room to at least tilt. When it didn't, she laughed again. She'd never been so happy. Never. Ever.

Olivia settled down to work, her mind half on what she was doing, the other half on Jeff. Pencil ready, she dialed the Information operator for Oxford, Mississippi, and was amazed to hear there were dozens of people with the names Clancy and Spencer. When the operator told her she could only give her three phone numbers at a time, Olivia groaned aloud. This was going to take forever. She opted for a coffee refill before she settled down to her calls.

By midafternoon, she'd whittled her list to six, maybe seven, possible people who fit the initials of Nate Clancy and Darryl Spencer. She didn't discount the fact that one or more of the numbers she'd crossed out might be listed under the names of the wives.

Olivia looked down at her watch. Time to think about something for dinner. Then she looked outside and was shocked speechless. Snow was coming down so heavily she couldn't see across the yard. She bolted from the office and ran to the kitchen for a better look. It looked like there was about four inches of fresh snow. Jeff would never make it. The thought was so devastating, she sat down, her eyes filling with tears. Hope arose with the thought that maybe it wasn't snowing in the District. But then hope was dashed as she told herself,

What a foolish thought. Of course it's snowing in Washington. The weather patterns were almost identical.

Still, on the off chance Jeff might make it, Olivia rummaged in her freezer for something to prepare for dinner. She finally selected three large pork chops that she'd stuffed weeks before, then frozen. She'd learned to cut corners when her father taught her how to cook. He always set aside one or two days a month to do nothing but cook and freeze. With both their late-day work schedules it was then a simple matter to take something out of the freezer to pop in the oven. A garlic sweet potato–turnip casserole, her father's favorite, went into the oven next to the pork chops. When the chops were almost done she would drizzle a sweet Vidalia onion relish over the top. A garden salad, some frozen rolls, and a cop-out frozen dessert would round out the meal. She rummaged in the freezer again before she withdrew a rock-solid peach cobbler that just needed to be put in the oven. She crossed her fingers that Jeff would show up.

Olivia walked over to the sliding doors and forced them open. The dogs looked up at her and took off running back through the house. She shrugged. How could she blame them? She put down fresh doggy pads by the door and returned to her office, where she continued making phone calls.

It was totally dark outside when she contacted a man who said his name was Nate Clancy. "No, ma'am, I handled the outlying areas. Darryl was the one who worked the Oxford area. He lives about a mile away. I can give you his phone number if you hold on. My wife, Emily, and Darryl's wife, Melissa, are best friends. I'll just be a minute."

Olivia's clenched fist shot in the air. She quickly scribbled down the number Nate Clancy read off to her. She thanked him and cut the connection.

Then she realized she was cold. The dogs must be cold, too—they were all huddled together in Alice's bed in the corner. She turned up the thermostats that controlled the heat in the front end and back end of the house. She turned on lights as she went along. Before she returned to her office, she checked the oven and built a roaring fire in the great room. The dogs scampered around her, yapping and growling. She slapped at her forehead. Of course! It was their suppertime. She trotted back to the kitchen to feed them. All day, she'd felt as if she was on another planet.

Olivia let her thoughts drift to Jeff and the snow outside. Would he make it? Wouldn't he make it? Of course he would. Maybe she should call him and tell him not to attempt the seventy-six-mile trip. She looked down at the sparkling ring on her finger and smiled. As much as she wanted to see her fiancé, she didn't want him to risk his life out on the roads. She called him but reached only his voice mail. She left a message telling him to stay put but to call her, then tried his cell phone, but a voice said she should try her call later.

The phone was ringing in her office when she started down the hall. Thinking it was Jeff returning her call, she clicked on and said, "Oh, you dear sweet man!"

The voice on the other end of the wire made Olivia cringe. "Obviously, Olivia, you were expecting someone else to be calling you. I'm sorry to disappoint you. This is Lea. I'm sure you know what's been going on with your father and me. At least that's what he led me to believe. How can you be so narrow-minded, so uncharitable in regard to Dennis and me? You could have made our lives so much easier. Dennis is your father. I treated you like a daughter, Olivia. I loved you because you were Dennis's daughter. Shame on you for being so selfish. You're just like your mother. If you loved Dennis, you would have found a way to make his life easier. It's all your fault that Dennis and I are separating. Your fault, Olivia! Do you hear me? I hope that money brings you nothing but misery. Are you listening to me, Olivia?" Lea screeched.

Olivia was too surprised to say anything. As she searched for words, the phone pinged in her ear. "Oh, God!" Tears burned her eyes as she grappled with what she'd just heard on the phone. She wasn't like Adrian Ames! She wasn't! Lea was the one who wanted the money! Not her father! Her father asked her to take out a mortgage. If he wanted the money, he would have asked for it. Wouldn't he? What if Lea was right? What if asking for the mortgage was to sidetrack her into thinking he didn't want the money to make her feel sorry for him? Lea was right, the money would make her father's life easier. Damn, she didn't know anything anymore.

The sudden desire to run away as far as she could go was so strong, she almost ran out of the room. She'd been deliriously happy a few minutes ago. Now, after one phone call, she was miserable. Her tears splashed down on the diamond on her finger. She cried harder as she dried off the ring.

Olivia squared her shoulders as she sat down at her desk. Lea could invade her thoughts only if she allowed it. Well, she wasn't going to allow it. Her face grim, she picked up the phone and dialed Darryl Spencer's phone number. It wasn't until she heard the man's voice that she realized she didn't have a reason for the phone call. She was going to have to wing it.

The voice on the phone was elderly, reedy, and thin-sounding. Olivia announced herself as Margaret Tyson, an intermediary in a forty-year-old insurance case. "I understand, Mr. Spencer, that you were the insurance investigator at the time. I'm sorry to say I am not able to divulge the name of my client at this time. My client is, however, prepared to pay back the money to Great Rock that they paid to the bank after the theft. Are you following me here, Mr. Spencer?"

"I think so. The company fired me after they paid out on the claim. The payout almost forced the company into bankruptcy. I was young back then and had never investigated anything like that claim. Mississippi forty years ago was a lot different than it is today. That's just another way of saying I didn't know what I was doing. But to this day, I still believe it was an inside job. There was something off-kilter about the owner of the bank, too. The company paid up real quick. I thought that was suspicious. At first the bank didn't even want to report the theft. I never could figure that out. There wasn't much follow-through, I can tell you that. Then they fired me, and I had to find other work because I'd just gotten married and we had a baby on the way. I did my best to nose around on my own time, but nothing ever came to light. That's about all I can tell you."

"My client wants to pay back the money, Mr. Simpson."

"Is your client the one who . . . made off with the bonds?"

"At this time, I'm not at liberty to say, Mr.

Spencer. You said you thought it was an inside job. I believe those were your words. Who did you think was responsible?"

Olivia could hear a woman's voice in the background shouting to her husband to shut up and mind his own business. The female voice went on to say they were too old to get involved or sued for something that happened forty years ago. Olivia could barely make out Spencer's thin voice when he told his wife to shush, that it was time to speak up.

"I always thought it was that smug young girl who worked there part-time. She was a smart-alecky one, she was. Cool as a Popsicle on a hot summer's day, she was. She looked me right in the eye, defiant, daring me to accuse her. I couldn't do it because I had no proof. Mr. Augustus wouldn't hear one bad word about that girl. She was a student at Ole Miss. I could tell you—" The wife's voice in the background turned shrill as she screamed at her husband to shut up.

There was a small silence on the other end of the phone line, but Olivia could hear husband and wife hissing at each other. Whatever it was Spencer's wife said to her husband, it was effective, because he backed away from what he had been about to say. "They watched the young woman for a long time, years actually. At least that was the rumor. She got married right after graduation and moved away, and they tracked her for years, but nothing ever came to light. That was rumored, too. The company just gave up, I guess. After a while, I didn't care anymore. Why does the person you represent want to pay back the money? I'm sure the company closed the books on the payout."

Olivia's gut churned. There was something Spencer wasn't telling her. Something his wife didn't want him to talk about. "Because it's the right thing to do, Mr. Spencer. My client also wants to pay the earnings the money would have generated if the insurance company had invested that sum of money."

Darryl Spencer whistled. The sound was as weak-sounding as the man's voice.

"Well, I'll be doggoned. Imagine that! Well, good luck, miss."

"Mr. Spencer, are you sure there's nothing else you want to tell me? You can think of me as a reporter, a reporter who never divulges her sources."

Spencer's silence went on too long. Finally, he said, "I told you all I know."

Olivia sighed. She knew the man was lying, but what could she do? "Thank you for your time, Mr. Spencer."

Olivia leaned back in her chair as she stared off into space.

Chapter 21

As the hours wore on, Olivia was unable to get the conversation with Darryl Spencer out of her mind. What did he know or suspect that he was afraid to tell her? She tried diverting her thoughts to other things, like Jeff, the snow, her dinner that was going to be dried out. Even the dogs couldn't distract her.

It was nine o'clock when Olivia sat down to eat the almost ruined dinner. She chewed her way through her somewhat dry pork chop as she struggled to make sense out of what Spencer hadn't told her. She wondered what would happen if she called him back. Even though he was an old man, his mind seemed sharp, his memory clear. He and his wife had probably talked her phone call to death. If she called him back that

night, she didn't think he'd part with anything. If she waited a day or so and caught
him off guard, he might open up.

But did she want to do that? Why bring
up the man's past? He didn't deserve to be
lied to and grilled just so she could honor
Adrian Ames's last wishes.

Olivia picked at the peach cobbler on
her plate. Where was Jeff? Why hadn't he
called her? Was he stuck out on the highway somewhere? She pushed her plate
away just as the front doorbell rang. The
dogs ran as fast as she did. The moment
she opened the door and Jeff stepped inside, she threw herself into his arms. The
dogs clamored for their share of attention.

"I couldn't call you—my cell battery died
on the way here. I'm starved, honey. Do you
have anything to eat?"

Olivia laughed as she helped Jeff off with
his coat. "I made dinner, but it's kind of
dried out. If you use a lot of gravy, it'll work.
I even made dessert. How bad is it out
there?"

Jeff grinned from ear to ear. "Bad enough
that I won't be able to get to the office tomorrow. That's why I wanted to make it out
here. I think the government will shut down

in the morning, so that means our office will be closed, too. It took me four hours to get out here. Half the time I couldn't see. I pretty much just followed the taillights in front of me."

Olivia beamed her pleasure as she dug into her peach cobbler while Jeff ate his dinner with gusto.

"This is really good, Olivia. I can't remember when I had stuffed pork chops last. My mother makes a casserole a little bit like this. I think I like this one better because I love garlic. I think I'm going to love being married to you if you promise to cook like this every night. I suspect we'll both have to sign up at the closest gym, though."

Olivia beamed at the compliment. Guys never told girls they cooked better than their mothers.

"Tell me, what kind of day did you have?" he asked her between bites.

Olivia told him and concluded, "I don't think it's my imagination, Jeff, I think Mr. Spencer knows something his wife didn't want him to tell me. If he doesn't know it for certain, he suspects something. I was going to call him back, but I don't want to upset him. The poor man doesn't have a dog in this fight, so why pester him?

"Tomorrow, I'm going to call Adrian Ames's attorney, make an appointment, and go on from there. I want this over and done with so I can get back to work."

Olivia poured more wine into Jeff's glass. "Good Lord, I forgot to tell you that Lea called me this afternoon. It was awful. To think I used to like that woman. Money has a way of changing everything for everyone. It's like people who win the lottery. All of a sudden they have all these new friends who want some of the jackpot. I have to decide what I'm going to do with her estate. Something good has to come out of all of this. I just don't know what it is. Right now, my brain feels freeze-dried.

"I want to pay back the money to the insurance company. That's a given. I'm pretty sure Mr. O'Brien can handle that part of it. Once that's done, I have to deal with the rest of the estate, and the payback is barely going to make a dent as far as the rest of the estate goes. I have a couple of ideas floating around inside my head, but I'm afraid to act on them because there's something I'm missing. When I sign off on this, I

want to be satisfied that I've done everything right to the best of my ability. Right
now, I am not satisfied.

"By any chance, Jeff, do you see anything
I'm not seeing? Do you have any ideas or
suggestions?"

Jeff shook his head as he yawned elabo-
rately. "I'm sorry, Olivia, I don't. O'Brien is
an excellent attorney. His firm is top-notch.
Work with them, and I'm sure everything will
be resolved to your satisfaction."

Olivia shrugged as she set about clearing
off the table. When he tried to help she
shooed Jeff and the dogs into the great
room. "Add some logs to the fire, okay?"

Carrying two glasses of wine, Olivia
turned off the kitchen light on her way to the
great room. The dogs looked up at her, their
tails swishing from side to side, as she took
in the situation. Jeff was sound asleep on
the couch. She covered him up before she
settled herself with the dogs on mounds of
pillows by the hearth. So much for romance.

Five days later, Olivia strode down the
hall to Prentice O'Brien's office. They made
small talk about the abominable weather

and canceled appointments in general before they settled down to business.

Olivia tugged at the skirt of her cranberry-colored suit. She opened her purse and withdrew the personal letter Allison Matthews had written to her. She watched the attorney as he read the letter. O'Brien's expression was totally blank when he raised his gaze to meet her own.

"Did you know any of that, Mr. O'Brien?"

"No, Ms. Lowell. I was your mother's attorney, not her confidant. I only met her in person twice. All our business was conducted over the phone or by fax. Now, what is it you want me to do?"

"I want you to find a way to pay back either the bank or the Great Rock Insurance Company of Mississippi without them knowing where the money came from. All of the money is to come from Adrian Ames's estate. I know the case has been closed as well as written off after forty years, but that doesn't change anything. It's the right thing to do, and I want you to do it. You transferred two million dollars into an account. I've withdrawn two hundred and twenty-five thousand. Here's the checkbook," Olivia said, handing it over. "Do you just want one check or the whole book?"

The attorney steepled his fingers against his nose as he stared at Olivia across his desk. "One check will do it. I can deposit the required amount into one of our escrow accounts. I don't anticipate a problem. Is there anything else you want me to do?"

"I'm working on it, Mr. O'Brien. How long will probate take?"

"You have plenty of time to make decisions, Ms. Lowell. Six to ten months, possibly sooner. I might be able to expedite things if you're in a hurry."

"I want it all to be settled as quickly as possible. I'm . . . working . . . What I mean is, I'm toying with several ideas, but nothing is concrete yet. You could start the paperwork on setting up several trusts. One is for Gwen's son, Timothy, and his three children; the other is for Jill's daughter and her children." Olivia reached into her purse again to withdraw a sheaf of papers. "I think you'll be able to locate both of them with the information I wrote down. I'm sorry it's not more conclusive, but it was the best I could do."

"I'll take care of it, Ms. Lowell. What about a trust for any children you might bear in the future? I urge you to do this. Children, as they grow up, want to know about their grandparents. I see the doubt on your face, and I understand your feelings, but, as you said a minute ago, it's the right thing to do. You can decide on an amount for the trusts and let me know at your own convenience. Eighteen years from now, college tuition rates will have quadrupled."

Olivia licked her dry lips. Everything the attorney was saying made sense. She knew Jeff would be agreeable. A trust set up for unborn children didn't mean she herself would be spending the tarnished money. She licked her lips again. "All right. I'll discuss it with my fiancé and get back to you."

"Have you given any thought to the houses and other properties? What about the boat your mother wanted you to purchase for your father?"

Instead of licking her lips, Olivia nibbled on the inside of her cheek. "Well . . . I haven't totally ruled that out, but I have to get back to you on that, too. I'm having a real hard time with all of this, Mr. O'Brien. I feel like I'm being torn in all directions. I didn't ask for this."

Prentice O'Brien leaned back in his chair.

"I've been a lawyer for a long time, Ms. Lowell. Some days I think I've seen and heard it all. One day, I think I might write a book. Then I tell myself no one would believe half of it. I say this because I want you to let go of all the hatred you're feeling toward your mother. I know you don't like me to use that word, but Adrian Ames was your mother. It is not written in stone that you have to love your mother. You don't. What you do have to do is let go of the hatred. If you don't, it will ruin your life. You need to think of this as a bump in the road that you have to cross over to reach your destination.

"I see that ring on your finger. It wasn't there when we spoke last. You're starting off on a new road now, so don't put speed bumps in the way. Like I said, I've seen families torn apart, relationships ruined in situations like this. I don't want to see you as a casualty of your own making.

"I was your mother's attorney for almost thirty years, and I didn't come to know her or understand her any better after all that time than I did at our first meeting. I doubt if anyone knew or understood Adrian Ames. Maybe her corporate attorneys understood her, but I don't see why they would. Maybe those two friends from her college days understood her, but I seriously doubt it."

Olivia clenched and unclenched her fists. Her voice was soft, almost gentle when she said, "She didn't want me. She referred to me as *it*. I think I have a right to feel as I do, Mr. O'Brien."

"Of course you do, but you have to let it go so you can move on and not be hampered by your mother's baggage. Think about it, Ms. Lowell. What exactly has changed in your life since we first spoke? Nothing, except you are suddenly a very rich woman. Everything you did or didn't do, you did willingly. No one forced you to do anything. You want to do the right thing, the decent thing, and setting up those trust funds proves what I just said. I think you should feel proud of how your father raised you. You're an honorable person, Ms. Lowell. Don't throw all of that away. If you don't take anything else away from this meeting, I want you to take this with you. In the end, your mother wanted to make it right."

Olivia bristled. "Then why didn't she do it herself? Why have me do it?"

The attorney seemed to be struggling for

words. "This is just a guess on my part. I think she wanted you to know what kind of person she was. If she had done it herself, you never would have known. There would have been no point in a confession on her part. Hey, I robbed a bank when I was in college—that kind of thing. No, that wasn't Adrian Ames. You can run with this in a hundred different directions. Don't do it. Move on, and don't look back. That's the best advice I can give you."

Olivia stood up, her camel-colored coat on her arm. She nodded and held out her hand. The attorney shook it before he walked her to the door. She was startled when he placed a fatherly hand on her shoulder. "It's all going to work out, Ms. Lowell."

"I hope so," Olivia mumbled.

Olivia sat in her car in the parking lot for a long time. She stared into space, going over and over in her mind what the attorney had said to her. When she finally turned the key in the ignition and drove off, she was clear in her mind that everything Prentice O'Brien said to her was sterling.

But knowing that and acting upon

O'Brien's sage advice were two different things.

Days and weeks flew by, and before Olivia knew it, spring arrived, dressed in every color of the rainbow against a backdrop of green.

Life was routine, so routine, in fact, that Olivia found herself almost bored. She worked steadily but counted the hours until Jeff would arrive nightly.

She finished up for the day, waved good-bye to a poodle named Tiffany and her owner, whose name was also Tiffany, popped open a bottle of cola, and settled back with feet on an ottoman. Her gaze settled on the calendar across the room. It was hard to believe that in another week she'd be turning the page to May. Then the first weekend of the month it would be the Apple Blossom Festival. She looked forward to taking Jeff to the festival.

Would her father come for the festival? He'd never missed one yet. How sad that she'd only heard from him once since he'd asked her to take out the home equity loan on the house. She hadn't heard another word from Lea, either. The March and April mortgage payments had arrived right on time, however. Maybe Dennis was waiting for her to call him. What good was calling someone who never answered the phone?

Olivia was on her way to the kitchen when the doorbell rang. She almost beat the dogs to the door. She laughed, signed her name for the DHL envelope, and carried it with her to the kitchen. The return address said the thick, heavy package was from Prentice O'Brien. She dropped it on the kitchen table, and her heart picked up an extra beat as she moved about the room. With the arrival of the package, everything was suddenly front and center again.

She fixed a cup of black rum tea to fortify herself before opening the package that glared up at her from the table. She stared at it for a while as she sipped her tea. Finally, she ripped at the tab and removed draft documents of the trust agreements. The enclosed letter said she was to read through the documents and get back to O'Brien.

She riffled through the pages. The contents could have been in a foreign language for all she understood. What she did understand was the numbers page that spelled out that all of Gwen's grandchildren's college expenses would be taken care of when it was time for them to go to college. Her son, Timothy, would receive $2000 a month for the rest of his life, while each child would receive $500 a month until he or she reached the age of thirty-five. Cost-of-living increases would be factored in yearly.

Jill's daughter's trust was basically the same in regard to the text, but the numbers were different. Since there were only two children, all college expenses would be paid, and each child would receive $750 a month until the age of thirty-five. Jill's daughter, Mary Louise, would receive $3500 a month for the rest of her life.

The trust booklet for her own unborn children was much thinner, the numbers similar. All college expenses would be paid in full; each child would receive $500 a month until the age of thirty-five. There was no provision for herself.

Everything was in order. All she had to do was sign it, and before long, the trusts would be active.

Olivia reached for the thin, bright red folder and opened it. A single sheet of paper announced that the annual meeting of the board of directors of Adrian's Treasures was scheduled for May 15, a little more than two weeks away. As Adrian Ames's sole heir, she was expected to conduct the meeting. Olivia could feel her eyes start to bulge. No, no, this was all wrong. She wasn't taking control of Adrian's business. No way was she going to the company's headquarters in Baltimore to preside over the annual meeting.

Her back ramrod-straight, her eyes sparking dangerously, Olivia dialed the attorney's private number. She hated it that she was trembling. She didn't bother with amenities when she heard his voice. She went right into her spiel. "No, I am not going to that board meeting. I told you, I don't want any part of Adrian Ames's estate or her business. What do you mean, I have to go? No, no I don't. Obviously, the company is, and has been, doing very well without Adrian at the helm. That has to mean there are some pretty competent people operating the company. Things can continue that way until all the business decisions are made."

Olivia closed her eyes as she listened to the attorney's words. "And who do you think is going to be making all those decisions? Adrian's Treasures has a great many people on its payroll. Those people have families and depend on the company for their salaries and their medical benefits. They want assurances that their livelihood will not change. I'm told morale is not the greatest at the moment. It's been months since Ms. Ames died. Seeing you presiding over the meeting, telling them things will continue, that their jobs are secure, is crucial. It won't take more than ten minutes of your time. Surely you can see your way clear to attending the meeting."

Olivia's shoulders slumped. "Since you put it like that, I guess I don't have any other choice. All right, I'll go. This has to be the end of it, though."

"Ms. Lowell, it isn't that simple. In fact, it's very complicated. I told you that more than once. The firm is working very hard on all matters. As I said, it's extremely complicated. The tax issue alone is mind-boggling. Now, tell me, do the trust documents meet with your approval?"

Olivia drummed her fingers on the countertop. "I didn't read them line for line, if that's what you mean. The numbers meet with my approval. How long will it take before you can start sending money to Gwen and Jill's children?"

"Six weeks, give or take a few weeks either side of it. Do you want me to send out letters ahead of time to apprise them of your intent?"

"No, not yet. I need to come up with something, some story that won't alert them to their mothers' . . . past history. They don't need that kind of grief. Is there anything else, Mr. O'Brien?"

"No, that covers everything for the moment. It's definite, then, that you will attend the meeting in Baltimore."

"Yes, Mr. O'Brien, I will attend the meeting."

Olivia sat down at the table. Her tea was cold, but she drank it anyway. Like it or not, good intentions or bad intentions, she was being sucked into Adrian Ames's world.

And there wasn't a damn thing she could do about it.

Chapter 22

Olivia stared at her reflection in the mirror hanging on the bathroom door. She should have bought a new suit. Or at least had the one she was wearing cleaned again, even though it came out of a plastic bag. Well, it would have to do. She continued to study herself with critical interest. The suit was tailored like any other business suit, charcoal gray, and she wore a crisp white blouse with it. No jewelry except her engagement ring on her left hand, her birthstone ring on her right hand, her watch, and her pearl earrings. She'd taken great pains with her hair and makeup, anguishing over the right eye shadow, just the right lipstick. Her hair was in a French twist. She grimaced. She looked trim, neat, and tidy.

Olivia was almost ready to leave her bedroom when she trotted back to the bathroom and spritzed herself with perfume. She likened the scent to body armor. Now she was ready to leave to make the long drive to Baltimore.

In the kitchen she put down fresh water and dry dog food for the dogs and pee pads by the door. "I'll be back by afternoon, so behave yourselves. Special treats when I get back."

The dogs looked up at her, seeming to understand everything she was saying. No dog-sitter today meant all kinds of wonderful things to do. Olivia eyed them suspiciously, knowing they were up to something. Whatever it was, she would deal with it when she got back.

A mighty sigh at the thought of what awaited her escaped Olivia's lips as she headed for the door—just as the bell rang. She opened it to see a chauffeured limo driver staring at her.

"Yes?"

"I'm David Lerner, your driver. If you're ready, we can leave now. I have coffee in the car and the morning paper, Ms. Lowell."

"Oh," was all Olivia could think of to say. A limo all the way to Baltimore. Well, la-di-da! Coffee and the morning paper. Like she was really going to drink the coffee and take a chance of spilling it down the front of her suit. Like she needed black newsprint all over her hands. She was cranky, there was no doubt about it.

She hadn't slept a wink. Knowing she'd be out of sorts, she'd told Jeff to stay in the District. She'd gone to bed at eleven and tossed and turned till one o'clock, when she got up and pressed her suit. At two o'clock she washed a load of clothes. At three o'clock she cooked bacon and eggs but ended up giving it to the dogs. At four o'clock, she vacuumed the great room, polished the furniture, and folded her laundry. At five o'clock, she took a shower and washed her hair. By seven she was dressed, made-up, and a bundle of nerves.

Here it was, 7:45, and she was in a stretch limo heading for Baltimore, compliments of Adrian's Treasures. She had to admit, it sure beat driving herself.

Olivia did her best to relax in the plush seat of the limo. She tried to think about Jeff and the wedding they were planning for the second week in September, but that didn't work. All she could see in her mind was a long conference table with a group of people eyeballing her, waiting to see what she was going to say about their futures. She wished now that she'd come up with a speech of sorts. Hello and good-bye wasn't going to do it.

Olivia closed her eyes and thought about all the movies she'd seen where the lead actors conducted board meetings. Usually they were men, with secretaries taking notes. Jeff had said she should just be herself. That piece of advice wasn't exactly what she wanted to hear. The board members wouldn't want to see her attitude in regard to Adrian Ames.

She'd called her father before going to bed, but, as had been the case lately, there had been no answer. She was on her own, but for some reason she couldn't get beyond hello and good-bye in her planned speech. Winging it wasn't something she was good at, but that's exactly what she would have to do—wing it. Maybe they'd kick her out. The thought pleased her.

As the miles clicked away, Olivia grew more nervous. She wished she had some chewing gum, something. When she was growing up, her father always gave her a stick of gum when she got nervous over something. Just the act of chewing seemed to calm her. She couldn't remember the last time she'd chewed gum. She wished now that she had left a message for her father to call her back. Maybe he was out on a charter and his cell phone was off. Anything was possible.

The minutes ticked by. Olivia inspected her manicure and cracked her knuckles, a very unladylike thing to do. She spent a few minutes inspecting her shoes, then another few minutes looking to see what exactly was in her purse. Junk.

Finally, the stretch limo slowed and turned into what looked like an industrial area. Tall eight- and ten-floor grimy redbrick buildings could be seen on both sides of the street. The moment the limo stopped, Olivia leaned forward. "Are we here? Is this the corporate headquarters?" There was doubt in her voice with the question.

"Yes, miss. I'll escort you inside. It looks quite different inside than it does out here." The door opened, and a hand reached in to help her out of the car. Swallowing hard, Olivia followed the chauffeur.

She watched as the man pressed a series

of numbers alongside an ugly steel door that opened soundlessly. He was right, the inside was beautiful. An atrium stood smack in the middle, the trees and plants lush and beautiful. Off to the side was a black marble reception desk with a neatly dressed middle-aged woman pecking away at a computer. Cozy sitting areas done in bright rainbow colors were welcoming to any new visitor. On one wall was a glass-enclosed guide to the different floors. She moved closer and studied the board. Floor two was New Products, floor three was Returns, floor four was Human Resources, floor five was Legal Services, floor six simply said Adrian Ames. She didn't get to see what was on floors seven and eight because the chauffeur nudged her elbow to follow him to the elevator.

"We're going to the seventh floor. It's the conference area and dining room," he said cheerfully. "You have ten minutes if you want to freshen up. The lavatory is to the right, the conference room is the second door on the left."

Freshen up. Oh yes. You bet she wanted to freshen up. Anything to postpone entering the conference room. Anything. Her stomach churned unbearably. She couldn't throw up, she just couldn't. Olivia looked down at her watch. Two minutes to go. The hell with two minutes. She marched forward and yanked at the door, almost knocking herself out with the wild *swoosh* of air she'd created. Second door on the left. She took a great, deep breath, held it for five seconds, exhaled, and walked down the hall. She didn't hesitate but grasped the knob and opened the door. She didn't blink at the men and women sitting around the table. Waiting for her.

She took everything in at a glance. The gorgeous spring flowers in the center of the polished teak table, the platters of pastries, the huge silver service on the sideboard with a waitress ready to serve everyone. She wasn't sure, but she thought she saw linen napkins on the sideboard.

Olivia walked around to the head of the table to the only vacant chair. Twelve people watched her progress. She sat down. Directly in her line of vision was a portrait of Adrian Ames. It startled her. Whoever painted the picture had captured the greed and coldness of the woman. She knew instinctively the portrait was meant to be intimidating. Maybe to other people. Never to her.

Olivia let her gaze circle the table. "Please, everyone, relax. I'm Olivia Lowell, Adrian Ames's daughter." She could hear vague greetings of hello, good morning, nice to meet you.

"I really don't have much to say at this time. I apologize for not coming in sooner but this . . . It was such a shock. I want you all to know that I do not intend to make any changes. I would like it if you'd notify all the department heads to tell their people that it will continue to be business as usual. I want to assure you that there are no plans to change membership on the board of directors. Nothing is going to change." Olivia took a deep breath and reached for the coffee cup the waitress was holding out to her. She set it down, looked around, and said, "Well, there is going to be one change. I'm going to implement a bonus program based on years of service to be paid before Christmas. In addition to the bonus program, I noticed that raises fell by the wayside a few years ago, so there will be a ten-percent raise across the board. It will be retroactive to January first of this year. A cost-of-living adjustment will go into effect every six months, January and June.

"If any of you have any questions, ask them now. I probably won't be able to answer them, but I'll try." Olivia looked around. They all looked so serious, so *suspicious.* Why was that? The bonus program and the raise should have caused some kind of positive reaction.

A woman in a severely cut navy blue suit raised her hand slightly. "Carol Vinter, Human Resources. How do we know you'll do what you say? Raises have been promised before but didn't materialize."

Aha. Adrian Ames was not a beloved boss. "When I say something, Carol, I mean it. I would like the legal department to draw up contracts for all of you. Lifetime contracts with everything spelled out. This might be a good time, ladies and gentlemen, to tell you I am not . . . I am not . . . *my mother!* In fact, I didn't even know that Adrian Ames was the woman who gave birth to me until after she died. I had been told my mother died when I was born. This whole"—Olivia waved her arms about— "*thing . . .* has been a bit of a shock to me. When I give you my word on something, it's sterling. That means you can take it to the bank. I am going to have many meetings with the legal department about turning this company over to the employees. I don't have the foggiest idea of how that can be done, but *it will be done*. Not right away, but soon. You can also take that one to the bank."

Olivia leaned back and reached for her coffee cup. She waited while her audience digested what she'd just said. After a few seconds, they all started to jabber at once. Some were smiling. She drained her coffee cup and held it up for a refill. Suddenly she was no longer nervous.

A fiftyish lawyer stood up and said, "We accept what you propose."

Olivia smacked her hands together. "Good! Can I go now?" That got a laugh. She stood up, shook hands with everyone, made small talk, then snatched a cinnamon apple pastry. She munched on it as she made her way down the hall. Her voice boomed before she stepped into the elevator. "Carry on!" Damn, she sounded like General George S. Patton. All she needed was a riding crop. She felt just like the general at that precise moment.

Curled up in the plush burgundy-colored seat, Olivia slept all the way back to Winchester.

The dogs greeted her with enthusiasm. She took a few minutes to play with them before letting them out in the garden. While they played, she popped open a cola and changed into jeans, T-shirt, and sneakers. She carried her cola and her portable phone out to the deck, where she called Prentice O'Brien to report on the meeting. She grinned from ear to ear when she heard the stuffy lawyer gasp and exclaim, "You can't do that!"

"Of course I can do that! I own Adrian's Treasures, Mr. O'Brien."

"But the tax—"

"Deal with it, Mr. O'Brien, or I will find someone else who will be more than happy to bill Adrian's Treasures all those delicious billable hours. I want you to do that raise-and-bonus thing right away. Right away means right away. Like *now*."

Power, Olivia thought, was an aphrodisiac all its own. She felt pleased with herself. She leaned back, the golden sun warming her. She dozed off, her dreams full of wedding dresses and lacy veils.

* * *

It was four o'clock when pandemonium erupted. The doorbell rang—her four o'clock appointment—and the phone lying beside her shrilled to life. She grabbed the phone on the run, heard Jeff's panic-filled voice, and knew instinctively it had something to do with Cecil. The dogs went wild when they saw the golden retrievers and their owner standing in the doorway to the studio. Playtime.

"Just a minute, Jeff," Olivia said, putting him on hold as she stuffed the portable into the pocket of her jeans.

"Mr. Donovan, right on time. Oh, you brought Sonia, Stash, *and* the pups! Okay, go on into the studio and put whatever costumes you want on the dogs. I think I might have a bit of an emergency here. I won't be long. There's a basket of dog treats on the shelf. Help yourself."

Her heart beating extra fast, Olivia clicked back to Jeff. "What? What's wrong?"

"You need to be sitting down for this, Olivia. Are you sitting down?"

"Yes, I'm sitting down. What is it, Jeff?"

"My boss just called me into his office. It seems they found a cousin of Lillian Manning's about twenty-six times removed. He's coming to town as soon as my boss sends him enough money to get his Harley fixed. He's going to move into Lillian's mansion and take care of Cecil. He sounds like one of those biker dudes you see on television all the time."

Olivia started to sputter. "But . . . Lillian appointed you as Cecil's handler. She wanted you to take care of Cecil. It said so in her will. They can't switch up now. You're going to fight this, aren't you? Tell them you want to see bona fide proof that he's related to Mrs. Manning."

"If he is, I'm out on the street. As in 'fired.' Lillian appointed me because she didn't think she had any other relatives. If I don't have a job, we can't get married, Olivia. Worse than that, we lose Cecil. The legal department is the one who found this guy. He didn't come to them. He didn't even know who Lillian Manning was. From what I can gather, which isn't much, he's shiftless, no job, just bums around doing odd jobs. Drinks a lot and sleeps even more. He was arrested on two separate drug charges. The investigative report said he's fathered seven children, all to different women, and pays no child support. He also spends a lot of time in jail. He happens to be roaming free right now. And he's only twenty-three years old. They're going to trust him to take care of Cecil!" Jeff's voice cracked with anger.

Olivia struggled with her breathing. Losing Cecil and not getting married. Talk about a double whammy. Well, that wasn't going to happen. Not if she had anything to say about it. "They would never give Cecil to someone like that! We'll go on television and the newspapers. Listen, Jeff, I have a family of dogs I have to photograph right now. Are you coming out this evening? If so, we'll talk and come up with a plan."

"Are you kidding! I'm halfway to your house right now. I just cut out the minute the old man told me the news. I'll see you in a bit."

Olivia bent down and picked up both Yorkies. She cuddled them close. She swore later to Jeff that they knew what was going on because their little hearts were beating trip-hammer fast. "Easy, easy," she crooned. "You're staying right here. No biker dude is getting his greasy hands on you two."

Olivia carried the two little dogs into the

studio, where she offered treats so everyone would calm down. Her mind a thousand miles away, she proceeded to photograph the beautiful retrievers and their frisky pups.

An hour later, Olivia was on her knees, aiming the camera at the three rambunctious pups, who were squabbling over a ball of bright red yarn. Their owner was laughing uproariously at their antics. The fattest pup bit the littlest one's ear. He in turn bit the darker-colored one on the tail as they got even more tangled in the red yarn. Sonia and Stash barked, then growled, hoping for obedience. When it didn't happen, the mother dog took matters into her own hands—or jaws, if you will—and picked up the fat one in her mouth and deposited him next to the owner's shoes. The father dog picked up the littlest one in his mouth, plopped him on a footstool, and barked, which meant, "Stay put." The darker-colored one looked around as he tried to untangle himself. When nothing happened, he lay down and went to sleep on top of the bright red ball of yarn. Olivia joined the pups' owner in laughter.

"That'll do it, Mr. Donovan. I'll call you in a week with the proofs."

"They keep me young, and they make me laugh," the old man said. "They're wonderful company. I'm keeping all three pups! The bed's going to be a little crowded, but what the heck. Once you get as old as I am, you don't need much sleep."

"Good for you, Mr. Donovan."

Olivia handed out more treats, tussled with the older dogs for a minute, then closed the door. She raced into the kitchen, where Jeff was standing by the window. When he turned she could see he was holding Cecil and Loopy. His eyes were bright with unshed tears.

Olivia could feel her own eyes fill up. "We'll make this come out right, Jeff. If I have to, I'll use every last cent of Allison Matthews's money to make sure you get to keep Cecil. That reject is *not* going to get Cecil. I mean it, Jeff!"

Chapter 23

Jeff hugged the two little terriers close to him as he followed Olivia into the great room. Overhead, the paddle fans whirred softly, late-afternoon sunshine creating a line of sunbeams on the wood floors. Olivia realized that Jeff was so focused on the dogs, he didn't notice all the fresh flowers sitting on the tables. The fact was, he didn't see anything, not even her.

"Damage control, Jeff. That's what we have to do right now. We need to go to the press and the local TV station here in Winchester. The bigger stations, and the AP wire service, will pick it up lickety-split. Cecil is news. We want to show what a great person you are and what good care you give Cecil. You're young, you're good-looking, and you're stable, with a good job.

Forget the fact that people hate lawyers. We'll pose together with the other dogs, showing what a wonderful life Cecil has. Then when that biker dude arrives, we'll arrange to have him photographed along with his police record.

"We'll call the SPCA and every animal organization in the country. The press will eat it up, and people will choose up sides. Your firm is not going to come out smelling real good if they stick with the biker. I think you should go into the office tomorrow to your boss and tell him exactly where you stand in regard to Cecil. You're not giving Cecil up, that's the bottom line. He was traumatized when Mrs. Manning died—he'll be worse if he's taken away from you. We aren't going to be shy about telling the press who I am and who Adrian Ames was. With all that money behind us to fight for Cecil, I think they'll buckle."

The two terriers whimpered in Jeff's tight embrace. "Okay, okay, I like the way that all sounds. But, Olivia, don't we need to know which dog is Cecil?"

Olivia's voice was soft and gentle. "I know which one he is, Jeff." She reached out for one of the terriers, who was whimpering the loudest. "This one is Cecil. He understands everything we've been saying. He knew there was trouble coming when you called earlier. I told you dogs are smart, and this little guy is at the top of the class. I put a little red mark on his tail with a Magic Marker when we were in the studio. This is Cecil!" she said, holding him out for Jeff's inspection. "And," she said, rubbing her nose playfully against Cecil's, "he's staying right here with us and his buddies. That's *my* bottom line."

Cecil looked up at Olivia with adoring eyes. He licked her chin and barked.

"See, he understands, and he *trusts* us. We are not going to let him down. We do have to act fast, though." Cecil squirmed in Olivia's arms. She lowered him to the floor, where he scampered off with his friends to do whatever they did when no one was watching.

Jeff rubbed at the stubble on his chin. "I'm not opposed to any of this, Olivia. I will get fired, that's a given. No one makes waves at my firm. I've never been fired before." His voice was so grim, Olivia winced.

"Fired and famous! Law firms will be forming a line to snap you up for standing by your principles. You'll probably end up with a better job than you have now. Worst-case scenario, you'll hang up your own shingle here in Winchester. The town can always use another lawyer. Bear in mind, animals and their welfare are as American as mom's apple pie and hot dogs. This will be human interest at its best."

"How'd you get so smart?" Jeff teased.

"I don't know about the smart part—I just want to marry you. Maybe that does make me smart. Besides, I love Cecil. We are not giving him up. Maybe something good will really come from Adrian Ames after all. Now, let's have a glass of wine while you tell me everything you know about Lillian Manning. Every single thing, no matter how small or inconsequential you might think it is. First thing tomorrow morning, I want to be geared up to put Operation Cecil into action. I have all kinds of ideas swimming around inside my head. Sort of like Plan A, Plan B, and, of course, Plan C in case things go awry."

Jeff's eyebrows shot upward, then he burst out laughing. "Remind me never to go up against you. You are devious, Olivia Lowell, and I love it!

"Okay, this is what I know about Lillian. She insisted I call her Lillian, said it didn't make her feel so old when people called her by her first name. She wasn't as rich as the papers made her out to be. The main reason she left her estate to Cecil was because she thought she didn't have any other relatives. I made sure to do an extensive search, and this guy didn't show up anywhere. It's possible he was born on the wrong side of the blanket. If Lillian had known about the guy the firm found, I'm sure she would have mentioned him with a bequest in her will. That's the only sticky part I can think of that might bite us. Well, maybe there is one other thing. Ambrose Martindale was a personal friend of Lillian Manning and handled her affairs for years and years until Lillian requested some 'young blood,' which is why he assigned me to manage her affairs and draw up her will. She and I really hit it off.

"I'm digressing. When everything was said and done, she had a little over five million dollars, not the hundred and fifty million the papers said she had, but certainly more than enough to see Cecil through his final years. There was a special fund she had set aside to pay for one cook/housekeeper for twelve years. She paid her property taxes on the house for those same twelve years. Of course, if they raise the taxes in the future, the funds will have to come from the main account. There were, like, six or seven bank accounts set up to pay various household bills, outside maintenance, car upkeep, that sort of thing. There isn't much in the accounts, but there is enough to take care of things. There was even an account set up for me as Cecil's handler. I never touched a penny of it. I couldn't take the money. Taking care of Cecil, ill prepared as I was, was more of a favor than a job. Lillian had it all down to a science. She said she wasn't taking any chances that things would go awry. According to her will—and, by the way, I drew up the will—after . . . after Cecil is gone, the remainder of her estate is to go to various animal funds. Those are the people we need to get in touch with so they can rally round to protect their future inheritance. I'm the executor of the will.

"Did I ever tell you that she had every picture you ever took of Cecil hanging in her bedroom? Didn't you ever wonder why she wanted so many pictures?"

"No, not really. I just knew she loved that little dog. She was so pleased when I made him Mister July on last year's calendar. She hugged me. She did tell me she loved Cecil more than she had loved either one of her husbands. We both had a good laugh over that. She had a wicked sense of humor. I liked that."

Jeff laughed. "She told me the same thing. Now what?"

Now what, indeed? "I'm going to call an old friend I grew up with who works at the *Winchester Star* and ask her to come by early in the morning. We want to get this in the papers *before* you get fired. While I'm doing that, you can get us some wine."

Wineglasses in hand, dogs at their side, Olivia and Jeff plotted and planned. Planned and plotted. They gave some thought to scheming and manipulating, but in the end they decided just to go for the jugular.

Dee Dee Pepper, Winchester's ace reporter and photographer, arrived at 509 Eagle Drive at 6:00 A.M. on a bright red motor scooter that matched her flaming red hair, which in turn matched her freckled face.

She hopped off the scooter, slung her camera over her shoulder, and marched up to the front door, where Olivia and Jeff were standing. The two women hugged, reminisced for a few minutes, then got down to business.

"Damn!" the reporter said when Olivia finally wound down. "We gotta do this real quick if you want it in tomorrow's paper, and you have to trust me, Ollie, okay? Hey," she hissed, "that's some good-lookin' guy you got there. Does he have a friend?"

Olivia laughed. "I don't know, but I'll ask. I'm going to kiss him good-bye now, so don't look!" Dee Dee grinned as she turned around.

The dogs liked the laughing young woman in the Doc Martens who romped in the yard with them as she snapped and snapped her camera. "Dogs need green grass, bushes to lift their legs on, and other dogs to play with for a full and rounded life," Dee Dee babbled as she continued clicking and clicking her Nikon. When Cecil dug up a bone from under an azalea bush, she snapped again as he proudly laid it at her feet.

The photo op took all of twenty-three

minutes before Dee Dee shoved the digital camera back into its case. "With the pictures I took of Jeff cuddling Cecil and the ones I just took, I feel we have a really good pictorial. After I download and tweak these, I'm going to write up my article. Since time is of the essence, I need to know if you trust me enough to go to press without your okay? I can fax it to you, but it will be after the fact. You okay with that, Ollie?"

"Sure. Just do a good job, okay? How can we get it in the *Post* and *USA Today*?"

Dee Dee laughed. "Hey, this is me. If I have to, I'll hand-deliver it to them. They'll run it tomorrow. You owe me, Ollie. Make sure you ask that hunk of yours to bring a friend out this way. I'm getting a little tired of being a bachelorette. I find myself longing for that little house with a white picket fence. My clock is ticking. Damn, he's good-lookin'. Way to go, Ollie."

Olivia took a step backward. The young woman was a whirlwind as she raced through the door and out to her motor scooter. Olivia knew she was in good hands.

And all of this had happened before she'd had her first cup of coffee.

Olivia crossed her fingers the way she used to do when she was little. Then she scooped up Cecil, checking to make sure she had the right dog, and whispered in his ear. The little guy yapped happily before she set him back on the floor.

After playing with the dogs for a while, Olivia was waiting for the coffee to brew when she looked at the clock on the kitchen wall. Jeff should be at the office already. Was he talking to his boss, or was he steeling himself to get up the nerve to do it? She crossed her fingers again as she made a wish that her fiancé wouldn't get fired, but she knew it was a fruitless wish. *Think positive, think positive*, she told herself over and over.

Jeff straightened his tie, smoothed back his unruly hair, and shrugged under his jacket so it would settle more evenly around his shoulders. Time to beard the lion. And Ambrose Martindale was a lion with a roar that had no equal. *Yeah, well, I can roar, too*, Jeff thought, when a vision of Cecil romping in the yard passed before him.

Jeff looked around his office, which he'd packed up on the fly. There wasn't much left—the pictures of his family, a shaving kit complete with toothbrush and a whitening toothpaste, along with his nail clippers. His briefcase, a gift from his parents when he'd graduated from law school and now containing the personal files he had downloaded from his computer, along with his day planner, had already been placed in the trunk of his car.

Standing in the doorway, Jeff wondered if he'd made a mistake in not calling Martindale's secretary to ask for an appointment. *Too late now,* he thought, taking the elevator to the top floor, where Ambrose Martindale reigned supreme.

The middle-aged secretary, who was stuffed into a peach-colored suit, looked like she could roar as loud as Martindale. She sat primly behind the polished desk that held only a computer and a phone console. She looked up from the computer screen, a frown on her face.

"Yes?"

"I'm Jeff Bannerman, I work on the sixth floor, and I'm also Cecil's handler. I need to speak with Mr. Martindale. *Now.*"

"Everyone wants to speak to Mr. Martindale. Unfortunately, that simply isn't possible today. Every minute of Mr. Martindale's day is accounted for, and your name is not on any of those minutes."

"Well, that's too bad," Jeff said. "Just tell him I am not giving up Cecil to some long-lost relative of Lillian Manning. Lillian wanted me to take care of Cecil, and that's what I'm going to do. If Mr. Martindale wants to sue me, tell him to feel free to do so, but also tell him I will go to the wall to keep Cecil. Another thing, tell him *I quit!*"

Jeff turned on his heel but not before the secretary's jaw dropped. She blinked rapidly as she tried to come to terms with the message she was to give to her boss.

Jeff was almost to the door when she said. "You're quitting over a dog, is that the gist of your message?"

"Not just any dog. Cecil is the dog that inherited Lillian Manning's estate. I'm his handler." He opened the door, then closed it behind himself with a loud bang. Well, quitting was better than getting fired. He supposed he would have to quickly type up his resignation and take it down to personnel. Well, hell, he could do that. As a matter of fact, it would give him great pleasure to do just that.

He'd quit, that was the important thing. He hadn't gotten fired.

The elevator stopped on the sixth floor, where he raced over to the secretary he shared with three other lawyers on his floor. "Type up a resignation letter and print it out so I can sign it. I want to drop it off at personnel on my way out. Snap to it, Hillary—I can't wait to get out of here." He realized suddenly that what he said was the truth. He really couldn't wait to get out of the steel-and-glass building with its recycled air and artificial plants. Hanging out his own shingle was starting to look better and better. His own boss. A small office in Winchester. His clients would be his neighbors, his friends. He'd be a member of the community. Yep, it was looking better and better.

Jeff scrawled his name above his printed name the minute the printer spit out his resignation letter. Holding it in his hand, he walked around the corner to his office, where he saw a tall man in a thousand-dollar suit standing in the doorway looking around.

Ambrose Martindale. The lion had come down to the cub's floor.

"Excuse me, sir," Jeff said, inching his

way past the tall, imposing figure. He wore gold cuff links. Ha!

"Ambrose Martindale," the tall man, said extending his hand. Jeff ignored it. "Are you Jeff Bannerman? I believe we spoke on the phone yesterday. When we finished our conversation, I was under the impression you were a team player and on board."

"Yes sir, I am Jeff Bannerman. One should never assume or presume anything in this life, as I've just found out," Jeff said, not missing a beat as he picked up the box with his personal belongings. "Here!" he said, holding out his resignation letter to the head of the firm. "You might as well take this and save me a trip to personnel." He was out the door a second later, heading for the elevator.

"Hold on there, young fellow. I want to talk to you!"

Jeff didn't bother to turn around. "Your secretary said every minute of your day was accounted for," he shouted over his shoulder, "and my name wasn't on any of those minutes. I'm in a hurry. By the way, I don't work here anymore. I quit. That's my resignation you're holding in your hand." Reaching the elevator, he stabbed at the down-arrow button and waited.

The thousand-dollar suit had finally caught up to him. The pewter-gray eyes flashed angrily. "I want to talk to you, young man. I will not tolerate such behavior. Lillian Manning was a personal friend for many years. I will not allow you to turn this . . . mess into a circus. Well?"

"I think, Mr. Martindale, you said everything you had to say to me yesterday. Today it's my turn. I'm not giving up Cecil to some drugged-up jailbird who didn't even know Lillian Manning. Mrs. Manning's will clearly states that I am to take care of Cecil. I don't want the money, I never drew a penny of it. If you want to sue me, sue me, but you're going to have one hell of a fight on your hands because I'll fight this firm till hell freezes over, and then I'll fight you on the ice.

"I wish I could say it's been a pleasure working here, but it hasn't been a pleasure, Mr. Martindale."

The elevator door slid open. Jeff stepped aside to allow three other lawyers, with whom he had a nodding acquaintance, to pass him. He stepped into the elevator just as the lion roared at him, "Get back here, Bannerman!"

"In your dreams, Martindale. In your dreams!" Jeff mumbled to himself as the elevator descended to the lobby.

Chapter 24

Olivia hopped into her car and headed for Valley Road to Gaunt's Drug Store, where she bought a prepaid phone card. She didn't know why, but each time she walked into the drugstore, she had a vision of Patsy Cline, the singer, behind the counter where she'd once worked as a soda jerk. The soda fountain was gone now, but there was a cutout of the singer in the front window these days.

Olivia stuck the card in her pocket and waved to the owner, Harold Madigan, as she left in search of the nearest phone booth, where she proceeded to make two phone calls. The first call was to the local TV channel. She rattled off Cecil's story and gave them Jeff's cell phone number to call for confirmation. With nothing exciting going on in Winchester at the moment, she knew the station would run with the information she provided. Her second call was to WINC, the local radio station, where she again rattled off the same information and offered up Jeff's cell phone number for confirmation for the second time.

Pleased with herself, she went back to her car and headed for South Pleasant Valley Road to Martin's, where she shopped for groceries to shore up her freezer and pantry. Her cell phone rang just as she inserted the key in the ignition. Joy and elation rang in her voice when she said, "Jeff! What happened? How did it go? Tell me everything! Did you get fired?"

"No, I didn't get fired! I quit, Olivia! I quit! I beat them to the punch. I'm unemployed! Do you still want me?"

Olivia laughed. "Do I need air to breathe? Of course I still want to marry you, and we are not postponing the wedding, either. What happened?"

"Listen, I have a call coming in. I'm on my way back to Winchester. We'll talk later. Love you!"

Before Olivia could return the endearment, the connection was broken. She smiled. Being in love was so wonderful. She beamed her happiness, waving to a few neighbors and acquaintances as she made her way out of the parking lot.

Her watch told her she had to hustle because she had an eleven o'clock appointment to photograph a schnauzer named Annabell—a holy terror who wanted nothing more than to bite everyone she came in contact with. It was obvious the dog's owner, a Mrs. Collins, had absolutely no control over the animal. Annabell also had a weak bladder. Olivia was not looking forward to dealing with Annabell and her owner, who always insisted on staying for the session so she could have "input."

Arriving home just at eleven, Olivia carried in her perishables and shoved everything in the refrigerator before she escorted a snapping, snarling Annabell into the studio.

Annabell's owner said she would not be able to stay owing to a hair-cutting appointment. "I'll be at Today's Hair in case you need to reach me." Olivia just nodded, relieved that she wouldn't have to contend with the arrogant woman. The angry dog was enough of a challenge.

The minute Mrs. Collins closed the door

behind her, Annabell hopped up on the bench and stared at Olivia as if to say, let's get with it. Olivia reached for her camera, focused, and snapped. Annabell stretched, yawned, moved to show her profile, first the left, then the right. Olivia clicked with the speed of light, muttering over and over, "You little ham! Keep this up and you definitely have a shot at being Ms. September. C'mon, c'mon, show me some leg!" Annabell dutifully stretched out her front leg and demurely looked downward. "Attagirl! You got it! Smile now!" Annabell showed her teeth. Olivia laughed till her sides hurt.

When Annabell had enough of the bench she hopped down and sprinted over to the red wagon and sat down. Again she posed, turning this way and that way. Olivia laughed and laughed. When Annabell had enough of the red wagon, she scooted out and ran over to the rocking horse, backed up a step, and hopped into the leather saddle. She reached for the leather strap and held it in her teeth. When the horse started to rock, Olivia sat down, angling the camera as she continued to laugh. "Good girl, Annabell! Yep, you are definitely Ms. September. And for being so good, here's a chewie!"

Olivia was still sitting on the floor laughing when Jeff walked into the studio. His hair was on end, his jacket slung over his shoulder, his tie askew. He looked like a wild man. Olivia continued to laugh as Annabell, clutching her chew, joined the other dogs. "You know what, Jeff? That dog hates her owner."

"That's a shame. The dog must be really unhappy. Where did he go?"

"He's a her. Her name is Annabell. When her owner is around she's just awful. The minute she left, she was just fine. She posed like a pro before she ran off to play with the others."

Jeff nodded as though he understood perfectly even though his mind was a million miles away.

"Tell me everything," Olivia prompted.

"Well, for starters, I didn't get an appointment with Mr. Martindale. His secretary told me every minute of his day was accounted for, and my name wasn't on any of those minutes, so I left a very curt, concise message and said I quit. I quit, Olivia. I didn't give the firm a chance to fire me. I knew I was going to quit, so I'd packed up my stuff before I went up to the lion's floor. Even downloaded my personal files and took my day planner, along with my briefcase, to the car. That's what everyone calls Martindale, the lion. I think he knows and is rather smug about the whole thing. I had Hillary type up my resignation and was on my way to personnel with it when Martindale caught up with me at the door to my office. I really didn't give him the time of day. He wasn't even sure who I was. Didn't do much for my confidence. Hell, I'd already bitten the bullet, so I just kept right on going to the elevator, talking to him over my shoulder. I even shoved my resignation in his hand, saving me a trip to personnel. That's about it. Oh, he said he wasn't going to allow me to turn this mess, that's what he called it, a mess, into a circus. I don't have a job, Olivia."

"I do. We won't starve. Now you are free and clear. Let's get to work on Cecil. You didn't say anything about the TV and radio stations. I gave them your cell phone number. Did they call you?"

Jeff slapped at his forehead. "Jeez, I almost forgot to tell you. Both stations called, and I gave them an earful. They sounded like they were on our side. Give me ten minutes to change my clothes, and I'm all yours."

Olivia stood up and was instantly kissed by Jeff. "Go!" she gasped before she pulled away. "Annabell's owner will be here any second. I have a few things I have to do in here because I have a one o'clock appointment with an Airedale. You can carry in the groceries I left in the car and make us lunch. I'm pretty hungry."

Jeff made a low, sweeping bow before he trotted off to do her bidding. He blew her a kiss that she returned with loud, smacking gusto.

Olivia's mood turned sour when the dogs barreled into the studio at the sound of Annabell's owner's car. The hair immediately went up on the schnauzer's back. Her new best friends joined in the frantic yapping. Olivia's heart thudded in her chest when the doorbell rang outside the studio. She opened the door, and Mrs. Collins, sporting a new haircut, sailed through. Olivia thought she looked like a broomstick with feathers on the end of it.

The woman tried to coax Annabell to her, and when the dog refused to listen, she started to scream about keeping Annabell in her crate for a week. Annabell sneaked around a stool and nipped her owner on her leg. Mrs. Collins howled. The other dogs, Cecil leading the pack, circled her showing their tiny teeth. Mrs. Collins continued to howl as she tried to catch Annabell, who raced away and tried to hide under the little red wagon. The little dog was trembling, and Olivia rushed to pick her up.

"Give her to me," her owner screeched. She reached out to snatch the dog, and Annabell snarled and bit down on her hand.

Olivia's heart was beating just as fast as the schnauzer's. What the heck was going on? What kind of dog owner was this? "I don't think so, Mrs. Collins. I'm not sure, but I think you've been abusing this dog. She isn't biting me, as you can plainly see. In fact, she's shaking badly, which tells me she's afraid of you. I think I'm going to call Animal Cruelty and let you fight it out with them. Be aware that if I file a complaint like that, it will get into the newspapers. Before that happens, why don't you let me buy Annabell from you?"

"Buy? Buy? You can have her! I've done everything I could for that stupid dog. She pees wherever she feels like it. I have to keep her in her crate most of the time or she'd ruin my entire house. My husband wanted this stupid dog, not me. She bites everyone. She's nothing but trouble. Don't bother calling Animal Cruelty, and don't think I'm paying for those photographs, either. She's all yours! And don't even think about giving her back!"

Olivia cuddled the schnauzer to her chest. The little dog was calmer now, as though she understood she wouldn't be leaving with the screeching woman.

Olivia sucked in her breath as she stroked the little dog. "I'm more than willing to pay for Annabell. She's a wonderful little dog. Which vet do you take her to?"

The woman laughed. "Figure it out for yourself!" She slammed the door behind her. The dogs started to bark and growl as they raced, a nanosecond too late, to the door.

Jeff poked his head in the door. "Lunch is ready!"

"We have a new dog!" Olivia said brightly. "Annabell will be staying with us from now on. She might be hungry, Jeff. By the way, what are we having for lunch?"

"BLTs with lots of leftover bacon for the dogs. I nuked it, so it's okay to give them as a treat. As you said, less nitrates that way. That's great, you can never have too many dogs," Jeff said, tickling Annabell behind the ears. "She's a cutie."

Olivia linked her arm with Jeff's. The dogs fell in line as they trooped into the kitchen. "I feel like the Pied Piper." Olivia giggled.

The minute Olivia and Jeff sat down to eat their lunch Cecil pawed Jeff's leg and Annabell pawed Olivia's leg. They weren't begging for food, they just wanted to be picked up and cuddled. Olivia bit down on her lower lip, but not before she saw Jeff's wet eyes. She pretended she didn't notice. "I think this little gal knows she's staying here, don't you?"

Jeff cleared his throat. "That would be my guess. I brought a copy of Lillian's will with me."

Alice and Loopy barked as Bea tried to outdo them both by growling. Cecil and Annabell joined the fray, and Olivia and Jeff were left to eat in peace and quiet.

The phone rang just as Olivia crunched up her napkin. She reached for it, clicked it on, and heard Miki Kenyon's voice. She wiggled her eyebrows at Jeff. She took the initiative. "Still can't find her, huh?"

"No, it's almost as though she dropped off the face of the earth." Miki was, of course, referring to Jill Laramie. "No charge, Ms. Lowell. Do you want us to keep trying, or do you want to let it go for now?"

"Right now I'm of a mind to let it all go, Miki. She's gone to ground. If I change my mind, I'll give you a call."

"Okay, honey, you're the boss. This is only the second time we failed to find our subject. She's good, I'll give her that. Take care. We'll talk again."

Olivia clicked off the connection. She looked over at Jeff. "That was the detective agency. Miki calls once a week. They still can't find Jill Laramie. I told her to let it go. Mr. O'Brien is supposed to be sending all of the money back to the bank. I'm surprised he hasn't called me. I guess there's a possibility he didn't send the check yet. Still, I made sure he knew how important it was to do it ASAP."

Jeff laughed. "You know us lawyers—we march to our own drummer." His eyes wide, he stared across the table at Olivia. "It's really starting to hit me now. I don't have a job. I've always had a job, from the time I was eleven and delivered papers."

"How about if I hire you as Advisor to the CEO of Adrian's Treasures? On a temporary basis, or until we can all figure out what to do with the company. Forever, if you like the job and whatever perks go with it. I'm going to need someone I can trust on the inside to report to me. The job has to go to someone. Who better than you? I was thinking the other day about asking my dad, but I don't think he'd do it for any amount of money. The job is yours if you want it. It would be a *real* job, Jeff, not something I'm making up just so you have a job. We could convert the garage to an office. I never keep my car in there anyway, and it's a double garage, which means there's plenty of room. More and more people are working at home these days, with all the modern technology available. You'd have to go to the corporate offices in Baltimore every so often, but that would be it. Will you at least think about it?"

"I will. I decided. I'll take the job!"

There was such relief in her fiancé's face, Olivia smiled. "Then all we have to do is negotiate a salary. What do you think is fair?"

They got down to it then, tooth and nail,

but it was all in fun. In the end, both agreed
that the position was worth $200,000 a year,
with medical benefits, a two-million-dollar
life insurance policy, and a 401(k). They
shook hands in a businesslike way. Then
Jeff really clinched the deal by kissing
Olivia.

Her eyes starry, Olivia whipped out her
cell phone with one hand and handed the
portable phone to Jeff with the other. "We
need to call all the animal organizations Lillian left bequests to and the ones who will
inherit . . . down the road. Then I think I
should take you to dinner at Two-Twenty
Seafood over on Route 7. It's on the out-
skirts of town. You'll love it. I want to celebrate having the good sense to hire you.

"Oh, one more thing. Do you have a friend
who might be interested in dating Dee Dee?
He has to be as good-looking as you and
just as nice."

"Damn, Olivia, I like the way you do business. It's a deal! I know just the guy—Tom
Ethridge. He has a law practice in Berryville
but lives in town. Let's make a date for this
weekend."

Olivia smacked her hands together. "I

love it when things work out. Just love it, love it, love it!"

The *Winchester Star* was hand-delivered the following morning by Dee Dee herself. She was beaming from head to toe as Olivia herded her and the dogs into the kitchen, where Jeff was making pancakes. "We got you a date for this Saturday," she hissed in her friend's ear. "How cool is that, my friend? Jeff said he's handsome, practices law over in Berryville, but lives right here in Winchester."

"Great! Now read my article. We got the top half of the fold, and it doesn't get any better than that. Jeff's firm called the paper four times before I left the office, and it's"— Dee Dee looked at her watch—"only seven-fifteen. My boss called Sally Blake to come in to help handle all the phone calls he knows will be coming in. This stuff is hot news for Winchester. What's really good is, we got the scoop. I owe you, Olivia."

Jeff turned off the stove to join the women at the table. Dee Dee handed him his own copy to peruse. He whistled at what he was reading. "You have a way with words, Ms. Pepper," he drawled. "The firm will be drawing up all kinds of motions. I'll bet they have people at the courthouse already just waiting to file those papers."

Olivia and Dee Dee looked at Jeff. "What kind of papers? What will they try to do?"

"Well, for starters, I can almost guarantee the firm is going to file a petition to have me removed as Cecil's handler. From there it will grow legs and take off. That means someone will be coming here with a court order to take Cecil away from us. They're going to say it's all about the money even though I never took a penny for his care."

As one, Olivia and Dee Dee exclaimed, "Over my dead body!"

Jeff leaned across the table. "Then, Ms. Pepper, write a follow-up for tomorrow's paper. What's the last second we can feed you news?"

Dee Dee hopped up from the chair she was sitting on. "Six this evening. Sorry about the pancakes, gotta run. Relax, Ollie, this is what I do to earn my living. No one is going to take Cecil. If I have to, I'll appeal to the whole town to come here and protest. If either of you has any ideas, this might be a good time to implement them, but don't tell me what they are." The combat boots stomped across the floor as the small pack of dogs raced her to the door. They gave her a rousing, yapping send-off.

"One stack of pancakes coming right up," Jeff said, heading for the stove. "This is going to be one hell of a day, Olivia. We need to fortify ourselves."

Little did he know how right he was.

Chapter 25

Jill Laramie's peach-colored spring jacket flapped in the early-morning breeze. Her stride was brisk as she made her way across the Ole Miss campus. Her destination was the library, where she went every day to read the morning papers. She could have subscribed to the papers or read them online, but she preferred to come here to the library and pretend she was part of the life there. She looked over her shoulder a half dozen times to see if anyone was following her. Satisfied there was no one on her trail, she walked even faster. She never felt safe these days unless she was inside a building.

It was no way to live, and she knew it. The anxiety and the stress had taken a toll on her these past few months. She hated looking in the mirror, hated the way she looked, hated the way she was living. On any given day she burst into tears at least a dozen times.

Jill nodded to several people she saw on a daily basis. One man in particular, a part-time professor at Ole Miss by the name of Alan Freeman, had invited her for coffee at Starbucks several times. If she wasn't so paranoid, she would have enjoyed a little get-together. He was more than a little interested, even inviting her to dinner and once to a concert. She'd declined all invitations with ridiculous excuses because she was afraid. Now she regretted those decisions. It was the story of her life—refusing to let anyone get close because at any given moment she might have to cut and run. Still, there was a lightness to her step when she made her way to the table where she usually sat to pore over the daily papers and saw Professor Freeman already at the table, a copy of *USA Today* in front of him.

Jill smiled, a genuine expression of warmth. She wished she could have met this man years ago. Before . . . before she'd ever met Allison Matthews.

Alan Freeman looked the part of the

absentminded professor. During the winter months he dressed in baggy tweeds. In the spring and summer he wore wilted seersucker. His hair was beyond the thinning stage, and his features were, at best, hawkish. It was his eyes, bright and curious, and his warm smile that drew her to him. He was gentle and soft-spoken. Outside the classrooms, he smoked a pipe, as did most of the older professors. A widower, he'd returned to Ole Miss when his wife of thirty years had died of ovarian cancer.

Alan only taught part-time because of his other interests, which were many and varied. He lived in a charming old house in Oxford. She'd driven by it one night just as it was turning dusk. She loved the old oaks, with their hanging moss, the Confederate jasmine that climbed and trailed over the ornate fencing and trellises. The house itself was set back from the street and surrounded by dozens of gardenia and azalea bushes. A magnificent magnolia tree, taller than the three-story house, stood sentinel at its side. Alan said that in June the tree was full of fragrant white flowers. The house, he'd gone on to say, had belonged first to his grandfather, then his own father, and now he owned it. He'd laughed, a wonderful sound, when he said the house was a work in progress, and the main reason why he only taught part-time. Jill suspected that Alan Freeman was independently wealthy.

If only she could live in a house like that with someone like Alan Freeman, her cup would, indeed, run over. It wasn't going to happen, though, and she knew it. Not with her past or current life. Still, it was fun to dream.

Jill sat down and smiled shyly at the man sitting across from her. "Anything new in the world today?"

Alan laughed, a quiet sound, as he pushed part of the paper across the table toward her. "I found this extremely interesting," he said, pointing to a large picture below the fold on the front page. "Great human interest. What do you think, Caroline?" Alan asked, using her new alias of Caroline Summers.

Jill stared down at a picture of Olivia Lowell holding a small dog. Next to her was a handsome young man. She was glad she wasn't holding the paper in her hands because she would have dropped it in shock.

Her hands in her lap, Jill speed-read the

article, knowing that Alan expected a comment. She hoped she could make her voice work. "Hmmm," she said. Her head bobbed up and down, her eyes behind their green contact lenses exceptionally bright.

"My wife and I had a dog once that we loved dearly. With no children of our own, Sophia, that was the dog's name, became our child. There was nothing we wouldn't have done for that dog. We were devastated when she died at the age of fifteen. We literally could not function for weeks. All we did was cry. I know how that young couple feels."

"Hmmm," Jill said again. What were the odds of her seeing this particular article at this particular time in her life? She allowed herself to slump down on the hard wooden chair. She was never going to get away from her past.

"I guess you had a similar experience, I can see it in your face. Listen, Caroline, let's go over to Starbucks and get a cup of coffee."

All she wanted to do was get out of there. Common sense told her an article like the one she'd just read didn't have anything to do with her. That same common sense told her where there was smoke, fire was sure to follow. Reporters were going to start digging, and when they found out that Olivia Lowell was Adrian Ames's daughter, the connection to Allison Matthews would be revealed as surely as night follows day. Sooner or later, the past was going to jump up and hit her hard. That was a given. A chill unlike anything she'd ever experienced rivered through her body.

Jill picked up her purse. It was time to run again. She felt like crying until she felt Alan's hand cup her elbow. She forced herself to look up at the man towering above her. She smiled. She knew then she didn't want to give *this* up, whatever *this* was or turned out to be. As much as she didn't want a cup of Starbucks coffee, she said, "Sounds good."

Just do something ordinary, she cautioned herself. *Coffee at Starbucks is ordinary. Try not to think about Olivia Lowell and the article in the paper. Oh, God, I don't want to run again. I don't have the stamina. I'm over sixty, and that's too old for this. I can't do this anymore.*

Jill looked around her garden apartment. In all the years since she'd graduated from college, this was the first place, the first time that she truly felt like she was home. The apartment was cozy, filled with brand-new furniture. She'd painted the walls herself, a shade of paint called Distant Mountain. It made the rooms look bigger. She cooked in the kitchen, did her laundry in a little closet off the master bedroom, soaked in the Jacuzzi with scented candles and fragrant bath salts. Subconsciously, she thought she'd made the decision to stay right there and stop running. For some ungodly reason, the apartment felt *permanent*. She'd paid her rent a year in advance when she'd signed the three-year lease, another sign she'd been thinking of the place as a permanent abode.

Who was she kidding? She could blast out of there with a moment's notice. *Old habits die hard*, she thought when she looked at the small travel bag that was packed in the corner. All she had to do was pick it up, and she was gone.

Her shoulders straightened as she walked over to the corner and picked up the bag. She plopped it down on the bed, opened it, and took everything out. She zipped the bag shut and shoved it into the closet. Everything else went in drawers or on hangers.

Done.

She was finished with running. She'd been running one way or another ever since Allison Matthews had revealed the role she and Gwen had to play *after* the robbery. But things got much worse the night that odious old man from the bank, Allison Matthews's former boss, decided that in addition to the usual services she provided, he wanted *her*, and for the three nights of the annual Faulkner conference, have her he did. And that was how she became pregnant with Mary Louise, and that was why she had been emotionally dysfunctional ever since, unable to be a mother to her child, a wife to her husband, a grandmother to her grandchildren. But now the running was over. Things had to change. And change they would.

Confession was good for the soul.

Sleeping soundly at night was something to dream about.

She wanted to get to know Alan Freeman better.

That was her bottom line.

Jill looked in her refrigerator, wondering

what she was going to make for dinner. She finally selected a small steak and set it on the sink to thaw. She made fresh coffee even though she didn't really want it. It was something to do while her mind raced.

The next two hours were spent on the phone and her laptop. After packing up her laptop, she made her dinner, ate quickly, washed the dishes, and changed her clothes.

At five o'clock Jill closed and locked her apartment door. She drove to Memphis, where she boarded a flight that would take her to Charleston, South Carolina. In Charleston she rented a car, drove to Summerville, and took a room at the Hampton Inn, which was just a mile or so away from where Gwen lived.

That night Jill Laramie slept like an innocent child. It was the first full night's sleep she'd had in over forty years.

The minute she woke and looked at her small travel clock, she knew she'd made the right decision in coming there.

Jill showered, dressed, and checked out. She didn't bother with coffee or breakfast but climbed in the car, looked down at the directions lying on the passenger seat of the car. Within minutes, she was knocking on the door of Gwen's trailer. When the door opened, the two women looked at each other and burst into tears. "Come in, come in," said Gwen.

Dozens of cats scattered in every direction. *At least Gwen has someone to love her*, Jill thought, her arm still around her old friend.

"Would you like some coffee? It's instant."

"Sure," Jill said, looking around. Everything was shabby but neat and tidy.

"I guess it's time, huh?" Gwen called from the kitchen area.

"I'm afraid so, Gwen. I don't know about you, but I can't live like this anymore. Let's just get it over with."

"But I thought . . ."

Jill whipped out a copy of *USA Today* and handed it to Gwen. "You don't have to be a rocket scientist to know how all of this is going to go down. You know how reporters are. I'm so sick of the lies, the running, can't take it anymore. I swear, Gwen, if that woman hadn't died, I think I was capable of killing her myself."

Gwen handed Jill a cup of coffee. She

slurped at her own. "I want to make sure I understand, Jill. Are you saying we're finally going to tell the *whole* truth and not that story we've stuck with all these years?"

Jill blinked as she sipped at the scalding coffee. "Yes." She looked around. "Why didn't you tell me you were living like this? I would have given you money."

"Because we agreed. I screwed up, and this is the result. I didn't want you to see what . . . You know what? It doesn't matter. When the girl came here, I stayed with our script."

"I did, too. Still, you should have told me. I would have helped you. Listen, I booked us on an afternoon flight to Washington, D.C. Can you find someone to take care of your cats till you get back? I'll give you the money, Gwen."

"What . . . what if I . . . can't come back? What happens to my cats?"

Jill pointed to the paper lying on Gwen's ample lap. "I don't think that girl will let anything happen to your cats. Now, do you have enough cat food to put out?"

"Just bought a big bag yesterday along with fresh kitty litter. They'll be good for a couple of days. Are you sure, Jill?"

Jill ran her hands through her hair. "I'm sure, Gwen. Look, no offense, but you and I have to go shopping. I saw a store called Belk's on my way here. We'll get you outfitted, have some lunch, then head for the airport. Is that okay with you?"

"I guess so. Should I call my son?"

"Not yet, Gwen. Things might not go our way, even though I think they will. Let's not look for trouble ahead of time. I didn't tell Mary Louise." Tears spurted in Jill's eyes.

"Don't cry, Jill. Now that we're at the end of the road, maybe somehow we can make it right. If we can't, then so be it."

"Do you need any help with the cats?"

"No, they all eat out of the same bowls. It won't take but a few minutes. If you're intent on fixing me up, I'll have to owe you, Jill."

"Oh, pooh, just forget that. I saw a beauty shop on the way, too. Want to get a haircut and shampoo? Does wonders for your self-confidence."

"Well, sure." Gwen laughed. "God, I've missed you, Jill. Do you think the girl believed all those stories we told her about not being in touch? I really don't think Allison ever bought into it. She knew that the two of us were close and she was the outsider."

"Who knows? At this point, Gwen, it doesn't even matter. One lie or a hundred lies, what difference does it make? None. Are you ready?"

"Just let me wash my hands and I'll be ready to go."

Outside, Gwen locked the door and reminded Jill about the missing step. Jill hopped over the space, and Gwen more or less lumbered down.

Jill turned to look at her friend of many years. "When this is all over, there is no way I'm letting you come back here. I'll buy you a van, and you can pack up the cats and move with me back to Mississippi. We aren't getting any younger, my friend. Something tells me we are going to need each other if the dark stuff hits the fan. You okay with that?"

"Will you have enough money left after you do the payback?" Gwen asked hesitantly.

"Not a lot, but enough for both of us if we get jobs. You can live with me until we find you a decent place that will allow all those cats. C'mon, now, we have some shopping to do."

"Jill, what about our kids?"

Jill stopped in her tracks. "We blew that one a long time ago, Gwen. I don't know about you, but I say we let sleeping dogs lie. I sure as hell don't want them knowing the *whole* sorry story, do you? Can you imagine how they'd react, your son a cop and all? Do you want to take that chance? I don't."

Gwen's voice was hesitant, doubtful. "My grandkids . . ."

"Yes, I know. Mary Louise has twins. I don't want to ruin their lives. It's time we took responsibility for our actions. Damn Allison Matthews! Do you think she's in hell, Gwen?"

Gwen straightened her plump shoulders. "I wouldn't be the least bit surprised," she responded hopefully.

"Okay, here's the plan once we get to D.C. I'm going to call Dennis Lowell and ask him to meet us there. He at least deserves to know our story and Allison's role in it. I'm going to call my ex, Gill. He deserves to know, too." She paused. "Do you want to call either one of your exes?"

"No. I think both of them are in jail somewhere. Let's not even go there, Jill."

"It's going to be tough for both of us to finally spill our guts."

Gwen laughed as Jill made a left turn at the light that would take them to Belk's. "Yeah, but think about how good it's going to feel to get this monkey off our shoulders. What's Ole Miss like these days, Jill?" she asked wistfully.

"You aren't going to believe the changes. It's wonderful. I think you're going to feel like I did. It was like going home again. Without the bad memories. They're all dead, Gwen. We outlived them all. We're the good guys, so that has to count for something. We'll make good lives for ourselves. Will you trust me?"

Gwen didn't have to think twice. "Of course I trust you."

Jill leaned over and patted her friend's hand. "Coming here was the best thing I ever did, Gwen. I just want you to know that."

Gwen squeezed Jill's fingers. When she spoke, her voice was little more than a hushed, apologetic whisper. "I hope she's roasting in hell, Jill."

Jill looked at her friend with wet eyes. She didn't say anything, but she nodded in agreement.

Chapter 26

Anita Wellesley adjusted her glasses as she filled out Form 246ZV12 for a temporary kennel license. When she reached the line that called for a signature, she bit down on her lip and signed it Olivia Lowell. She added Olivia's address next to the signature.

Ten minutes later, Anita walked out of the office holding the temporary license that said Olivia Lowell could operate a terrier rescue out of her home for a period of ninety days.

Anna Pellecone beamed her pleasure when Anita waved the temporary license in the air as she climbed into the specially out-fitted van. In the back, separated by a metal grille, eleven silver-toned Yorkshire terriers vented their displeasure at being cooped up in the van. Anna started to sing, and they quieted immediately, comforted by her sweet voice. One by one, they dozed off. When it was totally quiet, Anna spoke softly. "I hope this is the right thing to do, honey."

"It is, Mom. We can't let a bunch of vultures take that little dog away from Ms. Lowell and her fiancé. When she was at the house you could see how much she loved the dogs. You heard her, Mom. If we can help, we have to do it, and it's just temporary."

"Maybe we should have called her about your . . . your plan," the older woman fretted.

"Mom, didn't you see the news this morning? Her house is surrounded by TV people and media groups. We have to strike while we can before some smart-ass lawyer shows up with whatever it is lawyers show up with that will allow them to take the dog away from that couple. Our own organization, and everyone else I could think of, is already out there protesting. It's going to be a circus. I just hope we aren't too late as it is. Call her, Mom. I wrote the number on that sticky note on the back of the phone. Tell her to clear her driveway so I can back the van into her garage. If she's as smart as I think she is, she'll have it all figured out by the time we get there."

Anna Pellecone followed her daughter's instructions. When she hung up the phone, she was beaming. "I think she got it! She sounds real nervous, though—I could hear it in her voice. We cannot let those legal beagles take that little dog away from them, Anita."

"Mom, *hello!* Why do you think we're on our way to her house? I forged her name to a temporary kennel license. We've got eleven dogs in the back who look just like Cecil and Loopy, all silver in color, all with beige faces, short tails, and the same haircuts. No one is taking that dog! They won't know which one is Cecil. I think—and this is just a guess on my part—it's why she came to us in the first place, to get a dog just like Cecil. This way we now have an even dozen extras. It's a reprieve, though I have to be honest—I don't know how long we can hold out. I think it's a stroke of genius on our part. Uh oh, would you look at that street!" Anita said as she carefully turned the corner onto Eagle Drive.

Anna Pellecone rolled her window up

tight, grateful for the tinted glass. Anita drove down the street at a crawl, doing her best not to hit people running about. A child had set up a lemonade stand and was doing a brisk business. Farther down the street someone was selling yellow balloons with Cecil's name on them. He seemed to be doing a brisk business, too. Hundreds of people with their pets on leashes lined both sides of the street. A tethered goat was making all kinds of noises.

A circus.

Olivia opened the garage door the moment she spotted Anita's van. It just took seconds for Anita to turn into the driveway and enter the garage. The minute the van was secure inside, the garage door went down. Anita hopped out and ran to Olivia to hug her, the kennel license in her hand. She started to babble. She ended with, "I forged your name, but I don't think anyone is going to notice or say anything. I'm going to need some help getting these guys out of the van."

"Why . . . why are you doing this?" Olivia stuttered.

"Somebody needs to be in Cecil's corner.

Mom and I liked you. We just want to help. It's temporary, Olivia, but it might help."

Jeff was standing in the kitchen when Olivia opened the garage door. When the quartet of silver dogs, Cecil's body doubles, raced into the kitchen, "Wow!" was all he could think of to say.

Within seconds, Cecil was lost in the herd. Olivia clapped her hands in delight. "Let them come and try to take him! Just let them try! Oh, Anita, this is so great! Hey, where's your mom?"

"In the van. There wasn't enough room in the back for her wheelchair."

"I'll get her!" Jeff volunteered. He was back within minutes with Anna Pellecone in his arms. He set her down carefully on one of the kitchen chairs.

Anna looked around and smiled. "This is so nice, so cozy. The dogs will love it here." She looked over at Olivia. "You're going to find a lot of little puddles today, but by tomorrow they'll get the hang of going outdoors. A new place and all," she said by way of explanation. "Now, is there anything we can do in regard to that circus outside?"

"Just being here is more than enough. All those people outside, I just never . . . The phone is ringing off the hook. I haven't been answering it this morning. The wire services picked up my friend's story from our local paper. CBS and NBC are outside with their satellite trucks. Jeff and I are going to have to go out there pretty soon and make a statement."

Jeff held up his hand and pointed to the television sitting on the kitchen counter. "Who's that?" Olivia demanded.

"Shhh. It's Lillian Manning's long-lost relative. The tabloids found him. I think that's English he's speaking. Hard to tell with his drawl."

Olivia gasped. "That . . . that's who they want to give Cecil to?"

"Shhh, listen, Olivia."

A tall, lanky young man with long, greasy-looking hair scratched his skinny chest as he looked into the camera. "I cain't say I knowed the lady, but I does love dogs. Hound dogs in pertic'lar. I ain't even thought about the money. I seen a picture of the house that's mine now. I might git a pool table, mebbe a bowling alley." He hitched up jeans that were just as dirty as the shirt he was wearing. He puffed on a cigarette in between bursts of speech. "No, it ain't marijuana," he said, pointing the cigarette at the camera covering him. He let loose with a hacking cough and spit out of the corner of his mouth.

"Yeah, yeah, that's my hog," the lanky man responded to a question, pointing to a rusty-looking motorcycle. "I'm gittin' it fixed soons they send me some money. I need to go there to collect the dog and the money. Mebbe today. They said they wuz wiring the money to the cycle people. You want to talk to me anymore, you is going to have to pay me. That's all, folks. No more interviews. Don't *aks* me any more questions. I'm done."

The camera stayed on the dirty-looking man as he walked over to a trailer, where six or seven men who looked worse than he did were drinking from long-necked bottles of Bud. He reached for one and downed it in two gulps before tossing it into the air. One of his buddies whipped out a shotgun and shot the bottle in midair. A pack of skinny-looking wild dogs in the background barked shrilly at the sound of the shotgun blast. The scraggly-looking group cackled with delight before the camera crew switched back to the studio.

"Oh myyyyy God!" Olivia cried.

Her hand shook as she poured out coffee into the cups Jeff handed her.

"Olivia, think about it. That tabloid just did us the biggest favor of our lives. Half the world saw what we just saw. Does that guy look like someone you'd trust your dog with? I don't think so! I think once the firm gets a look at that particular segment, they're going to fall back and regroup."

Anita walked over to the sliding door, opened it, and stepped back as the herd of dogs whooped and yapped their way out to the yard. She smiled like a doting mother. "That's good for our side, isn't it?" she called over her shoulder. She motioned Olivia to the door. "See if you can pick Cecil out of the pack."

Olivia walked out onto the deck to check on the playful dogs. She whistled, then called Cecil's name. All the dogs beelined for the deck. She burst out laughing.

"I took all their collars off, but I know which one is which," Anita said. "This is a new batch of dogs, and none of them has been microchipped yet. We're going to start using the microchips soon. We're having a bake sale and car wash next weekend to raise funds to do it. Even though our vet discounts his time, we still have to pay him something."

Olivia wiped at the corners of her eyes. "If we pull this off, Anita, you aren't going to have to worry about anything again. Even if we don't pull it off, you still won't have to worry. How are we fixed for dog food?"

"I brought all we had at home. It will tide you over for a few days. I can get more on the way home. The other rescuers will help when we run short. We should get going. Mom doesn't like to be out too long. She's really going to miss the Yorkies, but we still have a poodle and a Scottie that have to be taken care of. I hope it all works out, Olivia. If you need me, call. I can be here in twenty minutes. Don't lose that license—put it someplace safe."

Olivia hugged her new friend. "Thanks, Anita. For everything."

"Good luck," Anita said as she entered the kitchen. "Okay, Mom, we're going home now. Jeff will carry you out to the car."

Olivia watched as Anita dropped to her knees and gathered the little herd of dogs close. She spoke softly, gently, promising to come back. She handed out treats, then sneaked out the door before the little dogs could realize she was gone.

Olivia walked around with a package of Tidy Wipes as she cleaned up puddles all around the house. The herd followed her, yipping happily as the old-timers brought out toys that squeaked and whistled. When she was finished she went back to the kitchen, where she washed her hands. She watched as Jeff made her a ham sandwich with a pickle and some chips on the plate.

"Now what?" Olivia asked, when she finished eating.

Jeff crossed his legs as he pushed his chair back from the table. "I guess it's time to turn the phone on. Then we need to go outside and make a statement. We have to stay on the good side of the press. They are on our side, you know." He looked down at his cell phone and pressed a button to review the calls that had come in while he had the phone turned off. "We can't keep it turned off, Olivia. Your dad might call. You might miss some new customers. So we have to deal with the pests."

Olivia grimaced. "You're right, Jeff," she said as she turned the phone back on. It rang almost immediately. A groan escaped her lips as she picked it up. "Olivia Lowell," she snapped into the mouthpiece. The moment she heard the voice on the other end of the phone, she sat down. "Yes, I'm home. Of course. Do you need directions? All right. The street is . . . It's kind of busy out there. Oh, you know, you saw it on television. I'll . . . I'll wait for you."

"What? What's wrong? Was that your dad? What, Olivia?" Jeff demanded, his brow furrowing at the tone of his fiancée's voice.

Olivia pointed to the phone she was still holding. "That was . . . that was . . . Jeff, it was Jill Laramie. Gwen is with her. They're on their way here. They're coming here, Jeff! What do you think that means?"

Jeff scratched his head. "Hopefully, something good. Why else would they both be coming here? You know what, Olivia, it could mean almost anything. Hey, someone's at the door!" The pack of dogs raced from the great room, down the hall, out to the kitchen, and the back door. Jeff and Olivia looked up in surprise when the door opened.

"Dad!" Olivia cried as she ran to him.

"Mr. Lowell!" Jeff said.

After Olivia introduced her fiancé to her father, Dennis looked down at the pack of dogs and laughed. "I bet they all answer to the name of Cecil, huh?"

Olivia nodded nervously. "What are you doing here, Dad? What's wrong? Did something happen? Oh, God, don't tell me the boat sank."

Dennis shrugged. "None of the above. Relax, Ollie. Jill called me yesterday and said I needed to get here as soon as possible. Gill, her ex, and Gwen are coming, too. I took that to mean it was something heavy coming down, so here I am."

Olivia sat down, her mind racing. "Jill just called. She and Gwen are on their way here as we speak. She . . . she didn't say anything about her ex-husband coming, though. Did she explain anything about that to you, Dad?"

Dennis rubbed at his chin before he took off the baseball cap. His head was damp with sweat. "Not a clue. She just said I needed to get here immediately. She prepaid a ticket for me, and I flew first class. I assumed it was critical for me to be here, so here I am. If you say she's due any minute, I guess we'll know soon enough. How about some coffee and a sandwich if it isn't too much trouble?"

Jeff stood at attention. This was Olivia's father. He needed all the Brownie points he could get. "No sir, no trouble at all. I'll be happy to make the sandwich for you. We just made coffee, too." Dennis winked at Olivia. She winked back and started to pace the confines of the kitchen. "Why are they coming here? Now! Why now? They must be up to something. Like I need this today."

"Calm down, Ollie," said Dennis. "Whatever it is, you can handle it. I'm thinking she's coming to give you a check. Then it will all be over. This business with Cecil will work out, too. Just try to calm down until we find out what's going on, Ollie." Turning to Jeff, he asked, with a twinkle, "Do you know anything about boats, Jeff?"

Jeff laughed ruefully. "Only that they operate on the water. I don't know the bow from the stern. I do know you're supposed to wear rubber-soled shoes, though. I probably saw that in a movie."

Dennis laughed. "If you want to, I can pencil you and Ollie into my schedule in September if you want to honeymoon in the area and go out to fish. Think about it—you don't have to give me your answer right now. All that open water. Catching a marlin, there's nothing like it. Even on a honeymoon."

For a brief moment, Jeff looked baffled at the offer. "Oh, I don't know, sir. I have a feeling I'd probably get seasick. I'm thinking that wouldn't be such a good thing on a honeymoon." He began to look desperate. "Of course, Olivia has something to say about it. We'll give your suggestion every bit of the thought it deserves."

Olivia thumped her hands down on the kitchen countertop. "Where are they? They said they were on the way. God, you don't think they're out there talking to all those media people, do you?"

"Ollie, count to ten and sit down. They'll get here when they get here. Stewing and fretting is not going to make it happen any sooner. If you want to go out and give the media statements, do it now. Maybe that will take the edge off things for you," Dennis said, tipping back the kitchen chair to stare at his agitated daughter. "I'll just sit here and wait for your guests."

Olivia stared at her father for a long time

before she reached for Jeff's hand. "Okay, let's do it."

When they reached the front door, Olivia looked up at her fiancé. "Do you think my dad knows something he isn't telling us? He looks so . . . at peace, so calm and relaxed. I don't think I've ever seen him look that way. He always seemed stressed out about something. You don't think he's sick, do you?" she asked, her voice tinged with worry.

"Oh, Olivia, no. My dad looked like that a month after he finally realized he didn't have to work at a job off the farm any longer. It took him that long to realize he didn't have to get up at dawn, go to work for someone else who had the authority to fire him at any given moment. It's called contentment. Everything is right with your dad's world now. He's here for you because you are the most important thing in the world to him. Relax. Look confident and square your shoulders. I'm the one they're going to attack. Smile. Don't let them trick you into saying anything you'll regret later on. All those guys out there do this for a living and know every trick there is. Quick, pick up one of the dogs, and let's get this over with."

Olivia bent over and picked up one of the little Yorkies. She brought him up to her cheek and whispered in his ear. He licked at her cheek. She smiled. He felt warm and sweet in her arms.

Olivia and Jeff walked to the end of the walkway and waited until a bank of microphones was moved in front of them. Jeff stepped forward. Olivia continued to cuddle the little dog close to her cheek.

"Can you turn Cecil around, Ms. Lowell, so we can get a better shot of him?" one of the photographers shouted. Olivia obediently turned the little dog around. The moment he saw and realized all the commotion, he burrowed into Olivia's neck.

"He's shy," Olivia said.

"Do you have a statement, Mr. Bannerman?"

"Nothing different from yesterday. We are not giving Cecil up. I was Mrs. Manning's attorney. I'm doing my best to do what she wanted. It's all in her will. If I have to, I'll go all the way to the Supreme Court. I want you all to understand something. This is not about money. We have no problem with Mrs. Manning's cousin inheriting her estate. He can have it all, but he cannot have the dog. A person's last will and testament has to be honored. I think that's all I have to say at the moment."

"Ms. Lowell, do you want to make a comment?"

"Actually, I do have something to say. Cecil adored Lillian Manning, and she adored him. That's why she provided so handsomely for him in her will. She knew Jeff would love him and take care of him. That was her wish. When Cecil came to us he was traumatized over losing his mistress. We worked with him. This is his new home now, and he loves it here. He has a lot of friends now. As you can see, he's a little frightened at the moment with all you people out here. He trusts us, he knows we're trying to do what's best for him. But like my fiancé says, we are not giving him up. No matter what." She turned slightly, and the dog in her arms licked her face before he snuggled back into her comforting embrace.

"Thank you all for letting us speak to you. Please, don't let them take Cecil away from us," Jeff said in his best courtroom voice.

"Hey, Mr. Bannerman," a reporter

shouted, "is it true you got fired because of Cecil? That sure is love and devotion."

Jeff turned around, his voice and expression serious. "I didn't get fired, I quit, and yes, it is love and devotion. I have another job, so Cecil isn't going to starve." He turned in full view of the camera, and said, "Thank you all for coming out here today to support us and Cecil. We appreciate it."

"Ambrose Martindale said you were a hothead. Is that true?"

Jeff tilted his head to the side and tweaked the dog's whiskers. "Only when it comes to Cecil. Other than that, I'm a pussycat." The dog in Olivia's arms barked loudly at his response. Everyone laughed.

As Olivia and Jeff retreated up the side-walk to the front door, Jeff said, "I think that went rather well. I know you want to run into the house, but don't. Walk slow and steady. We did good, Olivia. That doesn't mean we're home free yet. Some judge can still order us to give up Cecil, although I have no idea how they're going to pick him out of the crowd."

When Olivia set the little dog down in the foyer, he walked away, his tail swishing importantly. The others followed him into the great room and toward their basket of toys.

Olivia nodded. "Jill and Gwen should be here soon. While we're waiting, I'm going to call Mr. Prentice to see if he sent the check to the bank or the insurance company. Do you mind entertaining my dad for a little while? I want you to get to know him. My dad is a great guy. Maybe you should let the dogs out, too."

"Not a problem." Jeff kissed Olivia lightly on the tip of her nose before he made his way to the kitchen.

Chapter 27

While Dennis Lowell whipped up macaroni and cheese and hot dogs for an early supper, Olivia and Jeff tried to stay out of his way as they prepared to feed the herd of little dogs, who yapped expectantly.

Olivia scooped out dry dog food that Jeff mixed with canned dog food. "Where are they, Jeff? Do you think Jill changed her mind?" Olivia looked up at the clock on the kitchen wall. "It's almost five o'clock. She's hours late. Something must have gone wrong. And Prentice O'Brien hasn't returned my phone call, either. I bet they've all seen the circus outside and no one wants to get involved. What do you think?"

Jeff shrugged. A hundred answers flashed through his mind. "It could be something as simple as they got lost on the way here. I suppose it's possible Jill changed her mind. But if she wasn't sure she was going to go through with it, why would she have your father make the trip here at her expense? If you're asking me if she's jerking your chain, I think the answer is no. As for Mr. O'Brien, lawyers rarely call clients unless they have something to report. He probably hasn't heard back from the bank. In my opinion, I don't think the circus outside would deter someone like Jill or have any kind of effect on O'Brien.

"Wow! Look at these little guys chowing down!" Jeff laughed as the little dogs tumbled over one another in the quest for more to eat. He obliged by adding little bits of food to the brightly colored plastic plates. "Okay, guys, let's go outside," he said after the plates were empty, heading for the sliding doors. A blizzard of silver outran him.

While Jeff was outside with the dogs, Dennis said, "He seems like a nice guy, Ollie. I like him." As he turned the hot dogs over, he said with a sigh, "I haven't had a hot dog in years. All I eat is fish!"

"There's nothing wrong with fish. It's good for you. Omega-three or something. If you catch your own fish, you know it's fresh, and it is free. You okay, Dad?"

Dennis wiped his hands on a towel. "I'm fine, Ollie. For the first time in my whole life I am doing what I want to do. The charters are coming in steadily. The boat's good. If things keep up the way they are, I should be able to double up on the mortgage payments. How about you, Ollie? How's business?"

Olivia brought her father up to date. "I was going to ask you if you'd be interested in taking over as my advisor assistant to the CEO of Adrian's Treasures, but when all this stuff hit the fan, I gave the job to Jeff. I need someone on the inside until I can make more concrete decisions. You aren't upset over that, are you, Dad?"

"Heck, no. You know my feelings on that subject. Look, Ollie, do what you have to do and don't worry about what anyone else thinks. Now, how does your young man feel about all these dogs who look like Cecil? Does he think it's going to work out?"

Olivia threw her hands up in the air. "I don't know. If you're a dog expert, I suppose you could find differences, but at first I sure couldn't pick out Cecil. I had to mark his tail." She added, "They are so cute. They aren't castaways in the true sense. A couple of them belong to an older man who's having hip surgery. Anita is just caring for them. They make such wonderful companions for an older person. Anita and her mother take them to different nursing homes to cheer up the guests. Yorkies are extremely social. They take to strangers right away. Anita does a wonderful job—all rescue workers do. I'm going to set up a foundation with Allison's money to help her out. What do you think of that, Dad?"

Dennis was about to respond when the phone rang and the doorbell pealed at the same time. Father and daughter looked at each other for long seconds before Olivia raced for the front door and Dennis reached for the phone.

Through the frosted glass, Olivia could discern three figures. Her guests had arrived. She automatically smoothed down her hair before she took a deep breath and let it out slowly. She opened the door to see Jill, Gwen, and a tall, husky man she assumed to be Gill, Jill's ex-husband. But what really confused her was the huge white basket of red tulips in Jill's hands. Flowers! That must be a good portent.

"Come in."

"It's pretty busy out there," Gwen said, pointing over her shoulder.

"Olivia, this is my ex-husband, Gill Laramie," Jill said. "Did Dennis get here yet?"

Olivia reached out to shake Gill's hand. "Dad got here this morning. I was expecting you earlier."

"Gill's flight was delayed, so we had to wait for him. I should have called. I'm sorry." Jill held out the basket of tulips. The smile on her face was rueful when she said, "You looked like a tulip kind of person to me. It's what I call an 'I'm sorry' gift."

"I love tulips. My backyard is full of them in the spring. Please, come in. Can I get you anything? Some wine, coffee, a soft drink?" Olivia asked as she led the way into the great room.

"A beer would go nice," Gwen said. Gill nodded that he, too, would like a beer. Jill opted for a soft drink.

"I'll be just a minute," Olivia said, backing out of the room. She walked into the kitchen, where her father was just hanging up the phone. They both started to talk at once. Dennis's voice was deeper, huskier, and took precedence. "That was Prentice O'Brien, Ollie. He said the bank in Oxford returned the check, saying they were paid years ago, and the case is closed. He wants you to call him back and tell him if you want him to issue another check and forward it to Great Rock. I said you'd call him back."

Olivia nodded. "They're here, all three of them. The reason they are so late is they had to wait for Jill's ex-husband. His flight was late getting in. Two beers and a Coke. Do you want anything, Dad? Where's Jeff? Jill brought me a basket of tulips be- cause . . . because she thought I was a tulip kind of person. Does that make sense, Dad? Oh, God, I'm babbling again."

"Easy, Ollie, easy. You're in charge here. They came to you. C'mon, take a deep breath and relax. Nothing is going to hap- pen. This is just a discussion, an explana- tion so everyone can put it behind them. You are in control. Get Jeff, and I'll carry in the tray. It might be a good idea if you let the dogs stay outside for a little while."

"Okay. I'll get Jeff." From the doorway, Olivia motioned for Jeff to join her. She explained the situation, and somehow he managed to squeeze through the door, to the dogs' dismay. They howled and yapped as one at the loss of their overgrown playmate.

Inside the great room where the basket of tulips on the coffee table was the focal point, Olivia introduced Jeff to everyone before they sat down.

The sudden silence was louder than any summer thunder. Finally, Jill cleared her throat and started to talk as she fumbled in her purse. She withdrew a white envelope and held it toward Olivia. "The check is certified, so you don't have to worry about it clearing my account. It's mine and Gwen's share of the robbery. If you're wondering why the change of heart, it's because, as you said at our last meeting, it's the right thing to do. I also want to apologize for the merry chase I led you. And Gwen and I want to apologize to you for all the lies we told you. Both of us, believe it or not, are relieved that our past has finally caught up with us.

"Gwen and I talked it over, and decided to tell you that, yes, we've been in touch through the years out of necessity. The papers, the diary, the request Allison made of you to find us—all of that was lies. She knew where we were and how to get in touch with both of us if she wanted to. She chose to ignore us for good reason. She considered both of us as loose cannons. She was afraid that we would expose her dirty secret. Once she learned that we had freed ourselves from the trap she built for us, she disappeared from our lives. We never revealed her new name, and she never told the good ole boys about it."

Jill stopped long enough to take a deep breath. "The theft wasn't the simple operation that Allison made it out to be. It was something much worse, which she'd planned and plotted for a very long time. Somehow, Allison found out that Mr. Augustus, the owner of the bank, was involved in something with a few of his cronies. That's when she decided to steal one of the shipments of bearer bonds, being pretty sure he was in no position to go to the authorities. We didn't know all the details in the beginning. All we knew was that she needed us to pull off the robbery. We were young and stupid, and all that money was more than either one of us could turn our back on. Allison made it all sound so easy, so simple. Then she betrayed us, too—but by the time we found out, it was too late. We were in too deep.

"What she didn't tell us was that when Mr. Augustus began to suspect her, she made a deal with him. It was a pact with the devil himself. Mr. Augustus got the insurance money. She got the bonds. At first he didn't even know that anyone other than Allison was involved. Win-win, that kind of thing.

"A year *after*, and I stress the word *after*, we successfully pulled off the robbery, Allison told us about the string attached to the deal, courtesy of Mr. Augustus." Jill reached down for the can of Coke and took a long gulp. She set the can down on a paper napkin and prepared to continue.

Gwen reached over and patted Jill's hand. "I'll take it from here, Jill." She turned to face Olivia and the others. "Allison said it was no big deal. All we had to do was become couriers for future shipments of bearer bonds. Pure and simple, it was blackmail. Allison said she'd been doing it for a year, moving the bonds from D.C., where she was working, to Oxford. You see, after the robbery, it was no longer possible for the bank to get insurance on that kind of 'transaction,' so Mr. Augustus had to figure out a way to get someone who would not be suspected, and who he had leverage with, to transport the bonds. Once he knew that Allison was involved with the theft, she fit the bill perfectly. But then something happened, I don't know exactly what, and she could no longer get away the required four times a year. So she had to bring us into it. She told us how Mr. Augustus had begun to suspect her and forced her to agree to his scheme. When Allison told us about what we had to do, and where the money came from, Jill and I said no, absolutely not. Then Allison painted us a picture of prison life in Mississippi. In the end, we did it because we were literally scared out of our wits. It seems that these good ole boys were the ringleaders of a group that ran a number of houses of prostitution using underage girls—and boys. The bonds were the money-laundered proceeds from that activity.

"Years later, we were able to get out from under. After Allison divvied up the bonds, Jill and I found the courage to threaten the old geezers with exposure to the authorities.

We were prepared to go into hiding and turn over the evidence about their activities we had managed to gather over the years. Being the pillars of the community that they were, they didn't want to be *charged* with the crimes they had committed even if they couldn't be convicted.

"They all sat on boards. They were all wealthy. They donated handsomely to every charity in town. Their wives and children were what we called upper crust, however lowlife the men themselves were. They finally let us walk away when they realized we had the evidence, which we had arranged to be turned over to the authorities if anything happened to us. By then, of course, Allison had left Dennis, left Olivia, changed her name, and disappeared, so they couldn't find her.

"When I got married, I was a terrible wife. I couldn't love any man because I could no longer love myself. Later, I was a terrible mother. It was the same with Jill. I assume it was the same with Allison, and that's why she gave you up, Olivia. But she was so corrupt, I can't really be sure. I'm so sorry that I'm the one to be telling you this, but you came looking for us. If you hadn't, we probably never would have done anything. Allison must have wanted you to know just how base she was—otherwise, she wouldn't have sicced you onto us. She was an ugly, hateful person, and I no longer care why she did what she did. I think I speak for Jill, too."

It was Jill's turn again. "Yes, Gwen speaks for me. Of course, Gwen and I didn't want them to know about the prostitution ring, the money laundering, the robbery. We still don't want them to know. When you showed up, Olivia, Gwen and I both knew it was just a matter of time before it all came out. We came here to bare our souls to you. I gave you back the money. Please, will you let it all die a natural death now? Our children and grandchildren are innocent. No good can come of telling them how their parents and grandparents spent the years after college," Jill pleaded.

Then, without giving Olivia a chance to respond, she continued, "But now I have to reveal one last thing, after which you may understand why I have no contact with my family. Gill is not Mary Louise's natural father."

There were gasps all around the room.

"Two years after we were married, on one of the courier trips I had to take, Mr. Augustus threatened to tell my husband about the crime if I would not have sex with him. So I did. And that's when I became pregnant with Mary Louise."

"Oh, Jill, you poor darling," Gwen said. "Why didn't you tell me? I would have helped."

"How?" Jill replied. "We had no money. Remember, it was almost a year before we divvied up the bonds. Abortion was illegal. There was nothing to do, and I was so ashamed, I didn't want anyone to know."

A bomb could have exploded next door and no one would have noticed. In the background, the dogs barked.

Dennis Lowell dropped his head into his hands, finally coming to grips with the nature of the woman he had been unfortunate enough to marry. But could he really regret that marriage when they had created the wonderful daughter Olivia had turned out to be? Still, he made garbled noises behind his hands.

Olivia, finally realizing the extent to which she had been manipulated, sat in stunned silence, tears rolling down her cheeks. Jeff put his arm around her shoulders.

Gill Laramie gulped at his beer bottle.

"Not that this matters, but since we're telling you everything, we might as well tell you this, too. Gwen and I both went into therapy. We came to understand that Gwen had dealt with the guilt by marrying lousy husbands. She was relieved when they went through all the money. I, in turn, ran and hid. Speaking strictly for myself, there was no way I could love my daughter. Every time I looked at her I would think about the person who was her father and what I'd done. Gill did a better job of raising her than I ever could have. That's why I stayed out of their lives. You, Olivia, were the lucky one. Dennis, because he's a wonderful human being, loved you from the minute you were born and never let you know anything bad about your 'dead' mother. However evil Allison was, your father raised you to be a wonderful young woman. Don't you ever forget that."

Olivia, still dazed, had eyes only for her father. She wiped her tears on the sleeve of her pink shirt. She wanted to run to him, to have him tell her he would make this all come out right. Dennis looked up through his own tears and held out his arms. She bolted forward. "It doesn't matter to me, Dad. It doesn't. Please, Dad, tell me it doesn't matter to you. Please, Dad. Whatever that woman was like, it has nothing to do with us. Does it?"

"No, it doesn't, Ollie. Whatever your mother was, you're my daughter. And a better daughter no man could have. That's never going to change, no matter what."

Reassured, with her father's arms about her, Olivia looked at the other two women, who were also crying. She cleared her throat and wiped at her eyes again. "I know how hard it was to tell us about your past. I give you my word that I won't say anything to your families. What I will tell you is that I set up trust funds for your children and grandchildren with some of the monies from Adrian Ames's estate. Because it was the right thing to do." She wiped at her eyes again. "The bank sent back the check the attorney sent them to pay off the robbery. They said they were paid years ago by the insurance company and the case is closed. So the money goes back to you. Let's just say that the money you stole was advance payment for the services you were later required to perform. I, for one, have no intention of judging anyone. What are you going to do now?" Olivia held out the check, and both Gwen and Jill shook their heads as they reared back in their chairs. It was clear to everyone that they wanted nothing to do with the money.

Gill Laramie stood up, a look of revulsion on his face. There was no forgiveness of any kind in his expression. He looked down at his ex-wife, the revulsion directed at her. "I cannot believe you let me believe all these years that Mary Louise was my daughter. That was beyond cruel, Jill. All those years of struggling, trying to raise her, college, all of that. I think you're insane. You had free will. You didn't *have* to do what you did."

"Gill, please don't tell Mary Louise. Please."

"Don't worry, I'm not going to tell her. I hope to hell God punishes you for what you did. Stay out of her life, and the twins' lives, too. I hope I never have to see you again. You are despicable. Now, can someone call me a taxi to take me to the airport?"

Jeff jumped to his feet and went to the kitchen to call the taxi.

Dennis Lowell squeezed Olivia's shoulders. Olivia leaned into him, savoring the comfort and strength of his body. Whoever her mother had been, he was her dad. He would always be her dad.

Olivia looked at the two women, who looked drained. "What are you going to do now?"

"We're going back to Mississippi to pick up the pieces. We'll get jobs, live together till we can get our lives on track. Maybe God will smile on us and let us find a chance at some happiness."

"Is that decision carved in stone?" Olivia asked.

Gwen made a sound that passed for a laugh. "I live one day at a time. My biggest worry is how I can keep feeding my cats. Look, don't feel sorry for us. We'll find our way."

"I'm going to throw something out to you. Think about it. How would you two like to take over the operation of Adrian's Treasures? There's a big, fine house in the mountains that would be perfect for all those cats. There are any number of wonderful colleges in the area, if it's the academic ambiance you're looking for. You'll earn a hefty salary, but you'll be working for your money. You'll learn the business in no time. It's a win-win for both of you if you're interested."

"Take over Adrian Ames's business?" Jill gasped. "She would spin in her grave if she knew. I don't have to think about it—my answer is yes. Talk about divine retribution!"

"I'm in. As long as I can bring all my cats. Why would you do this for us?" Gwen asked, her eyes shining with unshed tears.

Olivia smiled through her own tears. "Because it's the right thing to do! Right, Dad?"

Dennis laughed. "Yes, it's the right thing to do, Ollie."

"There you go. My dad has the final word. Ladies, we have a deal!"

The front door closed, and the back slider opened. All the little Cecils bounded into the room. They yipped and yapped as they clamored for attention. The women obliged by tickling them behind the ears and rubbing their little pink bellies.

The worst was over.

Chapter 28

Olivia stared at the calendar hanging on the kitchen wall. Eight long days had passed since the "revelation" occurred. That's how she thought of the meeting she'd had with Jill, Gwen, Gill, and her father—as the revelation. Her stomach churned as she moved back to the table and her cup of coffee. She was waiting for Jeff to come downstairs so they could go to court for Cecil's scheduled hearing.

Eagle Drive was starting to come alive with the reporters and camera crews. She knew without looking out the front window that by seven everyone would be drinking coffee out of styrofoam cups, waiting for Jeff to leave the house. She wondered if they would pack up and follow him or stay on Eagle Drive. It would probably be half and half, she decided.

Olivia carried her coffee out to the deck, where the dogs were scampering around in the dew-moistened grass. How happy they all were! Just yesterday Jeff had taught the whole herd to jump through a hula hoop he'd found in the garage. The promise of a treat was reason enough to jump through the bright red hoop—except for Alice, who looked on with disdain at such shenanigans. However, when she saw the reward on the other end, she'd stirred herself and calmly approached the hoop and *stepped* through it. She did it five more times, earning a collection of six treats that she refused to share with anyone. Jeff laughed so hard he sat down and rolled on the grass, holding his sides.

Dogs were not dumb, was his assessment later, when he could breathe again. Especially not Alice.

Cecil pawed at Olivia's leg; he wanted to be picked up. Olivia obliged and crooned to him, "It's okay, Cecil. Trust me. Jeff isn't going to let anyone take you away. He's a lawyer. I know people hate lawyers, but he's one of the nice ones." Cecil licked at her chin before he snuggled into her arms. She hugged him.

Olivia sipped at her morning coffee as she thought about the past eight days—days that had rocked her to the core of her being. One of these days, when her life returned to normal, she was going to go into D.C. by herself and walk around the Tidal Basin to get her thoughts and feelings in order. She hadn't known it at the time because she was just a little girl, but her father had been in the habit of taking her there when he was stressed out about something. He'd hold her hand, talk to her about cartoons, roller-skating, sleepovers, all kinds of things until he worked out in his mind whatever was troubling him. Then they'd go for either a slice of pizza or an ice cream. Never both, and it was always her decision which one to have.

Since the revelation, her father had called every single day to reassure her of his love, to tell her that nothing had changed now that they knew what they knew about the woman who had given birth to her. She believed him because she loved him. She'd done her best to reassure him that she felt the same way, and she did.

The only change resulting from Gwen and Jill's revelation was how much more Olivia hated the woman known as Adrian Ames. But Adrian, as much as Allison, belonged to the past, and Olivia had felt a sense of peace come over her these last few days.

She thought back to the night of the revelation, when she'd seen her guests out the door, and although she hadn't meant to eavesdrop, had heard Jill's words carry up the driveway. She remembered seeing Jill put her hand on Gwen's arm and turn the other woman toward her so they were face to face, when she said, "Yes, I think she's in hell, Gwen." Then, arm in arm, the two had climbed into the rental car and left.

So many things had happened in the last eight days. Great Rock said their books were closed, too, and told Prentice O'Brien not to send them a check. The check from Jill and another check drawn on the funds the insurance company had refused, had gone into a special fund designated for animal rights, the homeless, soup kitchens, free medical and dental care for poor children, and everything else Olivia could think of to tack on to the new foundation.

Gwen and Jill were now living in Adrian

Ames's house and were talking about selling it and moving the executive suite to Mississippi if Olivia approved. Jeff said he thought it was a good idea and undertook to provide them legal advice in conjunction with the company's in-house legal department.

As her father had said, things had a way of working themselves out for the best if you were just patient. What a wise man he was.

Olivia was jolted from her thoughts when she heard a voice at the back gate. "Hey, Ollie, it's me, Dee Dee! Can I come in?"

Cecil was off Olivia's lap in the blink of an eye. The little herd escorted the reporter across the yard to the deck, which was a riot of bright red geraniums and Gerbera daisies in clay pots. A yellow butterfly settled on one of the blooms. Three of the little dogs watched the delicate butterfly but made no move to spring or pounce. Olivia smiled.

Dee Dee was breathless with her sprint across the yard. "Ollie, you have company! Your front doorbell should be ringing any second. I think it's your boyfriend's old boss. I saw his picture in the paper the other day. I can stay, can't I?" She pointed to the minirecorder in the pocket of her blouse. "It's on, and recording right now."

"Mr. Martindale is here? Oh myyyy God! I have to get Jeff. Court is this morning. What's he doing here? Of course you can stay."

Dee Dee shrugged. "Maybe he wants to settle before court. Lawyers do that all the time. He's got someone with him. I think it's Mrs. Manning's heir, but you won't recognize him. They really spruced him up. There goes the doorbell! What about the dogs?"

Olivia clenched and unclenched her fists as she tried to figure out what to do. She looked down at her watch. Jeff had exactly seven minutes if he wanted to make court on time. "Let's leave them out here for now. They'll stay right here by the door. If I nod, that means you let them in, okay? By the way, we're on for Saturday for a double date. Last Saturday was just too hectic. Among other things, we forgot the Apple Blossom Festival. Jeff says you're gonna love his friend. C'mon, let's see what Mr. Ambrose Martindale has to say."

Jeff was just opening the door when the two women joined him. Olivia looked the tall man over. He was everything Jeff had said he was. He was wearing a power suit in medium gray. His steel gray hair complemented a superior tan, probably from some tanning bed in his suite of offices. The man's scent was overpowering, as was the shine on his Bally shoes. The gold Rolex on his wrist winked in the foyer light. But it was his companion, a tall, thin man she'd seen on television over a week ago, who drew her attention.

Someone, probably Ambrose Martindale, had cleaned up this guy. He no longer looked like a shotgun-toting hillbilly drinking from a long-necked Bud bottle. He was dressed in dark blue Armani with a tie as powerful as the one Martindale was wearing. The pristine white shirt hugged his skinny neck like a vise. His straggly locks were gone, replaced with a regulation haircut. He looked more than presentable.

"May we come in, Jeffrey?"

Jeff didn't speak immediately but stepped forward, forcing both Martindale and the young man with him to step backward. Then he said calmly, "Why? What do you want, Ambrose? You shouldn't be here. I have to leave for court now. If you had called, I could have saved you the trip all the way out here." He took another step forward so the gaggle out front could get better pictures.

Martindale appeared unperturbed. "Allow me to introduce Everly Cracker. He's Mrs. Manning's heir. We would both like to talk to you. I can call the courthouse and explain that we're in negotiations. They'll just hear the case scheduled after ours. Judge Donner is a very understanding man and an old golfing buddy."

"There's nothing to negotiate, Ambrose. I'm not giving up Cecil to you or Mr. . . . Cracker. There's nothing else to discuss. Unless you're trying to tell me Judge Donner is predisposed to rule in your favor. That is what you're saying, isn't it?"

Martindale remained unruffled. "What I'm saying is, Judge Donner is a very understanding man, and we've been friends for over thirty years. I wouldn't be a bit surprised if he ruled in our favor. You're a hothead, Bannerman. I have every right to ask to see Cecil to see for myself that he is hale and hearty and being taken care of. Now, fetch him, please."

Jeff looked at Olivia and raised his eyebrows. Olivia in turn nodded to Dee Dee.

Jeff then whistled through his teeth to the crowd out front. "Hey, guys, it's time for you to meet Cecil. C'mon up!"

The silver stampede from the back deck was thunderous as Dee Dee hopped up on the foyer bench and started clicking her Nikon. The rush of human feet to the front door was pure pandemonium.

"Rats!" Cracker bellowed. "Somebody do something!" He flattened himself against the wall, his arms crossed against his skinny chest. "What the hell kind of place is this?"

"Shut up, Everly. Don't be stupid—they're dogs, not rats. What the hell is going on here, Bannerman?" Martindale demanded.

"I don't owe you any explanation, Martindale. I don't work for your firm anymore. I'm heading for court. You can do whatever you want. I'm going to make a motion for Judge Donner to recuse himself based on his long personal friendship with you. I'll also mention how understanding he is." This last was said loud enough for the reporters to catch every word.

"Stop being such an ass, Bannerman. I came all the way out here to talk to you to avoid a circus in court. Let's go someplace quiet so we can talk. Can't someone shut these dogs up? Which one is Cecil?"

Jeff smirked. "Cecil is the silver one with the beige face, short tail, perky ears!"

Martindale bent over to look at the yapping pack of dogs. "What are you trying to pull here? They all look like that!"

"They do, don't they? Call him by name. Cecil knows his name."

"These ain't dogs—these is rats. Don't you go thinkin' I'm takin' on some rat to git that old lady's money. I ain't takin' no rat! I ain't never seen dogs like this," Cracker said.

For the first time Martindale looked frazzled. "Shut up, Cracker. I told you, they're dogs and not rats. Act like you have half a brain, will you?"

"Are you sayin' I'm stupid?" Cracker's foot lashed out to kick one of the little dogs, but he scampered away when he saw the shiny Bruno Magli shoe aimed at his tiny head. Dee Dee got the shot dead center, as did the other photographers clustered in the doorway and foyer. In the midst of this, Martindale was shouting Cecil's name and couldn't understand why all the little dogs rushed to him.

"Take your pick, Martindale."

"I'll get you disbarred for this, Bannerman. Now, for the last time, which one is Cecil?"

"The long answer is, I don't know. The short answer is the same, I don't know. But as you can see, all the dogs are fine. They're healthy, and they are loved, and they belong together. Pick out Cecil, and let's get this show on the road."

"I can't pick him out, and you damn well know it, Bannerman. I'm ordering you to pick up that dog and show him to me. The courts are not going to view this kindly. How do I know that any of these dogs is Cecil? And isn't it against the law to have so many dogs in one house?" he blustered.

"Would you like to have an evidentiary hearing on the question of whether or not one of these dogs is Cecil? As Cecil's handler, Ms. Lowell's lawyer, and, most importantly, an officer of the court, I am prepared to so testify, as well as to present myriad witnesses who can support that proposition. Do you have any witnesses to the contrary?"

Before Martindale could respond, Olivia had the temporary kennel license in her hand. She waved it under Ambrose Martindale's nose. He backed up and blanched.

"Well?" Jeff said, tapping his foot impatiently.

"How about you, Mr. Cracker? Do you want to take a stab at picking out Cecil?" Jeff asked.

"I don't want no dog, 'specially one that looks like a rat. You can have him. Just give me my money and let me go home to that big fancy house. My friends are waitin' fer me. If I showed up with one of them there rats, they'd laugh me right out of there. I told you when I got here I didn' want no dog."

Olivia looked at the lanky man, her jaw dropping. "You don't want Cecil! Will you put that in writing?" *Please, God, let him know how to write.*

"Mr. Cracker is not putting anything in writing, so get that idea right out of your head, Ms. Lowell." Martindale bent over to peer at the sea of silver fur that was looking at him intently.

Olivia watched one of the little dogs—Cecil, she noted when she saw the little red mark on his tail—inch his way behind the lawyer. His head was down, as were his ears, his tiny little tail tucked tightly between his legs. She backed up a step and nudged Dee Dee to home in on Cecil, which she did just as the little dog took a mighty leap and sank his teeth into the seat of Martindale's expensive pants. Cecil hung on for dear life as the lawyer unsuccessfully tried to shake him loose.

Seeing their buddy having all the fun, the pack closed in, and in short order, Martindale looked like a Christmas tree bedecked with hanging terrier ornaments.

Everly Cracker chortled with laughter. "Ornery little cusses, ain't they? Gimme that paper so I kin git outta here."

The relief on Jeff's face was just short of comical. Not so Martindale's.

"What's it going to be, Martindale?"

"Get these dogs off me, Bannerman. I can sue you for this. I *will* sue you for this! They're shredding my suit. My three-thousand-dollar suit. All right, all right, if Mr. Cracker doesn't want the dog, you can keep him. Now, will you get these . . . rats off me!"

Olivia clapped her hands, and said, "Good boy, Cecil. C'mere, I have treats."

The little dogs formed two neat lines and

waited for their treats. "Say thank you, gentlemen." Olivia laughed. As one, the pack barked. She looked down to see the red spot on Cecil's tail. She scooped him up and whispered in his ear. "You get two treats because you bit that obnoxious guy's ass. Now scoot!" Cecil threw back his head and howled before sprinting off to the great room, where he showed he was staking out his position as top dog with two treats. In the blink of an eye, Alice snatched one of the two treats and raced off to her own bed, her tail moving at the speed of light. The pack knew Alice was the queen of 509 Eagle Drive, so no disputes arose.

Everly Cracker scrawled his name on the release form Jeff had withdrawn from his briefcase. Ambrose Martindale glowered for the benefit of the cameras. He tried to gather his dignity about him but failed miserably.

Dee Dee Pepper motioned Martindale toward the kitchen, while Jeff and Olivia talked to the reporters and the news crews outside on the lawn.

Dee Dee withdrew the minirecorder from her pocket. She pressed the ON button.

Ambrose's voice ricocheted around the kitchen.

"You even think about screwing with my friends, and I'll send this tape to the Bar Association. Are we clear on that, Mr. Martindale?" said Dee Dee.

Martindale huffed and puffed. "That's blackmail!"

"Call it whatever you want, Mr. Martindale. I prefer to call it insurance. It's a shame about your suit. What the heck, just bill Mrs. Manning's estate. Isn't that how you guys get suits like that in the first place? Bye," Dee Dee singsonged. "Gotta run. We're doing a special edition, and I have a deadline."

Dee Dee's Doc Martens thumped on the floor as she hurried to the front door. "I'll come by later with a copy of the paper," she told Olivia. "We're doing a special afternoon edition, and Cecil is going to get the whole front page. I'll try to get his picture above the fold. Invite me to supper so you can tell me about that guy you're going to fix me up with."

"You got it!" Olivia shouted as she and Jeff walked closer to the road, where they shook hands with all of Cecil's supporters.

They stood there a long time, holding hands, until Eagle Drive emptied out. "We did it, Jeff! Cecil is all ours. Hey, I gotta call my dad to tell him the good news!"

Jeff grinned from ear to ear as he trailed his fiancée into the house. Cecil was waiting for him at the door. He dropped to his knees and picked up the little dog. He didn't look at the tail—he knew it was Cecil. He didn't know how, he just did. "We got you, buddy, and let me tell you, you were worth the fight." Cecil did his best to stretch his tiny body lengthwise so he could cuddle into Jeff's neck. His little head sought for a soft spot, where he laid it. Jeff felt a lump settle in his throat.

Such devotion, such true love.

Chapter 29

Lucy the Saint Bernard and her two-month-old pup that Olivia had been photographing for the past two hours pranced alongside their owner, who was smiling benevolently as she led her dogs to her van.

Lucy had been a chore to photograph, as she did her best to make sure her new pup was in all the shots. Olivia had finally obliged, making the decision to give Lucy the December slot on next year's calendar. She frowned when she looked up to see Lucy trotting across the yard, a silver package between her teeth. She looked up at Olivia before she dropped it at her feet. Olivia blinked, half-expecting the huge dog to say, "Here's a wedding present." Of course she didn't, but she did bark, then waited for the obligatory "good girl" before she trotted back to the van.

Olivia's first wedding present.

Delivered by a Saint Bernard.

She picked it up but decided to wait for Jeff to open it.

Five more days!

Five more days until she became Mrs. Olivia Bannerman.

Olivia's heart kicked up a beat as she walked back into the house for a soda pop. She carried it out to the deck and sat down.

It was a glorious September day, as glorious as her mood. Her world was so right side up, it was downright scary.

Olivia settled herself more comfortably in the deck chair. She looked around her little domain. The grass wasn't quite as pretty as it had been before so many dogs began romping and digging, but it would come back. Then again, they hadn't had much rain, either, these last few months, and autumn and winter were just around the corner. She shivered in the afternoon sunshine, her eyes on the colorful pots of flowers, whose leaves were starting to turn yellow. Before long there would be a frost, and that would be the end of the bright blooms.

Some of the leaves were already starting to change color.

The phone rang. A smile stretched across her face. Jeff. He always called at this time of day. The smile stayed in her voice when she said hello.

"Do you still love me? said Jeff. "Five days to go!"

"No, I decided the meter reader is the man for me! Sorry. Five days! How many minutes and hours? Just tell me that, Jeff Bannerman!"

The soft laughter on the other end of the phone sent shivers up Olivia's spine. "I can't make it out this evening, Olivia. In fact, my desk here is so full, I probably won't make it out tomorrow, either. Tell me again why I took this short-term job."

"You wanted to help out a friend. That's what you said, Jeff. You had law firms lining up to sign you on after we settled Cecil's case. You turned them all down to help your friend establish his fledgling firm. Was it a mistake, Jeff? If it was, you can correct it. You have a job with Adrian's Treasures."

"Yes, I know. Was it a mistake? No, Olivia, it wasn't a mistake. Drew would have done it for me. In fact, he agreed to help me out when I open up a small office in Winchester—a project which, by the way, is looking better and better. I think I'm a small-town boy at heart. I want to get things squared away so I don't have to come back here after our honeymoon. Not to mention, all of this is pro bono. We almost have things taken care of. I begrudge the time I have to spend away from you and the dogs."

Olivia laughed. How was it possible to be so happy? "Jeff, Dee Dee Pepper called earlier this morning, and she said she's looking forward to following in our footsteps. I took that to mean her relationship is becoming serious."

"It is. Serious, I mean. I think we were a good influence on those two! Do you miss me? Do the dogs miss me?"

"Yes and yes. Oh, I almost forgot. We got a wedding present today. It was paw-delivered by a Saint Bernard named Lucy. I'll wait till you get here to open it. I was so excited—our first wedding present!"

"A Saint Bernard, huh? Gee, I can't wait. I gotta go, honey. I'll call you tonight."

Olivia leaned her head back on the deck chair to let the afternoon sun wash over her. The dogs meandered around the deck before they, too, found patches of sun not covered by the awning and stretched out. Why not? Dinner was still an hour away.

Olivia felt like singing but contented herself with humming the strains of "Here Comes the Bride" under her breath. It was all so very perfect. What did she ever do to gain such happiness? Especially with a mother like hers. Having her dad as both mother and father was the answer.

The last few months had been traumatic, but in the end, with her father's help, she'd managed to put all those events behind her. It was amazing, she thought, how things came together after Jill's brutal announcement that day in May. So much so that she and Jeff really were going to honeymoon on her father's boat. Dennis had clinched the deal by saying, "No radios, no televisions, and no telephones." Jeff had clapped her father on the back and said, "Sign us up!" And that had been the end of that.

Jill had called over the weekend to ask if she knew what the long-range weather forecast would be for the wedding, so she and Gwen would know what to wear. That call had been so far over the top that Olivia had laughed for an hour. She didn't know who was happier, Jill and Gwen or she and Jeff.

So out of all the ugliness, out of all the tragedy, much good had surfaced. Truth, hard as it was to bear sometimes, had healing powers. She, Gwen, Jill, and her father were the living proof.

Once in a while she had a twinge when she thought about the tricks she'd employed to keep Cecil out of Everly Cracker's clutches—who had been arrested twice since that fateful morning. Once for disturbing the peace and once for drunk driving. Dee Dee told her he was leaving with his cronies to go back to, as Dee Dee put it, whatever rock he'd crawled out from under. Cecil was safe and happy. In this case the end really had justified the means. Martindale, also according to Dee Dee, who had stayed on top of all developments the last few months, had taken a media licking and was cruising the Mediterranean.

Olivia yawned and stretched luxuriously. One by one, the dogs did the same thing. *Dinnertime*, she thought, looking down at her watch. From here on out, she had three whole weeks to do nothing but smile and be happy. Lucy the Saint Bernard had been her last client. Her day planner for the next three weeks held nothing but blank pages.

Life was so good.

Actually, life was wonderful.

The small house on Eagle Drive was filled to overflowing. Down the long hall away from the hubbub, in her bedroom, Olivia was getting dressed for the wedding ceremony, which was to take place in the great room. Dee, Gwen, and Jill were helping, their faces wreathed in smiles.

A tentative knock sounded. "Come in," Olivia called. Then, seeing who it was, she said, "Oh, Mrs. Bannerman! You look so pretty!"

The little lady who was Jeff's mother laughed. "Not half as pretty as you look. I wanted to give you something. It's not much, just a little handmade hankie that my grandmother gave to my mother, who gave it to me. You know, something old, something new, something borrowed, something blue." Her voice was shy and sweet as she handed over the small lace square. Olivia folded it neatly and inserted it in the sleeve of her wedding gown. "By the way, did I thank you for taking Jeff off our hands! The family was about to give up on him and accept the fact that he was going to be a bachelor forever."

Olivia hugged her. She whispered in the woman's ear. "I love your son very much. I will do everything in my power to make him happy. Thank you for having such a wonderful son."

Mrs. Bannerman smiled. "I'll leave you to finish dressing. I'll be the one crying in the front row."

When the door closed behind Mrs. Bannerman, Jill turned to Gwen, her eyes moist. "See? That's what we missed. Thank you, Olivia, for allowing us to share these moments with you. We both owe you so much. We'll never be able to thank you enough. We know we turned your life upside down, and for that we're sorry. We're living for the first time in forty years. Really living. It might not be perfect, but it's as good as it can get for now, and for that we will always be indebted to you."

Dee Dee, alert to every nuance of Olivia's expression, saw the tears that were about to overflow and stepped in. "I want you ladies to help dress *me* when I get married, too," she said, laughing. "Like Ollie, I don't have a mom. I can use all the help I can get."

"Really?" Gwen and Jill said in unison.

"Really," Dee Dee said and hugged both women.

Jill bit down on her lower lip. "And now for the veil! The veil makes it official. I love it that you chose such a simple gown—high neck, heavy satin, small train. It does you justice. The fresh flowers on the crown of the veil make it all just perfect."

"I love lilies of the valley," Gwen said in a choked voice. "I can smell them from here. You make a lovely bride, Olivia. May you always be as happy as you are right now."

"The music is starting. I have to run. Come on, ladies, let's go," Olivia cried.

"Ladies do not gallop!" Jill said. "We go first. We'll send your dad back, Olivia. Are you okay?"

"I am more than okay." Olivia smiled tremulously as she moved forward to wait for her father in the doorway.

How handsome he looks, she thought when Dennis appeared. Her second thought was how sad he looked. "Dad . . ." she said as he drew near.

"Ollie, you look so beautiful. My own little

angel." His voice was so husky, Olivia knew he was going to tear up just as she was about to do.

Olivia's voice was just as husky when she said, "You look pretty darn handsome yourself. Don't you dare make me cry now, you hear?"

Dennis cleared his throat. "Okay. Listen, Ollie. I'm not *giving* you away. I want you to know that. What I'm doing is, I'm . . . I'm *sharing* you with Jeff. I know giving the bride away is a wedding term, but I take it seriously. Just so we know."

Olivia's smile was of the megawatt variety. "I know, Dad. Listen, did you . . . ?"

"It's all taken care of, Ollie. We have to go now. There's a young man waiting for you who, the last time I looked, was about to collapse in sheer fright. What do you say we put him out of his misery?"

"I say let's do it!"

Thirty minutes later the minister concluded, "I now pronounce you husband and wife. You may kiss the bride."

And Jeff did, until her toes tingled, to the delight of everyone in attendance, even the dogs, who wore white satin collars in honor of the occasion.

Flower petals flew in all directions as the dogs scampered about trying to catch them. Pictures followed. Then it was time to leave for the reception in town.

Jeffrey and Olivia Bannerman stood in a small receiving line as the guests trooped out to the waiting cars. The newly married couple was the last to leave.

"Are you as happy as I am, Olivia?"

"Happier," Olivia responded.

"You can't be happier than I am," Jeff grumbled.

"Okay, how about as happy."

"Sounds good. Come on, honey, we have to get to the hall to greet our guests. Besides, I'm starved. I hope we're having something good for our wedding supper."

"I hope so, too. I can't remember what I ordered for us. Does it matter?"

"Nope. Not one little bit," Jeff said, kissing her on the lips, a kiss that said life was going to be wonderful for the two of them.

It was eleven o'clock when the deejay picked up his microphone to announce the last dance of the evening. "The bride and groom will now take the floor!" The guests formed a circle around the dance floor as the couple danced cheek to cheek to Whitney Houston singing, "I will always love you."

Then it was time to throw the bridal bouquet. Dee Dee caught it by jumping up in the air and clutching it with both hands. She gave a thumbs-up to Olivia, who laughed and laughed.

They were at the door when a gaggle of people approached them. Olivia turned to see Mary Louise Rafferty with her twin sons. Behind them were Gwen's son, Timothy, and his children. Both Mary Louise and Timothy looked as if they wanted to say something. Olivia brought her finger to her lips. "Shhh. Everyone deserves a second chance. This is your chance to be a real family. Don't blow it now."

"How'd you get so smart, Mrs. Bannerman?" Jeff asked, as they headed for the limo.

Olivia threw back her head and laughed. "By hanging around with you and my dad. By the way, he said he didn't *give* me to you. He's only *sharing* me with you."

Jeff held Olivia's train up as she slid into the limo. "He scared the living daylights out of me when he said the same thing to me.

He wagged his finger under my nose to make his point."

"He didn't!"

"He did!"

"What now, Mrs. Bannerman?"

"A kiss would be nice."

Jeff obliged.

"Are we going to live happily ever after, Jeff?"

"Hmm," Jeff said. "That's a yes, Mrs. Bannerman."

"That's good enough for me, Mr. Bannerman. Let's go home now!"

"Now, that's a plan if I ever heard one."